SHAKUNTALA

OR

THE FATAL RING.

SHAKUNTALA

OR

THE FATAL RING.

AN INDIAN DRAMA

BY

KALIDASA

REPRINTED FROM THE TRANSLATION OF

SIR WILLIAM JONES.

PUBLISHED BY

THE SOCIETY FOR THE RESUSCITATION
OF INDIAN LITERATURE.

GYAN

Published by

Gyan Publishing House
5, Ansari Road
Daryaganj, New Delhi-110002
Phone: 011-47034999, 9811692060
E-mail: books@gyanbooks.com

Distribution Network
gyanbooks.com
India, USA, Canada, UK, Australia, France

ISBN : 978-81-212-2752-0 (HB)
First Published, 1901

2nd Impression 2021

Printed at: Gyan Press, Delhi.

Shakuntala or The Fatal Ring
Author: Kalidasa

SHAKUNTALA;

OR

THE FATAL RING.

AN INDIAN DRAMA BY

KALIDASA.

REPRINTED FROM THE TRANSLATION OF

SIR WILLIAM JONES.

PUBLISHED BY

THE SOCIETY FOR THE RESUSCITATION
OF INDIAN LITERATURE.

CALCUTTA.

PRINTED BY H. C. DASS, ELYSIUM PRESS

1901.

PERSONS OF THE DRAMA.

DUSHMANTA	...	Emperor of India.
SHAKUNTALA	...	the Heroine of the piece.
ANASUYA PRIYAMVADA	}	Damsels attendant on her.
MADHAVYA	...	the Emperor's Buffoon.
GAUTAMI	...	an old female Hermit.
SHARNGARAVA SHARADWATA	}	two Brahmanas.
KANWA	...	Foster-Father of Shakuntala.
KUMBHILAKA	...	a Fisherman.
MISHRAKESHI	...	a Nymph.
MATALI	...	Charioteer of Indra.
A little Boy		
KASHYAPA ADITI	}	Deities, Parents of Indra.

Officers of State and Police, Brahmanas, Damsels, Hermits, Pupils, Chamberlains, Warders of Palace, Messengers, and Attendants.

PREFACE.

In one of the letters which bear the title of EDIFYING, though most of them swarm with ridiculous errors, and all must be consulted with extreme diffidence, I met, some years ago, with the following passage:—"In the north of India there are many books, called Nataka, which, as the Brahmanas assert, contain a large portion of ancient history without any mixture of fable," and having an eager desire to know the real state of this empire before the conquest of it by the Savages of the North, I was very solicitous, on my arrival in Bengal, to procure access to those books, either by the help of translations, if they had been translated, or by learning the language in which they were originally composed, and which I had yet a stronger inducement to learn from its connection with the administration of justice to the Hindus; but when I was able to converse with the Brahmanas, they assured me that the Natakas were not histories, and abounded with fables, that they were extremely popular works, and consisted of conversations in prose and verse, held before ancient Rajas in their public assemblies, on an infinite variety of subjects, and in various dialects of India: this definition gave me no very distinct idea; but I concluded that they were dialogues on moral or literary topics; whilst other

Europeans, whom I consulted, had understood from the natives that they were discourses on dancing, music, or poetry. At length a very sensible Brahmana, named Radhakanta, who had long been attentive to English manners removed all my doubts, and gave me no less delight than surprise, by telling me that our nation had compositions of the same sort, which were publicly represented at Calcutta in the cold season, and bore the name, as he had been informed, of plays. Resolving at my leisure to read the best of them, I asked which of their Natakas was most universally esteemed; and he answered without hesitation, Shakuntala, supporting his opinion, as usual among the Panditas, by a couplet to this effect: "The ring of Shakuntala, in which the fourth act, and four stanzas of that act, are eminently brilliant, displays all the rich exuberance of Kalidasa's genius." I soon procured a correct copy of it, and, assisted by my teacher Ramalochana, began with translating it verbally into Latin, which bears so great a resemblance to Sanskrit, that it is more convenient than any modern language for a scrupulous interlineary version: I then turned it word for word into English, and afterwards, without adding or suppressing any material sentence, disengaged it from the stiffness of a foreign idiom, and prepared the faithful translation of the Indian drama, which I now present to the public as a most pleasing and authentic picture of old Hindu manners, and one of the greatest curiosities that the literature of Asia has yet brought to light.

Dramatic poetry must have been immemorially ancient in the Indian empire: the invention of it is commonly ascribed to Bharata, a sage believed to have been inspired, who invented also a system of music which bears his name; but this opinion of its origin is rendered very doubtful by the universal belief, that the first Sanskrit verse ever heard by mortals was pronounced in a burst of resentment by the great Valmiki, who flourished in the silver age of the world, and was author of an Epic Poem on the war of his contemporary, Rama, king of Ayodhya; so that no drama in verse could have been represented before his time; and the Indians have a wild story, that the first regular play, on the same subject with the Ramayana, was composed by Hanumat or Pavana, who commanded an army of Satyrs or mountaineers in Ramas expedition against Lanka: they add, that he engraved it on a smooth rock, which, being dissatisfied with his composition, he hurled into the sea; and that, many years after, a learned Prince ordered expert diverse to take impresssions of the poem on wax, by which means the drama was in great measure restored; and my Pandita assures me that he is in possession of it.

By whomsoever or in whatever age this species of entertainment was invented, it is very certain, that it was carried to great perfection in its kind, when

Vikramaditya, who reigned in the first century before Christ, gave encouragement to poets, philologers, and mathematicians. at a time when the Britons were as unlettered and unpolished as the army of Hanumat: nine men of genius, commonly called the nine gems, attended his court, and were splendidly supported by his bounty: and Kalidasa is unanimously allowed to have been the brightest of them.—A modern epigram was lately repeated to me, which does so much honour to the author of Shakuntala, that I cannot forbear exhibiting a literal version of it: "Poetry was the sportful daughter of Valmiki, and, having been educated by Vyasa, she chose Kalidasa for her bridegroom after the manner of Vidarbha: she was the mother of Amara, Sundara, Sankha, Dhanika, but now, old and decrepit, her beauty faded, and her unadorned feet slipping as she walks, in whose cottage does she disdain to take shelter?" All the other works of our illustrious Poet, the Shakespeare of India, that have yet come to my knowledge, are a second play, in five acts, entitled Urvashi: an heroic poem, or rather a series of poems in one book, on the Children of the sun; another, with perfect unity of action, on the Birth of Kumara, god of war, two or three love-tales in verse, and an excellent little work on Sanskrit Metre, precisely in the manner of Terentianus; but he is believed by some to have revised the works of Valmiki and Vyasa, and to have corrected the perfect editions of them which are now current: this at least is admitted by all, that he stands next in reputation to those venerable bards; and we must regret, that he has left only to dramatic poems, especially as the stories in his Raghuvansha would have supplied him with a number of excellent subjects. Some of his contemporaries, and other Hindu poets even to our own times, have composed so many tragedies, comedies, farces, and musical pieces, that the Indian theatre would fill as many volumes as that of any nation in ancient or modern Europe, all the Panditas assert that their plays are innumerable; and, on my first inquiries concerning them, I had notice of more than thirty, which they consider as the flower of their Natakas, among which the Malignant Child, the Rape of Usha, the Taming of Durvasas, the Seizure of the Lock, Malati and Madhava, with five or six dramas on the adventures of their incarnate gods, are the most admired after those of Kalidasa.

They are all in verse, where the dialogue is elevated; and in prose, where it is familiar, the men of rank and learning are represented speaking pure Sanskrit, and the women Prakrit, which is little more than the language of the Brahmanas melted down by a delicate articulation to the softness of Italian; while the low persons of the drama speak the vulgar dialects of the several provinces which they are supposed to inhabit. The play of Shakuntala must have been very popular when it was first represented, for the Indian empire was then in full vigour, and the national vanity must have been highly flattered by the magnificent introduction of those kings and heroes in whom the Hindus gloried, the scenery must have been splendid and beautiful; and there is good reason to believe, that the court of Avanti was equal in brilliancy during the reign of Vikramaditya, to that of any monarch in any age or country.

Dushmanta, the hero of the piece, appears in the chronological tables of the Brahmanas among the children of the moon, and in the twentyfirst generation after the flood; so that, if we can at all rely on the chronology of tne Hindus, he was nearly contemporary with Obed or Jesse; and Puru, his most celebrated ancestor, was the fifth in descent from Budha, or Mercury, who married, they say, a daughter of the pious king, whom Vishnu preserved in an ark from the universal deluge; his eldest son Bharata was the illustrious progenitor of Kuru, from whom Pandu was lineally descended, and in whose family the Indian Apollo became incarnate; whence the poem, next in fame to the Ramayana, is called Mahabharata. As to the machinery of the drama, it is taken from the system of mythology, which prevails to this day, and which it would require a large volume to explain; but we cannot help remarking, that the deities introduced in the Fatal Ring are clearly allegorical personages, Marichi, the first production of Brahma or the Creative Power, signifies light, that subtil fluid which was created before its reservoir, the sun, as water was created before the sea; Kashyapa, the offspring of Marichi, seems to be a personification of infinite space, comprehending innumerable worlds; and his children by Aditi, or his active power (unless Aditi mean the primeval day, and Diti, his other wife, the night), are Indra, or the visible firmament, and the twelve A'dityas, or suns, presiding over as many months. On the characters and conduct of the play I shall offer no criticism, because I am convinced that the tastes of men Differ as much as their sentiments and passions; and that, in feeling the beauties of art, as in smelling flowers, tasting fruits, viewing prospects, and hearing melody, every individual must be guided by his own sensations and the incommunicable associations of his own ideas. This only I may add, that if Shakuntala should ever be acted in India, where alone it could be acted with perfect knowledge of Indian dresses, manners, and scenery, the piece might easily be reduced to five acts of a moderate length, by throwing the third act into the second, and the sixth into the fifth; for it must be confessed that the whole of Dushmanta's conversation with his buffoon, and great part of his courtship in the hermitage, might be omitted without any injury to the drama. It is my anxious wish that others may take the pains to learn Sanskrit, and may be persuaded to translate the works of Kalidasa: I shall hardly again employ my leisure in a task so foreign to my professional (which are, in truth, my farvourite) studies, and have no intention of translating any other book from any lgnauage, except the Law Tract of Manu, and the new Digets of Indian and Arabian laws; but to show, that the Brahmanas, at least, do not think polite literature incompatible with jurisprudence, I cannot avoid mentioning, that the venerable compiler of the Hindu Digest, who is now in his eighty-sixth year, has the whole play of Shakuntala by heart, as he proved when I last conversed with him, to my entire conviction. Lest, however, I should hereafter seem to have changed a resolution which I mean to keep inviolate, I think it proper to say, that I have already translated four or five other books, and among them the Hitopadesha which I undertook, merely as an exercise in learning Sanskrit, three years before I know that Mr. Wilkins, without whose aid I should never have learnt it, had any thought of giving the same work to the public.

THE PROLOGUE.

A Brahmana *pronounces the benediction.*

Water was the first work of the Creator; and Fire receives the oblations ordained by law; the Sacrifice is performed with solemnity; the Two Lights of heaven distinguish time; the subtil Ether, which is the vehicle of sound, pervades the universe; the Earth is the natural parent of all increase; and by Air all things breathing are animated: may ISHA, the God of Nature, apparent in these eight forms, bless and sustain you!

The Manager *enters.*

Man. What occasion is there for a long speech?—*(Looking towards the dressing-room.)*—When your decorations, Madam, are completed, be pleased to come forward.

An Actress *enters.*

Actr. I attend, Sir.—What are your commands?

Man. This, Madam, is the numerous and polite assembly of the famed Hero, our king Vikramaditya, the patron of every delightful art; and before this audience we must do justice to a new production of Kalidasa, a dramatic piece, entitled Shakuntala, or, The Fatal Ring; it is requested, therefore, that all will be attentive.

Actr. Who, Sir, could be inattentive to an entertainment so well intended?

Man. (*smiling.*) I will speak, Madam, without reserve.—As far as an enlightened audience receive pleasure from our theatrical talents, and express it, so far, and no farther, I set a value on them; but my own mind is diffident of its powers, how strongly soever exerted.

Actr. You judge rightly in measuring your own merit by the degree of pleasure which this assembly may receive; but its value, I trust, will presently appear.—Have you any farther commands?

Man. What better can you do, since you are now on the stage, than exhilarate the souls, and gratify the sense, of our auditory with a song?

Actr. Shall I sing the description of a season? and which of the seasons do you choose to hear described!

Man. No finer season could be selected than the summer, which is actually begun, and abounds with delights. How sweet is the close of a summer day, which invites our youth to bathe in pure streams, and induces gentle slumber under the shades refreshed by sylvan breezes, which have passed over the blooming Patalis and stolen their fragrance!

Actr. (*Singing.*) "Mark how the soft blossoms of the Nagakeshara are lightly kissed by the Bees! Mark how the damsels delicately place behind their ears the flowers of Shirisha!"

Man. A charming strain! the whole company sparkles, as it were, with admiration; and the musical mode to which the words are adapted, has filled their souls with rapture. By what other performance can we ensure a continuance of their favour?

Actr. Oh! by none better than by the Fatal Ring, which you have just announced.

Man. How could I forget it! In that moment I was lulled, to distraction by the melody of thy voice, which allured my heart, as the king Dushmanta is now allured by the swift antelope.

[*They both go out.*

—:o:—

SHAKUNTALA

OR

THE FATAL RING.

ACT I.

SCENE—A FOREST.

Dushmanta, *in a car, pursuing an antelope, with a bow and quiver, attended by his* Charioteer.

Char. [*Looking at the antelope, and then at the King.*]—When I cast my eye on that black antelopé, and on thee, O King, with my braced bow, I see before me, as it were, the God Mahesha chasing a hart, with his bow, named Pinaka, braced on his left hand.

Dushm. The fleet animal has given us a long chase. Oh! there he runs, with his neck bent gracefully, looking back, from time to time, at the car which follows him. Now, through fear of a descending shaft he contracts his forehand, and extends his flexible haunches; and now, through fatigue, he pauses to nibble the grass in his path with his mouth half opened. See how he springs and bounds with long steps, lightly skimming the ground, and rising high in the air! and now so rapid is his flight that he is scarce discernible!

Char. The ground was uneven, and the horses were checked in their course. He has taken advantage of our delay. It is level now, and we may easily overtake him.

Dushm. Loosen the reins.

Char. As the king commands.—[*He drives the car first at full speed and then gently.*]—He could not escape. The horses were not even touched by the clouds of dust which they raised; they tossed their manes, erected their ears, and rather glided than galloped over the smooth plain.

Dushm. They soon outrain the swift antelope.—Objects which, from their distance, appeared minute presently became larger: what was really divided, seemed united, as we passed; and what was in truth bent, seemed straight. So swift was the motion of the wheels, that nothing, for many moments, was either distant or near. [*He fixes an arrow in his bow-string.*

Behind the scenes.] He must not be slain. This antelope, O King, has an asylum in our forest; he must not be slain.

Char. [*Listening and Looking.*] Just as the

animal presents a fair mark for your arrow, two hermits are advancing to interrupt your aim.

Dushm. Then stop the car.

Char. The king is obeyed. [*He draws in the reins.*

Enter a Hermit *and his* Pupil.

Herm. [*Raising his hands.*] Slay not, O mighty sovereign, slay not a poor fawn, who has found a place of refuge. No surely, no; he must not be hurt. An arrow in the delicate body of a deer would be like fire in a bale of cotton. Compared with thy keen shafts, how, weak must be the tender hide of a young antelope. Replace quickly, oh! replace the arrow which thou hast aimed. The weapons of you kings and warriors are destined for the relief of the oppressed, not for the destruction of the guiltless.

Dushm. (*Saluting them*) It is replaced.

[*He places the arrow in his quiver.*

Herm. (*with joy*) Worthy is that act of thee, most illustrious of monarchs; worthy, indeed, of a prince descended from Puru. Mayst thou have a son adorned with virtues, a sovereign of the world!

Pup. (*Elevating both his hands*). Oh! by all means may thy son be adorned with every virtue, a sovereign of the world!

Dushm. (*Bowing to them*). My head bears with reverence the order of a Brahmana.

Herm. Great king, we came hither to collect wood for a solemn sacrifice; and this forest, on the banks of the Malini, affords an asylum to the wild animals protected by Shakuntala, whom our holy preceptor Kanwa has received as a sacred deposit. If you have no other avocation, enter yon grove, and let the rights of hospitality be duly performed. Having seen with your own eyes the virtuous behaviour of those whose only wealth is their piety, but whose worldly cares are now at an end, you will then exclaim, "How many good subjects are defended by this arm, which the bowstring has made callous!"

Dushm. Is the master of your family at home?

Herm. Our preceptor is gone to Somatirtha, in hopes of deprecating some calamity, with which destiny threatens the irreproachable Shakuntala; and he has charged her, in his absence, to receive all guests with due honour.

Dushm. Holy man, I will attend her; and she, having observed my devotion, will report it favourably to the venerable sage.

Both. Be it so; and we depart on our own business.

[*The Hermit and his Pupil go out.*

Dushm. Drive on the car. By visiting the abode of holiness, we shall purify our souls.

Char. As the king (may his life be long!) commands. [*He drives on.*

Dushm. [*Looking on all sides.*] That we are near the dwelling-place of pious hermits, would clearly have appeared, even if it had not been told.

Char. By what marks?

Dnshm. Do you not observe them? See under yon trees the hallowed grains which have been scattered on the ground, while the tender female parrots were feeding their unfledged youmg in their pendant nests. Mark in other places the shining pieces of polished stone which have bruised the oily fruit of the sacred Ingudi. Look at the young fawns, which having acquired confidence in man, and accustomed themselves to the sound of his voice frisk at pleasure, without varying their course. Even the surface of the river is reddened with lines of consecrated bark, which float down its stream. Look again; the roots of yon trees are bathed in the waters of holy pools, which quiver as the breeze plays upon them; and the glowing lustre of yon fresh leaves is obscured, for a time by smoke that rises from oblations of clarified butter. See too, where the young roes graze, without apprehension from our approach on the lawn before yonder garden, where the tops of the sacrificial grass, cut for some religious rite, are sprinkled around.

Char. I now observe all those marks of some holy habitation.

Dushm. [*Turning aside.*] This awful sanctuary, my friend, must not be violated. Here, therefore, stop the car, that I may descend.

Char. I hold in the reins. The king may descend at his pleasure.

Dushm. [*Having descended and looking at his own*

dress.] Groves devoted to religion must be entered in humble habiliments. Take these regal ornamentals:—[*the charioteer receives them,*]—and, whilst I am observing those who inhabit this retreat, let the horses be watered and dressed.

Char. Be it as you direct! [*He goes out.*

Dnshm. [*Walking round and looking.*] Now then I enter the sanctuary.—[*He enters the grove.*]—Oh! this place must be holy. My right arm throbs. [*Pausing and considering.*]—What new acquisition does this omen promise in a sequestered grove? But the gates of predestined events are in all places open.

Behind the scenes.] Come hither, my beloved companions; oh! come hither.

Dushm. [*Listening.*] Hah! I hear female voices to the right of yon arbour. I am resolved to know who are conversing.—[*He walks round and looks.*]—There are some damsels, I see, belonging to the hermit's family who carry water-pots of different sizes proportioned to their strength, and are going to water the delicate plants. Oh! how charmingly they look! If the beauty of maids who dwell in woodland retreats cannot easily be found in the recesses of a palace, the garden flowers must make room for the blossoms of the forest which excel them in colour and fragrance. [*He stands gazing at them.*

Enter Sakuntala, Anasuya *and* Priyamvada.

Ana. O my Sakuntala, it is in thy society that the trees of our father Kanwa seem to be delightful;

it well becomes thee, who art soft as the fresh-blown Mallika, to fill with water the canals which have been dug round these tender shrubs.

Shak. It is not only in obedience to our father that I thus employ myself, though that were a sufficient motive, but I really feel the affection of a sister for these young plants. [*Watering them.*

Pri. My beloved friend, the shrubs which you have watered flower in the summer, which is now begun; let us give water to those which have passed their flowering time; for our virtue will be the greater when it is wholly disinterested.

Shak. Excellent advice! [*Watering other plants.*

Dushm. (*Aside in transport.*) How! is that Kanwa's daughter, Sakuntala?—(*With surprise*)—The venerable sage must have an unfeeling heart, since he has allotted a mean employment to so lovely a girl, and has dressed her in a coarse mantle of woven bark. He, who could wish that so beautiful a creature, who at first sight ravishes my soul, should endure the hardships of his austere devotion, would attempt, I suppose, to cleave the hard wood Sami with a leaf of the blue lotus. Let me retire behind this tree, that I may gaze on her charms without diminishing her confidence. *He retires.*

Shak. My friend Priyamvada has tied this mantle of bark so closely over my bossom that it gives me pain; Anasuya, I request you to untie it.

[*Anasuya unties the mantle.*

Pri. *(Laughing.)* Well, my sweet friend, enjoy, while you may, that youthful prime which gives your bosom so beautiful a swell.

Dushm. (*Aside.*) Admirably spoken Priyamvada! No: her charms cannot be hidden, even though a robe of intertwisted fibres be thrown over her shoulders, and conceal a part of her bosom, like a veil of yellow leaves enfolding a radiant flower. The water-lily, though dark moss may settle on its head, is nevertheless beautiful; and the moon with dewy beams is rendered yet brighter by its black spots. The bark itself acquires elegance from the features of a girl with antelope's eyes, and rather augments than diminishes my ardour. Many are the rough stalks which support the water-lily; but many and exquisite are the blossoms which hang on them.

Shak. [*Looking before her.*] Yon Amra tree, my friends, points with the finger of its leaves, which the gale gently agitates, and seems inclined to whisper some secret. I will go near it.

[*They all approach the tree.*

Pri. O my Shakuntalâ, let us remain some time in this shade.

Shak. Why here particularly?

Pri. Because the Amra tree seems wedded to you who are graceful as the blooming creeper which twines round it.

Shak. Properly are you named Priyamvadá, or speaking kindly.

Dushm. [*Aside.*] She speaks truly. Yes; her lip glows like the tender leaflet; her arms resemble two flexible stalks; and youthful beauty shines, like a blossom, in all her lineaments.

Ana. See, my Shakuntalâ, how yon fresh Mallika, which you have surnamed Vanatoshini, or Delight of the Grove, has chosen the sweet Amra for her bridegroom.

Shak. [*Approaching, and looking at it with pleasure.*] How charming is the season, when the nuptials even of plants are thus publicly celebrated!

[*She stands admiring it.*

Pri. [*Smiling.*] Do you know, my Anasuyâ, why Shakuntala gazes on the plants with such rapture?

Ana. No indeed: I was trying to guess. Pray, tell me.

Pri. "As the Grove's Delight is united to a suitable tree, thus I too hope for a bridegroom to my mind"—that is her private thought at this moment.

Shak. Such are the flights of your own imagination.

[*Inverting the water-pot.*

Ana. Here is a plant, Shakuntala, which you have forgotton, though it has grown up, like yourself, under the fostering care of our father Kanwa.

Shak. Then I shall forget myself.—O wonderful!—[*Approaching the plant.*]—O priyamvada!—*looking at it with joy,*]—I have delightful tidings for you.

Pri. What tidings, my beloved, for me?

Shak. This Mádhavi-creeper, though it be not the usual time for flowering, is covered with gay blossoms from its root to its top.

Both. [*Approaching it hastily.*] Is it really so, sweet friend?

Shak It is so? Look yourselves.

Pri. [*With eagerness.*] From this omen, Shakuntalá, I announce you an excellent husband, who will very soon take you by the hand.

[*Both girls look at Shakuntala.*

Shak. [*Displeased.*] A strange fancy of yours.

Pri. Indeed, my beloved, I speak not jestingly. I heard something from our father Kanwa. Your nurture of these plants has prospered; and thence it is, that I foretell your approaching nuptials.

Ana. It is thence, my Priyamvadá, that she has watered them with so much alacrity.

Shak. The Mádhavi plant is my sister; can I do otherwise than cherish her?

[*Pouring water on it.*

Dusnm. (*Aside.*) I fear she is of the same religious order with her foster-father. Or has a mistaken apprehension risen in my mind? My warm heart is so attached to her, that she cannot but be a fit match for a man of a military class. The doubts which awhile perplex the good, are soon removed by the prevalence of their strong inclinations. I am enamoured of her, and she cannot, therefore, be the daughter of a Bráhmana, whom I could not marry.

Shak. (*Moving her head.*) Alas! a bee has left the blossom of this Malliká, and is fluttering round my face.

[*She expresses uneasiness.*

Dushm. (*Aside, with affection.*) How often have I seen our court damsels affectedly turn their heads aside from some roving insect, merely to display their graces! but this rural charmer knits her brows, and gracefully moves her eyes through fear only, without art or affectation. Oh! happy bee, who touchest the corner of that eye beautifully trembling; who, approaching the tip of that ear, murmurest as softly as if thou wert whispering a secret of love; and who sippest nectar, while she waves her graceful hand, from that lip, which contains all the treasures of delight! Whilst I am solicitious to know in what family she is born, thou art enjoying bliss, which to me would be supreme felicity.

Shak. Disengage me, I entreat, from this importunate insect, which quite baffles my efforts.

Pri. What power have we to deliver you? The king Dushmanta is the sole defender of our consecrated groves.

Dushm. (*Aside.*) This is a good occasion for me to discover myself. (*Advancing a little.*) I must not, I will not, fear. Yet—(*checking himself and retiring,*)—my royal character will thus abruptly be known to them. No; I will appear as a simple stranger, and claim the duties of hospitality.

Shak. This impudent bee will not rest. I will remove to another place.—(*Stepping aside and looking round.*—Away ! away ! He follows me wherever I go. Deliver me, oh ! deliver me from this distress.

Dushm. (*Advanciny hastily.*) Ah ! while the race of Puru govern the world, and restrain even the most profligate, by good laws well administered, has any man the audacity to molest the lovely daughters of pious hermits ?

[*They loak at him with emotion.*

Ana. Sir, no man is here audacious ; but this damsel, our beloved friend, was teased by a fluttering bee.

[*Both girls look at* Shakuntalá.

Dushm. (*Approaching her.*) Damsel, may thy devotion prosper !

[Shakuntalá *looks on the ground bashful and silent.*

Ana. Our guest must be received with due honours.

Pri. Stranger, you are welceme. Go, my Shakuntalá ; bring from the cottage a basket of fruits and flowers. This river will, in the mean time, supply water for his feet.

[*Looking at the water-pots.*

Dushm. Holy maid, the gentleness of thy speech does me sufficient honour.

Ana. Sit down awhile on this bank of earth, spread with the leaves of Saptaparna : the shade is refreshing, and our lord must want repose after his journey.

Dushm. You too must all be fatigued by your hospitable attentions : rest yourselves, therefore, with me.

Pri. (*Aside to* Shakuntalá.) Come, let us all be seated; our guest is contented with our reception of him.

[*They all seat themselves.*

Shak. (*Aside.*) At the sight of this youth I feel an emotion scarce consistent with a grove devoted to piety.

Dushm. (*Gazing at them alternately.*) How well your friendship agrees, holy damsels, with the charming equality of your ages, and of your beauties !

Pri. (*Aside to* Anasúyá.) Who can this be, my Anasuyá ? The union of delicacy with robustness in his form, and of sweetness with dignity in this discourse, indicate a character fit for ample dominion.

Ana. (*Aside to* Priyamvadá.) I too have been admiring him. I must ask him a few questions.—(*Aloud*)—Your sweet speech, sir, gives me confidence. What imperial family is embellished by our noble guest ? What is his native country ? Surely it must be afflicted by his absence from it. What, I pray, could induce you to humiliate that exalted form of yours by visiting a forest peopled only by simple anchorites ?

Shak. (*Aside.*) Perplex not thyself, O my heart ! let the faithful Anasuya direct with her counsel the thoughts which rise in thee.

Dushm. (*Aside*). How shall I reveal, or shall I disguise myself?—(*Musing.*)—Be it so—(*Aloud to* Anasuya.) Excellent lady, I am a student of the Veda, dwelling in the city of our king descended from Puru; and, being occupied in the discharge of religious and moral duties, come hither to behold the sanctuary of virtue.

Ana. Holy men, employed like you, are our lords and masters.

(Shakuntala *looks modest, yet with affection; while her companions gaze alternately at her and at the king.*)

Ana. (*Aside* to Shakuntala.) Oh! if our venerable father were present.

Shak. What if he were?

Ana. He would entertain our guest with a variety of refreshments.

Shak. (*Pretending displeasure.*) Go too; you had some other idea in your head; I will not listen to you.

[*She sits apart.*

Dushm. (*Aside* to Anasuya *and* Priyamvada.) In my turn, holy damsels, allow me to ask one question concerning your lovely friend.

Both. The request, sir, does us honour.

Dushm. The sage Kanwa, I know, is ever intent upon the great Being; and must have declined all earthly connections. How then can this damsel be, as it is said, his daughter?

Ana. Let our lord hear. There is in the family of Kusha, a pious prince of extensive power, eminent in devotion and in arms.

Dushm. You skpeak, no doubt, of Kaushika, the sage and monarch.

Ana. Know, sir, that he is in truth her father; while Kanwa bears that reverend name, because he brought her up, since she was left an infant.

Dushm. Left? the word excites my curiosity; and raises in me a desire of knowing her whole story.

Ana. You shall hear it, sir, in few words.—When that sage king had begun to gather [the fruits of his austere devotion, the gods of Swarga became appresive of his increasing power and sent the nymph Menaka to frustrate, by her allurements, the full effect of his piety.

Dushm. Is a mortal's piety so tremendous to the inferior deities? What was the event.

Ana. In the bloom of the vernal season, Kaushika, beholding the beauty of the celestial nymph, and wafted by the gale of desire—

[*She stops and looks modest.*

Dushm. I now see the whole. Shakuntala then is the daughter of a king, by a nymph of the lower heaven.

Ana. Even so.

Dushm. *(Aside.)* The desire of my heart is gratified—*(Aloud)*—How, indeed, could her transcendent beauty be the portion of mortal birth? You light, that sparkles with treamulous beams, proceeds not from a terrestrial cavern.

[Shakuntala *sits modestly, with her eyes on the ground.*

Dushm. (*Again-aside*) Happy man that I am! Now has my fancy an ample range; yet, having heard the pleasantry of her companions on the subject of her nuptials, I am divided with anxious doubt, whether she be not wholly destined for a religious life.

Pri. (*Smiling, and looking first at* Shakuntala, *then at the king*). Our lord seems desirous of asking other questions.

[Shakuntala *rubukes* Priyamvada *with her hand.*

Dushm. You know my very heart. I am, indeed, eager to learn the whole of this charmer's life; and must put one question more.

Pri. Why should you muse on it so long?—(*Aside*). One would think this religious man was forbidden by his vows to court a pretty woman.

Dushm. This I ask. Is the strict rule of a hermit so far to be observed by Kanwa, that he cannot dispose of his daughter in marriage, but must check the natural impulse of juvenile love? Can she (oh preposterous fate!) be destined to reside for life among her favourite antelopes, the black lustre of whose eyes is far surpassed by hers?

Pri. Hitherto, sir, our friend has lived happy in this consecrated forest, the abode of her spiritual father; but it is now his intention to unite her with a bridegroom equal to herself.

Dushm. (*Aside, with ecstacy*) Exult, oh my heart, exult. All doubt is removed; and what before thou wouldst have dreaded as a flame, may now be approached as a gem inestimable.

Shak. (*seeming angry*) Anasuya, I will stay here no longer.

Ana. Why so, I pray?

Shak. I will go to the holy matron Gautami, and let her know impertinently our Priyamvada has been brattling.

Ana. It will not be decent, my love, for an inhabitant of this hallowed wood to retire before a guest has received complete honour.

Shakuntala, *giving no answer. Offers to go.*

Dushm. (*Aside.*) Is she then departing?—(*He rises, as if going to stop her, but checks himself.*)—The actions of a passionate lover are as precipitate as his mind is agitated. Thus I, whose passion impelled me to follow the hermit's daughter, am restrained by a sense of duty.

Pri. (*Going up to* Shakuntala.) My angry friend, you must not retire.

Shak. (*stepping back and frowning.*) What should detain me?

Pri. You owe me the labour, according to our agreement, of watering two more shrubs. Pay me first to acquit your conscience, and then depart if you please.

Holding her,

Dushm. The damsel is fatigued, I imagine, by pouring so much water on the cherished plants. Her arms, graced with palms like fresh blossoms, hang carelessly down; her bosom heaves with strong breathing; and now her dishevelled locks, from which the string has dropped, are held by one of her lovely hands. Suffer me, therefore, thus to discharge the debt. *Giving his ring to* Priyamavada.—*Both damsels, reading the name* Dushmanta *inscribed on the ring, look with surprise at each other.*)—It is a toy unworthy of your fixed attention; but I value it as a gift from the king.

Pri. Then you ought not, sir, to part with it. Her debt is from this moment discharged on your word only.

[*She returns the ring.*

Ana. You are now released, Shakuntala, by this benevolent lord,—or favoured, perhaps, by a monarch himself. To what place will you retire?

Shak. (*Aside*). Must I not wonder at all this if I preserve my senses?

Pri. Are not you going, Shakuntala?

Shak. Am I your subject? I shall go when it pleases me.

Dushm. (*Aside looking at* Shakuntala). Either she is affected towards me, as I am towards her, or

I am distracted with joy. She mingles not her discourse with mine; yet, when I speak, she listens attentively. She commands not her actions in my presencé; and her eyes are engaged on me alone.

Behind the scenes). Oh pious hermits, preserve the animals of this hallowed forest! The king Dushmanta is hunting in it. The dust raised by the hoofs of his horses, which pound the pebbles ruddy as early dawn, falls like a swarm of blighting insects on the consecrated boughs which sustain your mantles of woven bark, moist with the water of the stream in which you have bathed.

Dushm. (*Aside.*) Alas! my officers, who are searching for me, have indiscreetly disturbed this holy retreat.

[*Again behind the scenes.*] Bewere, ye hermits, of yon elephant, who comes overturning all that oppose him; now he fixes his trunk with violence on a lofty branch that obstructs his way; and now he is entangled in the twining stalks of the Vratati. How are our sacred rites interrupted! How are the protected herds dispersed! The wild elephant, alarmed at the new appearance of a car, lays our forest waste.

Dushm. (*Aside.*) How unwillingly am I offending the devout foresters! Yes; I must go to them instantly.

Pri. Noble stranger, we are confounded, with

dread of the enraged elephant. With your permission, therefore, we retire to the hermit's cottage.

Ana. O Shakuntala, the venerable matron will be much distressed on your account. Come quickly that we may be all safe together.

Shak. (*Walking slowly.*) I am stopped. Alas! by a sudden pain in my side.

Dushm. Be not alarmed, amiable damsels. It shall be my care that no disturbance happen in your sacred groves.

Pri. Excellent stanger, we were wholly unacquainted with your station; and you will forgive us, we hope, for the offence of intermitting awhile the honours due to you: but we humbly request that you will give us once more the pleasure of seeing you though you have not now been received with perfect hospitality.

Dushm. You depreciate your own merits. The sight of you, sweet damsels, has sufficiently honoured me.

Shak. My foot, O Anasuya, is hurt by this pointed blade of Kusha grass; and now my loose vest of bark is caught by a branch of the Kuruvaka. Help me to disentangle myself, and support me.

[*She goes out looking from time to time at* Dushmanta, *and supported by the damsels.*]

Dushm. (*Sighing*) They are all departed; and I too, alas! must depart. For how short a moment have I been blessed with a sight of the imcomparable

Shakuntala! I will send my attendants to the city, and take my station at no great distance from this forest. I cannot, in truth, divert my mind from the sweet occupation of gazing on her. How, indeed, should I otherwise occupy it? My body moves onward but my restles heart runs back to her; like a light flag borne on a staff against the wind, and fluttering in an opposite direction. [*He goes out.*

ACT II.

SCENE I—A Plain, *with royal pavilions on the skirt of the forest.*

Madhavya. (*Sighing and lamenting.*) Strange recreation this!—Ah me! I am wearied to death.—My royal friend has an unaccountable taste.—What can I think of a king so passionately fond of chasing unprofitable quadrupeds?—" Here runs an antelope!—there goes a boar!"—Such is our only conversation.—Even at noon in excessive heat, when not a tree in the forest has a shadow under it, we must be skipping and prancing about like the beasts whom we follow.—Are we thirsty? We have nothing to drink but the waters of mountain torrents, which taste of burned stones and mawkish leaves.—Are we hungry? We must greedily devour lean vension, and that commonly roasted to a stick.—Have I a moment's repose at night?—My slumber is disturbed by the din of horses and elephants, or by the song of slave-girls hollooing out, "More venision, more venision!"—Then comes a cry that pierces my ear, "Away to the forests, away!" —nor are these my only grievances: fresh pain is now added to the smart of my first wounds; for, while we were separated from our king, who was chasing a foolish deer, he entered, I find, yon lonly place, and there, to my infinite grief, saw a certain girl, called Shakuntala, the daughter of a hermit; from that moment not a word of returning to the city!—These distressing thoughts have kept my eyes open the whole night.—Alas! when shall we return?—I cannot set eyes on my beloved friend Dushmanta since he set his heart on taking another wife.—[*Stepping aside and looking*]—Oh! there he is.—How changed!—He carries a bow, indeed, but wears for his diadem a garland of wood-flowers.—He is advancing; I must begin my operations.—(*He stands leaning on a staff.*)—Let me thus take a moment's rest.

Dushmanta *enters, as described.*

Dushm. (*Aside, sighing.*) My darling is not so easily attainable; yet my heart assumes confidence from the manner in which she seemed affected: surely though our love has not hitherto prospered, yet the inclinations of us both are fixed on our union.—(*Smiling.*)—Thus do lovers agreeably beguile themselves, when all the powers of their souls are intent on the objects of their desire!—But am I beguiled? No; when she cast her eyes even on her companions, they sparkled with tenderness; when she moved her graceful arms, they dropped, as if languid with love; when her friend remonstrated against her departure, she spoke angrily—all this was, no doubt, on my account.—Oh! how quick-sighted is love in discerning his own advantages!

Madh. (*Bending downward as before.*) Great prince! my hands are unable to move; and it is with my lips only that I can mutter a blessing on you. May the king be victorious!

Dushm. (*Looking at him and smiling.*) Ah! what has crippled thee, friend Madhavya?

Madh. You strike my eyes with your own hand and then ask what made it weep.

Dushm. Speak intelligibly. I know not what you mean.

Madh. Look at yon Vetasa tree bent double in the river. Is it crooked, I pray, by its own act, or by the force of the stream?

Dushm. It is bent, I suppose, by the current.

Madh. So am I by your Majesty.

Dushm. How so, Madhavya?

Madh. Does it become you, I pray to leave the great affairs of your empire, and so charming a mansion as your palace, for the sake of living here like a forester? Can you hold a council in a wood? I, who am a reverend Brahmana, have no longer the use of my hands and feet; they are put out of joint by my running all day long after dogs and wild beasts. Favour me, I entreat, with your permission to repose but a single day.

Dushm. (*Aside*). Such are this poor fellow's complaints; whilst I, when I think of Kanwa's daughter, have as little relish for hunting as he; how can I brace this bow, and fix a shaft in the string, to shoot at those beautiful deer who dwell in the same groves with my beloved, and whose eyes derive lustre from hers?

Madh. (*Looking steadfastly at the king.*) What scheme is your royal mind contriving? I have been crying, I find, in a wilderness.

Dushm. I think of nothing but the gratification of my old friend's wishes.

Madh. (*Joyfully.*) Then may the king live long!

[*Rising, but counterfeiting feebleness.*

Dushm. Stay and listen to me attentively.

Madh. Let the king command.

Dushm. When you have taken repose, I shall want your assistance in another business, that wil give you no fatigue.

Madh. Oh! what can that be, unless it be eating rice-pudding?

Dushm. you shall know in due time.

Madh. I shall be delighted to hear it.

Dushm. Hola! who is there?

[*The* Chamberlain *enters.*]

Cham. Let my sovereign command me.

Dushm. Raivatak, bid the General attend.

Cham. I obey.—(*He goes out and returns with the General.*)—Come quickly, Sir, the king stands expecting you.

Gen. (*Aside looking at* Dushmanta.) How comes it that hunting, which moralists reckon a vice, should be a virtue in the eyes of a king? Thence it is, no doubt, that our emperor, occupied in perpetual toil, and inured to constant heat, is become so lean, that the sunbeams hardly affect him; while he is so tall, that he looks to us little men, like an elephant gazing on a mountain: he seems all soul.—(*Aloud, approaching the king.*)—May our monarch ever be victorious! This forest, O king, is infested by beasts of prey; we see traces of their huge feet in every path. What orders is it your pleasure to give?

Dushm. Bhadrasena, this moralizing Madhavya has put a stop to our recreation by forbiding the pleasures of the chase.

Gen. (*Aside to Madhavya.*) Be firm to your word, my friend; whilst I sound the king's real inclinations.—(*Aloud.*)—O! Sir, the fool talks idly. Consider the delights of hunting. The body, it is true, becomes emaciated, but it is light and fit for exercise. Mark how the wild beasts of various kinds are variously affected by fear and by rage! What pleasure equals that of proud archer, when his arrow hits the mark as it flies?—Can hunting be justly called a vice? No recreation, surely, can be comapred with it.

Madh. (*Angrily.*) Away, thou false flatterer! The king, indeed, follows his natural bent, and is excusable; but thou, son of a slave-girl, has no excuse.—Away to the wood!—How I wish thou hadst been seized by a tiger or an old bear, who was prowling for a skakal like thyself!

Dushm. We are now, Bhadrasena, encamped near a sacred hermitage; and I cannot at present applaud your panegyric on hunting. This day, therefore, let the wild buffalos roll undisturbed in the shallow water or toss up the sand with their horns; let the herd of antelopes, assembled under the thick shade, ruminate without fear; let the large boars root up the herbage on the brink of yon pool; and let this my bow take repose with a slackened string.

Gen. As our lord coommands.

Dushm. Recall the archers who have advanced before me, and forbid the officer to go very far from this hallowed grove. Let them beware of irritating the poius: holy men are eminent for patient virtues, yet conceal within their bosoms a scorching flame; as carbuncles are naturally cool to the touch; but, if the rays of the sun have been imbibed by them, they burn the hand.

Madh. Away now, and triumph on the delights of hunting.

Gen. The king's orders are obeyed.

[*He goes out.*

Dushm. (*To his attandants.*) Put off your hunting apparel; and thou, Raivataka, continue in waiting at a little distance.

Cham. I shall obey. [*Goes out.*

Madh. So! you have cleared the stage; not even a fly is left on it. Sit down, I pray, on this pavement of smooth pebbles, and shade of this tree shall be your canopy: I will sit by you; for I am impatient to know what will give me no fatigue.

Dushm. Go first, and seat thyself.

Madh. Come, my royal friend.

[*They both sit under a tree.*

Dushm. Friend Madhavya, your eyes have not been gratified with an object which best deserves to be seen.

Madh. Yes truly; for a king is before them.

Dushm. All men are apt, indeed, to think favourably of themselves; but I meant Shakuntala, the brightest ornament of these woods.

Madh. [*Aside.*] I must not foment this passion.—[*Aloud.*]—What can you gain by seeing her? She is a Brahmana's daughter, and consequently no match for you!

Dushm. What! Do people gaze at the new moon, with uplifted heads and fixed eyes, from a hope of possessing it? But you must know, that the heart of Dushmanta is not fixed on an object which he must for ever despair of attaining.

Madh. Tell me how.

Dushm. She is the daughter of a pious prince and warrior, by a celestial nymph; and, her mother having left her on earth, she has been fostered by Kanwa, even as a fresh blossom of Malati, which droops on its pendant stalk, is raised and expanded by the sun's light.

Madh. [*Laughing.*] Your desire to possess this rustic girl, when you have women bright as gems in your palace already, is like the fancy of a man, who has lost his relish for dates and longs for the sour tamarind.

Dushm. Did you know her, you would not talk so wildly.

Madh. Oh! certainly, whatever a king admires must be superlatively charming.

Dushm [*Smiling.*] What need is there of long description? When I meditate on the power of Brahma, and on her lineaments, the creation of so transcendent a jewel outshines, in my apprehension, all his other works! She was formed and moulded in the eternal mind, which had raised with its utmost exertion, the ideas of perfect shapes and thence made an assemblage of all abstract beauties.

Madh. She must render, then, all other handsome women contemptible.

Dushm. In my mind she really does. I know not yet what blessed inhabitant of this world will be the possessor of that faultless beauty, which now resembles a blossom whose fragrance has not been diffused;

a fresh leaf, which no hand has torn from its stalk; a pure diamond, which no polisher has handled; new honey, whose sweetness is yet untasted; ot rather the celestial fruit of collected virtues, to the perfection of which nothing can be added.

Madh. Make haste, then, or the fruit of all virtues will drop into the hand of some devout rustic, whose hair shines with oil of Ingudi.

Dushm. She is not her own mistress; and her foster father is at a distance.

Madh. How is she disposed towards you?

Dushm. My friend, the damsels in a hermit's family are naturally reserved: yet she did look at me, wishing to be unperceived; then she smiled, and started a new subject of conversation. Love is by nature averse to a sudden communication, and hitherto neither fully displays, nor wholly conceals, himself in her demeanor towards me.

Madh. (*Laughing.*) Has she thus taken possession of your heart on so transient a view?

Dushm. When she walked about with her female friends I saw her yet more distinctly, and my passion was greatly augmented. She said sweetly, but untrully. "My foot is hurt by the points of the Kusha grass:" then she stopped; but soon, advancing a few paces, turned back her face, pretending a wish to disentangle her vest of woven bark from the branches in which it had not really been caught.

Madh. You began with chasing an antelope, and

have now started a new game: thence it is, I presume, that you are grown so fond of a consecrated forest.

Dushm. Now the business for you, which I mentioned, is this: you, who are a Brahmana, must find some expedient for my second entrance into that asylum of virtue.

Madh. And the advice which I give is this: remember that you are a king.

Dushm. What then?

Madh. "Hola! bid the hermits bring my sixth part of their grain." Say this, and enter the grove without scruple.

Dushm. No, Madhavya; they pay a different tribute, who, having abandoned all the gems and gold of this world, possess riches far superior. The wealth of princes, collected fram the four orders of their subjects, is perishable; but pious men give us a sixth part of the fruits of their piety, fruits which never perish.

Behind the scenes.] Happy men that we are! we have now attained the object of our desire.

Dushm. Hah! I hear the voices of some religious anchorites.

The Chamberlain *enters.*

Cham. May the king be victorious!—Two young men, sons of a hermit, are waiting at my station, and soliciting an audience.

Dushm. Introduce them without delay.

Cham. As the king commands.—(*He goes out,*

and re-enters with two Brahmanas.)—Come on; come this way.

First Brahm. (*Looking at the king.*) Oh! what confidence is inspired by his brillliant appearence!—¡Or proceeds it rather from his disposition to virtue and holiness?—Whence comes it, that my fear vanishes?—He now has taken his abode in a wood which supplies us with every enjoyment; and with all his exertions for our safety, his devotion increases from day to day.—The praise of a monarch who has conquered his passions ascends even to heaven: inspired bards are continually singing, "Behold a virtuous prince!" but with us the royal name stands first: "Behold, among kings, a sage!"

Second Brahm. Is this, my friend, the truly virtuous Dushmanta?

First Brahm. Even he.

Second Brahm. It is not then wonderful, that he alone, whose arm is lofty and strong as the main bar of his city gate, possesses the whole earth, which forms a dark boundary to the ocean; or that the gods of Swarga, who fiercely contend in battle with evil powers, proclaim victory gained by his braced bow, not by the thunderbolt of INDRA.

Both. (*Approaching him.*) O king, be victorious!

Dushm. (*Rising.*) I humbly salute you both.

Both. Blessings on thee!

Dushm. (*Respectfully.*) May I know the cause of this visit?

First Brahm. Our sovereign is hailed by the pious inhabitants of these woods; and they implore—

Dushm. What is their command?

First Brahm. In the absence of our spiritual guide, Kanwa, some evil demons are disturbing our holy retreat. Deign, therefore, accompanied by thy charioteer, to be the master of our asylum, if it be only for a few short days.

Dushm. [*Eagerly.*] I am highly favoured by your invitation.

Madh. [*Aside*]. Excellent promoters of your design. They draw you by the neck, but not against your will.

Dushm. Raivataka, bid my charioteer bring my car, with my bow and quiver.

Cham. I obey. [*He goes out.*

First Brahm. Such condescension well becomes thee, who art an universal guardian.

Second Brahm. Thus do the descendants of Puru perform their engagement to deliver their subjects from fear of danger.

Dushm. Go first, holy men: I will follow instantly.

Both. Be ever victorious! [*They go out.*

Dushm. Shall you not be delighted, friend Madhavya, to see my Shakuntala?

Madh. At first I should have had no objection; but I have a considerable one since the story of the demons.

Dushm. Oh! fear nothing: you will be near me.

Madh. And you, I hope, will have leisure to protect me from them.

The Chamberlain *re-enters.*

Cham. May our lord be victorious!—The imperial car is ready; and all are expecting your triumphant approach. Karabhaka too, a messenger from the queen-mother, is just arrived from the city.

Dushm. Is he really come from the venerable queen.

Cham. There can be no doubt of it.

Dush. Let him appear before me.

[*The* Chamberlain *goes out, and returns with the* Messenger.

Cham. There stands the king—O Karabhaka, approach him with reverence.

Mess. [*Prostrating himself.*] May the king—be ever victorious!—The royal mother sends this message——

Dushm. Declare her command.

Mess. Four days hence the usual fast for the advancement of her son will be kept with solemnity; and the presence of the king (may his life be prolonged!) will then be required.

Dushm. On one hand is a commission from holy Brahmanas; on the other, a command from my revered parent: both duties are sacred, and neither must be neglected.

Madh. [*Laughing.*] Stay suspended between them both, like king Trishanku between heaven and earth: when the pious men said, "Rise!" and the gods of Swarga said, "Fall!"

Dushm. In truth I am greatly perplexed. My mind is principally distracted by the distance of the two places where the two duties are to be performed; as the stream of a river is divided by rocks in the middle of its bed.—[*Musing.*]—Friend Madhavya, my mother brought you up as her own son, to be my play-fellow, and to divert me in my childhood. You may properly act my part in the queen's devotions. Return then to the city, and give an account of my distress through the commission of these reverend Brahmanas.

Madh. That I will:—but you could not really suppose that I was afraid of demons!

Dushm. How come you, who are an egregious Brahmana, to be so bold on a sudden!

Madh. Oh! I am now a young king.

Dushm. Yes, certainly; and I will despatch my whole train to attend your highness, whilst I put an end to the disturbance in this hermitage.

Madh. *(Strutting).* See, I am a prince regnant.

Mushm. (*Aside*). This buffoon of a Brahmana has a slippery genius. He will perhaps disclose my present pursuit to the women in the palace. I must try to deceive him.—*Taking* Madhavya *by the hand.*)—I shall enter the forest, be assured, only through respect for its pious inhabitants; not from any inclination for the daughter of a hermit. How far am I raised above a girl educated among antelopes; a girl, whose heart must ever be a stranger to love!—The tale was invented for my diversion.

Madh. Yes, to be sure; only for your diversion.

Dushm. Then farewell, my friend; execute my commission faithfully, whilst I proceed—to defend the anchorites. [*All go out.*

ACT III.

SCENE—The Hermitage *in a Grove.*

The Hermit's Pupil *bearing consecrated grass.*

Pupil.—(*Meditating with wonder*). How great is the power of Dushmanta!—The monarch and his charioteer had no sooner entered the grove than we continued our holy rites without interruption,—What words can describe him?—By his barely aiming a shaft, by the mere sound of his bow-string, by the simple murmur of his vibrating bow, he disperses at once our calamities.—Now then I deliver to the priests this bundle of fresh Kusha grass to be scattered round the place of sacrifice.—(*Looking behind the scenes.*)—Ah! Priyamvada, for whom are you carrying that ointment of Ushira root, and those leaves of water-lilies?—(*Listening attentively*)—What say you?—That Shakuntala is extremely disordered by the sun's heat, and that you have procured for her a cooling medicine! Let her, my

Priyamvada, be diligently attended; for she is the darling of our venerable father Kanwa.—I will administer, by the hand of Gautami, some healing water consecrated in the ceremony called Vaitina.

(*He goes out.*

Dushm. I well know the power of her devotion; that she will suffer none to dispose of her but Kanwa, I too well know. Yet my heart can no more return to its former placid state, than water can re-ascend the steep, down which it has fallen.—O God of Love, how can thy darts be so keen, since they are pointed with flowers?—Yes, I discover the reason of their keenness. They are tipped with the flames which the wrath of Hara kindled, and which blaze at this moment like the Barava fire under the waves; how else couldst thou, who wast consumed even to ashes, be still the inflamer of our souls? By thee and by the moon, though each of you, seems worthy of our confidence, we lovers are cruelly deceived. They who love as I do, ascribe flowery shafts to thee, and cool beams to the moon, with equal impropriety; for the moon sheds fire on them with her dewy rays, and thou pointest with sharp diamonds those arrows which seem to be barbed with blossoms. Yet this God, who bears a fish on his banners, and who wounds me to the soul, will give me real delight, if he destroy me with the aid of my beloved, whose eyes are large and beautiful as those of a roe. O powerful divinity, even when I thus adore thy attributes, hast thou no compassion? Thy fire, O Love, is fanned into a blaze by a hundred of my vain thoughts. Does it become thee to draw thy bow even to thy ear, that the shaft aimed at my bosom may inflict a deeper wound? Where now can I recreate my afflicted soul by the permission of those pious men whose uneasiness I have removed by dismissing my train?—(*Sighing*)—I can have no relief but from a sight of my beloved.—*(Looking up.)*—This intensely hot noon must, no doubt, be passed by Shakuntala with her damsels on the banks of this river over-shadowed with Tamalas.—It must be so.—I will advance thither.—*(Walking round and looking.)*—My sweet friend has, I guess, been lately walking under that row of young trees; for I see the stalks of some flowers, which probably she gathered, still unshrivelled; and some fresh leaves, newly plucked, still dropping milk.—(*Feeling a breeze.*)—Ah! this bank has a delightful air! Here may the gale embrace me, wafting odours from the water-lilies, and cool my breast, inflamed by the bodiless god, with the liquid particles which it catches from the waves of the Malini.—(*Looking down.*)—Happy lover! Shakuntala must be somewhere in this grove of flowering creepers; for I discern on the yellow sand at the door of yon arbour some recent footsteps, raised a little before and depressed behind by the weight of her elegant limbs—I shall have a better view from behind this thick foliage.—(*He conceals himself, looking vigilantly.*)—Nor are my eyes fully gratified.—The darling of my heart, with her two faithful attendants, reposes on a smooth rock strewn with fresh flowers.—These branches will hide me, whilst I hear their charming conversation.

[*He stands concealed and gazes.*

Shakuntala *and her two damsels discoverd,*

Both. [*Fanning her.*] Say, beloved Shakuntala, does the breeze, raised by our fans of broad lotus leaves, refresh you?

Shak. [*Mournfully.*] Why, alas! do my dear friends take this trouble?

[*Both look sorrowfully at each other.*]

Dushm [*Aside.*] Ah! she seems much indisposed. What can have been the cause of so violent a a fever? Is it what my heart suggests? Or— (*musing*)—I am perplexed with doubts. The medicine extracted from the balmy Ushira has been applied, I see, to her bosom; her only bracelet is made of thin filaments from the stalks of a water-lily, and even that is loosely bound on her arm. Yet, even thus disordered, she is exquisitely beautiful. Such are the hearts of the young! Love and the sun equally inflame us; but the scorching heat of summer leads not equally to happiness with the ardour of youthful desires.

Pri. (*Aside to* Anasuya). Did you not observe how the heart of Shakuntala was affected by the first sight of our pious monarch? My suspicion is, that her malady has no other cause.

Ana. (*Aside to* Priyamvada.) The same suspicion had risen in my mind. I will ask her at once.—(*Aloud.*)—My sweet Shakuntala, let me put one question to you. What has really occasioned your indisposition?

Dushm,. (*Aside*). She must now declare it. Ah! though her bracelets of lotus are bright as moonbeams, yet they are marked. I see with black spots from internal ardour.

Shak. (*Half raising herself.*) Oh! say what you suspect to have occasioned it.

Ana. Shakuntala, we must necessarily be ignorant of what is passing in your breast; but I suspect your case to be that which we have often heard related in tales of love. Tell us openly what causes your illness. A physician, without knowing the cause of a disorder, cannot even begin to apply a remedy.

Dushm. (*Aside*). I flatter myself with the same suspicion.

Shak. (*Aside.*) My pain is intolerable; yet I cannot hastily disclose the occasion of it.

Pri. My sweet friend, Anasuya, speaks rationally. Consider the violence of your indisposition. Every day you will be more and more emaciated, though your exquisite beauty has not yet forsaken you.

Dushm. (*Aside.*) Most true. Her forehead is

parched; her neck droops; her waist is more slender than before; her shoulders languidly tall; her complexion is wan; she resembles a Madhavi creeper, whose leaves are dried by a sultry gale; yet even thus transformed, she is lovely, and charms my soul.

Shak. (*Sighing.*) What more can I say? Ah! why should I be the occasion of your sorrow?

Pri, For that very reason, my beloved, we are solicitous to know your secret; since, when each of us has a share of your uneasiness, you will bear more easily your own portion of it.

Dushm. (*Aside.*) Thus urged by two friends, who share her pains as well as her pleasures she cannot fail to disclose the hidden cause of her malady; while I, on whom she looked at our first interview with marked affection, am filled with anxious desire to hear her answer.

Shak. From the very instant when the accomplished prince, who has just given repose to our hallowed forest, met my eye—

[*She breaks off and looks modest.*

Both. Speak on, beloved Shakuntala.

Shak. From that instant my affection was unalterably fixed on him—and thence I am reduced to my present langour.

Ana. Fortunately your affection is placed on a man worthy of yourself.

Pri. Oh! could a fine river have deserted the sea and followed into a lake?

Dushm. (*Joyfully.*) That which I was eager to know, her own lips have told. Love was the cause of my distemper, and love has healed it; as a summer's day, grown black with clouds, relieves all animals from the heat which itself had caused.

Shak. If it be no disagreeable task, contrive, I entreat you, some means by which I may find favour in the king's eyes.

Dushm. (*Aside.*) That request banishes all my cares, and gives me rapture even in my present situation.

Pri. (*Aside to* Anasuya.) A remedy for her, my friend, will scarce be attainable. Exert all the powers of your mind; for her illness admits of no delay.

Ana. (*Aside to* Priyamvada.) By what expedient can her cure be both accelerated and kept secret?

Pri. (*As before.*) Oh! to keep it secret will be easy; but to attain it soon almost insuperably difficult.

Ana. (*As before.*) How so?

Pri. The young king seemed, I admit, by his tender glances, to be enamoured of her at first sight; and he has been observed, within these few days, to be pale and thin, as if his passion had kept him long awake.

Dushm. (*Aside*). So it has. This golden bracelet sullied by the flame which preys on me, and which no dew mitigates, but the tears gushing nightly from the eyes, has fallen again and again on my wrist, and has been replaced on my emaciated arm.

Pri, *(Aloud.)* I have a thought, Anasuya—Let us write a love-letter, which I will conceal in a flower and, under the pretext of making a respectful offering deliver it myself into the king's hand.

Ana. An excellent contrivance! It pleases me highly; but what says our beloved Shakuntalá ?

Shak. I must consider, my friend, the possible consequences of such a step.

Pri. Think also of a verse or two, which may suit your passion, and be consistent with the character of a lovely girl born in an exalted family.

Shak. I will think of them in due time; but my heart flutters with the apprehension of being rejected.

Dushm. (*Aside.*) Here stands the man supremely blessed in thy presence, from whom, O timid girl, thou art apprehensive of a refusal! Here stands the man, from whom, O beautiful maid, thou fearest rejection, though he loves thee distractedly. He who shall possess thee will seek no brighter gem; and thou art the gem which I am eager to possess.

Ana. You depreciate, Shakuntala, your own incomparable merits. What man in his senses would intercept with an umbrella the moonlight of autumn, which alone can allay the fever caused by the heat of the noon ?

Shak. (*Smiling.*) I am engaged in thought.

[*She meditates.*

Dushm. Thus then I fix my eyes on the lovely poetess, without closing them a moment, while she measures the feet of her verse : her forehead is gracefully moved in cadence, and her whole aspect indicates pure affection.

Shak. I have thought of a couplet ; but we have no writing implements.

Pri. Let us hear the words ; and then I will mark them with my nail on this lotus leaf, soft and green as the breast of a young parroquet ; it may easily be cut into the from of a letter.—Repeat the verses.

Shak. "Thy heart, indeed, I know not : but mine, Oh ! cruel, love warms by day and by night ; and all my faculties are centered on thee."

Dushm. (*Hastily advancing, and pronouncing a verse in the same measure.*) "Thee, O slender maid, love only warms ; but me he burns ; as the day-star only stifles the fragrance of the night-flower, but quenches the very orb of the moon."

Ana. (*Looking at him joyfully.*) Welcome, great king ; the fruit of my friend's imagination has ripened without delay.

Shakuntala *expresses an inclinatian to rise.*

Dushm. Give yourself no pain. Those delicate limbs, which repose on a couch of flowers, those arms, whose bracelets of lotus are disarranged by slight pressure, and that sweet frame, which the hot moon seems to have disordered, must not be fatigued by ceremony.

Shak. (*Aside.*) O my heart, canst thou not rest at length after all thy sufferings ?

Ana. Let our sovereign take for his seat a part of the rock on which she reposes.

[Shakuntala *makes a little room.*

Dushm. (*Seating himself.*) Priyamvada, is not the fever of your charming friend somewhat abated ?

Pri. (*Smiling.*) She has just taken a salutary medicine, and will soon be restored to health. But, O mighty prince, as I am favoured by you and by her, my friendship for Shakuntala prompts me to converse with you for a few moments.

Dushm. Excellent damsel, speak openly ; and suppress nothing,

Pri. Our lord shall hear.

Dushm. I am attentive,

Pri. By dispelling the alarms of our pious hermits, you have discharged the duty of a great monarch.

Dushm. Oh ! talk a little on other subjects.

Pri Then I must inform you that our beloved companion is enamoured of you, and has been reduced to her present langour by the resistless divinity, Love. You only can preserve her inestimable life.

Dushm. Sweet Priyamvada, our passion is reciprocal ; but it is I who am honoured.

Shak. (*Smiling, with a mixture of affection and resentment.*) Why should you detain the virtuous monarch, who must be afflicted by so long an absence from the secret apartments of his palace ?

Dushm. This heart of mine, Oh thou who art of all things the dearest to it, will have no object but thee, whose eyes enchant me with their black splendour, if thou wilt but speak in a milder strain. I, who was nearly slain by Love's arrow, am destroyed by the speech.

Ana. (*Laughing.*) Princes are said to have many favourite consorts. You must assure us, therefore, that our beloved friend shall not be exposed to affliction through our conduct.

Dushm. What need is there of many words? Let there be ever so many women in my palace, I will have only two objects of perfect regard; the sea-girt earth, which I govern, and your sweet friend, whom I love.

Both. Our anxiety is dissipated.

[Shakuntala *strives in vain to conceal her joy.*

Pri. (*Aside* to Anasuya.) See how our friend recovers her spirits by little and little, as the pea-hen, oppressed by the summer heat, is refreshed by a soft gale and a gentle shower.

Shak. (*To the damsels.*) Forgive, I pray, my offence in having used unmeaning words: they were uttered only for your amusement in return for your tender care of me.

Pri. They were the occasion, indeed, of your serious advice. But it is the king who must forgive; who else is offended?

Shak. The great monarch will, I trust, excuse

what has been said either before him or in his absence.—(*Aside to the damsels.*)—Intercede with him, I entreat you.

Dushm. (*smiling.*) I would cheerfully forgive any offence, lovely Shakuntala, if you, who have dominion over my heart, would allow me full room to sit by you, and recover from my fatigue, on this flowery couch pressed by your delicate limbs.

Prt. Allow him room ; it will appease him, and make him happy.

Shak. (*Pretending anger aside to* Priyamvada.) Be quiet, thou mischief-making girl ! Dost thou sport with me in my present weak state.

Ana. (*Looking behind the scenes.* O ! my Priyamvada, there is our favourite young antelope running wildly and turning his eyes on all sides ; he is, no doubt, seeking his mother, who has rambled in the wide forest. I must go and assist his search.

Pri. He is very nimble ; and you alone will never be able to confine him in one place. I must accompany you. [*Both going out.*

Shak. Alas ! I cannot consent to your going far ; I shall be left alone.

Both. (*smiling.*) Alone ! with the sovereign of the world by your side ! [*They go out.*

Shak. How could my companions both leave me ?

Dushm. Sweet maid, give yourself no concern. Am not I, who humbly solicit your favour, present in the room of them ?—(*aside.*)—I must declare my passion.—(*Aloud.*)—Why should not I, like them, wave this fan of lotus leaves, to raise cool breezes and dissipate your uneasiness? Why should not I, like them, lay softly in my lap those feet, red as water-lilies, and press them, O my charmer, to relieve your pain?

Shak. I should offend against myself, by receiving homage from a person entitled to my respect.

[*She rises and walks slowly through weariness.*

Dushm. The moon, my love, has not yet passed: and your sweet limbs are weak. Having left couch where fresh flowers covered your bosom, you can ill sustain this intense heat with so languid a frame.

[*He gently draws her back.*

Shak. Leave me, Oh leave me. I am not, indeed, my own mistress, or——the two damsels were only appointed to attend me. What can I do at present?

Dushm. (*Aside.*) Fear of displeasing her makes me bashful.

Shak. (*Overhearing him.*) The king cannot give offence. It is my unhappy fate only that I accuse.

Dushm. Why should you accuse so favourable a destiny?

Shak. How rather can I help blaming it, since it has permitted my heart to be affected by amiable qualities, without having left me at my own disposal?

Dushm. (*Aside.*) One would imagine that the charming sex, instead of being, like us, tormented with love, kept love himself within their hearts, to torment him with delay.

[Shakuntala *going out.*

Dushm. (*Aside.*) How! Must I then fail of attaining felicity?—(*Following her, and catching the skirt of her mantle.*)

Shak. (*Turning back.*) Son of Puru, preserve thy, reason; oh! preserve it.—The hermits are busy on all sides of the grove.

Dushm. My charmer, your fear of them is vain. Kanwa himself, who is deeply versed in the science of law, will be no obstacle to our union. Many daughters of the holiest men have been married by the ceremony called Gandharva, as it is practised by Indra's band, and even their fathers have approved them.—(*Looking round.*)—What say you? Are you still inflexible? Alas! I must then depart.—(*Going from her a few paces, then looking back.*

Shak. (*Moving also a few steps, and then turning back her face.*) Though I have refused compliance, and have only allowed you to converse with me for a moment, yet—O son of Puru—let not Shakuntala be wholly forgotten.

Dushm. Enchanting girl, should you be removed to the ends of the world, you will be fixed in this heart, as the shade of a lofty tree remains with it even when the day is departed.

Shak. (*Going out, aside.*) Since I have heard his protestations, my feet move, indeed, but without advancing. I will conceal myself behind those flowering Kuruvakas, and hence I shall see the result of his passion.—(*She hides herself behind the shrubs.*)

Dushm. (*Aside.*) Can you leave me beloved Shakuntala; me who am all affection? Could you not have tarried a single moment? Soft is your beautiful frame, and indicates a benevolent soul; yet your heart is obdurate, as the tender Shirisha hangs on a hard stalk.

Shak. (*Aside.*) I really have now lost the power of departing.

Dushm. (*Aside.*) What can I do in this retreat since my darling has left it?—(*Musing and looking round.*)—Ah! my departure is happily delayed. Here lies her bracelet of flowers, exquisitely perfumed by the root of Ushira which had been spread on her bosom: it has fallen from her delicate wrist, and is become a new chain for my heart.

Taking up the bracelet with reverence.

Shak. (*Aside looking at her hand.*) Ah me! such was my langour, that the filaments of lotus stalks which bound my arm dropped on the ground unperceived by me.

Dushm. (*Aside placing it in his bosom.*) Oh! how delightful to the touch! From this ornament of your lovely arm, Oh my darling, though it be inanimate and senseless, your unhappy lover has regained confidence,—a bliss which you refused to confer.

4

Shak. (*Aside.*) I can stay here no longer. By this pretext I may return.

[*Going slowly towards him.*

Dushm. (*With rapture.*) Ah! the empress of my soul again blesses these eyes. After all my misery I was destined to be favoured by indulgent heaven. The bird Chataka, whose throat was parched with thirst, supplicated for a drop of water, and suddenly a cool stream poured into his bill from the bounty of a fresh cloud.

Shak. Mighty king, when I had gone half way to the cottage, I perceived that my bracelet of thin stalks had fallen from my wrist; and I return because my heart is almost convinced that you must have seen and taken it. Restore it, I humbly entreat, lest you expose both yourself and me to the censure of the hermits.

Dushm. Yes, on one condition I will return it.

Shak. On what condition? Speak——

Dushm. That I may replace it on the wrist to which it belongs.

Shak. (*Aside.*) I have no alternative.

[*Approaching him.*

Dushm. But in order to replace it, we must both be seated on that smooth rock. [*Both sit down.*

Dushm. (*Taking her hand.*) O exquisite softness! This hand has regained its native strength and beauty, like a young shoot of Kamalata; or it resembles rather the God of love himself, when, having been consumed by the fire of Hara's wrath, he was restored to life by a shower of nectar sprinkled by the immortals.

Shak. (*Pressing his hand.*) Let the son of my lord make haste to tie on the bracelet.

Dushm. (*Aside, with rapture.*) Now I am truly blessed.—That phrase, the son of my lord, is applied only to a husband.—(*Aloud.*)—My charmer, the clasp of this bracelet is not easily loosened; it must be made to fit you better.

Shak. (*Smiling.*) As you please.

Dushm. (*Quittiug her hand.*) Look, my darling; This is the new moon which left the firmament in honour of superior beauty, and, having descended on your enchanting wrist, has joined both its horns round it in the shape of a bracelet.

Shak. I really see nothing like a moon; the breeze, I suppose, has shaken some dust from the lotus flower behind my ears, that has obscured my sight.

Dushm. (*Smiling.*) If you permit me, I will blow the fragrant dust from your eye.

Shak. It would be a kidness; but I cannot trust you.

Dushm. Oh! fear not, fear not. A new servant never transgresses the command of his mistress.

Shak. But a servant over assiduous deserves no confidence.

Dushm. (*Aside.*) I will not let slip this charming

occasion.—(*Attempting to raise her head*—Shakuntala *faintly repels him, but sits still.*)—O damsel with an antelope's eyes, be not apprehensive of my indiscretion.—(Shakuntala *looks up for a moment and then bashfully drops her head.*—Dushmanta, *aside, gently raising her head.*)—That lip, the softness of which is imagined, not proved, seems to pronounce, with a delightful tremor, its permission for me to allay my thirst.

Shak. The son of my lord seems inclined to break his promise.

Dushm. Beloved, I was deceived by the proximity of the lotus to that eye which equals it in brightness. [*He blows gently on her eye.*

Shak. Well; now I see a prince who keeps his word as it becomes his imperial character. Yet I am really ashamed, that no desert of mine entitles me to the kind service of my lord's son.

Dushm. What reward can I desire, except that which I consider as the greatest, the fragrance of your delicious lip?

Shak. Will that content you?

Dushm. The bee is contented with the mere odour of the water-lily.

Shak. If he were not, he would get no remedy.

Dushm. Yes, this and this—(*Kissing her eagerly.*)

Behind the scenes.] Hark! the Chakravaka is

calling her mate on the bank of the Malini: the night is beginning to spread her shades.

Shak. (*Listening alarmed.*) O Son of my lord, the matron Gautami approaches to enquire after my health. Hide yourself, I entreat, behind yon trees.

Dushm. I yield to necessity. [*He retires.*

Gautami *enters with a vase in her hand.*

Gaut (*Looking anxiously at* Shakuntala.) My child, here is holy-water for thee.—What! hast thou no companion here but the invisible gods,—thou who art so much indisposed?

Shak. Both Priyamvàda and Anasuya are just gone down to the river.

Gaut. (*Sprinkling her.*) Is thy fever, my child, a little abated? [*Feeling her hands.*

Shak. Venerable matron, there is a change for the better.

Gaut. Then thou art in no danger. Mayst thou live many years! The day is departing; let us both go to the cottage.

Shak. [*Aside, rising slowly.*] O my heart, no sooner hadst thou begun to taste happiness, than the occasion slipped away.—(*She advances a few steps, and returns to the arbour.*) O bower of twining plants by whom my sorrows have been dispelled, on thee I call; ardently hoping to be once more happy under thy shade. [*She goes out with* Gautami.]

Dushm. (*Returning to the bower, and sighing*) How, alas, have my desires been obstructed! Could

I do less than kiss the lips of my charmer, though her modest cheeks were half adverted; lips whose sweetness had enchanted me, even when they pronounced a denial? Whither now can I go? I will remain a while in this arbour of creepers, which my darling's presence illuminated.—(*Looking round.*) Yes; this her seat on the rock, spread with blossoms, which have been pressed by her delicate limbs.—Here lies her exquisite love-letter on the leaf of a water-lily; here lay her bracelet of tender filaments which had fallen from her sweet wrist.—Though the bower of twining Vetasas be now desolate, since my charmer has left it, yet, while my eyes are fixed on all these delightful memorials of her, I am unable to depart.—(*Musing*).—Ah! how imperfectly has this affair been conducted by a lover, like me, who, with his darling by his side, has let the occasion slip. Should Shakuntala visit once more this calm retreat the opportunity shall not pass again unimproved: the pleasures of youth are by nature transitory.—Thus my foolish heart forms resolutions, while it is distracted by the sudden interruption of its hapiness. Why did it ever allow me to quit without effect the presence of my beloved?

(*Behind the scenes.*) O king, while we are beginning our evening sacrifice, the figures of blood-thirsty demons, embrowned by clouds collected at the departure of day, glide over the sacred heart, and spread consternation around

Dushm. Fear not, holy men.—Your king will protect you.

[*He goes out.*

ACT IV.

SCENE.—*A Lawn before the Cottage.*

The two damsels are discovered gathering flowers.

Anasuya. O my Priyamvadà, though your sweet friend has been happily married, according to the rites of Gandharva, a bridegroom equal in rank and accomplishments yet my affectionate heart is not wholly free from care ; and one doubt gives me particular uneasiness.

Pri. What doubt, my Anasuya?

Ana. This morning the pious prince was dismissed with gratitude by our hermits, who had then completed their mystic rites; he is now gone to his capital, Hastinapura, where, surrounded by a hundred women in the recesses of his palace, it may be doubted whether he will remember his charming bride.

Pri. In that respect you may be quite easy. Men so well informed and well educated as he, can never be utterly destitute of honour.—We have another thing to consider. When our father Kanwa shall return from his pilgrimage, and shall hear what has passed, I can not tell how he may receive the intelligence.

Ana. If you ask my opinion, he will, I think, approve of the marriage.

Pri. Why do you think so ?

Ana. Because he could desire nothing better, than that a husband so accomplished and so exalted should take Shakuntala by the hand. It was, you know, the declared object of his heart, that she might be suitably married : and, since Heaven has done for him what he most wished to do, how can he possibly be dissatisfied.

Pri. You reason well ; but—(*Looking at her basket.*)—my friend, we have plucked a sufficient store of flowers to scatter over the place of sacrifice.

Ana. Let us gather more to decorate the temples of the goddesses who have procured for Shakuntala so much good fortune.

[*They both gather more flowers.*

Behind the scenes.) It is I——Hola !

Ana. (*Listening.*) I hear the voice, as it seems of a guest arrived in the hermitage.

Pri. Let us hasten thither. Shakuntala is now reposing ; but though we may, when she wakes, enjoy her presence, yet her mind will all day be absent with her departed lord.

Ana. Be it so ; but we have occasion, you know, for all these flowers. [*They advance.*

(*Again behind the scenes.*) How ! Dost thou show no attention to a guest ? Then hear my imprecation—"He on whom thou art meditating, on whom alone thy heart is now fixed, while thou neglectest a pure jem of devotion who demands hospitality, shall forget thee when thou seest him next as a man restored to sobriety forgets words he uttered in a state of intoxication."

[*Both damsels look at each other with affection.*

Pri. Woe is me! Dreadful calamity! Our beloved friend has, through mere absence of mind, provoked by her neglect, some holy man who expected reverence.

Ana. (*Looking.*) It must be so; for the choleric Durvasa is going hastily back.

Pri. Who else has power to consume, like raging fire, whatever offends him? Go, my Anasuya; fall at his feet, and persuade him, if possible, to return: in the meantime, I will prepare water and refreshments for him.

Ana. I go with eagerness. [*She goes out.*

Pri. (*Advancing hastily, her foot slips.*) Ah! through my eager haste I have let the basket fall; and my religious duties must not be postponed.

[*She gathers fresh flowers.*

Anasuya *re-enters.*

Ana. His wrath, my beloved, passes all bounds.—Who living could now appease him by the humblest prostration or entreaties! yet at last he little relented.

Pri. That little is a great deal for him.—But inform me how you soothed him in any degree.

Ana. When he positively refused to come back, I threw myself at his feet, and thus addressed him: "Holy sage, forgive, I entreat, the offence of an amiable girl, who has the highest veneration for you, but was ignorant, through distraction of mind, how exalted a personage was calling to her."

Pri. What then? What said he?

Ana. He answered thus: "My word must not be recalled; but the spell which it has raised shall be wholly removed when her lord shall see his ring." Saying this, he disappeared.

Pri. We may now have confidence; for before the monarch departed, he fixed with his own hand on the finger of Shakuntala the ring, on which we saw the name Dushmanta engraved, and which he will instantly recognize. On him therefore alone will depend the remedy for our misfortune.

Ana. Come, let us now proceed to the shrines of the goddesses, and implore their succour.

[*Both advance.*

Pri. (*Looking.*) See, my Anasuya, where our beloved sits, motionless as a picture, supporting her languid head with her left hand. With a mind so intent on one object, she can pay no attention to herself, much less to a stranger.

Ana. Let the horrid imprecation, Priyamvada, remain a secret between us two; we must spare the feelings of our beloved, who is naturally susceptible of quick emotions.

Pri. Who would pour boiling water on the blossom of a tender Mallika. [*Both go out.*

A Pupil *of* Kanwa *enters.*

Pup. I am ordered by the venerable Kanwa, who is returned from the place of his pilgrimage, to observe the time of the night, and am, therefore, come forth to see how much remains of it.—(*Walking round, and observing the heavens.*)—On one side, the moon, who kindles the flowers of the Oshadi, has nearly sunk in western bed; and, on the other, the sun, seated behind his charioteer Aruna, is beginning his course: the lustre of them both is conspicuous, when they rise and when they set; and by their example should men be equally firm in prosperous and in adverse fortune.—The moon has now disappeared, and the night-flower pleases no more: it leaves only a remembrance of its odour, and languishes like a tender bride whose pain is intolerable in the absence of her beloved.—The ruddy morn impurples the dew-drops on the branches of yonder Vadari; the peacock, shaking off sleep, hastens from the cottages of hermits interwoven with holy grass; and yonder antelope, springing hastily from the place of sacrifice, which is marked with his hoofs, raises himself on high, and stretches his graceful limbs.—How is the moon fallen from the sky with diminished beams! the moon who had set in foot on the head of Sumeru, king of mountains, and had climbed, scattering the rear of darkness even to the central palace of Vishnu!—Thus do the great men of this world ascend with extreme labour to the summit of ambition, but easily and quickly descend from it.

Anasuya *enters meditating*.

Ana. (*Aside.*) Such has been the affection of Shakuntala, though she was bred in austere devotion, averse from sensual enjoyments!—How unkind was the king to leave her!

Pup. (*Aside*). The proper time is come for performing the Homa: I must apprise our preceptor of of it. [*He goes out.*

Ana. The shades of night are dispersed; and I am hardly awake; but were I ever so perfectly in my senses, what could I now do? My hands move not readily to the usual occupations of the morning.—Let the blame be cast on love only, by whom our friend has been reduced to her present condition, through a monarch who has broken his word.—Or does the imprecation of Durvasa already prevail?—How else could a virtuous king, who made so solemn an engagement, have suffered so long a time to elapse without sending even a massage?—Shall we convey the fatal ring to him?—Or what expedient can be suggested for the relief of this incomparable girl, who mourns without ceasing?—Yet what fault has she committed?—With all my zeal for her happiness, I cannot summon courage enough to inform our father Kanwa that she is pregnant. What then, oh! what step can I take to relieve her anxiety?

Priyamavada *enters.*

Pri. Come, Anasuya, come quickly. They are making suitable preparations for conducting Shakuntala to her husband's palace.

Ana. (*With surprise.*) What say you, my friend?

Pri. Hear me. I went just now to Shakuntala, meaning only to ask if she had slept well—

Ana. What then? Oh! what then?

Pri. She was sitting with her head bent on her knee, when our father Kanwa, entering her appartment, embraced and congratulated her.—"My sweet child," said he, "there has been a happy omen: the young Brahmana who officiated in our morning sacrifice, though his sight was impeded by clouds of smoke, dropped the clarified butter in the very centre of the adorable flame.—Now, since the pious act of my pupil has prospered, my foster child must not be suffered any longer to languish in sorrow; and this day I am determined to send thee from the cottage of the old hermit who bred thee up, to the palace of the monarch who has taken thee by the hand."

Ana. My friend, who told Kanwa what passed in his absence?

Pri. When he entered the place where the holy fire was blazing, he heard a voice from heaven pronouncing divine measures.—

Ana. (*Amazed.*) Ah! you astonish me.

Pri. Hear the celestial verse:—"Know that thy

adopted daughter, O pious Brahmana, has received from Dushmanta a ray of glory destined to rule the world, as the wood Shami becomes pregnant with mysterious fire."

Ana. (*Embracing* Priyamvada.) I am delighted, my beloved; I am transported with joy. But—since they mean to deprive us of our friend so soon as to-day, I feel that my delight is at least equalled by my sorrow.

Pri. Oh! we must submit patiently to the anguish of parting. Our beloved friend will now be happy; and that should console us.

Ana. Let us now make haste to dress her in bridal array. I have already, for that purpose, filled the shell of a cocoa-nut, which you see fixed on an Amra tree, with the fragrant dust of Nagakesharas; take it down, and keep it in a fresh lotus leaf, whilst I collect some Gorochana from the forehead of a sacred cow, some earth from consecrated ground, and some fresh Kusha grass, of which I will make a paste to ensure good fortune.

Pri. By all means.

[*She takes down the perfume.*—Anasuya *goes out.*

[*Behind the scenes.*] O Gautami, bid the two Mishras, Sharngarava and Sharadwata, make ready to accompany my child Shakuntala.

Pri. (*Listening.*) Lose no time, Anasuya, lose no time. Our father Kanwa is giving others for the intended journey to Hastinapura.

Anasuya *re-enters with the ingredients of her charm.*

Ana. I am here; let us go, my Priyamvada.

[*They both advance.*

Pri. (*Looking.*) There stands our Shakuntala, after her bath at sunrise, while many holy women, who are congratulating her, carry baskets of hallowed grain; let us hasten to greet her.

Enter Shakuntala, Gautami, *and female Hermits.*

Shak. I prostrate myself before the goddess.

Gaut. My child, thou canst not pronounce too often the word goddess: thus wilt thou procure great felicity for thy lord,

Herm. Mayst thou, O royal bride, be delivered of a hero.

[*The* Hermits *go out.*

Both damsels. (*Approaching* Shakuntala.) Beloved friend, was your bath pleasant?

Shak. O! my friends, you are welcome: let us sit a while together. [*They seat themselves.*

Ana. Now you must be patient, whilst I bind on a charm to secure your return.

[*Wiping off her tears.*

Pri. Beloved, it is unbecoming to weep at a time when you are going to be so happy.—(*Both damsels burst into tears as they dress her.*)—Your elegant person deserves richer apparel: it is now decorated with such rude flowers as we could procure in this forest.

Kanwa's pupil *enters with rich clothes.*

Pup. Here is a complete dress. Let the queen wear it auspiciously; and may her life be long!

[*The women look with astonishment.*

Gaut. My son, Harita, whence came this apparel.

Pup. From the devotion of our father Kanwa.

Gaut. What dost thou mean?

Pup. Be attentive. The venerable sage gave this order: "Bring fresh flowers for Shakuntala from the most beautiful trees;" and suddenly the wood-nymphs appeared raising their hands, which rivalled new leaves in beauty and softness. Some of them wove a lower mantle bright as the moon, the presage of her felicity; another pressed the juice of Laksha to stain her feet exquisitely red; the rest were busied in forming the gayest ornaments; and they eagerly showered their gifts on us.

Pri. (*Looking at* Shakuntala.) Thus it is, that even the bee, whose nest is within the hollow trunk, does homage to the honey of the lotus flower.

Gaut. The nymphs must have been commisioned by the goddess of the king's fortune, to predict the accession of brighter ornaments in his palace.

[Shakuntala *looks modest.*

Pup. I must hasten to Kanwa, who has gone to bathe in the Malini, and let him know the signal kindness of wood-nymphs.

[*He goes out.*

Ana. My sweet friend, I little expected so splendid a dress:—how shall I adjust it in properly?—(*Considering*)—Oh! my skill in painting will supply me with some hints; and I will dispose the drapery according to art.

Shak. I well know your affection for him.

Kanwa *enters meditating*

Kan. (*Aside.*) This day must Shakuntala depart: that is resolved; yet my soul is smitten with anguish.—My speech is interrupted by a torrent of tears, which my reason suppresses and turns inward; my very sight is dimmed.—Strange that the affliction of a forester, retired from haunts of men, should be so excessive!—Oh! with what pangs must they, who are fathers of families, be afflicted on the departure of a daughter! (*He walks round musing.*

Pri. Now, my Shaknntala, you are becomingly decorated; put on this lower vest, the gift of sylvan goddesses.

[Shakuntala *rises, and puts on the mantle.*

Gaut. My child, thy spiritual father, whose eyes overflow with tears of joy, stands desiring to embrace thee. Hasten, therefore, to do him reverence.

[Shakuntala *modestly bows to him.*

Kan. Mayst thou be cherished by thy husband, as Sharmishtha was cherished by Yayati! Mayst thou bring forth a sovereign of the world, as she brought forth Puru!

Gaut. This, my child, is not a mere benediction; it is a boon actually connferred.

Kan. My best beloved, come and walk with me round the sacrificial fire.—*(They all advance.)*—May these fires preserve thee! Fires which spring to their appointed stations on the holy hearth, and consume the consecrated wood, while the fresh blades of mysterious Kusha lie scatterd around them!—Sacramental fires, which destroy sin with the rising fumes of clarified butter!—(Shakuntala *walks with solemnity ronnd the hearth.*) Now set out, my darling, on thy auspicious journey.—*(Looking round.)*—Where are the attendants, the two Mishras?

Enter Sharngarava *and* Sharadwata.

Both. Holy sage, we are here.

Kan. My son, Sharngarava, show thy sister her way.

Sharn. Come damsel. *They all advance.*

Kan. Hear, all ye trees of this hallowed forest: ye trees, in which the sylvan goddesses have their abode; hear, and proclaim, that Shakuntala is going to the palace of her wedded lord; she who drank not, though thirsty, before you were watered: she who cropped not, through affection for you, and of your fresh leaves, though she would have been pleased with such an ornament for her locks; she whose chief delight was in the season when your branches are spangled with flowers!

CHORUS *of invisible* WOOD-NYMPHS] May her way be attended with prosperity! May propitious breezes sprinkle, for her delight, the odoriferous dust of rich blossoms! May pools of clear water, green with the leaves of the lotus, refresh her as she walks! and may shady branches be her defence from the scorching sunbeams! *All listen with admiration.*

Sharn. Was that the voice of the Kokila wishing a happy journey to Shakuntala?—Or did the nymphs, who are allied to the pious inhabitants of these woods, repeat the warbling of the musical bird, and make its greeting their own?

Gaut. Daughter, the sylvan goddesses, who love their kindred hermits, have wished you prosperity, and are entitled to humble thanks.

[Shakuntala *walks round, bowing to the nymphs.*

Shak. (*Aside to* Priyamvada.) Delighted as I am, O Priyamvada, with the thought of seeing again the son of my lord, yet, on leaving this grove, my early asylum, I am scarce able to walk.

Pri. You lament not alone.—Mark the affliction of the forest itselfswhen the time of your departure approaches!—The female antelope browses no more on the collected Kusha grass; and the pea-hen ceases to dance on the lawn; the very plants of the grove, whose pale leaves fall on the ground, lose their strength and their beauty.

Shak. Venerable father, suffer me to address this Madhavi creeper, whose red blossoms inflame the grove.

Kan. My child, I know thy affection for it.

Shak. (*Embracing the plant.*) O most radiant of twining plants, receive my embraces, and return them with thy flexible arms; from this day, though removed to a fatal distance, I shall for ever be thine. —O Beloved father, consider this creeper as myself.

Kan. My darling, thy amiable qualities have gained thee a husband equal to thyself; such an event has been long, for thy sake, the chief object of my heart; and now, since my solicitude for thy marriage is at an end, I will marry thy favourite plant to the bridegroom A'mra, who sheds fragrance near her.— Proceed, my child on thy journey.

Shak. (*Approaching the two damsels.*) Sweet friends, let this Madhavi creeper be a precious deposit in your hands.

Ana. and Pri. Alas! in whose care shall we be left? [*They both weep.*

Kan. Tears are in vain, Anasuya: our Shakuntala ought rather to be supported by your firmness, than weakened by your weeping.

[*All Advance.*

Shak. Father! when yon female antelope, who now moves slowly from the weight of the young ones with which she is pregnant, shall be delivered of them, send me, I beg, a kind message with tidings of her safety.—Do not forget.

Kan. My beloved, I will not forget it.

Shak. (*Advancing, then stopping.*) Ah! what

is it that clings to the skirts of my robe, and detains me? [*She turns round and looks.*

Kan. It is thy adopted child, the little fawn, whose mouth, when the sharp points of Kusha grass had wounded it, has been so often smeared by thy hand with the healing oil of Ingudi, who has been so often fed by thee with a handful of Shyamaka grains, and now will not leave the footstep of his protectress.

Shak. Why dost thou weep tender fawn for me, who must leave our common dwelling-place?—As thou wast reared by me when thou hadst lost thy mother, who died soon after thy birth, so will my foster-father attend thee, when we are separated, with anxious care.—Return, poor thing, return—we must part. [*She burst into tears.*

Kan. Thy tears, my child, ill suit the occasion: we shall all meet again: be firm: see the direct road before thee, and follow it.—When the big tear lurks beneath thy beautiful eye-lashes, let thy resolution check its first efforts to disengage itself.—In the passage over this earth, where the paths are now high, now low, and the true path seldom distinguished, the traces of thy feet must needs be unequal: but virtue will press the right onward.

Sharn. It is a sacred rule, holy sage, that a benevolent man should accompany a traveller till he meet with abundance of water; and that rule you have carefully observed; we are now near the brink of a large pool. Give us. therefore, your commands, and return.

Kan. Let us rest awhile under the shed of this Vata tree.—(*They all go to the shade.*) What message can I send with propriety to the noble Dushmanta? [*He meditates.*

Ana. (*Aside to* Shakuntala.) My beloved friend, every heart in our asylum is fixed on you alone, and all are afflicted by your departure.—Look, the bird Chakravaka, called by his mate, who is almost hidden by waterlilies, gives her no answer; but having dropped from its bill the fibres of lotus stalks which he had plucked, gazes on you with inexpressible tenderness.

Kan. My son Sharngarava, remember, when thou shalt present Shakuntala to the king, to address him thus in my name; "Considering us hermits as virtuous, in deed, but rich only in devotion, and considering also thy own exalted birth, retain thy love for this girl, which arose in thy bosom without anys interference of her kindred; and look on her among thy wives with the same kindness which they experience: more than that connot be demanded; since particular affection must depend on the will of heaven."

Sharn. Your massage, venerable man, is deeply rooted in my remembrance.

Kan. (*Looking tenderly at* Shakuntala.) Now, my darling, thou too must be gently admonished.—

We, who are humble foresters, are yet acquainted with the world which we have forsaken.

Sharn. Nothing can be unknown to the wise.

Kan. Hear, my daughter.—When thou art settled in the mansion of thy husband, show due reverence to him, and to those whom he reveres; though he has other wives, be rather an affectionate handmaid to them than a rival.—Should he displease thee, let not thy resentment lead thee to disobedience —In thy conduct to thy domestics be rigidly just and impartial: and seek not eagerly thy own gratification.—By such behaviour young women become respectable; but perverse wives are the bane of a family.—What thinks Gautami of this lesson?

Gaut. It is incomparable:—My child, be sure to remember it.

Kan. Come, my beloved girl, give a parting embrace to me and to thy tender companions.

Shak. Must Anasuya and Priyamvada return to the hermitage?

Kan. They too, my child, must be suitably married; and it would not be proper for them yet to visit the city; but Gautami will accompany thee.

Shak. (*Embracing him.*) Removed from the bosom of my father, like a young sandal tree, rent from the hills of Malaya, how shall I exist in a strange soil!

Kan. Be not so anxious. When thou shalt be mistress of a family, and consort of a king, thou mayst, indeed, be occasionally perplexed by the intricate affairs which arise from exuberence of wealth, but wilt then think little of this transient affliction, especially when thou shalt have a son (and a son thou wilt have) bright as the rising day-star.—Know also with certainty that the body must necessarily, at the appointed moment, be separated from the soul: who, then, can be immoderately afflicted, when the weaker bonds of extrinsic relations are loosened, or even broken.

Shak. (*Falling at his feet.*) My father, I thus humbly declare my veneration for you.

Kan. Excellent girl, may my effort for thy happiness prove successful.

Shak. (*Approaching her two companions.*) Come, then, my beloved friends, embrace me together.

[*They embrace her.*

Ana. My friend, if the virtuous monarch should not at once recollect you, only show him the ring on which his own name is engraved.

Shak. (*Starting.*) My heart flutters at the bare apprehension which you have raised.

Pri. Fear not, sweet Shakuntala: love always raises ideas of misery, which are seldom or never realised.

Sharn. Holy sage, the sun has risen to a considerable height; let the queen hasten her departure.

Shak. (*Again embracing* Kanwa.) When, my

father, oh! when again shall I behold this asylum of virtue?

Kan. Daughter, when thou shalt long have been wedded, like this fruitful earth, to the pious monarch, and shalt have borne him a son, whose car shall be matchless in battle, thy lord shall transfer to him the burden of empire, and thou, with thy Dushmanta, shalt again seek tranquility before thy final departure, in this loved and consecrated grove.

Gaut. My child, the proper time for our journey passes away rapidly: suffer thy father to return.—Go, venerable man, go back to thy mansion, from which she is doomed to be so long absent.

Kan. Sweet child, this delay interrupts my religious duties.

Shak. You, my father, well perform them long without sorrow; but I, alas! am destined to bear affliction.

Kan. O! my daughter, compel me not to neglect my daily devotions.—(*Sighing.*)—No, my sorrow will not be diminished.—Can it cease, my beloved, when the plants which rise luxuriantly from the hallowed grains which thy hand has strewn before my cottage, are continually in my sight? Go, may thy journey prosper.

[Shakuntala *goes out with* Gautami, *and the two* Mishras.

Both damsels. (*Looking after* Shakuntala *with*

anguish.) Alas! alas! our beloved is hidden by the thick trees.

Kan. My children, since your friend is at length departed, check your immoderate grief, and follow me.

[*They all turn back.*

Both. Holy father, the grove will be a perfect vacuity without Shakuntala.

Kan. Your affection will certainly give it that appearance.—(*He walks round meditating.*)—Ah me!—Yes; at last my weak mind has attained its due firmness after the departure of my Shaknutala. —In truth a daughter must sooner or later be the property of another; and, having now sent her to her lord, I find my soul clear and undisturbed, like that of a man who has restored to its owner an inestimable deposit which he long had kept with solicitude. [*They go out.*

ACT V.

SCENE—The Palace.

An old Chamberlain *enters.*

Chamberlain. (*Sighing.*) Alas! what a decrepit old age have I attained!—This wand, which I first held for the discharge of my customary duties in the secret apartments of my prince, is now my support, whilst I walk feebly through the multitude of years which I have passed.—I must now mention to the king, as he goes through the Palace, an event which concern himself: it must not be delayed. (*Advancing slowly.*) —What is it?—Oh! I recollect, the devout pupils of Kanwa desire an audience.—How stange a thing is human life!—The intellect of an old man seems at one time luminous, and then on a sudden is involved in darkness, like the flame of a lamp at the point of extinction.—(*He walks round and looks.*)—There is Dushmanta: he has been attending to his people, as to his own family; and now with a tranquil heart seeks a solitary chamber; as an elephant, the chief of his herd, having grazed the hole morning, and being heated by the meridian sun, repairs to a cool station during the oppressive heat.—Since the king is just risen from his tribunal, and must be fatigued, I am almost afraid to inform him at present that Kanwa's pupils are arrived; yet how should they who support nations enjoy rest?—The sun yokes his bright steeds for the labour of many hours; the gale breathes by night and by day; the prince of serpents continually sustains the weight of this earth; and equally incessant is the toil of that man, whose revenue arises from a sixth part of his people's income.

[*He walks about.*

Enter Dushmanta, Madhavya, *and Attendants.*

Dushm. (*Looking oppressed with business.*) Every petitioner having attained justice, is departed happy; but kings who perform their duties conscientiously are afflicted without end.—The anxiety of acquiring dominion gives extreme pain: and when it is firmly established, the cares of supporting the nation incessantly harass the sovereign; as a large umbrella, of which a man carries the staff in his own hand, fatigues while it shades him.

Behind the scenes.] May the king be victorious!

[*Two* Bards *repeat stanzas.*]

First. Bard. Thou seekest not thy own pleasure: no; it is for the people that thou art harassed from day to day. Such, when thou wast created, was the disposition implanted in thy soul! Thus a branchy tree bears on his head the schorching sunbeams, while his broad shade allays the fever of those who seek shelter under him.

Second Bard. When thou wieldest the rod of justice, thou bringest to order all those who have deviated from the path of virtue: thou biddest contention cease thou wast formed for the preservation of thy people: thy kindred possess, indeed, considerable wealth; but so boundless is thy affection, that all thy subjects are considered by thee as thy kinsmen.

Dushm. (*Listening.*) That sweet poetry refreshes me after the toil of giving judgments and public orders.

Madh. Yes; as a tried bull is refreshed when the people say, "There goes the lord of cattle."

Dushm. (*Smilling.*) Oh! art thou here, my friend: let us take our seats together.

[*The king and* Madhavya *sit down.—*
Music behind the scenes.

Madh. Listen, my royal friend, I hear a well-tuned Vina sounding, as if it were in concert with the lutes of the gods, from yonder apartment.—The queen Hansamati is preparing, I imagine, to greet you with a new song.

Dushm. Be silent, that I may listen.

Cham. (*Aside.*) The king's mind seems intent on some other business. I must wait his leisure.

[*Retiring on one side.*

SONG. [*Behind the scenes.*]

"Sweet bee, who, desirous of extracting fresh honey, wast wont to kiss the soft border of the new-blown A'mra flower, how canst thou now be satisfied with the water lily, and forget the first object of thy love?"

Dushm. The ditty breathes a tender passion.

Madh. Does the king know its meaning? It is too deep for me.

Dushm. (*Smiling.*) I was once in love with Hansamati. and am now reproved for continuing so long absent from her.—Friend Madhavya, inform the queen in my name that I feel the reproof.

Madh. As the king commands; but——(*Rising slowly.*)—My friend, you are going to seize a sharp lance with another mans' hand. I cannot relish your commission to an enraged woman.—A hermit cannot be happy till he has taken leave of all passions whatever.

Dushm. Go, my kind friend; the urbanity of thy discourse will appease her.

Madh. What an errand! [*He goes out.*

Dushm. (*Aside.*) Ah! what makes me so melancholy on hearing a mere song on absence, when I am not in fact separated from any real object of affection?—Perhaps the sadness of men, otherwise happy, on seeing beautiful forms and listening to sweet melody, arises from some faint remembrance of past joys and the traces of connections in a former state of existence. [*He sits pensive and sorrowful.*

Cham. (*Advancing humbly.*) May our sovereign be victorious!—Two religious men, with some women, are come from their abode in a forest near the Snowy Mountains, and bring a message from Kanwa.—The king will command.

Dnshm. (*Surprised.*) What! are pious hermits arrived in the company of women?

Cham. It is even so.

Dushm. Order the priest Somarata, in my name to shew them due reverence in the form appointed by the Veda,; and bid him attend me. I shall wait for my holy guests in a place fit for their reception.

Cham. I obey. [*He goes out*

Dushm. Warder, point the way to the hearth of the consecrated fire.

Ward. This, O king, this is the way.—(*He walks before.*)—Here is the entrance of the hallowed enclosure; and there stands the venerable cow to be milked for the sacrifice, looking bright from the recent sprinkling of mystic water.—Let the king ascend.

[Dushmanta *is raised to the place of sacrifice on the shoulders of his warders.*]

Dushm. What message can the pious Kanwa have sent me?—Has the devotion of his pupils been impeded by evil spirits.—or by what other calamity?—or has any harm, alas! befallen the poor herds who graze in the hallowed forest?—Or have the sins of the king tainted the flowers and fruits of the creepers planted by female hermits? My mind is entangled in a labyrinth of confused apprehensions.

Ward. What our sovereign imagines, cannot possibly have happened; since the hermitage has been rendered secure from evil by the mere sound of his bowstring. The pious men, whom the king's benevolence has made happy, are come, I presume, to do him homage.

Enter Sharnagarava, Sharadwata, *and* Gautami, *leading* Shakuntala *by the hand*; *and before them the old* Chamberlain *and the* Priest.

Cham. This way, respectable stangers; come this way.

Sharn. My friend Sharadwata, there sits the king of men, who has felicity at command, yet shews equal respect to all: here no subject, even of the lowest class, is received with contempt. Nevertheless, my soul having ever been free from attachment to wordly things, I consider this hearth, although a crowd now surround it, as the station merely of consecrated fire.

Sharad. I was not less confounded than yourself on entering the populous city; but now I look on it, as a man just bathed in pure water, on a man smeared with oil and dust, as the pure on the impure, as the waking on the sleeping, as the free man of the captive, as the independent on the slave.

Priest. Thence it is, that men, like you two, are so elevated above other mortals.

Shak. (*Perceiving a bad omen.*) Venerable mother, I feel my right eye throb! What means this involuntary motion?

Gaut. Heaven avert the omen, my sweet child! May every delight attend thee.

[*They all advance.*

Priest. (*Shewing the king to them.*) There, holy men, is the protector; who has taken his seat, and expects you.

Sharn. This is what we wished; yet we have no private interest in the business. It is ever thus: trees are bent by the abundance of their fruit; clouds are brought low, when they teem with salubrious rain; and the real benefactors of mankind are not elated by riches.

Ward. O king, the holy guests appear before you with placid looks, indicating their affection.

Dushm. (*Gazing at* Shakuntala.) Ah! what damsel is that whose mantle conceals the far greater part of her beautiful form? She looks, among the hermits, like a fresh green bud among faded and yellow leaves.

Ward. This at least, O king, is apparent; that she has a form which deserves to be seen more distinctly.

Dushm. Let her still be covered; she seems pregnant; and the wife of another must not be seen even by me.

Shak. (*Aside with her hand to her bosom.*) O my heart, why dost thou palpitate?—Remember the beginning of thy lord's affection, and be tranquil.

Priest. May the king prosper! The respectable guests have been honoured as the law ordains: and they have now a message to deliver from their spiritual guide; let the king deign to hear it.

Dushm. (*With reverence.*) I am attentive.

Both Mishras. (*Extending their hands.*) Victory attend thy banners!

Dushm. I respectfully greet you both.

Both. Blessing on our sovereign.

Dushm. Has your devotion been uninterrupted?

Sharn. How should our rites be disturbed, when thou art the preserver of all creatures? How, when the bright sun blazes, should darkness cover the world?

Dushm. (*Aside.*) The name of royalty produces, I suppose, all worldly advantages!—(*Aloud*)—Does the holy Kanwa then prosper?

Sharn. O king, they who gather the fruits of devotion may command prosperity. He first inquires affectionately whether thy arms are successful, and then addresses thee in these words :—

Dushm. What are his orders ?

Sharn. "The contract of marriage, reciprocally made between thee and this girl, my daughter, I confirm with tender regard ; since thou art celebrated as the most honourable of men, and my Shakuntala is Virtue herself in a human form, no blasphemous complaint will henceforth be made against Brahma for suffering discordant matches : he has now united a bride and bridegroom with qualities equally transcendent. –Since, therefore, she is pregnant by thee, receive her in thy palace, that she may perform, in conjunction with thee, the duties prescribed by religion."

Gaut. Great king, thou hast a mild aspect ; and I wish to address thee in few words.

Dushm. (*Smiling.*) Speak, venerable matron.

Gaut. She waited not the return of her spiritual father; nor were thy kindred consulted by thee. You two only were present, when your nuptials were solemnized ; now, therefore, converse freely together in the absence of all others.

Shak. (*Aside.*) What will my lord say ?

Dushm. (*Aside, perplexed.*) How strange an adventure !

Shak. (*Aside.*) Ah me! how disdainfully he seems to receive the message!

Sharn. (*Aside.*) What means that phrase which I overheard, "How strange an adventure?"—(*Aloud.*)—Monarch, thou knowest the hearts of men. Let a wife behave ever so discreetly, the world will think ill of her, if she live only with her paternal kinsmen; and a lawful wife now requests, as her kindred also humbly entreat, that whether she be loved or not, she may pass her days in the mansion of her husband.

Dushm. What sayest thou?—Am I the lady's husband?

Shak. (*Aside with anguish.*) O my heart, thy fears have proved just.

Sharn. Does it become a magnificent prince to depart from the rules of religion and honour, merely because he repents of his engagements?

Dushm. With what hope of success could this groundless fable have been invented?

Sharn. (*Angrily.*) The minds of those whom power intoxicates are perpetually changing.

Dushm. I am reproved with too great severity.

Gaut. (*To* Shakuntala.) Be not ashamed, my sweet child; let me take off thy mantle, that the king may recollect thee. [*She unveils her*

Dushm. (*Aside, looking at* Shakuntala.) While I am doubtful whether this unblemished beauty which is displayed before me has not been possessed by another, I resemble a bee fluttering at the close of night over a blossom filled with dew; and in this state of mind, I neither can enjoy nor forsake her.

Ward. (*Aside to* Dushmanta.) The king best knows his rites and his duties; but who would hesitate when a woman, bright as a gem, brings lustre to the apartments of his place?

Sharn. What, O king, does thy strange silence import?

Dushm. Holy man, I have been meditating again and again, but have no recollection of my marriage with this lady. How then can I lay aside all consideration of my military tribe, and admit into my palace a young woman who is pregnant by another husband?

Shak. (*Aside.*) Ah! Woe is me.—Can there be a doubt even of our nuptials?—The tree of my hope, which had risen so luxuriantly, is at once broken down.

Sharn. Beware, lest the godlike sage, who would have bestowed on thee, as a free gift, his inestimable treasure, which thou hadst taken, like a base robber, should now cease to think of thee, who art lawfully married to his daughter, and should confine all his thoughts to her whom thy perfidy disgraces.

Sharad Rest awhile, my Sharngarava; and thou Shakuntala, take thy turn to speak; since thy lord has declared his forgetfulness.

Shak. (*Aside.*) If his affection has ceased, of what use will it be to recall his remembrance of me?—Yet, if my soul must endure torment, be it so; I will speak to him.—(*Aloud to* Dushmanta.) O my husband!—(*Pausing.*)—Or (if the just application of that sacred word be still doubted by thee) O son of Puru, is it becoming, that, having been once enamoured of me in the consecrated forest. and shown the excess of thy passion, thou shouldst this day deny me with bitter expressions.

Dushm. (*Covering his ears.*) Be the crime removed from my soul!—Thou hast been instructed for some base purpose to vilify me, and make me fall from the dignity which I have hitherto supported; as a river which has burst its bank and altered its placid current, overthrows the trees that had risen aloft on them.

Shak. If thou sayst this merely from want of recollection, I will restore thy memory by producing thy own ring with thy name engraved on it!

Dushm. A capital invention.

Shak. (*Looking at her finger.*) Ah me! I have no ring.

[*She fixes her eyes with anguish on* Gautami.

Gaut. The fatal ring must have dropped, my child, from thy hand, when thou tookest up water to pour on thy head in the pool of Shachitirtha, near the station of Shakravatara.

Dushm. (*Smiling.*) So skilful are women in finding ready excuses!

Shak. The power of Brahma must prevail: I will yet mention one circumstance.

Dushm. I must submit to hear the tale.

Shak. One day in a grove of Vetasas, thou tookest water in thy hand from its natural vase of lotus leaves—

Dushm. What followed?

Dhak. At that instant a little fawn, which I had reared as my own child, approached thee; and thou saidst with benevolence: "Drink thou first, gentle fawn." He would not drink from the hand of a stranger, but received water eagerly from mine; when thou saidst, with increasing affection: "Thus every creature loves its companions; you are both foresters alike, and both alike amiable."

Dushm. By such interested and honied falsehoods are the souls of voluptuaries ensnared.

Gaut. Forbear, illustrious prince, to speak harshly. She was bred in a sacred grove where she learned no guile.

Dushm. Pious matron, the dexterity of females, even when they are untaught, appears in those of a species different from our own.—What would it be if they were duly instructed!—The female Kokilas, before they fly towards the firmament, leave their eggs to be hatched, and their young fed by birds who have no relation to them.

Shak. (*With anger.*) Oh! void of honour, thou measurest all the world by thy own bad heart. What prince ever resembled, or ever will resemble, thee, who wearest the garb of religion and virtue, but in truth art a base deceiver like a deep well whose mouth is coverd with smiling plants!

Dushm. (*Aside.*) The rusticity of her education makes her speak thus angrily and inconsistently with female decorum.—She looks indignant; her eye glows; and her speech, formed of harsh terms, falters as she utters them. Her lips, ruddy as the Bimba fruit, quiver as if it were nipped with frost; and her eyebrows, naturally smooth and equal, are at once irregularly contracted.—Thus having failed in circumventing me by the apparent lustre of simplicity, she has recourse to wrath, and snaps in two the bow of Kama, which, if she had not belonged to another, might have wounded me.—(*Aloud.*)—The heart of Dushmanta, young woman, is known to all; and thine is betrayed by thy present demeanor.

Shak. (*Ironically.*) You king are in all cases to be credited implicitly; you perfectly know the respect which is due to virtue and to mankind; while females, however modest, however virtuous, know nothing and speak nothing truly.—In a happy hour I came hither to seek the object of my affection; in a happy moment I received the hand of a prince descended from Puru; a prince who had won my confidence by the honey of his words, whilst his heart concealed the weapon that was to pierce mine.

[*She hides her face and weeps.*

Sharn. This insufferable mutability of the king's temper kindles my wrath. Henceforth let all be circumspect before they form secret connections: a friendship hastily contracted, when both hearts are perfectly known, must ere long become enmity.

Dushm. Wouldst thou force me then to commit an enormous crime, relying solely on her smooth speeches?

Sharn. (*Scornfully*). Thou hast heard an answer. —The words of an incomparable girl, who never learned what iniquity was, are here to receive no credit; while they, whose learning consists in accusing others, and inquiring into crimes, are the only persons who speak truth!

Dushm. O man of unimpeached veracity, I certainly am what thou describest; but what would be gained by accusing thy female associate?

Sharn. Eternal misery.

Dushm. No; misery will never be the portion of Puru's descendants.

Sharn. What avails our altercation?—O king, we have obeyed the commands of our preceptor, and now return. Shakuntala is by law thy wife, whether thou desert or acknowledge her; and the dominion of a husband is absolute.—Go before us, Gautami.

[*The two Mishras and* Gautami *returning.*

Shak. I have been deceived by this perfidious man; but will you, my friends, will you also forsake me?

[*Following them.*

Gaut. (*Looking back*) My son, Shakuntala follows us with affectionate supplications. What can she do here with a faithless husband; she who is all tenderness?

Sharn. (*Angrily to* Shakuntala.) O wife, who seest the faults of thy lord, dost thou desire independence?

[Shakuntala *stops and trembles.*

Sharad. Let the queen hear. If thou beest what the king proclaims thee, what right hast thou to complain? But if thou knowest the purity of thy own soul, it will become thee to wait as a handmaid in the mansion of thy lord. Stay, then, where thou art; we must return to Kanwa.

Dushm. Deceive her not, holy men, with vain expectations. The moon opens the night-flower; and the sun makes the water-lily blossom: each is confined to its own object: and thus a virtuous man abstains from any connection with the wife of another.

Sharn. Yet thou, O king, who fearest to offend religion and virtue, art not afraid to offend religion and virtue, art not afraid to desert thy wedded wife; pretending that the variety of thy public affairs has made thee forget thy private contract.

Dushm. (*To his Priest.*) I really have no remembrance of any such engagement; and I ask thee, my spiritual counsellor, whether of the two offences be the greater, to forsake my own wife, or to have an intercourse with the wife of another?

Priest. *(After some deliberation.)* We may adopt an expedient between both.

Dushm. Let my venerable guide command.

Priest. The young woman may dwell till her delivery in my house.

Dushm. For what purpose?

Priest. Wise astrologers have assured the king, that he will be the father of an illustrious prince, whose dominion will be bounded by the western and eastern seas; now, if the holy man's daughter shall bring a son whose hands and feet bear the marks of extensive sovereignty, I will do homage to her as my queen, and conduct her to the royal apartments; if not, she shall return in due time to her father.

Dushm. Be it as you judge proper.

Priest. (*To* Shakuntala.) This way, my daughter, follow me.

Shak. O earth! mild goddess, give me a place within thy bosom!

[*She goes out weeping with the Priest; while the two Mishras go out by a different way with* Gautami.—Dushmanta *stands meditating on the beauty of* Shakuntala; *but the imprecation still clouds his memory.*

Behind the scenes.) Oh! miraculous event!

Dushm. (*Listening.*) What can have happened?

The Priest *enters.*

Priest. Hear, O king, the stupendous event. When Kanwa's pupils had departed, Shakuntala, bewailing her adverse fortune, extended her arms and wept; when——

Dushm. What then?

Priest. A body of light, in a female shape, descended near Apsarastirtha, where the nymphs of heaven are worshippd; and having caught her hastily in her bosom, disappeared.

[*All express astonishment.*

Dushm. I suspected from the beginning some work of sorcery.—The business is over; and it is needless to reason more on it.—Let thy mind Somarata be at rest.

Priest. May the king be victorious!

[*He goes out.*

Dushm. Chamberlain, I have been greatly harassed: and thou, Warder, go before me to a place of repose.

Ward. This way; let the king come this way.

Dushm. (*Advancing, aside.*) I cannot with all my efforts recollect my nuptials with the daughter of the hermit; yet so agitated in my heart, that it almos induces me to believe her story.

[*All go out*

ACT VI.

Scene—A Street.

Enter a Superintendent of Police with two Officers, leading a man with his hands bound.

First Officer. (*Striking the Prisoner.*) Take that, Kumbhilaka, if Kumbhilaka be thy name; and tell us now where thou gottest this ring, bright with a large gem, on which the king's name is engraved.

Kumbh. (*Trembling.*) Spare me, I entreat your honours to sparc me; I am not guilty of so great a crime as you suspect.

First Off. O distinguished Brahman, didst thou then receive it from the king as a reward of some important service?

Kumbh. Only hear me; I am a poor fisherman dwelling at Shakravatara—

Second Off. Did we ask, thou thief, about thy tribe or thy dwelling place?

Sup. O Suchaka, let the fellow tell his own story.—Now conceal nothing, sirrah.

First Off. Dost thou hear? Do as our master commands.

Kumbh. I am a man who support my family by catching fish in nets or with hooks, and by various other contrivances.

Sup. (*Laughing.*) A virtuous way of gaining a livelihood!

Kumbh. Blame me not, master. The occupation of our forefathers, how soever, low must not be forsaken; and a man who kills animals for sale may have a tender heart though his act be cruel.

Sup. Go on, go on.

Kumbh. One day having caught a large Rohit fish, I cut it open, and saw this bright ring in its stomach; but when I offered to sell it, I was apprehended by your honours. So far only am I guilty of taking the ring. Will you now continue beating and bruising me to death?

Sup. (*Smelling the ring.*) It is certain, Jaluka, that this gem has been in the body of a fish. The case requires consideration; and I will mention it to some of the king's household.

Both Off. Come on cut purse.

[*They advance.*

Sup. Stand here, Suchaka, at the great gate of the city, and wait for me, while I speak to some of the officers in the palace.

Both Off. Go, Rajayukta. May the king favour thee. [*The Superintendent goes out.*

Second Off. Our master will stay, I fear, a long while.

First Off. Yes; access to kings can only be had at their leisure.

Second Off. The tips of my fingers itch, my friend Jaluka, to kill this cutpurse.

Kumbh. You would put to death an innocent man.

First Off. (*Looking.*) Here comes our master.— The king has decided quickly. Now, Kumbhilaka;

you will either see your companions again, or be the food of shakals and vultures.

The Superintendent re-enters.

Sup. Let the fisherman immediately——

Kumbh. (*In an agony.*) Oh ! I am a dead man.

Sup.——be discharged.—Hola ! set him at liberty. The king says he knows his innocence ; and his story is true.

Second Off. As our master commands.—The fellow is brought back from the mansion of Yama, to which he was hastening.

[*Unbinding the fisherman.*

Kumbh. (*Bowing.*) My lord, I owe my life to your kindness.

Sup. Rise, friend ; and hear with delight that the king gives thee a sum of money equal to the full value of the ring ; it is a fortune to a man in thy station. [*Giving him the money.*

Kumbh. (*With rapture.*) I am transported with joy.

First Off. This vagabond seems to be taken down from the stake, and set on the back of a state elephant.

Second Off. The king, I suppose, has a great affection for his gem.

Sup. Not for its intrinsic value : but I guessed the cause of his ecstasy when he saw it.

Both Off. What could occasion it ?

Sup. I suspect that it called to his memory some person who has a place in his heart; for though his mind be naturally firm, yet, from the moment when he beheld the ring, he was for some minutes excessively agitated.

Second Off. Our master has given the king extreme pleasure.

First Off. Yes; and by the means of this fish-catcher. [*Looking fiercely at him.*

Kumbh. Be not angry.—Half the money shall be divided between you to purchase wine.

First Off. Oh! now thou art our beloved friend.—Good wine is the first object of our affection.—Let us go together to the vintners.

[*They all go out.*

SCENE.—*The* Garden *of the* Palace.

The Nymph Mishrakeshi *appears in the air.*

Mishr. My first task was duly performed when I went to bathe in the Nymph's pool; and I now must see with my own eyes how the virtuous king is afflicted.—Shakuntala is dear to this heart, because she is the daughter of my beloved Menaka, from whom I received both commissions.—(*She looks round.*)—Ah! on a day full of delights the monarch's family seem oppressed with some new sorrow.—By exerting my supernatural power I could know what has passed; but respect must be shown to the desire of Menaka. I will retire, therefore, among those plants, and observe what is done without being visible.

[*She descends, and takes her station.*]

Enter two Damsels, *attendants on the* God *of* Love

First Dams. (*Looking at an A'mra flowers*) The bloossoms of yon A'mra, waving on the green stalk, are fresh and light as the breath of this vernal month. I must present the goddess Rati with a basket of them.

Second Dams. Why, my Parabhritika, dost thou mean to present it alone?

First Dams. O my friend Madhukarika, when a female Kokila, which my name implies, sees a blooming A'mra, she becomes entranced, and loses her recollection.

Second Dams. (*With transport*). What! is the season of sweets actually returned?

First Dams. Yes; the season in which we must sing of nothing but wine and love.

Second Dams. Support me, then, while climb up this tree, and strip it of its fragrant gems, which we will carry as an offering to Kama.

First Dams. If I assist, I must have a moiety of the reward which the god will bestow.

Second Dams. To be sure, and without any previous bargain. We are only one soul, you know, though Brahma has given it two bodies.—(*She climbs up, and gathers the flowers.*)—Ah! the buds are hardly opened.—Here is one a little expanded, which diffuses a charming odour.—(*Taking a handful of buds*)—This flower is sacred to the god who bears a fish on his banner.—O sweet blossom, which I now consecrate, thou well deservest to point the sixth arrow of Kamadeva, who now takes his bow to pierce myriads of youthful hearts.

[*She throws down a blossom.*

The old Chamberlain *enters.*

Cham. (*Angrily*) Desist from breaking off those half opened buds; there will be no jubilee this year; our king has forbidden it.

Both Dams. Oh! pardon us. We really knew not the prohibition.

Cham. You knew it not!—Even the trees which the spring was decking, and the birds who perch on them, sympathize with our monarch. Thence it is, that yon buds, which have long appeared, shed not yet their prolific dust; and the flower of the Kuruvaka, though perfectly formed, remains veiled in a closed chalice; while the voice of the Kokila, though the cold dews fall no more, is fixed within his throat; and even Smara, the god of desire, replaces the shaft half drawn from his quiver.

Mishr. (*Aside.*) The king, no doubt, is constant and tender-hearted.

First Dams. A few days ago, Mitravasu, the governor of our province, dispatched us to kiss the feet of the king, and we come to decorate his groves and gardens with various emblems, thence it is, that we heard nothing of his interdict.

Cham. Beware then of reiterating your offence.

Second Dams. To obey our lord will certainly be our delight; but if we are permitted to hear the story, tell us, we pray, what has induced our sovereign to forbid the usual festivity.

Mishr. (*Aside.*) Kings are generally fond of gay entertainments; and there must be some weighty reason for the prohibition.

Cham. (*Aside.*) The affair is public; why should I not satisfy them.—(*Aloud*)—Has not the calamitous desertion of Shakuntála reached your ears?

First Dams. We heard her tale from the governor as far as the sight of the fatal ring.

Cham. Then I have little to add.—When the king's memory was restored, by the sight of his gem, he instantly exclaimed: "Yes, the incomparable Shakuntala is my lawful wife; and when I rejected her, I had lost my reason."———He showed strong marks of extreme affliction and penitence; and from that moment he has abhorred the pleasures of life. No longer does he exert his respectable talents from day to day for the good of his people; he prolongs his nights without closing his eyes, perpetually rolling on the edge of his couch; and when he rises, he pronounces not one sentence aptly; mistaking the names of the women in his apartments, and through distraction calling each of them Shakuntala; then he sits abashed, with his head long bent on his knees.

Mishr. (*Aside.*) This is pleasing to me, very pleasing.

Cham. By reason of the deep sorrow which now prevails in his heart, the vernal jubilee has been interdicted.

Both Dams. The prohibition is highly proper.

Behind the scenes. Make way! The king is passing.

Cham. (*Listening.*) Here comes the monarch; depart therefore, damsels, to your own province.

[*The two damsels go out.*

Dushmanta *enters in penetential weeds, preceded by a Warder, and attended by* Madhavya.

Cham. (*Looking at the king.*) Ah! how majestic are noble forms in every habiliment!—Our prince, even in the garb of affliction, is a venerable object.—Though he has abandoned pleasure, ornaments, and business; though he is become so thin, that his golden bracelet falls loosened even down to his wrist; though his lips are parched with the heat of his sighs, and his eyes are fixed open by long sorrow and want of sleep, yet am I dazzled by the blaze of virtue which beams in his countenance like a diamond exquisitely polished.

Mishr. (*Aside, gazing on* Dushmanta.) With good reason is my beloved Shakantala, though disgraced and rejected, heavily oppressed wirh grief through the absence of this youth.

Dushm. (*Advancing slowly, in deep meditation.*) When my darling with an antilope's eyes would have reminded me of our love, I was assuredly slumbering; but excess of misery has awakened me.

Mishr. (*Aside.*) The charming girl will at last be happy.

Madh. (*Aside.*) This monarch of ours is caught again in the gale of affection; and hardly know a a remedy for his illness.

Cham. (*Approaching* Dushmanta.) May the king be victorious!—Let him survey yon fine woodland, these cool walks, and this blooming garden; where he may repose with pleasure on banks of delight.

Dushm. (*Not attending to him.*) Warder, inform the chief minister in my name, that having rasolved on a long absence from the city, I do not mean to sit for some time in the tribunal; but let him write and despatch to me all the cases that may arise among my subjects.

Ward. As the king commands. [*He goes out*

Dushm. (*To the* Chamberlain.) And thou, Parvatayana neglect not thy stated business.

Cham. By no means. [*He goes out.*

Madh. You have not left a fly in the garden.—Amuse yourself now in this retreat, which seems pleased with the departure of the dew season.

Dushm. O Madhavya, when person accused of great offences prove wholly innocent, see how their accusers are punished!—A phrensy obstructed my remembrence of any former love for the daughter of the sage; and now the heart-born god, who delights in giving pain, has fixed in his bow-string a new shaft pointed with the blossom of an Amra.—The fatal ring having restored my memory, see me deplore with tears of repentance the loss of my best beloved, whom I rejected without cause; see me overwhelmed with sorrow, even while the return of spring fills the hearts of all others with pleasure.

Madh. Be still, my friend, whilst I break Love's arrows with my staff.

[*He strikes off some flowers from an Amra tree.*

Dushm. (*Meditating.*) Yes, I acknowledge the supreme power of Brahma.—(*To* Madhavya.)—Where now, my friend, shall I sit and recreate my sight with the slender shrubs which bear a faint resemblance to the shape of Shakuntala?

Madh. You will soon see the damsels skilled in painting, whom you informed that you would spend the forenoon in yon bower of Madhavi creeper; and she will bring the queen's picture which you commanded her to draw.

Dushm. My soul will be delighted even by her picture.—Show the way to the bower.

Madh. This way, my friend.—(*They both advance,* Mishrakeshi *following them.*)—The arbour of twining

Madhavis, embellished with fragments of stone like bright gems, appears by its pleasantness, though without a voice, to bid thee welcome.—Let us enter it, and be seated. [*They both sit down in the bower.*

Mishr. (*Aside.*) From behind these branchy shrubs I shall behold the picture of my Shakuntala.—I will afterwards hasten to report the sincere affection of her husband. [*She conceals herself.*

Dushm. [*Sighing.*] O my approved friend, the whole adventure of the hermitage is now fresh in my memory.—I informed you how deeply I was affected by the first sight of the damsel; but when she was rejected by me you were not present. Her name was often repeated by me (how, indeed, should it not?) in your conversation.—What! hast thou forgotten, as I had the whole story.

Mishr. [*Aside*] The sovereigns of the world must not, I find, be left an instant without the objects of their love.

Madh. Oh no: I have not forgotten it; but at the end of our discourse you assured me that your love-tale was invented solely for your diversion; and this in the simplicity of my heart, I beleived,—Some great event seems in all this affair to be predestined in heaven.

Mishr. (*Aside.*) Nothing is more true.

Dushm. (*Having meditated.*) O my friend, suggest some relief for my torment.

Madh. What new pain torments you? Virtuous

men should never be thus afflicted: the most violent wind shakes not mountains.

Dushm. When I reflect on the situation of your friend Shakuntala, who must now be greatly affected by my desertion of her, I am without comfort.—She made an attempt to follow the Brahmanas and the matron; Stay, said the sage's pupil, who was revered as the sage himself: Stay, said he, with a loud voice. Then once more she fixed on me, who had betrayed her, that celestial face, then bedewed with gushing tears; and the bare idea of her pain burns me like an envenomed javelin.

Mishr. (*Aside.*) How he afflicts himself! I really sympathize with him.

Madh. Surely some inhabitant of the heavens must have wafted her to his manson.

Dushm. No; what male divinity would have taken the pains to carry off a wife so firmly attached to her lord? Menaka, the nymph of Swarga, gave her birth; and some of her attendant nymphs have, I imagine, concealed her at the desire of her mother.

Mishr. (*Aside.*) To reject Shakuntala, was, no doubt, the effect of a delirium, not the act of a waking man.

Ma'dh. If it be thus, you will soon meet her again.

Dushm. Alas.! why do you think so?

Ma'dh. Because no father and mother can long endure to see their daughter deprived of her husband.

Dushm. Was it sleep that impaired my memory?

Was it delusion ? Was it an error of my judgment ? Or was it the destined reward of my bad actions ? Whatever it was, I am sensible that, untill Shakuntala return to these arms, I shall be plunked in the abyss of affliction.

Ma'dh. Do not despair : the fatal ring itself an example that the lost may be found.—Events which were foredoomed by Heaven must not be lamented.

Dushm. (*Looking at his ring.*) The fate of this ring, now fallen from a station which it will not easily regain, I may at least deplore.—O gem, thou art removed from the soft finger, beautiful with ruddy tips, on which a place had been assigned thee, and, minute as thou art, thy bad qualities appear from the similarity of thy punishment to mine.

Mishr. (*Aside.*) Had it found a way to any other hand its lot would have been truly deplorable.—O Menaka, how wouldst thou be delighted with the conversation which gratifies my ears !

Mádh. Let me know, I pray, by what means the ring obtained a place on the finger of Shakuntala.

Dushm. You shall know, my friend.—When I was coming from the holy forest to my capital, my beloved, with tears in her eye, thus addressed me : "How long will the son of my lord keep me in his remembrance ?"

Mádh. Well ; what then ?

Dushm. Then, fixing this ring on her lovely finger, I thus answered : "Repeat each day one of the three syllables engraved on this gem; and before thou hast spelled the word Dushmanta, one of my noblest officers shall attend thee, and conduct my darling to her palace."—Yet I forgot, I deserted her in my phrensy.

Mishr. (*Aside.*) A charming interval of three days was fixed between their seperation and their meeting, which the will of Barhma rendered unhappy.

Madh. But how came the ring to enter, like a hook, into the mouth of a carp?

Dushm. When my beloved was lifting water to her head in the pool of Shachitirt'ha, the ring must have dropped unseen.

Madh. It is very probable.

Mishr. (*Aside.*) Oh! it was thence that the king, who fears nothing but injustice, doubted the reality of his marriage; but how, I wonder, could his memory be connected with a ring?

Dushm. I am really angry with this gem.

Madh. (*Laughing.*) So am I with this staff.

Dushm. Why so, Madhavya?

Madh. Because it presumes to be so straight when I am so crooked.—Impertinent stick!

Dushm. (*Not attending to him.*) How, O ring, couldst thou leave that hand adorned with soft long fingers, and fall into a pool decked only with water-lilies?—The answer is obvious; thou art irrational.—But how could I, who was born with reasonable soul, desert my only beloved?

Mishr. (*Aside.*) He anticipates my remark,

Madh. (*Aside.*) So; I must wait here during his meditations, and perish with hunger.

Dushm. O my darling, whom I treated with disrespect, and forsook without reason, when will this traitor, whose heart is deeply stung with repentant sorrow, be once more blessed with a sight of thee?

A Damsel *enters with a picture.*

Dams. Great king, the picture is finished.

[*Holding it before him.*

Dushm. (*Gazing on it.*) Yes; that is her face: those are her beautiful eyes; those her lips embellished with smiles, and surpassing the red lustre of the Karkandhu fruit; her mouth seems, though painted, to speak, and her countenanee darts beams of affection blended with a variety of melting time.

Madh. Truely, my friend, it is a picture sweet as love itself: my eye glides up and down to feast on every particle of it; and it gives me as much delight as if I were actually conversing with the living Shakuntala.

Mishr. (*Aside.*) An exquisite piece of painting! —My beloved friend seems to stand before my eyes.

Dushm. Yet the picture is infinitely below the original, and my warm fancy, by supplying its imperfections, represents, in some degree, the loveliness of my darling.

Mishr. (*Aside.*) His ideas are suitable to his excessive love and severe penitence.

Dushm. (*Sighing.*) Alas! I rejected her when she lately approached me, and now I do homage to her picture; like a traveller who negligently passes by a clear and full rivulet, and soon ardently thirst for a false appearance of water on the sandy desert.

Madh. There are so many female figures on this canvas, that I cannot well distinguish the lady Shakuntala.

Mishr. (*Aside.*) The old man is ignorant of her transcendent beauty! her eyes, which fascinated the soul of this prince, never sparkled, I suppose, on Madhavya.

Dushm. Which of the figures do you conceive intended for the queen?

Madh. (*Examining the picture.*) It is she, I imagine, who looks a little fatigued; with the string of her vest rather loose; the slender stalks of arms falling languidly; a few bright drops on her face, and some flowers dropping from her united locks. That must be the queen; and the rest, I suppose, are her damsels.

Dushm. You judge well; but my affection requires somethitg more in the piece. Besides, through some defect in the colouring, a tear seems trickling down her cheeks, which ill suits the state in which I desired to see her painted.—(*To the* Damsel.)—The picture O Chaturika, is unfinished.—Go back to the painting room and bring the implements of thy art,

Dams. Kind Madhavya, hold the picture while I obey the king.

Dushm. No; I will hold it.

[*He takes the picture: and the* Damsel *goes out.*

Madh. what else is to be painted?

Mishr. (*Aside.*) He desires, I presume, to add all those circumstances which became the situation of his beloved in the hermitage·

Dushm. In this landscape, my friend, I wish to see represented the river Malini, with some amorous Flamingos on its green margin; farther back must appear some hills near the mountain Himalaya, surrounded with herds of Chamaras; and in the foreground. a dark spreading tree, with some mantles of woven bark suspended on its branches to be dried by the sunbeams; while a pair of black antelopes couch in its shade, and the female gently rubs her beatiful forehead on the horn of the male.

Madh. Add what you please; but, in my judgment, the vacant places should be filled with old hermits, bent, like me, towards the ground.

Dushm. (*Not attending to him.*) Oh! I had forgotten that my beloved herself must have some new ornaments.

Madh. What, I pray?

Mishr. (*Aside.*) Such, no doubt, as become a damsel bred in a forest.

Dushm The artist had omited a Shirisha flower with its preduncle fixed behind her soft ear, and its filaments waving over part of her cheek; and between her breasts must be placed a knot of delicate fibres from the stalks of water-lilies, like the rays of an autumnal moon.

Madh. Why does the Queen cover part of her face, as if she was afraid of something, with the tips of her fingers that glow like the flowers of the Kuwalaya?—Oh! I now perceive an impudent bee, that thief of odours, who seems eager to sip honey from the lotus of her mouth.

Dushm. A bee! drive off the importunate insect.

Madh. The king has supreme power over all offenders.

Dushm. O male bee, who approachest the lovely inhabitants of a flowery grove, why dost thou expose thyself to the pain of being rejected?—See where thy female sits on a blossom, and, though thirsty, waits for thy return: without thee she will not taste its nectar.

Mishr. (*Aside.*) A wild, but apt, address!

Madh. The perfidy of male bees is proverbial.

Dushm. (*Angrily.*) Shouldst thou touch, O bee, the lip of my darling, ruddy as a fresh leaf on which no wind has yet breathed, a lip from which I drank sweetness in the banquet of love, thou shalt, by my order be imprisoned in the centre of a lotus.—Dost thou still disobey me?

Madh. How can he fail to obey, since you denounce so severe a punishment?—(*Aside, laughing.*)

He is stark mad with love and affliction: whilst I, by keeping him company, shall be as mad as he without either.

Dushm. After my positive injunction, art thou still unmoved?

Mishr. (*Aside.*) How does excess of passion alter even the wise!

Madh, Why, my friend, it is only a painted bee.

Mishr. (*Aside.*) Oh! I perceive his mistake: it shows the perfection of the art. But why does he continue musing.

Dushm. What ill-natured remark was that?—Whilst I am enjoying the rapture of beholding her to whom my soul is attached, thou, cruel remembrancer, tellest me that it is only a picture.

[*Weeping.*

Mishr. (*Aside.*) Such are the woes of a separated lover! He is on all sides entangled in sorrow.

Dushm. Why do I thus indulge unremitted grief? That intercourse with my darling which dreams would give, is prevented by my continued inability to repose; and my tears will not suffer me to view her distinctly even in this picture.

Mishr. (*Aside.*) His misery acquits him entirely of having deserted her in his perfect senses.

The Damsel *re-enters.*

Dams. As I was advancing, O king, with my box of pencils and colours—

Dushm. (*Hastily.*) What happened?

Dams. It was forcibly seized by the queen Vasumati, whom her maid Pingalika had apprised of my errand; and she said: "I will myself deliver the casket to the son of my lord."

Madh. How came you to be released?

Dams. While the queen's maid was disengaging the skirt of her mantle, which had been caught by the branch of a thorny shrub, I stole away.

Dushm. Friend Madhavya, my great attention to Vasumati has made her arrogant; and she will soon be here; be it your care to conceal the picture.

Madh. (*Aside.*) I wish you would conceal it yourself.—(*He takes the picture and rises.*)—(*Aloud.*)—If, indeed, you will disentangle me from the net of your secret apartments, to which I am confined, and suffer me to dwell on the wall Meghachchhanna which encircles them, I will hide the picture in a place where none shall see it but pigeons. [*He goes out.*

Mishr. (*Aside.*) How honourably he keeps his former engagements, though his heart be now fixed on another object.

A Warder *enters with a leaf.*

Ward. May the king prosper.!

Dushm. Warder, hast thou lately seen the queen Vasumati?

Ward. I met her, O king; but when she perceived the leaf in my hand, she retired.

Dushm. The queen distinguishes time: she would not impede my public business.

Ward. The chief minister sends this message: "I have carefully stated a case which has arisen in the city, and accurately committed it to writing: let the king deign to consider it."

Dushm. Give me the leaf.—(*Receiving it, and reading*)—" Be it presented at the foot of the king, that a merchant named Dhanavriddhi, who had extensive commerce at sea, was lost in a late shipwreck; he had no child born; and has left a fortune of many millions, which belong, if the king commands, to the royal treasury."—(*With sorrow.*)—Oh! how great misfortune it is to die childless! Yet with his affluence he must have had many wives:—let an inquiry be made whether any one of them is pregnant.

Ward. I have heard that his wife, the daughter of an excellent man, named Sa'ketaka, has already performed the ceremonies usual on pregnancy.

Dushm. The child, though unborn, has a title to his father's property.—Go: bid the minister make my judgment public.

Ward. I obey. [*Góing.*

Dushm. Stay a while.—

Ward. (*Returning.*) I am here.

Dushm. Whether he had or had not left offspring the estate should not have been forfeited.—Let it be proclaimed, that whatever kinsman any one of my subjects may lose, Dushmanta (excepting always the case of forfeiture for crimes) will supply, in tender affection, the place of that kinsman.

Ward. The proclamation shall be made.

[*He goes out.*

[Dushmanta *continues meditating.*

Re-enter Warder.

Ward. O king! the royal decree, which proves that your virtue are awake after a long slumber, was heard with bursts of applause.

Dushm. (*Sighing deeply.*) When an illustrious man dies, alas, without an heir, his estate goes to a stranger; and such will be the fate of all the wealth accumulated by the sons of Puru.

Ward. Heaven avert the calamity! [*Goes out.*

Dushm. Woe is me! I am stripped of all the felicity which I once enjoyed.

Mishr. (*Aside*) How his heart dwells on the idea of his beloved!

Dushm. My lawful wife, whom I basely deserted, remains fixed in my soul; she would have been the glory of my family, and might have produced a son brilliant as the richest fruit of the teeming earth.

Mshr. [*Aside.*] She is not forsaken by all; and soon, I trust, will be thine.

Dams. (*Aside.* What a change has the minister made in the king by sending him that mischievous leaf! Behold, he is deluged with tears.

Dushm. Ah me! the departed souls of my ancestors, who claim a share in the funeral cake, which

I have no son to offer, are apprehensive of losing their due honour, when Dushmanta shall be no more on earth ;—who then, alas, will perform in our family those obsequies which the Veda prescribes? My forefathers must drink, instead of a pure libation, this flood of tears, the only offering which a man who dies chidless can make them. [*Weeping.*

Mishr. (*Aside.*) Such a veil obscures the king's eyes, that he thinks it total darkness, though a lamp be now shining brightly.

Dams. Afflict not yourself immoderately: our lord is young; and when sons illustrious as himself shall be born of other queens, his ancestors will be redeemed from their offences committed, here below.

Dushm. (*With agony.*) The race of Puru, which has hitherto been fruitful and unblemished, ends in me; as the river Saraswati disappears in a region unworthy of her divine stream. [*He faints.*

Dams. Let the king resume confidence.—

[*She supports him.*

Mishr. (*Aside.*) Shall I restore him? No, he will speedily be roused—I heard the nymph Devajanani consoling Shakuntala, in these words: "As the gods delight in their portion of sacrifices, thus wilt thou soon be delighted by the love of thy husband.' I go, therefore, to raise her spirits, and please my friend Menaka with an account of his virtues and his affection.

[*She rises aloft and disappears.*

Behind the Scenes.] A Brahmana must not be slain: save the life of a Brahmana.

Dushm. (*Reviving and listening.*) Hah! was not that the plaintive voice of Madhavya?

Dams. He has probably been caught with the picture in his hand by Pingalika, and the other maids.

Dushm. Go, Chaturika, and reprove the queen in my name for not restraining her servants.

Dams. As the king commands. [*She goes out.*

Again behind the scenes.] I am a Brahmana and must not be put to death.

Dushm. It is manifestly some Brahmana in great danger.—Hola! who is there?

The old Chamberlain *enters.*

Cham. What is the king's pleasure?

Dushm. Inquire why the faint-hearted Madhavya cries out so piteously.

Cham. I will know in an instant.

He goes out, and returns trembling.

Dushm. Is there any alarm, Parvatayana?

Cham. Alarm enough!

Dushm. What causes thy tremour?—Thus do men tremble through age: fear shakes the old man's body, as the breeze agitates the leaves of the Pippala.

Cham. Oh! deliver thy friend.

Dushm. Deliver him! from what?

Cham. From distress and danger.

Dushm. Speak more plainly.

Cham. The wall which looks to all quarters of heavens, and is named from the clouds which cover it, Meghachchhanna—

Dushm. What of that?

Cham. From the summit of that wall, the pinnacle of which is hardly attainable even by the blue-necked pigeons, and evil being, invisible to human eyes, has violently carried away the friend of your childhood.

Dushm. (*Starting up hastily.*) What! are even my secret apartments infested by supernatural agents?—Royalty is ever subjected to molestations.—A king knows not even the mischiefs which his own negligence daily and hourly occasions!—how then should he know what path his people are treading and how should he correct their manners when his own are uncorrected?

Behind the scenes.) Oh, help! oh, release me.

Dushm. (*Listening and advancing.*) Fear not, my friend, fear nothing.—

Behind the scenes.) Not fear, when a monster has caught me by the nape of my neck, and means to snap my back-bone as he would snap a sugar cane!

Dushm. (*Darting his eyes round*). Hola! my bow—

A Warder *enters with the king's bow and quiver.*

Ward. Here are our great heroe's arms.

[Dushamanta *takes his bow and an arrow.*

Behind the scenes). Here I stand; and thirsting

for thy fresh blood, will slay thee struggling as a tiger slays a calf.—Where now is thy protector, Dushmanta, who grasps his bow to defend the oppressed?

Dushm. (*Wrathfully*). The demon names me with defiance.—Stay, thou basest of monsters.--Here am I, and thou shalt not long exist.—(*Raising his bow.*) Show the way, Parvatayana, to the stares of the terrace.

Cham. This way great king!

All go out hastily.

The SCENE *changes to a broad* TERRACE.
Enter Dushmanta.

Dushm. (*Looking round.*) Ah! the place is deserted.

Behind the scenes]. Save me, oh! save me.—I see thee, my friend, but thou canst not discern me, who, like a mouse in the claws of a cat, have no hope of life.

Dushm. But this arrow shall distinguish thee from thy foe, in spite of the magic which renders thee invisible.—Madhavya, stand firm; and thou, blood-thirsty fiend, think not of destroying him whom I love and will protect.—See, I thus fix a shaft which shall pierce thee, who deserves death, and shall save a Brahmana who deserves long life; as the celestial bird sips the milk, and leaves the water which has been mingled with it. [*He draws the bowstring.*

Enter Matali *and* Madhavya.

Mat. The god Indra has destined evil demons to fall by thy shafts; against them let thy bow be drawn, and cast on thy friends eyes bright with affection.

Dushm. (*Astonished, giving back his arms.*) Oh! Matali, welcome; I greet the driver of Indra's car.

Madh. What! this cut-throat was putting me to death, and thou greetest him with a kind welcome!

Mat. (*Smiling.*) O king, live long and conquer! Hear on what errand I am dispatched by the ruler of the firmament.

Dushm. I am humbly attentive.

Mat There is a race of Danavas, the children of Kalanemi whom it is found hard to subdue—

Dushm. This I have heard already from Narada.

Mat. The god with an hundred sacrifices, unable to quell that gigantic race, commissions thee, his approved friend, to assail them in the front of battle; as the sun with seven steeds despairs of overcoming the dark legions of night, and gives way to the moon, who easily scatters them. Mount, therefore, with me, the car of Indra, and, grasping thy bow, advance to assured victory.

Dushm. Such a mark of distinction from the prince of good genii honours me highly; but say why you treated so roughly my poor friend Madhavya.

Mat. Preceiving that, for some reason or another, you were grievously afflicted, I was desirous to rouse your spirits by provoking you to wrath.—The fire blazes when wood is thrown on it; the serpent, when provoked, darts his head against the assailant; and a man capable of acquiring glory, exerts himself when his courage is excited.

Dushm. (*To* Madhavya.) My friend, the command, of Devaspati must instantly be obeyed; go, therefore, and carry the intelligence to my chief minister; saying to him in my name: "Let thy wisdom secure my people from danger while this braced bow has a different employment."

Madh. I obey; but wish it could have been employed without assistance from my terror.

[*He goes out.*

Mat. Ascend, great king.

[Dushmanta *ascends, and* Matali *drives off the car.*

ACT VII.

Dushmanta *with* Matali *in the car of* Indra, *supposed to be above the clouds.*

Dushm. I am sensible, O Matali, that, for having executed the commission which Indra gave me, I deserved not such a profusion of honours.

Mat. Neither of you is satisfied. You who have conferred so great a benefit on the god of thunder, consider it as a trifling act of devotion; whilst he recons not all his kindness equal to the benefit conferred.

Dushm. There is no comparison between the service and the reward.—He surpassed my warmest expectation, when, before he dismissed me, he made me sit on half of his throne thus exalting before all the inhabitants of the Empyreum; and smiling to see his son Jayanta, who stood near him, ambitious of the same honour, perfumed my bosom with essence of heavenly sandal wood, throwing over my neck a garland of flowers blown in paradise.

Mat. O king, you deserve all imaginable rewards from the sovereign of good genii, whose empyreal seats have twice been disentangled from the thorns of Danu's race; formerly by the claws of the man-lion, and lately by thy unerring shafts.

Dushm. My victory proceeded wholly from the auspices of the god; as on earth, when servants prosper in great enterprises, they owe their success to the magnificence of their lords.—Could Aruna dispel the shades of night if the deity with a thousand beams had not placed him before the car of day?

Mat. That case, indeed, is parallel.—(*Driving slowly.*)—See, O king, the full exaltation of the glory, which now rides on the back of heaven! The delighted genii have been collecting, among the trees of life, those crimson and azure dyes, with which the celestial damsels tinge their beautiful feet! and they now are writing thy actions in verses worthy of divine melody.

Dushm. (*Modestly.*) In my transport, O Matali,

after, the rout of giants, this wonderful place had escaped my noticc.—In what path of the winds are we now journeying.

Mat. This is the way which leads along the triple river, heaven's brightest ornament, and causes you lumanaries to roll in a circle with diffused beams; it is the course of a gentle breeze which supports the floating forms of the gods; and this path was the second step of Vishnu, when he confounded the proud Vali.

Dushm. My internal soul, which acts by exterior organs, is filled by the sight with a charming complacency.—(*Looking at the wheels.*)—We are now passing, I guess, through the region of clouds.

Mat. Whence do you form that conjecture?

Dushm. The car itself instructs me that we are moving over clouds pregnant with showers; for the circumference of its wheels disperses pellucid water; the horses of Indra sparkle with lighting; and I now see the warbling Chatakas descend from their nests on the summits of mountains.

Mat. It is even so; and in another moment you will be in the country which you govern.

Dushm. (*Looking down.*) Through the rapid, yet imperceptible, descent of the heavenly steeds, I now perceive the allotted station of men.—Astonishing prospect! It is yet so distant from us, that the low lands appear confounded with the high mountain tops; the trees erect their branchy shoulders, but seem leaf-less; the rivers look like bright lines, but their waters vanish; and, at this instant, the globe of earth seems thrown upwards by some stupendous power.

Mat. (*Looking with reverence on the earth.*) How delightful is the abode of mankind!—O king, you saw distinctly!

Dushm. Say, Matali, what mountain is that which, like an evening cloud, pours exhilarating streams, and forms a golden zone between the western and eastern seas?

Mat. That, O king, is the mountain of Gandharva, named Hemakuta; the universe contains not a more excellent place for the successful devotion of the pious. There Kashyapa, father of the immortals, ruler of men, son of Marichi, who sprang from the self-existent, resides with his consort Aditi, blessed in holy retirement.

Dushm. (*Devoutly*). This occasion of attaining good fortune must not be neglected: may I approach the divine pair, and do them complete homage?

Mat. By all means.—It is an excellent idea!—We are now descended on earth.

Dushm. (*With wonder*). These chariot-wheels yield no sound; no dust arises from them; and the descent of the car gave me no shock.

Mat. Such is the difference, O king, between thy car and that of Indra!

Dushm. Where is the holy retreat of Marichi?

Mat. (*Pointing.*) A little beyond that grove,

where you see a pious Yogi, motionless as a pollard, holding his thick bushy hair, and fixing his eyes on the solar orb.—Mark; his body is half covered with a white ant's edifice made of raised clay; the skin of a snake supplies the place of his sacredotal thread, and part of it girds his loins; a number of knotty plants encircle and wound his neck; and surrounding birds' nests almost conceal his shoulders.

Dushm. I bow to a man of his austere devotion.

Mat. (*Checking the reins.*) Thus far, and enough. —We now enter the sanctuary of him who rules the world, and the groves which are watered by streams from celestial sources.

Dushm. This asylum is more delightful than paradise itself; I could fancy myself bathing in a pool of nectar.

Mat. (*Stopping the car*). Let the king descend.

Dushm. (*Joyfully descending.*) How canst thou leave the car?

Mat. On such an occasion it will remain fixed: we may both leave it.—This way, victorious hero, this way.—Behold the retreat of the truly pious.

Dushm. I see with equal amazement both the pious and their awful retreat.—It becomes, indeed, pure spirits to feed on balmy air in a forest blooming with trees of life; to bathe in rills dyed yellow with the golden dust of the lotus, and to fortify their virtue in the mysterious bath; to mediate in caves, the pebbles of which are unblemished gems; and to restrain their passions, even though nymphs of exquisite beauty frolic around them: in this grove alone is attained the summit of true piety, to which other hermits in vain aspire.

Mat. In exalted minds the desire of perfect excellence continually increases.—*(Turning aside.)*—Tell me Vriddha Sakalya, in what business is the divine son of Marichi now engaged?—What sayest thou?—Is he conversing with the daughter of Daksha, who practises all the virtues of a dutiful wife, and is consulting him on moral questiens?—Then we must await his leisure. —(*To* Dushmanta.) Rest O king, under the shade of this Ashoka tree, whilst I announce thy arrival to the father of Indra.

Dushm. As you judge right.—[Matali *goes out.*—Dushmanta *feels his right arm throb.*]—Why O my arm, dost thou flatter me with a vain omen?—My former happiness is lost, and misery only remains.

Behind the scenes.] Be not so restless; in every situation thou showest thy bad temper.

Dushm. (*Listening.*) Hah! this is no place, surely, for a malignant disposition.———Who can be thus rebuked?—(*Looking with surprise.*)—I see a child, but with no childish countenance or strength, whom two female anchorites are endeavouring to keep in order; while he forcibly pulls towards him, in rough play, a lion's whelp with a torn mane, who seems just dragged from the half-sucked nipple of the lioness!

A little Boy *and two female* Attendants *are discovered, as described by the king.*

Boy. Open thy mouth, lion's whelp, that I may count thy teeth.

First Atten. Intractable child! Why dost thou torment the wild animals of this forest, whom we cherish as if they were our own offspring?——Thou seemest even to sport in anger.——Aptly have the hermits named thee Sarvadamana, since thou tamest all creatures.

Dushm. Ah! what means it that my heart inclines to this boy as if he were my own son?—(*Meditating.*) —Alas! I have no son; and the reflection makes me once more soft-hearted.

Second Atten. The lioness will tear thee to pieces if thou release not her whelp.

Boy. (*Smiling.*) Oh! I am greatly afraid of her to be sure! [*He bites his lip, as in defiance of her.*

Dushm. (*Aside, amazed.*) The child exhibits the rudiments of heroic valour, and looks like fire which blazes from the addition of dry fuel.

First Atten. My beloved child, set at liberty this young prince of wild beasts; and I will give thee a prettier plaything.

Boy. Give it first.—Where is it?

[*Stretching out his hand.*

Dushm. (*Aside, gazing on the child's palm.*) What! the very palm of his hand bears the marks of empire; and whilst he thus eagerly extends it, shows its lines of exquisite network, and glows like a lotus expanded at early dawn, when the ruddy splendour of its petals hides all other tints in obscurity.

Second Atten. Mere words, my Suvrata, will not pacify him.—Go, I pray, to my cottage, where thou wilt find a plaything made for the hermit's child, Sankochana: it is a peacock of earthenware painted with rich colours.

First Atten. I will bring it speedily.

She goes out.

Boy. In the meantime I will play with the young lion.

Second Atten. (*Looking at him with a smile.*) Let him go I entreat thee.

Dushm. (*Aside.*) I feel the tenderest affection for this unmanageable chid.—(*Sighing.*)—How sweet must be thee delight of virtuous fathers, when they soil their bosoms with dust by lifting up their playful children, who charm them with inarticulate prattle, and show the white blossoms of their teeth, while they laugh innocently at every trifling occurrence.

Second Atten. (*Raising her finger.*) What! dost thou show no attention to me?—(*Looking round.*)—Are any of the hermits near?—(*Seeing* Dushmanta.)—Oh! let me request you, gentle stranger, to release the lion's whelp, who cannot disengage himself from the grasp of this robust child.

Dushm. I will endeavour.—(*Approaching the* boy, *and smiling.*)—Oh! thou, who art the son of a pious anchorite, how canst thou dishonour thy father, whom thy virtues would make happy, by violating the rules of this consecrated forest? It becomes a black serpent only, to infest the boughs of a fragrant sandal tree.

[*The* Boy *releases the lion.*

Second Atten. I think you, courteous guest; but he is not the son of an anchorite.

Dushm. His actions, indeed, which are conformable to his robustness, indicate a different birth; but my opinion arose from the sanctity of the place which he inhabits.—(*Taking the* Boy *by the hand.*)—(*Aside.*)—Oh! since it gives me such delight merely to touch the hand of this child, who is the hopeful scion of a family unconnected with mine what rapture must be felt by the fortunate man from whom he sprang?

Second Atten. (*Gazing on them alternately.*) Oh wonderful!

Dushm. What has raised your wonder?

Second Atten. The astonishing resemblance between the child and you, gentle stranger, to whom he bears no relation.—It surprised me also to see, that although he has childish humours, and had no former acquaintance with you, yet your words have restored him to his natural good temper.

Dushm. (*Raising the* Boy *to his bosom.*) Holy matron, if he be not the son of a hermit, what then is the name of his family?

Second Atten. He is descended from Puru.

Dushm. (*Aside.*) Hah! thence, no doubt, springs his disposition, and my affection for him.—(*Setting him down.*)—(*Aloud.*)—It is, I know, an established usage among the princes of Puru's race, to dwell at first in rich palaces with jewelled walls, where they protect and cherish the world, but in the decline of life to seek humbler mansions near the roots of venerable trees, where hermits with subdued passions practise austere devotion.—I wonder, however, that this boy who moves like a god, could have been born of a mere mortal.

Second Atten. Affable stranger your wonder will cease when you know that his mother is related to a celestial nymph, and brought him forth in the sacred forest of Kashyapa.

Dushm. (*Aside.*) I am transported.—This is a fresh ground of hope.—(*Aloud.*)—What virtuous monarch took his excellent mother by the hand?

Second Atten. Oh! I must not give celebrity to the name of a king who deserted his lawful wife.

Dushm. (*Aside.*) Ah! she means me.—Let me now ask the name of the sweet child's mother.—(*Meditating.*)—But it is against good manners to inquire concerning the wife of another man.

The First Attendant *re-enters with a toy.*

First Atten. Look, Sarvadamana, look at the beauty of this bird, Shakunta-lavanyam.

Boy. (*Looking eagerly round.*) Shakuntala! Oh, where is my beloved mother? [*Both* Attendants *laugh.*

Frist Atten. He tenderly loves his mother, and was deceived by an equivocal phrase.

Second Atten. My child, she meant only the beautiful shape and colours of this peacock.

Dushm. (*Aside.*) Is my Shakuntala then his mother? Or has that dear name been given to some other woman?—This conversation resembles the fallacious appearance of water in a desert, which ends in bitter disappointment to the stag parched with thirst.

Boy. I shall like the peacock if it can run and fly; not else. [*He takes it.*

First Atten. (*Looking round in confusion.*) Alas, the child's amulet is not on his wrist!

Dushm. Be not alarmed. It was dropped while he was playing with the lion: I see it, and will put it into your hand.

Both. Oh! beware of touching it.

First Atten. Ah! he has actually taken it up.

[*They both gaze with surprise on each other.*

Dushm. Here it is; but why would you have restrained me from touching this bright gem?

Second Atten. Great monarch, this divine amulet has a wonderful power, and was given to the child by the son of Marichi, as soon as the sacred rites had been performed after his birth; whenever it fell on the ground, no human being but the father or mother of this boy could have touched it unhurt.

Dushm. What if a stranger had taken it?

9

First Atten. It would have become a serpent and wounded him.

Dushm. Have you seen that consequence on any similar occasion?

Both. Frequently.

Dushm. (*With transport.*) I may then exult on the completion of my ardent desire.

[*He embraces the child.*

Second Atten. Come, Suvrata, let us carry the delightful intelligence to Shakuntala, whom the harsh duties of a separated wife have so long oppressed.

[*The* Attendants *go out.*

Boy. Farewell; I must go to my mother.

Dushm. My darling son, thou wilt make her happy by going to her with me.

Boy. Dushmanta is my father; and you are not Dushmanta.

Dushm. Even thy denial of me gives me delight.

Shakuntala *enters in mourning apparel, with her long hair twisted in a single braid, and flowing down her back.*

Shak. (*Aside.*) Having heard that my child's amulet has proved its divine power, I must either be strangely diffident of my good fortune, or that event which Mishrakesi predicted has actually happened.

[*Advancing.*

Dushm. (*With a mixture of joy and sorrow.*) Ah! do I see the incomparable Shakuntala clad in sordid, weeds?—Her face is emaciated by the performance of austere duties; one twisted lock floats over her shoulders; and with a mind perfectly pure, she supports the long absence of her husband, whose unkindness exceeded all bounds.

Shak. (*Seeing him, yet doubting.*) Is that the son of my lord grown pale with penitence and affliction?—If not, who is it, that sullies with his touch the hand of my child, whose amulet should have preserved him from such indignity?

Boy. (*Going hastily to* Shakuntala.) Mother, here is a stranger who calls me son.

Dushm. Oh! my best beloved, I have treated thee cruelly; but my cruelty is succeeded by the warmest affection; and I implore your remembrance and forgiveness.

Shak. (*Aside.*) Be confident, O my heart!—(*Aloud.*)—I shall be most happy when the king's anger has passed away.—(*Aside.*)—This must be the son of my lord.

Dushm. By the kindness of heaven, O loveliest of thy sex, thou standest again before me, whose memory was obscured by the gloom of fascination; as the star Rohini at the end of an eclipse rejoins her beloved moon.

Shak. May the king be——[*She bursts into tears.*

Dushm. My darling, though the word victorious be suppressed by thy weeping, yet I must have victory, since I see thee again, though with pale lips and a body unadorned.

Boy. What man is this, mother,

Shak. Sweet child, ask the divinity who presides over the fortunes of us both. [*She weeps.*

Dushm. O my only beloved, banish from thy mind my cruel desertion of thee.—A violent phrensy overpowered my soul.—Such, when the darkness of illusion prevails are the actions of the best intentioned; as a blind man, when a friend binds his head with a wreath of flowers, mistakes it for a twining snake, and foolishly rejects it. [*He falls at her feet.*

Shak. Rise, my husband, oh! rise—My happiness has been long interrupted; but joy now succeeds to affliction, since the son of my lord still loves me.—(*He rises.*)—How was the remembrance of this unfortunate woman restored to the mind of my lord's son?

Dushm. When the dart of misery shall be wholly extracted from my bosom, I will tell you all; but since the anguish of my soul has in part ceased, let me first wipe off that tear which trickles from thy delicate eye-lash; and thus efface the memory of all the tears which my delirium has made thee shed.

[*He stretches out his hand.*

Shak. (*Wiping off her tears, and seeing the ring on his finger.*) Ah! is that the fatal ring?

Dushm. Yes; by the surprising recovery of it my memory was restored.

Shak. Its influence, indeed, has been great; since it has brought back the lost confidence of my husband.

Dushm. Take it then, as a beautiful plant receives a flower from the returning season of joy.

Shak. I cannot again trust it.—Let it be worn by the son of my lord.

Mátali *enters.*

Mát. By the will of heaven the king has happily met his beloved wife, and seen the countenance of his little son.

Dushm. It was by the company of my friend that my desire attained maturity.—But say, was not this fortunate event previously known to Indra?

Mát. (*Smiling.*) What is unknown to the gods?—But come; the divine Maricha desires to see thee.

Dushm. Beloved, take our son by the hand; and let me present you both to the father of immortals.

Shak. I really am ashamed, even in thy presence, to approach the deities.

Dushm. It is highly proper on so happy an occasion.—Come I entreat thee.

[*They all advance.*

The SCENE *is withdrawn, and* Kasyapa *is discovered on a throne conversing with* Aditi

Kash. (*Pointing to the king.*) That, O daughter of Daksha, is the hero who led the squadrons of thy son to the front of battle, a sovereign of the earth, Dushmanta; by the means of whose bow the thunderbolt of Indra (all its work being accomplished) is now a mere ornament of his heavenly palace.

Adi. He bears in his form all the marks of exalted majesty.

Mát. (*To* Dushmanta.) The parents of the twelve Adityas, O king, are gazing on thee, as on their own offspring, with eyes of affection.—Approach them, illustrious prince.

Dushm. Are those, O Matali, the divine pair, sprung from Marichi and Daksha?—Are those the grand-children of Barhma, to whom the self-existent gave birth in the beginning: whom inspired mortals pronounce the fountain of glory apparent in the form of twelve suns; they who produced my benefactor, the lord of a hundred sacrifices, and ruler of three worlds?

Mat. Even they.—(*Prostrating himself with* Dushmanta.)—Great beings, the king Dushmanta, who has executed the commands of your son Vasava, falls humbly before your throne.

Kash. Continue long to rule the world.

Adi. Long be a warrior with a car unshattered in combat.

[Shakuntala *and her son prostrate themselves.*

Kash. Daughter, may thy hasband be like Indra; May thy son resemble Jayanta! and mayst thou (whom no benediction could better suit) be equal in prosperity to the daughter of Puloman!

Adi. Preserve, my child, constant unity with thy lord: and may this boy, for a great length of years, be the ornament and joy of you both! Now be seated near us. [*They all sit down.*

Kash, (*Looking at them by turns.*) Shakuntala is the model of excellent wives; her son is dutiful; and thou, O king, hast three rare advantages, true piety, abundant wealth, and active virtue.

Dushm. O divine being, having obtained the former object of my most ardent wishes, I now have reached the summit of earthly happiness through thy favour, and thy benizon will ensure its permanence.—First appears the flower, then the fruit; first coulds are collected, then the shower falls; such is the regular course of causes and effects; and thus, when thy indulgence preceded, felicity generally followed.

Mat. Great indeed, O king, has been the kindness of the primeval Brahmanas.

Dushm. Bright son of Marichi, this thy handmaid was married to me by the ceremony of Gandharvas, and, after a time, was conducted to my palace by some of her family; but my memory having failed through delirium, I rejected her, and thus committed a grievous offence against the venerable Kanwa, who is of thy divine lineage; afterwards, on seeing this fatal ring, I remembered my love and my nuptials; but the whole transaction yet fills me with wonder. My soul was confounded with strange ignorance that obscured my senses; as if a man were to see an elephant marching before him, yet to doubt what animal it could be, till he discovered by the traces of his large feet that it was an elephant.

Kash. Cease, my son, to charge thyself with an offence committed ignorantly, and, therefore, innocently—Now hear me——

Dushm. I am devoutly attentive.

Kash. When the nymph Menaka led Shakuntala from the place where thy desertion of her had afflicted her soul, she brought her to the palace of Aditi; and I knew, by the power of meditation on the Supreme Being, that thy forgetfulness of thy pious and lawful consort had proceeded from the imprecation of Durvasas, and that the charm would terminate on the sight of thy ring.

Dushm. (*Aside.*) My name then is cleared from infamy.

Shak. (*Aside.*) Happy am I that the son of my lord, who now recognises me, denied me through ignorance, and not with real aversion,—The terrible imprecation was heard, I suppose, when my mind was intent on a different object, by my two beloved friends, who, with extreme affection, concealed it from me to spare my feelings, but advised me at parting to show the ring if my husband should have forgotten me.

Kash. (*Turning to* Shakuntala.) Thou art apprised, my daughter, of the whole truth, and must no longer resent the behaviour of thy lord.—He rejected thee when his memory was impaired by the force of a charm, and when the gloom was dispelled, his conjugal affection revived; as a mirror whose surface has been sullied, reflects no image; but exhibits perfect resemblances when its polish has been restored.

Dushm. Such, indeed, was my situation.

Kash. My son Dushmanta, hast thou embraced thy child by Shakuntala, on whose birth I myself performed the ceremonies prescribed in the Veda?

Dushm. Holy Maricha, he is the glory of my house.

Kash. Know too, that his heroic virtue will raise him to a dominion extended from sea to sea: before he has passed the ocean of mortal life, he shall rule, unequalled in combat, this earth with seven peninsulas; and, as he now is called Sarvadamana, because he tames even in childhood the fiercest animals, so, in his riper years, he shall acquire the name of Bharata, because he shall sustain and nourish the world.

Dushm. A boy educated by the son of Marichi, must attain the summit of greatness.

Adi. Now let Shakuntala, who is restored to happiness, convey intelligence to Kanwa of all these events; her mother Menaka is in my family, and knows all that has passed.

Shak. The goddess proposes what I most ardently wish.

Kash. By the force of true piety the whole scene will be present to the mind of Kanwa.

Dushm. The devout sage must be still excessively indignant at my frantic behaviour.

Kash. (*Meditating*). Then let him hear from me the delightful news, that his foster-child has been tenderly received by her husband and that both are happy with the little warrior who sprang from them.—Hola! who is in waiting?

A Pupil *enters.*

Pup. Great being, I am here.

Kash. Hasten, Gulava, through the light air, and in my name inform the venerable Kanwa that Shakuntala has a charming son by Dushmanta, whose affection for her was restored with his remembrance on the termination of the spell raised by the angry Durvasas.

Pup. As the divinity commands. (*He goes out.*)

Kash. My son, re-ascend the car of Indra with thy consort and child, and return happy to thy imperial seat.

Dushm. Be it as Maricha ordains.

Kash. Henceforth may the god of the atmosphere with copious rain give abundance to thy affectionate subjects; and mayst thou with frequent sacrifices maintain the Thunderer's friendship! By numberless interchanges of good-offices between you both, may benefits reciprocally be conferred on the inhabitants of the two worlds!

Dushm. Powerful being, I will be studious, as I am able, to attain that felicity.

Kash. What other favours can I bestow on thee?

Dushm. Can any favours exceed those already bestowed?—Let every king apply himself to the attainment of happiness for his people; let Saraswati, the goddess of liberal arts, be adored by all readers of the Veda; and may Shiva, with an azure neck and red locks, eternally potent and self-existing, avert from me the pain of another birth in this perishable world, the seat of crimes and of punishments.

[*All go out.*]

THE END.

VIKRAMA & URVASI.

OR

THE HERO AND THE NYMPH.

A DRAMA,

TRANSLATED FROM THE ORIGINAL,
SANSKRIT.

BY

H. H. WILSON.

PUBLISHED BY
THE SOCIETY FOR THE RESUSCITATION
OF INDIAN LITERATURE.

CALCUTTA:
PRINTED BY H. C. DAS, ELYSIUM PRESS,

1901.

INTRODUCTION.

—:o:—

The Drama of Vikrama and Urvasi is one of the three plays attributed to Kalidasa, already advantageously known to the Western world as the author of Sakuntala. The introductory observation of the Manager in the prelude is our evidence to this effect; and it is corroborated by the correspondence of these two compositions in many of their characteristic merits and defects. The subject of each is taken from heroic mythology, and a royal demigod and nymph of more than human mould are the hero and heroine of either; there is the same vivacity of description, and tenderness of feeling in both; the like delicate beauty in the thoughts, and extreme elegance in the style. It may be difficult to decide to which the palm belongs; but the story of the present play is perhaps more skilfully woven and the incidents rise out of each other more naturally than in Sakuntala; while on the other hand, there is perhaps no one personage in it, so interesting as the heroine of that drama.

Although, however, there is no reason to doubt that this play is the work of the same hand as that translated by Sir William Jones, the concurrence does not throw any further light upon the date or history of the author. We can only infer, from the observance of the same chaste style of composition and the absence of any forced construction or offensive conceits, that they are both the production of a period anterior to the reign of Bhoja, when his Kalidasa, a man of fancy and taste, could descend to write a whole poem, the Nalodaya, for instance, in a strain of verbal paltering and a succession of jingling sounds.

The richness of the Prakrit in this play, both in structure and in its metrical code, is very remarkable. A very great portion, especially of the fourth act, is in this language, and in that act also a considerable variety of metre is introduced; it is clear, therefore, that this form of Sanskrit must have been highly cultivated long before the play was written, and this might lead us to doubt whether the composition can bear so remote a date as the reign of Vikramaditya (56 B.C.) It is yet rather uncertain whether the classical language of Hindu literature had at that time received so high a polish as appears in the present drama, and still less, therefore, could the descendants have been exquisitely refined, if the parent was comparatively rude. We can scarcely conceive that the cultivation of Prakrit preceded that of Sanskrit, when we advert to the principles on which the former seems to be evolved from the latter; but it must be confessed that the relation between Sanskrit and Prakrit has been hitherto very imperfectly investigated, and is yet far from being understood.

The mythological notions of the author, as inferable from the benedictory stanzas, opening all the three plays attributed to him, is rather adverse to a remote antiquity, as the worship of any individual deity as the Supreme Being, and with Bhakti or faith, appears to be an innovation in Hindu ritual and theology of a comparatively modern period. At the same time, the worship of Siva undoubtedly prevailed in the Dekhin at the commencement of the Christian era, and Vikramaditya, the patron of Kalidasa, is traditionally represented as devoted to Siva and his consort.

It may be thought some argument for the comparative antiquity of the present drama, that it tells the story of Pururavas very differently from the Puranas, in several of which it may be found. We may suppose, therefore, that the play preceded those works; as, had it been subsequently composed, the poet would either spontaneously, or in deference to sacred authority, have adhered more closely to the Puranik legend. The difference in the Puranas also indicates that corruption of taste, which we cannot hesitate regarding as the product of more modern and degenerate days.

The loves of Pururavas and Urvasi are related in various Puranas. The following is the story as it appears in the Vishnu Purana, in which and in the Padma,* it is more fully and connectedly detailed than perhaps in any other composition of the same class.

Urvasi, the Apsaras, or one of the nymphs of heaven so named, having incurred the displeasure of Mitra and Varuna, was sentenced by them, to become the consort of a mortal, and in consequence of this curse she became enamoured of the king Pururavas, the son of Budha and Ila. Forgetting her celestial duties, and foregoing the delights of Swarga, she introduced herself to the monarch, and her charms did not fail to make an impression on his heart. She was delicately and symmetrically formed, was graceful in her gesture, and fascinating in her manners; her voice was music; her countenance was dressed in smiles, and her beauty was such as might enchant the world: no wonder therefore, that Pururavas was at once inspired with fervent love. Confiding in his rank and renown, the king did not hesitate to propose a matrimonial alliance to the nymph of heaven; she was nothing loth, but had not the power to comply, without previously exacting

* It is the subject also of a work of some length in Telugu, called the Kaviraja-monoranjanam, or Pururava charitram composed by Avyaya, the minister of a petty prince in the Dekhin, the Raja of Condavir.

the bridegroom's consent to two conditions. Pururavas hesitated not to accede to the stipulations.

Urvasi had with her two pet-rams, creatures of heavenly and illusive natures, and one of her conditions was, that the king should take these animals under his own charge, and guard against their being ever carried away by fraud or force.

The other stipulation was, that the nymph was never to behold the person of the king divested of his raiment. On the ready accession of Puraravas to these terms Urvasi became his bride, and they dwelt together in the forest of Chitraratha, near Alaka, the capital of Kuvera, for sixty-one years,* in perfect happiness and undiminished affection.

The absence of Urvasi was very soon felt in the upper sphere, and the inhabitants of Swarga found their enjoyments stale and unprofitable, no longer heightened by the agreeable manners and entertaining society of the nymph. The whole body of Apsaras, Siddhas, Gandharvas, and other tenants of Indra's heaven, regretted her loss and determined to attempt her recovery as soon as the period of her exile, as denounced by the imprecation, should have expired. When this period arrived, they deputed

* This is, however, a mere moment in the extravagant duration of the life of Pururavas according to the Puranas; there is nothing of the kind in the play.

some of the Gandharvas on the expedition, who undertook to bring about the violation of the terms on which the alliance of the king and the nymph depended. When this intent they entered the sleeping chamber of the monarch, and carried off one of the rams. The bleat of the animal woke Urvasi, who echoed its cries with her lamentations, and aroused the prince. Apprehensive, however, of appearing before his bride undressed, Pururavas hesitated to pursue the thief, and thus incurred the angry reproaches of his spouse for his indifference to her loss. Presently the Gandharvas bore away the second ram, and the grief of Urvasi, was afresh excited; the king's indignation also could no longer be restrained, and, determined to pursue and punish the ravishers, he leaped naked out of bed, trusting that the darkness of night would screen him from the eye of his consort. This was what his enemies desired, and he was no sooner off the couch than a vivid flash of lightning revealed him to view, and put an end to his union with the nymph of Swarga. Urvasi immediately disappeared accompanying the Gandharvas to the halls of Indra.

When Pururavas was conscious of his loss, his grief was so intense that it affected his intellects, and he long wandered frantic over the world in quest of his bride. After many years had elapsed he came no a lake in Kurukshetra, where he found several tymphs sporting on the bank; amongst them, was

Urvasi. Recognizing her at once, he ran to her and with wild energy implored her return; the nymph, however, was no longer disposed, even if she had been permitted, to comply with his wishes, and was deaf to all his entreaties; and at last she succeeded in convincing him of the unreasonableness of his solicitations, and prevailed on him to resume his station, and the duties of a king, engaging on those terms to pay him an annual visit. Pururavas, however, reluctantly, was compelled to submit, and returned sorrowfully but composed to his capital. His annual interviews with Urvasi were punctually repeated, and the fruit of this intercourse was the birth of six sons,* Ayus, Dhimat, Amavasu, Viswavasu, Satayus and Srutayus, who were the progenitors of the lunar race of kings.

The occasional interviews with his bride granted to Pururavas were far from satisfying his desires, and he still sighed for the permanent enjoyment of her society. The Gandharvas at last, pitying his distress, engaged to promote his reunion with the nymph, and sent the king a brazier charged with fire, with which they directed him to perform a sacrifice in the forest, to attain the gratification of all his wishes. The king repaired to the woods, but reflecting that he had

* All this part of the story, Urvasi's loss and recovery, and the birth of Ayus, are totally different in the play.

quitted Urvasi in order to celebrate this rite, giving up the substance for the shadow, he returned to seek the nymph, leaving the vessel of fire in the thicket. Not finding his consort, he again directed his steps to the forest, but there the brazier was gone, and on the spot where it had stood, a sami* and Aswattha† tree had spruug up. After a little consideration Pururavas broke a branch from either tree and carried them back to the palace, where, reciting the Gayatri‡ and rubbing the sticks together he generated fire with the friction: this primeval fire he divided into three portions, and with them he performed various sacrifices, and oblations, until he obtained the rank of a Gandharva, and being elevated to the regions of Swarga, there enjoyed the constant society of his beloved Urvasi§.

The latter circumstances of this legend seem to indicate the introduction of fire-worship into India by Pururavas, considered as a historical personage.‖

---

* Mimosa suma.

† Religious fig.

‡ The holiest verse of the Vedas.

§ The play makes no allusion to these incidents, closing witn the appearance of the elder son, Ayus.

‖ The three fires are: the garhapatya, or perpetual fire maintained by a house holder; Ahavaniya, or consecrated fire taken from the preceding and prepared for receiving oblations; and dakshinagni,

There may have been some old tradition to that effect, whence the Pauranik writers derive the ground work of their fable; but it is not noticed in the play; neither is any allusion made to it in the version of this story in another work in which it is found, the Vrihat-Katha, whch differs in many particulars from both the play and the Puranas. The story there, however, is very concisely narrated, and the author has clearly taken merely the personages and course of the fable from what was currently known, and given his own colouring to the incidents. It adds, therefore, nothing to the history of the narrative, and may be either anterior or subsequent to the forms in which it is now presented to English readers. Another authority, however, the, Matsya Purana, tells the story more agreeably to the tenor of the drama, as follows:

" When a year had elapsed, the divine Tara bore a son of surpassing splendour, arrayed in celestial raiment of a yellow colour, and richly decorated with heavenly gems. From his youth he was versed in regal duties, and was so skilled in the training of elephants that he taught the art, and acquaired the appellation of Gajavedhaka. The gods being assembled at the mansion of her husband, Vrihaspati,

---

fire, taken from either of the former and placed towards the south.

to perform the rites due to his birth, inquired of Tara whose son he was, and with much reluctance she acknowledged the royal Soma was his father. Soma therefore took the boy, and named him Budha, and gave him dominion on the earth, and inaugurated him supreme over the world. Brahma and the rest conferred upon him the dignity of a planetary power, and then took their departure.

"The holy Budha begot by Ila a son, who performed by his own might a hundred Ashwamedhas. He was named Pururavas, and was revered by all worlds. He worshipped Vishnu on the peaks of Himalaya, and thence became the monarch of the seven fold earth. Kesin and myriads of Daityas fell before his prowess, and Urvasi, fascinated by his personal graces, became his bride.

Virtue, wealth, and Desire, once paid this monarch a visit, curious to ascertain which of them held the first place in his esteem. The king received them with respect, but paid to virtue his profoundest homage. Wealth and Desire were offended by the preference shown to their companion. Wealth denounced a curse upon him, that Avarice should occasion his fall; and Desire declared that he should be separated from his bride, and on that account suffer distraction in the forest of Kumara on the Gandhamadana mountain; but Virtue declared that he should enjoy a long and pious life, that his descendants should continue to multiply as long as the sun and moon endured and should ever enjoy the dominion of the earth. After this the divinities disappeared.

"Pururavas was in the habit of paying a visit to Indra every day. Having ascended his car, accompanying the Sun in his southern course he beheld on one occasion the demon Kesin seize and carry off the nymphs Chitralekha and Urvasi. The king attacked the demon, and destroyed him with the shaft of Vayu by which he not only rescued the nymphs, but established, Indra on his throne, which the demon had endangered. For this service Indra repaid the monarch with his friendship, and gave him additional power, splendour, and glory.

"Having invited the king to a festival, at which was represented the celebrated story of Lakshmi's election of a husband, the invention of Bharata, Indra commanded Menaka, Rambha, and Urvasi to perform their respective parts. Urvasi, who represented Lakshmi, being engrossed by admiration of the king, forgot what she had to enact, and thereby incurred the high displeasure of the sage, who sentenced her to separation from the prince on earth, and condemned her to pine fifty-five years transformed to a vine, until restored to the regrets of Pururavas. Urvasi having made the king her lord, resided with him, and after the term of the course had expired bore him eight sons: Ayus, Dhritayus, Aswayus, Dhanayus, Dhritimat, Vasu, Diviyata, and Satayus, all endowed with more than human power.

This story is evidently that of the play, although related less in detail, and with a few variations according to Pauranik taste, but it is clear that it is either derived from a common source with the narration of the drama, or which is not improbable, that it has borrowed from the latter its general complexion. The nature of the relation which exists between the fiction, as it appears in the drama, and in the Puranas, our readers will be able to appreciate for themselves after perusal of the former.

DRAMATIS PERSONÆ

OF THE PRELUDE.

MANAGER. ACTOR.

OF THE PLAY

MEN.

Pururavas—King of Pratishthana.

Ayus—The son of Pururavas.

Manavaka—The Vidushaka and confidential-companion of the King.

Chitraratha—King of Gandharvas, the attendants on Indra.

Narada—The divine sage, the son of Brahma.

Chamberlain.

A Forester.

Paila.
Galava. } Two disciples of the sage Bharata.

WOMEN.

Urvasi—An Apsaras, or nymph of Indra's heaven.

Chitralekha—Another nymph, her friend.

Sahajanya.
Rambha. } Nymphs.*
Menaka.

---

* According to the Kasi-Khanda there are thirty-five millions of these nymphs, but only one thousand

Ausinari—The queen of Pururavas and daughter of the king of Kasi or Benares.

Nipunika—One of her attendants.

PERSONS SPOKEN OF.

Indra—The chief of all the inferior deities, and sovereign of Swarga or Paradise.

---

and sixty are the principal. Of these, however, not more than five or six are the subject of Pauranika or poetical narrations, or Urvasi, Menaka, Rambha, Tillottama, and Alambusa. In their birth and denomination they offer some analogy to the goddess. Aphrodite: like her they arose from the sea; and as her name is referred to aphros, "foam or spray," so that of the Apsarasas is from ap "water" and saras "who moves." Their origin is thus related in the first book of the Ramayana :—

"Then from the agitated deep upsprung.
The legion Apsarasas, so named,
That to the watery element they owed
Their being. Myriads were they born, and all
In vesture heavenly clad, and heavenly gems:
Yet more divine their native semblance, rich
With all the gifts of grace, and youth, and beauty.
A train innumerous followed: yet thus fair.
Nor god nor demon sought their wedded love
Thus, Raghava, they still remain—their charm
The common treasure of the host of heaven."

Kesin—A Daitya or Titan, an enemy of the gods.

Bharata—A holy sage, the inventor of dramatic composition.

Guards.—Nymphs, etc.

Scene in the First Act, the Peaks of Himalaya; in the second and third, the palace of Pururavas at Pratisthana; in the fourth, the forest of Akalusha; and in the fifth again, at the palace.

Time, uncertain.

VIKRAMA & URVASI.

PRELUDE.

ENTER THE MANAGER.

May that Siva * who is attainable by devotion and and faith ;† who is the sole male‡ of the Vendanta,§ spread through all space, to whom alone the name of Lord‖ is applicable, and who is saught with suppres-

---

* The term used in the text is Sthanu, a name of Siva, from Stha to stay or be, the existent or eternal.

† Bhakti, faith, and Yoga the practise of abstract meditation.

‡ The ekapurusha, the active instrument in creation.

§ The theological and metaphysical portion of the Vedas.

‖ Iswara, which is derived from is, to have power, or as, to pervade: in the latter case the vowel is changed.

sed breath* by those who covet final emancipation,† bestow upon you final felicity.

---

* The exercise of Pranayama, or breathing through either nostril alternately, and then closing both during the repetition mentally of certain formulœ.

† Inferior enjoyment of heaven is not an object of desire to the more enthusiastic of the Hindus, as it is but finite, and after its cessation the individual is born again in the world, and exposed to the calamities of a frail existence. The great aim of devotion is union with the supreme, and universal spirit, in which case the soul no more assumes a perishable shape. The character of this benediction corresponds with that of Sakuntala and the Malavikagnimitra, and all three indicated the author's belonging to that modification of the Hindu faith in which the abstract deism of the Vedanta is qualified by identifying the supreme, invisible, and inappreciable spirit with a delusive form, which was the person of Rudra or Siva. It is of a more practical character, therefore, than pure Vedantism, and it is equally different from both metaphysical and theistical Sankhya. It is, in fact, the doctrine of the Saiva Puranas. (See As Res., vol xvii.) The Brahmans of the south and west are mostly of this sect, and whatever Sankara Swamin may have taught, it is that of his descendants the Dasnami—

Man. (Looking off the stage.) Ho! Marisha,* come hither.

(ENTER ACTOR.)

Act.—Here am I, sir.

Man.—Many assemblies have witnessed the compositions of former dramatic bards:† I therefore propose to exhibit one not hitherto represented, the drama‡ of Vikrama and Urvasi.§ Desire the company to be ready to do justice to their respective parts.

Gosains. The sect is probably the oldest of all now existing in India.

* A term by which it is proper to address one of the principal performers.

† Kalidasa is therefore not the oldest dramatic writer.

‡ The Trotaka, a drama in five, eight, or nine acts, the characters of which are mixed, or heavenly and human.

§ Mr Lenz, in his very excellent edition and version of this play (Berline, 1833), seems to think the title, Urvasi—Vikarma, Urvasiœ incessus, would be preferable to that of Vikaramorvasi, as the latter, If not a dwandwa compound, is not comformable to rule: the latter is matter of little moment with the poets; and that Vikramorvasi is the author's reading, appears from the text. The addition of Nama Vikramorvasi na ma trotakam, makes no difference, as

Act.—I shall, sir,

Man.—I have now only to request the audience that they will listen to this work of Kalidas with attention and kindness, in consideration of its subject and respect for the author.‖

(Behind the Scenes.)

---

indeed the commentator shows who entitles his comment, Vikramorvasi prakasika, the explanation of the Vikrama and Urvasi. With regard to the meaning of Vikrama, which is properly "heroism" it may be observed that it is often used in a way where "king" or "hero" alone can be signified by it; thus Vikramaditya is as often called simply Vikrama as not. The traditions relating to him are termed the Vikramacharita: the nine gems are said to be ratnani-nova Vikramasya. The word is applied also attributively, as Dipakornir iti kkyato rajabhud rajya Vikramah. There was a king named Dipakarni, the Vikrama of the realm. Here it might be thought equivalent to the Alexander or the Cœsar of his age, but it could not be so employed as a synonym of the Hindu Alexander himself, nor could it be so used in the universally current (in India) ltitle of the play. There can be no doubt therefore, that by a poetic license heroism is here put for hero and the compound is of the Dwandwa class, in despite of the grammarians.

‖ The original may be so understood, although

Help, help! if in the middle sky
A friend be found, to aid us fly.

Man.—What sounds are these in the air, that like the plaintive bleat of lambs, break in upon my speech? Was it the murmur of the bee or koil's distant song, or do the nymphs of heaven as they pass above warble their celestial strains? Ah, no! it is the cry of distress. The fair creation of the saint, the friend of Nara, Urvasi, has been carried off by a demon on her return from the halls of the sovereign of Kailasa,* and her sisters are invoking some friendly power to their aid.

[EXIT.

ACT I.

SCENE FIRST.

Part of the Himalaya Range of Mountains.

Enter in the Air a Troop of Apsarasas or Nymphs of Heaven.

Nymphs—Help, help! if any friend be nigh.
To aid the daughters of the sky!

---

it is not quite clear.—Pranayishu dakshinyavasad yadi va sadvastu-purusha-bahumnat-srinuta manobhir avahitaih kriyam imam Kalidasasya. It is of little consequence, except that in the sense preferred it indicates the fame of the author to be established when this piece was written.

* Kuvera, the god of wealth, whose capital Alaka is supposed to be situated on mount Kuvera.

Enter Pururavas* in a heavenly car, driven by his charioteer.

Brahma.

Daksha. Atri.

Aditi-Kasyapa. Soma.

Vaivaswata, the sun.

Ila. Budha—Ila.

Pururavas.

Pur.—Suspend your cries; in me behold a friend,
Pururavas, returning from the sphere,
Of the wide-glancing sun: command my aid,
And tell me what you dread.

Rambha—A demon's violence.

Pur.—What violence presumes the fiend to offer,

Menaka—Great king, it thus has chanced; we measured back
Our steps from an assembly of the gods,
Held in Kuvera's† hall. Before us stepped.
The graceful Urvasi the nymph whose charms,

---

* Pururavas is a king of high descent, being sprung by his mother Ila from the sun, and his father Budha from the moon, being the grand-son of the latter and great-grandson of the former. His origin is ultimately derived from Brahma, thus:

† The God of riches.

Defeated Indra's stratagems and shamed
The loveliness of Sri,† the brightest ornament
Of heaven : when on our path the haughty Danava,
Kesin, the monarch of the golden city.‡
Sprang fierce and bore the struggling nymph away.

Pur.—Which path pursued the wretch ?

Sahajanya—'Tis yonder,

Pur.—Banish your fears ;
I go to rescue and restore your friend.

Rambha.—The act is worthy of your high descent.

Pur.—Where wait you my return ?

Rambha.—Here, on this peak.

The towering Hemakuta.§

Pur.—(To the Charioteer.) Bend our course
To yonder point, and urge rapid steeds
To swiftest flight. 'Tis done; before the car
Like volleyd dust the scattering clouds divide,
The whirling wheel deceives the dazzled eye,
And double round the axle seems to circle.
The waving chowrie on the steed's broad brow,
Points backward, motionless as in a picture;
And backward streams the banner from the breeze.

---

† The wife of Vishnu, goddess of prosperity and beauty.

‡ Hiranyapura is the name in the text.

§ The golden or snowy peak.

We meet immovable.* We should outstrip.
The flight of Vainateya,† and must surely
Overtake the ravisher.

[EXEUNT.]

Rambha.—Now, sisters, on, and blithely seek
The golden mountain's glittering peak;
Secure the king extracts the dart,
That rankles in each anxious heart.

Menaka.—We need not fear.

Rambha.—Yet heard to quell the demon race.

Menaka.—The brood of hell.

---

* A very similar description, but less picturesque and just, occurs in the beginning of Sakuntala, and the truth of it is rendered less striking by a loose translation. Sir William Jones translates Nishkampa Chamara sikha, "they tossed their manes," when it means "their manes and the chowries on their heads are unagitated, "that is, they point against the wind without waving a predicate much more indicative of a rapid advance against the breeze than the undulation of either. The chamara or chowrie, the white bushy tail of the Tibet cow, fixed on a gold or ornamented shaft, rose from between the ears of the horse like the plume of the war horse of chivalry; the banner or banneret, with the device of the chief, rose at the back of the car; sometimes several little triangular flags were mounted on its sides.

† Garuda, the son of Vinata.

Shall feel his prowess. Aid to bring
From mortal realms to Swarga's king.
He comes, and to his hand is given
Command o'er all the host of heaven.

[THEY PROCEED.

Rambha.—Joy, sisters, joy, the king advances;
High O'er you ridgy rampart dances
The deer emblazoned banner. See
The heavenly car rolls on;—tis he.

Enter Pururavas in his car slowly; Urvasi in the car faintly, supported by Chitralekha.

Chitral.—Dear friend, revive.

Pur.—Fair nymph, resume your courage.
Still wields the thunderer his bolt, and guards
The triple world from harm; the foes of heaven
Are put to flight:—why cherish this alarm
When its just cause is o'er? unclose those lids;
The lotus opens when the night retires.

Chitral.—Alas! her sighs alone declare her conscious.

Pur.—Soft as the flower, the timid heart not soon
Foregoes its fears. The scarf that veils her bosom
Hides not its flutterings, and the panting breast
Seems as it fell the wreath of heavenly blossoms
Weigh too oppressively.

Chitral.—Revive, my friend;

This weakness ill becomes a nymph of heaven.

Pur.—Have patience; she recovers, though but faintly. So gently steals the moon upon the night
Retiring tardily; so peeps the flame
Of evening fires through smoky wreaths; and thus,
The Ganges slowly clears her troubled wave,
Engulphs the ruin that the tumbling bank
Had hurled across her agitated course,
And flows a clear and stately stream again.

Chitral.—Awake, dear friend, the enemies of heaven
Are baffled in despair.

Urv.—(Reviving.) By Indra's prowess.

Chitral.—By prowess not inferior to Mahendra's.
By this most holy prince, Pururavas.

Urv.—(Looking at Pururavas; then apart.)
What thanks I owe the Danava!

Pur.—(After looking at Urvasi; then apart.)
What marvel,
The nymphs celestial blushed with humbled charms,
When, to rebuke their wantonness, the sage
Willed that this wondrous beauty should appear.
The creature of a sage!—it cannot be:
How could an aged anchoret, grown old
In dull devotion, and to feeling dead,
Conceive such matchless beauty—oh no! love

Himself was her creator, whilst the moon
Gave her his radience, and the flowery spring
Taught her to madden men and gods with passion.

Urv.—Where are our friends!

Chitral.—The king will lead us to them.

Pur.—Trust me, they mourn your loss; nor is it strange
That they, your friends, should miss you, when the eye
In whose delighted path you once have moved
Cannot but grieve to lose your lovely presence.

Urv.—(Apart.) Delightful words! they fall like drops of nectar.
Nor wonder nectar from the moon should flow.
(Aloud.) Not less my eagerness to see again
The friends I love.

Pur.—Behold them there! they keep
Their anxious watch on Hemakuta's brow,
And mark your coming, safe from the demon's grasp,
Like the bright moon emerging from eclipse.

Chitral.—Why do you gaze on me, dear friend?

Urv.—The same delight and pain my eyes imbibe as—

Chitral.—Whose?

Urv.—My friends.

Rambha.—Attended by each brilliant star,
like Chandra in his radiant car,
The king appears, and with him borne

Behold our sister nymphs return.

Menaka.—For both the boons our thanks be poured!
The prince unharmed and friends restored.

Shahajanya.—Now, sister, see how hard to quell
By mortal might the sons of hell.

Pur.—To yonder lofty mountain guide the car.
(Apart.) Not vain our journey hitherward: 'tis much
In the unsteady rolling of the chariot
But for a moment to have touched the form
Of this celestial nymph; the blissful contact
Shoots ecstasy through every fibre. Here (aloud).
Arrest our course. The maid's companion choir
Press on to her embrace, like flowery vines,
That bend to catch the beauty of the spring.

Chorus.—Joy to the king. Propition heaven
Has victory to his prowess given.

Pur.—Behold in these my triumph!
Presenting Urvasi and Chitralekha.

Urv.—My dear, dear sisters, little did I hope.
But late to feel once more this loved embrace.
[EMBRACES THEM.

Chorus.—May countless ages blest survey
The mighty Pururavas' sway.
[A NOISE WITHOUT.

Charioteer.—(To the king.)
Sire, from the east the rushing sound is heard

Of mighty chariots; yonder like clouds they roll
Along the mountain cliffs now there alights
A chief in gorgeous raiment, like the blaze
Of lightning playing on the towering precipice.

Nymphs.—Our king, great Chitraratha.

Enter Chitraratha, the king of Gandharvas (attended).

Chitrar.—Illustrious, victor, friend of Indra, hail!

Pur.—King of the heavenly quiristers, receive
The welcome of a friend. What brings you hither?

Chitrar.—When Indra learnt from Narada the rape
Of this fair damsel by the Daitya, Kesin,
He bade me gather the Gandharva train
And hasten to her rescue. I obeyed;
But ere we marched, news of your triumph came
And stopped our progress. For your friendly aid
I bear you now our monarch's thanks, and more—
His wish to see you in the heavently courts
Your worth has opened to your welcome visit.
This service is most dear to him. The nymph
Is now your boon–first given by Narayana
To grace the halls of swarga now redeemed
From hands profane by your resistless valour.

Pur.—You rate the deed too high. Not mine the glory,
But his the thunderer's, from whom derived
The strength of those who conquer in his cause.
The very echo of the lion's roar
As through the rocky rifts it spreads and deepens,
Appals the mighty elephant.

Chitrar.—'Tis well.
This modesty becomes your worth. Humility
Is ever found the ornament of valour.

Pur.—Excuse me to the monarch. Other claims
Demand my distant presence; lead the nymph
Back to the king.

Chitrar.—Your will shall be obeyed.

Urv.—(Apart to Chitralekha.)
Speak for me, my dear friend; my lips refuse
To bid adieu to my protector.—Speak.

Chitral.—(To the king.)
Illustrious sir, my friend commands me ask
Your leave to carry back with her to heaven,
As one she dearly cherishes, your fame.

Pur.—Farewell!—I trust ere long to meet again.
The Gandharvas and Apsarasas ascend;
(Urvasi loiters and pretends to be stopped.)

Urv.—A moment pause! (To Chitralekha.) Dear girl, this straggling vine
Has caught my garland—help me to get loose.

Chitral.—No easy task, I fear you seem entangled

Too fast to be set free: but come what may,
Depend upon my friendship.

Urv.—Thanks, thanks,
Be mindful of your promise.

[CHITRALEKHA EMPLOYED IN DISENGAGING HER.

Pur.—A thousand thanks, dear plant, to whose kind aid
I owe another instant, and behold
But for a moment and imperfectly,
Those half-averted charms.

Charioteer.—Come, royal sir,
Let us depart. The demon foes are hurled
Deep in the ocean wave, just punishment
For their rebellion against Swarga's king.
Now let the shaft, whose headlong force resembles,
The blast of fate, sleep in its wonted quiver,
As cowers the snake within his gloomy covert.

[THEY MOUNT.

Pur.—Ascend the car.

Urv.—Ah! me; ah! when again
Shall I behold my brave deliverer!

[DEPARTS WITH CHITRALEKHA AND THE NYMPHS.

Pur.—(Looking after her.)
What idle dreams does fantic love suggest?
What arduous tasks inspire! The beauteous nymph
Bears off my heart in triumph through the path
Her sire immortal treads: so flies the swan

Through the mid air, charged with its precious spoil,
The milky nectar of the lotus stem.

[Exit in his car.

END OF THE FIRST ACT.

ACT II.

THE GARDEN OF THE PALACE OF PURURAVAS AT PRAYAGA (ALLAHABAD.)

Enter Manavaka, the Vidushaka.

It is mighty inconvenient this, for a Brahman like myself, one so much sought after and subject to such frequent invitation, to be burthened with the king's secret! Going so much into company as I do, I shall never be able to set a guard upon my tongue. I must be prudent, and will stay here by myself in this retired temple, until my royal friend comes forth from the council-chamber. (Sits down and covers his face with his hands.)

Enter Nipunika, an Attendant on the Queen.

The daughter of the king of Kasi is quit sure, that since the king returned from the regions of the sun, he is no longer the same; he must have left his heart behind him,—what else can be the reason? I must try and find it out. If that crafty Brahman be in the secret, I shall easily get at it. A secret can rest no longer in his breast than morning dew upon the grass. Where can he be?—eh!—yes, there he sits deep in thought, like a monkey in a picture. Now to atack him, that is all I have to do, Arya Manavaka, I salute you!

Man.—Prosperity attend you. (Apart.) The king's secret is bursting forth at the mere sight of that hussy Nipunika. (Aloud.) Well, Nipunika, how is it you leave your music practice for the garden?

Nip.—The queen has sent me to pay you a visit, sir.

Man.—And what may be her Majesty's commands?

Nip.—She bids me say that she has ever esteemed you as her good friend, and that it is, therefore, with some surprise she finds you utterly indifferent to her present anxiety.

Man.—Why, what's the matter? Has my royal friend done anything to displease her?

N*ip.*—Oh, that is not the point! my mistress knows [the cause of his melancholy well enough; nay more, he let out the secret himself, and, in a fit of absence, addressed the queen by the very name of his new love.

Man.—(Apart.) Indeed! Oh if his Majesty cannot keep his own secrets, why should I be plagued with them? (Aloud.) Why, what the deuce, Nipunika, did he call the queen?—Urvasi?

Nip.—And, pray, who is Urvasi?

Man.—The nymph, the Apsaras. Ever since the king saw her, he has been out of his senses; he not only neglects her grace, but annoys me and spoils my dinner.

Nip,—(Apart.) So, so; I have settled that matter, as I expected. (Aloud.) Well, I must return to the queen. What am I to say her?

Man.—Tell her I am weary of attempting to cure my friend, the king, of this idle fancy of his. The only remedy is the sight of her lotus countenance.

Nip.—You may depend upon me.

[EXIT.

The Warder. (Without.)

All hail to the monarch who toils through the day,
To shed o'er his subjects the light of his sway,
As travels unceasing the sun in his sphere
To chase from the universe darkness and fear.
The lord of lone splendour an instant suspends
His course at mid-noon ere he westward descends;
And brief are the moments our young monarch knows,
Devoted to pleasure or paid to repose.

Man.—(Listening.) Ha! my royal friend has arisen from his seat, and is coming hither; I will await him.

Enter Pururavas.

Pur.—One glance sufficed; the unerring shaft of love
Laid bare the path, and gave a ready access

To that celestial nymph, to seat herself
Throned in my heart.

Man.—(To himself.) Ah! that is exactly what the poor daughter of *Kasiraja* complains of.

Pur.—(To the *Vidushaka.*) You have kept my secret safe?

Man.—(Apart.) That baggage must have betrayed me! Why else should he ask the question?

Pur.—(Alarmed.) How, you are silent?

Man.—Don't be alarmed; the fact is, that my tongue is so accustomed to the restraint I have put upon it, that I cannot answer off hand even your inquiries.

Pur.—'Tis well! Now then for recreation—
What shall I do?

Man.—Pay a visit to the kitchen.

Pur.—With what intent?

Man.—Why, the very sight of the savoury dishes in course of preparation will be sufficient to dissipate all melancholy ideas.

Pur.—With you it may, for what you covet there
You may obtain; what my desires affect
Is hopeless! Where should I then seek diversion.

Man.—May I ask if the person of your Highness was not beheld by the lady Urvasi?

Pur.—What then?

Man.—Why, then, I should think her not quite so uncomeatable.

Pur.—The fit compeer of beauty such as hers
Must needs be more than human.

Man.—What you say only adds to my surprise.
What signified madam Urvasi's unrivalled beauty?
Am I not equally without a peer, in ugliness?

Pur.—Words cannot paint her every excellence.
Hear her Manavaka, described in brief.

Man.—I am all attention.

Pur.—Her loveliness yields splendour to her ornaments,
Her purity gives fragrance to her perfumes;
All the similitudes that poets use
To picture beauty, it were gross flattery
To them, to name with her surprising charms.

Man.—This is mighty well! but in the will-o'-the-wisp fancy for such super-human excellence, I should think your Majesty had taken the *chataka* for your model. Where, please you, shall we go.

Pur.—To melancholy moods the only solace
Is solitude;—go onwards to the grove.

Man.—(Apart.) What absurdity (Aloud.)

This way, sir; here is the boundary of the grove, and the southern wind advances with due civility to meet you.

Pur.—He comes to teach me, as he amorous sports
Amongst the blossoms of the *madhavi*
And dances frolic with the *Kunda* flowers,
With all the impassioned fervour of desire

And graceful ingenuity of love—
I mark in him my pictured sentiments.

Man.—The only likeness I see is your mutual perseverance. But here we are; please you to enter?

Pur.—Precede! I fear my coming hither vain,
Nor yield these shades relief to my affliction
Though with intent to gain tranquillity,
I seek these paths of solitude and peace;
I feel like one contending with the stream,
And still borne backwards by the current's force

Man.—Why entertain such feelings?

Pur.—How avoid them?
What I affect is of no light attainment:
The very thought presumption, and now love,
The five armed god, whose shafts already pierce me,
Call to his aid these passion-breathing blossoms,
The mango's fragrant flowers and pallid leaves,
Light wafted round us by the southern breeze.

Man.—Away with despondence! Be assured that in a little time *Ananga* will be your friend, and help you to obtain your desires.

Pur.—I take your words as ominous.

Man.—But now let your Highness notice the beauty of this garden, heralding, as it were, the presence of the spring

Pur.—I mark it well. In the *Kuravaka*,
Behold the painted fingers of the fair
Red tinted on the tip and edged with ebony;
Here the *asoka* puts forth nascent buds
Just bursting into flowers, and here the mango
Is brown with blossoms, on whose tender crests
Scant lies the fragrant down; methinks I see
The pride of spring on either hand attended
By budding infancy and flowering youth.

Man.—The bower of jasmines yonder, with its slab of black marble, is studded thick with blossoms, and the bees crowd about them in heaps; it invites your majesty to repose.

[THEY ENTER THE ARBOUR.

Pur.—As you please.

Man.—Now, seated in this shade, you may dissipate your cares by contemplating the elegant plants around us.

Pur.—How should I learn composure? As my eye
Rests on the towering trees, and from their tops
Sees the lithe creeper wave, I call to mind
The graces that surpass its pendulous elegance.
Come, rouse your wit, and friendship may inspire

Some capable expedient to secure me
The object of my wishes.

Man.—Well, I will turn the matter over in my mind; but you must not disturb my cogitations by your sighs.

Pur.—(Feeling his eyes twinkle.)

The moon-faced maid is far beyond my reach;
Then, why should love impart such flattering tokens.
They teach my mind to feel as if enjoyed
The present bliss, hope scarcely dares imagine.

[THEY RETIRE.

Enter Urvasi and Chitralekha in the air.

Chitral.—Tell me, dear girl, your purpose: whither go we?

Urv.—Nay, tell me first, do you recall the promise
You made me jestingly upon the brow
Of *Hemakuta*, when your friendly hand
Detached my vesture from entangling thorns?
If it be still within your recollection,
You need not ask me whither we proceed.

Chitral.—You see the moon of monarchs, Pururavas.

Urv.—Right, girl, though ill it argue of my modesty.

Chitral.—Whom have you sent the envoy of your Coming?

Urv.—None, but my heart; that has long gone before me.

Chitral.—But first consider.

Urv.—Love impels me; how can I delay?

Chttral.—I have no more to offer.

Urv.—Assist me with your counsel, which way best
We may proceed, to meet with no impediment.

Chitral.—There is no fear: the all-wise preceptor
Of the immortals has imparted to you
The spell that renders you invincible,
And mightier than the mightest foe of heaven.

Urv.—My heart is confident, and yet my fears
Will sometimes bid me doubt.

Chitral.—Behold where meet
Ganga and *Jamuna*, in the bright mirror
Of the broad waves, the palace of the king,
The crest-borne gem of *Pratishthana* views
Complacently its own reflected glory.

Urv.—The scene in truth might tempt us to believe
The fields of heaven were here in prospect spread—
But where to find its lord, the pitying friend
Of all the helpless children of misfortune!

Chitral.—Let us alight and hide us in this garden,
Whose groves may vie with Indra's, till we learn
Some news of him we seek.
Yonder I view him!

[THEY DESCEND.

He waits thy coming to display his beauty
With undiminished brightness, like the moon,

That newly risen, expects a while his bride
The soft moonlight, ere he put forth his radiance.

Urv.—More graceful seems he than when first he met my gaze,

Chitral.—No doubt; come, let us approach.

Urv.—No, hold a moment! let us conceal ourselves
In veiling mist, and lurking thus unseen
About the arbour, we may overhear
What thoughts he utters in this solitude,
Communing with one only friend.

They become invisible to the king and the Vidusaka.

Man.—I have it; difficult as it is, I have hit upon a plan for securing you an interview with your charmer.

Urv.—(Behind.) How! who! what female is so blest to be
The object of his anxious thoughts

Chitral.—Employ
Your meditation to discover her.

Urv.—I fear too soon to know what may befall.

Man.—Did your majesty hear me observe I had Devised an expedient?

Pur.—Say on; what is it?

Man.—This it is: let your Majesty cherish a comfortable nap; your union will then be effected by your dreams; or delineate a portrait of the lady Urvasi and recreate your imagination by gazing on her picture.

Urv.—Be of good cheer, my heart!

Pur.—I fear me both impracticable.

How can I hope to taste repose that dreams
Might give me Urvasi, while fierce the shaft
Of *Kama*, rankles in my breast! And vain
The task her blooming graces to portray;
And tears of hopeless love at every line
Would fill my eyes, and hide her beauties from me.

Chitral.—You hear?

Urv.—I do,—yet scarcely yet confide.

Man.—Ah well! my ingenuity extends no farther.

Pur.—Cold and relentless; little does she know,
Or knowing, little heeds my fond despair.
Yet cannot I reproach the archer god,
Although, by giving to my hope such aim,
He tortures me with barren, wild desires.

Chitral.—What say you now?

Urv.—I grieve that he should deem me
Cold and unfeeling. I cannot now appear
Before I make these charges some reply:
I'll make a *Bhurja* leaf, and will inscribe
My thoughts on it, and cast it in his way,

[She writes upon the leaf and lets it fall near the Vidusaka who picks it up?

Man.—Holla! what is here, the slough of a snake dropped upon me to eat me up.

Pur.—It is no snake skin, but a leaf and something written on it.

Man.—No doubt, the lady Urvasi, unperceived, has over-heard your lamentations and sends this billet to console you.

Pur.—Hope dawns upon my passion. (Reads the leaf.) Your guess was right.

Man.—Oblige me, then, by letting me hear what is written.

Urv.—Indeed! Sir, you are curious.

Pur.—(Reads).

"Thou wrongest me, lord, to think I do not feel
Alike the pains that o'er thy bosom steal.
The breeze that softly floats through heavenly bowers,
Reclined upon my couch of coral flowers,
Sheds not on me its cool reviving breath,
But blows the hot and scorching gale of death:
O'er all my form the fevered venom flies,
And each bright bud beneath me droops and dies."

Man.—I hope you are pleased. You have now as much cause for rapture, as I should consider it to be civilly asked to dinner when I felt hungry.

Pur.—How say you! cause for rapture? This dear leaf
Conveys indeed assurance most delightful:
Yet still I sigh to interchange our thoughts,
Met face to face, and eye encountering eye

Urv.—Our sentiments accord.

Pur.—The drops that steal

Fast from my tremulous fingers may efface
These characters traced by her tender hand :
Take you the leaf, and as a sacred trust
With care preserve it.

Man.—Phoo! what matters it now? Since by the assenting sentiments of the lady Urvasi, your desire has borne flowers, will it not bear fruit?

Urv.—Now, Chitralekha, whilst I summon courage
To issue into view, do you appear,
And give the monarch notice of my purpose.

Chitral.—I shall obey. (Becomes visible.) Hail, to the king!

Pur.—Fair damsel, you are welcome; yet forgive me
The less, your lovely friend comes not along:
The sacred streams before us show less stately
Until they flow in unison.

Chitral.—Royal Sir,
The cloud precedes the lightning,

Pur.—Where is Urvasi?
You are inseperable,

Chitral.—She salutes the king,
And makes this her request.

Pur.—Say, her command.

Chitral.—Once, by the enemy of the gods assailed
And captive made, your valiant arm redeemed her,
Again in peril, she applies to you,
And claims your guardian shield against a foe

More formidable still, from *Madana*,
Whom you have armed against her,

Pur.—You tell me gentle nymph, your fair friend pines
With amorous passion ; but you do not see,
The ardour that consumes this heart forlher.
Alike our glowing flame ; then quickly aid
Our union to cement as close combines
Iron with iron, when each fiery bar
With equal radiance glows.

Chitral.—Appear, my friend !
The potent deity with like relentlessness
Afflicts the prince, and now to you I call
The herald of his sufferings.

Urv.—Faithless friend,
Thus to desert me !

Chitral.—It will soon be seen
Which merits best the title of deserter ;
But now be present.

Urv.—(Appearing) Triumph to the king !

Pur.—The wish is victory,
When from the sovereign of the gods transferred
By lips celestial to a mortal monarch.

[Takes her hand and leads her to a seat.]

Man.—Fair lady, I am the Brahman of the king, and his friend, and so may claim some notice. (Urvasi bows to him smiling). Prosperity attend you.

A messenger of the gods in the air.

Mess.—Ho, Chitralekha! Urvasi, repair
Swift to the palace of the Lord of air;
There your appointed duties to fulfil,
And give expression to the wondrous skill
Of Bharata, your master. To the dome
Divine, the world's protecting rulers come,
Eager to view the scene that genius fires,
That passion animates, and truth inspires.

Chitral.—Hear you, my friend! be speedy in your parting.

Urv.—I cannot speak.

Chitral.—My friend, great prince requests
Permission to depart. She owes obedience
To heaven's high king, and dreads last her delay
Incur his wrath.

Pur.—Not mine to interrupt
The tasks your mighty Lord assigns.
Farewell!
Do not forget me!

[Urvasi and Chitralekha depart.

Pur.—(To the Vidusaka.) She disappears! What else deserves my gaze?

Man.—Why, perhaps, this. (Looking for the Bhurja leaf.) (Apart.) Bless me, I have been so fascinated myself by the smiles of the lady Urvasi, that the leaf with her billet upon it has unconsciously slipped out of my hands.

Pur.—You were about to speak.

Man.—Yes, I was going to say, do not lose your fortitude. The nymph is firmly attached to you, and her going hence will not relax the attachment.

Pur.—Of that I feel assured. The sighs that heaved
Her panting bosom as she hence departed,
Exhaled her heart, and lodged it in my bosom,
Free to dispose of it, although her person
Be forced to wait upon a master's will.

Man.—(Apart.) [I am all in a flutter lest he should ask me for that abominable leaf.

Pur.—What shall console my eyes! Give me the leaf.

Man.—The leaf! dear me, it is not here! it was a leaf of heaven, and must have gone after Urvasi.

Pur.—Heedless blockhead!

Man.—Let us search for it. Here, here!

[They search for the leaf and retire.

Enter in the foreground, Ausinari, the queen with Nipunika and Attendants.

Ausi.—You saw his highness, you are sure

Nipunika.

Entering the arbour with Manavaka.]

Nip.—Why should your Majesty doubt my report?

Ausi.—Well, let us seek him then, and unobserved,
Amidst these shades we may detect the truth
But what is you that meets us like a shred
Of some rent garment, floating on the wind?

Nip.—A bhojpatra leaf;—There seems to be some marks like letter's upon it; it is caught by your

Grace's anklet. (Picks it up) Will it please you read it?

Ausi.—Glance o'er its tenor, and if not unfit
To meet our ear, peruse what there is written.

Nip.—It looks like a memorial verse. Eh, no! now it strikes me, they must be lines addressed by Urvasi to the king; this is some carelessness, now, of that blockhead Manavaka.

Ausi.—Read, I shall conceive its purport.

Nip.—(Reads the line as above.)

Ausi.—Enough!—proceed; and with this evidence
We shall confound our nymph enamoured swain.

They go round the arbour, the king and Manavaka advance.

Man.—Eh! is not that the leaf yonder on the mount just on the edge of the garden?

Pur.—Breeze of the south, the friend of love and spring,
Though from the flower you steal the fragrant down
To scatter perfume, yet why plunder me
Of those dear characters, her own fair hand,
In proof of her affection, traced? Thou knowest,
The lonely lover that in absence pines
Lives on such fond memorials.

Man.—No, I was mistaken; I was deceived by the tawny hue of the peacock's tail.

Pur.—I am every way unhappy.

Ausinari and her train advance.

Ausi.—Nay my good lord,

I pray you be consoled, If, as I deem,

The loss of this occasion your distress.

[OFFERING THE LEAF.

Pur.—(Apart.) The queen, (Aloud.) Madam! you are welcome.

Ausi.—You do not think me so.

Pur.—(To the Vidusaka apart.) What is to be done?

Man.—I don't know: what excuse can a free-booter offer when he is taken in the fact?

Pur.—This is no time to jest, (Aloud) believe me, Madam,

This leaf was not the object of my search,

Nor cause of my anxiety.

Ausi.—Excuse me,

If I suspect that your denial seeks,

But to conceal the truth.

Man.—Your grace had better order dinner: that will be the most effectual remedy for his Majesty's bile.

Ausi.—You hear Nipunika, this most sage counsellor,

And how he would remove his friend's distress.

Man.—Why not, madam? Is not every body put into good humour by hearty meal?

Pur.—Peace, blockhead! you but heighten my offence.

Ausi.—Not yours the offence, my lord: 'tis mine, who tarry,
Here, where my presence is not wished; 'tis soon.
Removed. [GOING.

Pur.—Yet stay, I own myself to blame,—
Curb your resentment, that alone convicts me:
When monarchs are incensed it cannot be
But that their slaves are guilty.

[FALLS AT HER FEET.

Ausi.—Think me not
So light of purpose, as to be beguiled
By such assumed respect. You make my Lord,
An awkward penetent: I cannot trust you.

Nip.—Come, madam, come.

[THE QUEEN REPELS THE KING AND EXIT.

Man.—Her Majesty has gone off in a hurry like a river in the rains; you may rise. (To the king, who has continued prostrate.)

Pur.—I might have spared myself the pains.
A woman is clear sighted, and mere words,
Touch not her heart. Passion must give them credit.
The lapidary, master of his craft,
With cold indifference eyes the spurious gem.

Man.—You care very little about this, I suppose; the eye that is dazzled with light cannot bear the lamp.

Pur.—Not so. 'Tis true that Urvasi engrosses
My heart, but Kasiraja's daughter claims
My deference; less indeed, that her contempt
Disdains my postrations, and this scorn
Will justify requital.

Man.—Well, let us have done with her Majesty, and think a little of a famished Brahman. It is high time to bathe and eat.

Pur.—'Tis past mid-day. Exhausted by the heat,
The peacock plunges in the scanty pool
That feeds the tall tree's root: the drowsy bee
Sleeps in the hollow chamber of the lotus
Darkened with closing petals; on the brink
Of the now tepid lake the wild duck lurks
Amongst the sedgy shade; and even here,
The parrot from his wiry bower complains,
And calls for water to allay his thirst.

[EXEUNT.

END OF THE SECOND ACT.

ACT III.

Scene I.—The Hermitage of Bharata.

Enter Galava and Pailava, two of his disciples.

Gal.—Well, friend Pailava, what news? Whilst you were at Madhava's palace with the sage, I have been obliged to stay at home to look after the holy fire. Were the immortals pleased with the specimen of our master's skill?

Pail.—How could they choose but be pleased?—there was eloquence and melody for them. The drama was Laksmi's choice of a lord; the nymph Urvasi quite lost herself in the impassioned passage.

Gal.—There is something not quite right implied in your applause.

Pail.—Very true, for unluckily Urvasi stumbled in her part.

Gal.—How so?

Pail.—You shall hear. Urvasi played Lakshmi; Menaka was Varuni. The latter says:—

Lakshmi, the mighty powers that rule spheres
Are all assembled: at their head appears
The blooming Kesava. Confess to whom
Inclines your heart?——

Her reply should have been—To Purushottama; but instead of that—To Pururavas escaped her lips.

Gal.—The intellectual faculties are but the slaves of destiny. Was not the sage much displeased?

Pail.—He immediately denounced a curse on her but she found favour with Mahendra.

Gal.—How so?

Pail.—The sentence of the sage was, that she had forgotten her part, so she she should lose her divine knowledge. But when the performance was over, Indra observing her, as she stood apart, ashamed and disconsolate, called her to him. The mortal, who engrossed her thoughts, he said, had been his friend in the hour of peril; he had aided him in conflict with the enemies of the gods, and was entitled to his acknowledgment. She must accordingly repair to the monarch, and remain with him till he beholds the offspring she shall bear him.

Gal.—This was like Mahendra; he knows all hearts.

Pail.—Come, come! we have been chattering here till it is almost the time when our preceptor performs his ablutions. Come, we have no time to lose; let us attend him.

[EXEUNT.

SCENE II.—PART OF THE GARDEN OF THE PALACE

Enter the Chamberlain.

As long as life is vigorous, man endures labour for the sake of procuring wealth; when farther advanced in age, his tools are lightened by the participation of his children; but for me, my strength is daily undermined and my body exhausted by this servitude. Waiting on women is the devil. I am now to find the king, and tell him that her Majesty, having dismissed all anger and resentment, is desirous of paying her homage to him this evening, for the completion of the vow in which she has engaged. The close of the day is agreeable enough here in the palace. The peacocks nod upon their perches and the doves flock to the turret tops, scarcely distinguishable from the incense that flows through the lattices of the lofty chambers. The venerable servant of the inner apartment are all busily engaged in propitiatory rites, and substituting lamps for the offering of flowers that decorated the holy shrines throughout the day. Ah! here comes the prince, attended by the damsel train with flambeaux in their delicate hands : he moves like a mountain, around whose stately skirts the slender *karnikara* spreads its brilliant blossoms. I will wait him here.

Enter Pururavas and Vidushaka, with female attendants carrying torches.

So ends the day: the anxious cares of state
Have left no interval for private sorrow.
But how to pass the night: its dreary length
Affords no promise of relief.

Chamberlain.—(Advances.) Glory to the kng! So please your Gace, her Majesty expresses a wish to be honoured with your presence on the terrace of the pavilion of gems, to witness from it the entrance of the moon into the asterism Rohini.

Pur.—Go, my friend, apprise her majesty
She may dispose of us.

[Exit Chamberlain.

What object, think you, that the queen, in Truth,
Proposes by the vow she has asssumed ?

Man.—I suppose she repents of her pettishness, and wishes to be friends with you again. This is but an excuse to bring you to her presence, when she may efface the recollection of the indignity with which she treated you.

Pur.—'Tis very likely. Prudent wives full soon
Repent the scorn that urged them to repel
An humbled husband, and are glad to seek
Some fair pretext to win his love again—
We will indulge her Grace. On to the chamber.

Man.—'Tis here. Ascend these steps of crystal, smooth shining as the waters of the Ganges. The pavilion of gems is particularly lovely when evening sets in. (They ascend.) The moon is just about to rise; the east is tinged with red.

Pur.—'Tis even so: illumined by the rays
Of his yet unseen orb, the evening glooms
On either hand retire, and in the midst
The horizon glows, like a fair face that
Betwixt the jetty curls on either brow
In clusters pendulous. I could gaze for ever!

Man.—Ho! here he comes, the king of the Brahmans, as beautiful as a ball of a dall of almonds and sugar.

Pur.—Oh, base similitudes! Your thoughts, my friend,
Have rarely nobler prompter than your stomach

[*Carries his hands to his forehead, and bows to the moon now risen*

Hail glorious lord of night! whose tempered fires
Are gleaned from solar fountains, but to yield
The virtuous frut eternal, as they light
The flame of holy sacrifice, whose stores
Ambrosial serve but to regale the gods
And the immortal fathers of mankind.
All hail to thee! whose rising ray dispels
The glooms of eve, and whose pale cresent crowns
The glorious diadem of Mahadeva.

Man.—Enough, sir; your grandfather bids you, by me his interpreter, sir, that he may repose himself.

Pur.—(Makes the Vidusaka sit and then seats himself)
The splendour of the moon is light enough:
Remove the torches and command my train
Retire to rest.

Att.—As you command. [Withdraws with the torch-bearers.)

Pur.—I think we may not yet expect the queen:

And now we are alone, I would impart
My thoughts.

Man.—Out with them; there is no appearence of her yet, and it is well to keep up your spirits with hope.

Pur.—You counsel well. In truth, my fond desire
Becomes more fervid as enjoyment seem
Remote, and fresh impediments obstruct
My happiness like an impetuous torrent,
That, checked by adverse rocks, awhile delay
Its course, till high with chafing waters swollen
It rushes past with aggravated fury.

Man.—There is one thing to be said: notwithstanding your anxiety has made you something thinner, it has rather improved than impaired your personal appearance. I argue from this that a meeting with the nymph is not very distant.

Pur.—My right arm by its glad pulsation soothes
My grief, like you, with hope inspiring words.

Man.—A Brahmán's words, be assured, are never uttered in vain.

Enter above in a heavenly car Urvasi and Chitralekha: Urvasi in a purple dress with pearl ornaments.

Urv.—Now my dear girl,
What say you? Do these purple robes become me?
Thus trimmed with pearls?

Chitral.—I cannot think of words

To speak my admiration—only this,
Would I were Pururavas.

Urv.—My dear friend,
I feel my strength desert me; bring him quickly,
Or quickly lead me to his royal palace.

Chitral.—We are there. Behold it,
White gleaming in the moonlight, whilst below
The Yamuna's blue waters wash its foot;
Like the snow tufted summits of Kailasha,
Rising in radiance from their bosky base.
Advance.

Urv.—One moment—exercise the power
Of meditative vision. Where is the king,
The master of my heart, and what employs him?

Chitral.—(Apart.) I will rouse her fears.
I see him; in a fit solitude he waits
Impatiently the coming of the bride.

[URVASI EXPRESSES DESPAIR.

How silly wench! what else would you desire
Should be his occupation?

Urv.—Ah, my friend,
My fluttering heart is easily alarmed.

Chitral.—In the pavilion of bright gems awaits
The king, his trusty friend alone attends him,
Let us thither.

Urv.—Proceed,

[THEY DESCEND AND LEAVE THE CAR.

Pur.—As spreads the moon its lustre, so my love
Grows with advancing night.

Urv.—Ah me! I fear
Even yet to trust. Let us remain invisible,
And overhear their conference, till doubt
Be all dispersed.

Chitral.—Be it as you will.

Man.—The rays of the moon are charged with ambrosia; do you find no benefit from them?

Pur.—Small is their power, or that of aught to mitigate
The pangs of love. Soft beds of fragrant flowers,
Sandal's cool unguent, strings of gelid pearl,
And these mild tempered rays exhaust on me
In vain their virtue; nothing can allay
The fever of my heart. She, she alone,
The goddess I adore, or secret converse,
That ever speaks for her, can yield me rest.
These limbs that pressed her side, when on we drive
Through fields of ether, are still worm with life;
All else a lifeless load that burthens earth.

Urv.—I need no more cocealment.

[SHE ADVANCES

Woe is me; [HASTILY
He deigns not to regard me.

Chitral.—In your haste

You have forgotten to put off the veil
That screens you from his sight.

(Behind.) This way, your Grace.

[ALL LISTEN; URVASI THROWS HERSELF INTO THE ARMS OF CHITRALEKHA.

Man.—The queen is here! we had better be mute.

Pur.—Assume the resemblance of indifference.

Urv.—What shall we do?

Chiiral.—Remain invisible.

Not long her purposed stay; by her attire
She holds some sacred vow.

Enter the Queen, with attendants bearing offerings; the Queen is dressed in white; flowers are her only ornaments.

Queen,—This union with the constellation yields
New brillance to the lord of Rohini.

Att.—Such effect attends your Grace's encounter with his Majesty.

Man.—(To Pururavas.) She comes, I imagine, to offer her benedictions; or under the resemblance of a solemn vow, she wishes to obliterate the recollection of the indignity with which she lately repelled your advances. Well, I think her Majesty looks very charming today.

Pur.—In truth she pleases me. Thus chastely robed
In modest white, her clustering tresses decked
With sacred flowers alone, her haughty mein
Exchanged for meek devotion; thus arrayed
She moves with heightened charms.

Queen.—(Advancing.) Hail to the king!

Att.—Hail to the king!

Pur.—Madam, you are welcome to a seat [Leads her

Urv.—(Behind.) She merits to be called divine; the
Bride
Of heaven's great king boasts not surpassing
dignity.

Chitral.—Your commendations speak you free from
envy.

Queen.—My gracions lord, I would perform a rite
Of which you are the object, and must beg you
Bear with the inconvenience that my presence
May for brief time occasion you.

Pur.—You do me wrong;
Your presence is a favour.

Man.—May such inconvenience often befall me as to pronounce a benediction on like occasions.

Pur.—(To the queen.) How call you your observance

Nip.—(On the queen's turning to her.) The conciliation of regard.

Pur.—Is it even so? Yet trust me, it is needless
To wear this tender form, as slight and delicate
As the lithe lotus stem, with rude austerity.
In me behold your slave, whom to propitiate
Claims not your care; your favour is his happiness.

Urv.—(Smilling scornfully.) He pays her mighty
deferenc.

Chitral.—So he should—

When the heart strays, the tongue is most profuse
Of bland professions to the slighted wife.

Queen.—Not vain my vow, since it already wins me
My lord's complacent speech.

Man.—Enough said on both sides; these civilities require no further reply.

Queen.—Come, girls, the offerings, that I may present them
To the bright deity, whose rays diffuse
Intenser lustre on these splendid walls.

Att.—Here are the perfumes, madam, here are the flowers.

[*The attendants take a tray of sweetmeats first to the Vidusaka and then to the Kanchukin*

Man.—Prosperity attend your Highness; may your fast prove fortunate.

Chamberlain.—Prosperity to the queen!

Queen.—Now, with your Grace's leave, I pay you homage.

[*Presents oblations to the king; bows, and falls at his feet, then rises.*

Resplendent pair who o'er night preside,
Lord of the Deer-borne banneret, and thou
His favourite, Rohini hear and attest
The sacred promise that I make my husband.
Whatever nymph attract my lord's regard,
And share with him the mutual bonds of love,

I henceforth treat with kindness and complacency.

Urv.—Oh, my dear friend, how much these words assuage
The apprehension of my heart.

Chitral.—She is a lady
Of an exalted spirit, and a wife
Of duty most exemplary. You now
May rest assured, nothing will more impede
your union with your love.

Man.—(Apart to Pururavas.) The culprit that escapes before his hand is cut off, determines never to run such a risk again. (Aloud.) What, then, is his Majesty indifferent to your Grace!

Queen.—Wise sir, how think you? To promote his happiness
I have resigned my own. Does such a purpose
Prove him no longer dear to me!

Pur.—I am not what you doubt me; but the power
Abides with you: do with me as you will.
Give me to whom you please, or if you please
Retain me still your slave.

Queen.—Be what you list.
My vow is plighted, nor in vain the rite,
If it afford you satisfaction. Come,
Hence, girls, 'tis time we take our leave.

Pur.—Not so:
So soon to leave me is no mark of favour.

Queen.—You must excuse me, I may not fore go
The duties I have solemnty incurred.
[EXIT WITH TRAIN.

Urv.—Why, girl, I doubt the Raja still affects
His queen, so be it; it is now too late
For me to hope my heart can be reclaimed.

Chitral.—Away with doubt; you have no need to fear.

Pur.—Is the queen far removed?

Man.—You may say whatever you wish, safely enough. You are fairly given over by her, like a sick man by his physician.

Pur.—I fear I am, by faithless Urvasi,
Would she were here; and that the gentle music
Of her rich anklets murmured in my ears;
Or that her lotus hands, as with light step
She stole behind me, spread a tender veil
Before my eyes; that in this shady bower
She deigned descend spontaneous, or drawn hither
With welcome violence by some fair friend,—
Ha! the lovely daughter of Narayan!
[*Urvasi has advanced behind the king and covers his eyes with her hands.*

Vid.—How knows your Grace?

Pur.—It must be Urvasi,—
No other hand could shoot such ecstacy
Through this emaciate frame. The solar ray

Wakes not the night's fair blossom—that alone
Expands when conscious of the moon's dear presence.

Urv. (Appearing.) Joy to the king!

Pur.—All hail, bright nymph of heaven!

[LEADS HER TO A SEAT.

Chitral.—(Advancing.) Be the king blest!

Pur—I feel I am already.

Urv.—The queen, my friend, has just presented me
This pious prince, and therefore I approach
This person, as the object of my love.
You cannot say I claimed a part in him
Before the right was granted me.

Man.—What! were you here ever since sunset?

Pur.—I have no purpose to dispute the claim.
But let me ask, if such assent were needed,
Who was it that first granted you permission
To rob me of my heart.

Chitral.—My friend, I know,
Can proffer no reply—then let this be.
Now grant me my request; I must depart
To minister to Surya at the term
Of the spring festival: till my return
Be careful that this nymph have never cause
To mourn the heaven she has resigned for thee.

Man.—Heaven, indeed! why should she ever think of such a place?—a place where they neither think, nor eat, nor close their eyes even for a twinkle.

Pur.—The Heaven of Indra is the eternal source
Of joy ineffable : it can not be
The cares of Pururavas should efface
The memory of immortal bliss—
Yet, nymph, of this be confident, my soul
Shall know no other sovereign than your friend.

Chitral : 'Tis all I ask : be happy, Urvasi,
And bid me now adieu !

Urv. (Embracing her,) Forget me not.

Chitral.—That I should rather beg of you, thus blest
With one the only object of your wishes.

[Bows to the king and Exit.

Man.—Fate is propitious and crowns your Majesty's desires.

Pur.—'Tis true, I reach the height of my ambition.
The haughty canopy that spreads its shades
Of universal empire over the world ;
The footstool of dominion, set with gems,
Torn from the glittering brows of prostrate kings,
Are in my mind less glorious than to lie
At Urvasi's fair feet and do her bidding.

Urv.—I have not words to speak my gratitude.

Pur.—Now I behold thee thus ! how changed is all
The current of my feelings—these mild rays,
Cool, vivifying, gleam ; the shafts of Madana
Are now most welcome—all that was but late
Harsh and distasteful to me, now appears
Delightful by your absence.

Urv.—I lament,
I caused my lord to suffer pain so long.
Pur.—Nay, say not so! the joy that follows grief
Gains richer zest from agony foregone.
The traveller who faint pursues his track
In the fierce day, alone can tell how sweet
The grateful shelter of the friendly tree.
Man.—The moon is high; it were as well to go in.
Pur.—Conduct the way: and dearest, may the hours
With thee be still prolonged, as when, without thee,
They brought the day.
[*Exeunt into the pavilion.*

END OF THE THIRD ACT.

ACT IV.

SCENE.—THE FOREST OF AKALUSHA ON THE SKIRTS OF GANDHAMADANA, ONE OF THE MOUNTAINOUS CARRIERS OF MERU.

Strains without.

Soft voices low sound in the sky,
Where the nymphs a companion deplore,
And lament, as together they fly,
The friend they encounter no more.
So, sad and melodious awakes
The plaint of the swan o'er the stream,
Where the red lotus blossoms, as breaks
On the wave, the day's orient beam.

Enter Chitralekha and Sakajanya.

Chitral.—(Looking up.)
The swans along the stream that sail,
A fond companion's loss bewail—
With murmuring songs they soothe their grief,
Or find from tender tears, relief.

Sah.—Now Chitralekha, what has changed to cloud
Your countenance! it indicates your heart
Is ill at ease: what causes your distress!
Tell me, that I may share and soothe your sorrow.

Chitral.—It is not all unknown to you. Engaged
Amidst our band in paying wonted service

To the all seeing Sun, I have not shared
The vernal sports, my Urvasi away.

Sah.—This we all know, and know your mutual love.

Chitral.—Whilst dwelling on her memory, anxious to learn
Some tidings of her, I employed my power
Of bringing absent objects to my view;
And by this art I learn what much alarms me.

Sah,—Say on.

Chitral.—The king, by Urvasi's persuasion,
Resigned of late the reins of rule and sought
With her groves of Gandhamadana.

Sah,—Amid such lovely scenes, the amorous pair
Would most enjoy each other's company.
What followed?

Chitral.—Whilst wandering pleasantly along the brink
Of the Mandakini, a nymph of air,
Who gambolled on its sandy shore, attracted
The monarch's momentary glance—and this
Aroused the zealous wrath of Urvasi.

Sha.—Ugenerous girl! although it proves her love,
Yet destiny is mightier.

Chitral.—Thus incensed,
My friend disdainfully repelled her lord;
In sooth, her mind was darkened by the curse
The save sage erewhile denounced; and troubled thus,
She heedlessly forgot the law that bars

All female access from the hateful groves
Of Kartikeya. Trespassing the bounds
Proscribed, she suffers now the penalty
Of her transgression, and to a slender vine
Transformed, there pines till time shall set her free.

Sah.—How vain the hope to shun the will of fate!
What other cause could interrupt a love
So fervent.—Where is now the king?

Chitral.—He roams,
Frantic with sorrow, through the wood, in search
Of his lost bride, nor night nor day desists
From the sad quest. These rising clouds that teach
Passion to pious sages angur ill
For his alleviation—I much fear
There is but little hope of remedy—

[*Repeats the first stanza, "The swans along the stream that sail,"* &c.

Sah.—But think you there is no expedient then
To reunite these lovers?

Chitral.—There is but one.
The Sacred gem that owes its ruby glow
To the bright tint of Gauri's sacred feet,
Alone effects their union.

Sah.—Le us hope it—
Their delicate forms endure not agony
Violent and protracted, and the gods

Can surely never purpose such a pair
Should wholly perish; they will soon devise
Some means of their relief, to their high power
We leave them.—Come. The glorious sun reveals
His countenance; let us depart and pay
Our wonted adorations. (sings.)
Amidst the lake, where the lotus shining,
Its flower unfolds to the sunny beam,
The swan, for her lost companion pining,
Swims sad and slow o'er the lonely stream.

[EXEUNT.

ANOTHER PART OF THE FOREST.

(Strains without)

Air.

The lord of the elephant train
Now wanders afar from his mate,
And franticly comes, to complain
To the woods of his desolate state.
Distraction his vigour consumes,
As he plunges amidst the dark bowers,
While o'er his vast bulk sweatly blooms
The garland of wild forest flowers.

Enter Pururavas hastily, looking up to the heavens, his dress discorded, and his general appearance indicative of insanity.

Hold, treacherous fiend, suspend thy flight, forbear

Ah! whither wouldst thou bear my beauteous bride?
And now his arrows sting me—thick as hail
From yonder peak whose sharp top pierces heaven,
They shower upon me.

[*Rushes forward as to the attack—then pauses and looks upwards.*

Air.

The lonely cygnet breasts the flood,
Without his mate, in mournful mood;
This ruffled plumage drooping lies,
And trickling tears suffuse his eyes.

It is no demon—but a friendly cloud;
No hostile quiver—but the bow of Indra:
The cooling rain drops fall, not barbed shafts;
And I mistake the lightning for my love.

[*Faints—then revives, and rising.*

Air.

I madly thought a fiend conveyed
Away from me my fawn-eyed maid:
'Twas but a cloud that rained above
With the lightning for its love.

Where can she bend her steps—or is she here
Invisible, in anger? If she seek
The skies, her love for me will soon revive.
Once mine again, not all the demon host
That brave the gods, should force her from my arms.

Alas! no more my gaze delighted dwells
Upon her loveliness—How sad the chance!
Fate heaps calamities with diligent malice
On those whom once misfortune has assailed.
Hence have I lost my love, when genial airs
And overshadowing clouds, veiling the day,
Had shed intenser rapture on her presence.

Air.

Ye clouds whose ceaseless torrents shed
New glories through the gloomy air,
A while your angry showers forbear,
No burst upon this humbled head—
Give me to find my love, and then fulfil
Your wrath—Content, I bow me to your will
Away with this humility; the wise
Call kings the lords of time—I will assert
My power, and bid the seasons stay their course.

Air.

The tree of heaven invites the breeze,
And all its countless blossoms glow;
They dance upon the gale; the bees
With sweets inebriate, murmuring low,
Soft music lend, and gushes strong
The Koil's deep thick warbling song.

No, I will not arrest the march of time,
For all around behold my state apparelled;
The clouds expand my canopy—their lightnings
Gleam as its glittering fringe. Rich chowries wave

Of many-coloured hues from flowering trees.
The shrieking pea-fowl, clamorous in their joy,
Are the loud heralds of a sovereign's honours;
And those bright torrents, flashing o'er the brows
Of the tall mountains, are the wealthy streams,
Poured forth profuse from tributary realms.
Fie on it, what have I to do with pomp
And kingly pride? my sole sad business here
To thread the woods in search of my beloved.

Air.

The monarch of the woods
With slow desponding gait
Wanders through vales and floods,
And rocks and forest bowers,
Gemmed with new springing flowers,
And mourns heart broken for his absent mate.
Ah me! whatever I behold but aggravates
My woe. These bright and pendulous flowers,
Surcharged with dew, resemble those dear eyes
Glistening with starting tears. How shall I learn
If she have passed this way? The yielding soil,
softened by showers, perchance may have retained
The delicate impression of her feet,
And show some vestige of their ruby tincture.
Where in this lonely thicket may I hope
To gain some tidings of her? You proud bird,
Perched on the jutting crag, that stately stands
With neck outstretched and spreading tail to tell
His raptures to the clouds, haply may give
Some kind intelligence.

Air.

The royal elephant, the dread of all his rival foes,
With downcast eye and tardy tread,
Through tangled thickets goes;
To solitary grief a prey,
This loved companion for away,

Air.

I will speak to this peacock—oh tell,
If, free on the wing as you soar,
In forest, or meadow, or dell,
You have seen the loved nymph I deplore—
You will know her, the fairest of damsels fair,
By her large soft eye, and her graceful air.

[*Advancing to the bird, and bowing.*

Bird of the dark-blue throat and eye of jet,
Oh tell me, have you seen the lovely face
Of my fair bride, lost in this dreary wilderness?
Her charms deserve your gaze. How! no reply?
He answers not, but beats a measure. How!
What means this merry mood? Oh yes, I know
The cause. He now may boast his plumage
Without a peer, nor shame to show his glories
Before the floating tresses of my Urvasi.
I leave him, nor will waste a thought on one
Who feels no pity for another's woes.

[PROCEEDS—MUSIC.

Yonder amidst the thick and shady branches
Of the broad jambu, cowers the koil—faint

Her flame of passion in the hotter breath of noon.
She of the birds is wisest fame I will address her.

Air.

Majestic as sails the mighty cloud
Along the dusky air,
The elephant cometh hither to shroud
In the thickets his despair.
From his heart all hope of delight is riven,
And his eyes with tears o'er flow,
As he roams the shades, where the sons of heaven
Descend to sport below.

Air.

Say, nursling of a starnger nest,
Say, hast thou chanced my love to see,
Amidst these gardens of the beasts,
Wandering at liberty,
Or warbling with a voice divine.
Melodious strains more sweet than thine?

[*Approaches and kneels*

Sweet bird—whom lovers deem Love's messenger,
Skilled to direct the god's envenomed shafts
And tame the proudest heart; oh, hither guide
My lovely fugitive, or leads my steps
To where she strays,

[*Turns to his left, and as if replying.*

Why did she leave
One so devoted to her will? In wrath

She left me, but the cause of anger lives not
In my imagination; the fond tyranny
That women exercise o'er those who love them
Brooks not the slightest show of disregard.
How now! the bird has flown. 'Tis ever thus—
All coldly listen to another's sorrows.
Unheeding my affliction, lo, she speeds,
Intent on joy expected, to yon tree,
To banquet on the luscious juice the jambu
From its now ripe and roseate fruit distills.
Like my beloved, the bird of tuneful song
Deserts me. Let her go—I can forgive her,
[PROCEEDS.
Ha!—On my right amidst the wood I hear—
A tinkling melody. 'Tis the sweet chime
My fair one's anklets echo to her footstops.
Air.
Through the woods the stately elephant strays,
And his glances despair express;
On his limbs the enfeebling malady preys,
And his steps are slow with distress;
In his eyes the starting tear drops swell,
As his thoughts on his lost companion dwell.
Alas the gathering of the the clouds deceives
The swan, who hails rejoicingly the time
For periodic flight to a *Manasa*.
I hear his song of gladness, not the sound
Of tinkling anklets. Ere yet the troop begins
Its distant march I will address the chief.

Ho! monarch of the tribes that breast the stream,
Forebear a while your course; forego the provender
Of lotus stems, not needed yet, and hear
My suit—redeem me from despair—impart
Some tidings of my love; 'tis worthier far
To render kindly offices to others
Than meanly labour for a selfish good.
Though bent on Manasa, he gazes on me,
As if to own he had beheld my love.
Why seek to veil the truth? If my beloved
Was never seen by thee as graceful straying
Along the flowery borders of the lake,
Then whence this elegant gait?—'Tis hers and thou
Hast stolen it from her, in whose every step
Love sports; thy walk betrays thee; own thy crime,
And lead me quickly to her. (Laughs.) Nay, he fears
Our royal power—the plunderer flies the king.

[PROCEEDS—MUSIC.

Yonder I see the Chakwa, with his mate;
Of him I will inquire.

Air.

In groves of tall trees with bright blossoms blooming,
And vocal with many sweet murmured tones,
The lord of the herd, whom grief is consuming,
Distracted, the loss of his mate bemoans.

Air. *After a pause.*

Ah no, the replies, I taste, on the wing,
The joys of the cool returning spring,
And as each feather thrills with delight,
I mark not the fair that meet my sight.

Yet tell me—hast thou seen her? Know'st thou not
Who asks thy answer? The great king of day
And monarch of the night are my progenitors:
Their grandson I, and by their own free choice,
The lord of Urvasi and of the earth.
How—silent? Thou mightst measure my affliction.
By what thou feelest; all the air resounds
With thy incessant plaints, if, but a moment,
Thy fair companion nestling hides in sport
Amongst the lotus leaves, and flies thy view.
Alas! to one whom fate has cursed like me,
Nought is propitious; I will ask no more.

[PROCEEDS—MUSIC.

How beautiful the lotus!—it arrests
My path and bids me gaze on it—the bees
Murmur amidst its petals—like the slip
Of my beloved it glows, when that has been
Somewhat too rudely slipped by mine, and sweetly
Protests against such violence—I will woo
Tis honey riffler to become my friend.

[ADVANCES.

Air.

Unheeding the cygnet at first,
His beak in the nectar of passion dips;

But fiercer and fiercer his thirst—
As deeper he lips.
Say, plunderer of the honeyed dew, hast thou
Beheld the nymph whose large and languid eye
Voluptuous rolls, as if it swam with wine?
And yet methinks 'tis idle to inquire;
For had he tasted her delicious breath,
He now would scorn the lotus. I will hence.

[PROCEEDS.

Beneath the shade of yon Kadamba tree.
The royal elephant reclines, and with him,
His tender mate. I will approach—yet hold,
From his companion he accepts the boughs
Her trunk has snapped from the balm-breathing tree,
Now rich with teeming shoots and juicy fragrance.

[ADVANCES, THEN PAUSES.

He crushed it! it may proceed.

Air

King of the forest, whose sports have felled
The stateliest trees, the thicket's pride;
Oh, say, in these shades hast thou beheld,
More bright than the moon, my wandering bride?

[ADVANCING A FEW PACES.

Chief of the mighty herd, say, hast thou seen
My love; like the young moon her delicate frame,
And with eternal youth her beauties glow;

Her voice is music—her long tresses wear
The jasmine's golden hue. Hadst thou afar
Beheld her charms, they must have fixed thy gaze.
Ha, he replies! That kind assenting roar
Conveys some intimation—oh repeat
The sound—consider that we should befriend
Each other, bound by various common ties.
Thou art the sovereign of the forest, me
They term the king of men. Thy bounty sheds
Thy frontal fragrance on the air; my wealth
On all is showered profuse. Amongst the bands
Of lovely nymph, obedient to my will,
One only Urvasi commands my love;
As thou hast chosen this, thy favourite,
From all the herd. Thus far our fates accord;
And never be the pangs of separation,
Such as distract my bosom, known to thee;
Propitious be thy fortunes. Friend, farewell.

[PROCEEDS.

What have we here? Deep in the mountain's breast
A yawning chasm appears: such shades are ever
Haunts of the nymphs of air and earth. Perchance
My Urvasi now lurks within the grotto
In cool seclusion—I will enter. All
Is utter darkness. Would the lightning's flash
Now blaze to guide me—no, the cloud disdains,
Such is my fate perverse, to shed for me
Its many-channelled radiance. Be it so.

I will retire—but first the rock address.

Air

With horny hoofs and a resolute breast
The hoar through the thicket stalks;
He ploughs up the ground, as he piles his quest
In the forest's gloomiest walks.

Say, mountain, whose expansive slope confines
The forest verge, oh tell me, hast thou seen
A nymph as beauteous as the bride of love,
Mounting with slender frame thy steep ascent,
Or weary resting in thy crowning woods?
How—no reply! remote he hears me not;
I will approach him nearer.

Air.

From thy crystal summits the glistening springs
Rush down the flowery sides,
And the spirit of heaven delightedly sings
As among thy peaks he hides.
Say, mountain so favoured, have the feet
Of my fair one pressed this clam retreat?

Now, by my hopes, he answers! he has seen her—
Where is she?—say. Alas! again deceived—
Alone I hear the echo of my words,
As round the cavern's hollow mouth they roll
And multiplied return. Ah, Urvasi! (Faints.)

[RECOVERS, AND SITS AS EXHAUSTED.

Fatigue has overcome me. I will rest
Upon the borders of this mountain torrent,

And gather vigour from the breeze that gleans
Refreshing coolness from its gelid waves.
Whilst gazing on the stream, whose new swollen
waters
Yet turbid flow, what strange imaginings
Possess my soul and fill it with delight!
The rippling wave is like her arching brow;
The fluttering line of storks, her timid tongue;
The foamy spray, her white loose-floating vest;
And this meandering course the current tracks,
Her undulating gait; all these recall
My soon-offended love—I must appease her.

Air.

Be not relentless, dearest,
Not wroth with me for ever.
I mark where thou appearest
A fair and mountain river.
Like Ganga proud thou showest,
From heavenly regions springing;
Around thee, as thou flowest,
The birds their course are winging.
The timid dear confiding,
Thy flowering borders throng;
And bees, their store providing,
Pour forth enraptured song.

Air.

In the lowering east the king of the deep
Expects his coming bride;

His limbs are the clouds that darkly sweep
The skirts of the heaving tide;
And his tossing arms are the tumbling waves,
Where the gale o'er the heaving billows raves.

With rapture he dances, the lord of the main,
And proud in his state appears;
His steps are pursued by the monster train,
The deep sea darkness rears;
And the curlew, the swan, and glistening shell,
And the lotus, the monarch's glory swell.

The bellowing surges his fame resound,
And dash at the gates of heaven;
The sea with the sky they threat to confound,
But back with shame are driven;
For now the young rains are armed for their right,
And their prowess arrests old Ocean's might.

[APPROACHES AND BOWS.

O nymph adored, what crime have I committed,
That thus you fly from one so wholly yours,
Who now implores your pity, and with terror
Anticipates your loss? Relent—return—
This is not Urvasi. She would not quit me
Even for the Ocean king. What's to be done?
Fortune crowns those who yield not to despair—
I'ld back to where my love first disappeared.
Yonder the black deer couchant lies; of him
I will inquire. O antelope, behold,

The royal elephant Airavata,
Scorched by the pangs of solitude, explores,
In search of his lost mate, the groves of Nandana;
Whose close embowering walks are resonant
With the glad koil's song, as pleased he sips
The juicy nectar of the clustering blossoms.
How! he averts his gaze, as he disdained
To hear my suit! Ah, no!—he anxious marks
His doe approches him—tardily she comes,
Her frolic fawn impeding her advance.

Air.

A nymph of heaven has left her sphere
To make a heavenly region here,
And treads this sacred ground;
Her slender waist, her swelling hips,
Her languid eye, her ruby lips,
With youth unfading crowned.
Oh tell me, through the tangled maze,
If wandering she has met thy gaze
Deer of the soft black eye,
Ere yet beneath the yawning brink
Of sorrow's gulph, immersed I sink?
Befriend me, or I die— [ADVANCHES.
Lord of the bounding herds, say, hast thou seen
My fair, whose large and languid eye resembles
That of thy tender mate? He heeds me not,
But springs to meet his doe. Be happy both,
Though fate still adverse frowns on my desires.

[PROCEEDS AND PAUSES.

How now! what stream of ruddy radiance breaks
Through the cleft rock? No flame could have survived!
The fast descending torrents; 'tis perchance
Some sanguine fragment of the lion's feast.
No-'tis a gem more roseate than the blush
Of the *asoka* blossom, and the sun
Would grasp it with his beams; it pleases me,
And I will make it mine.

Air.

With tearful eye and dejected gaze,
Despairing his love to meet,
All lonely the royal elephant strays,
Through the forest's still retreat.

Why should I take the jewel? She whose brow
Bound with *Mandara* fillet, best had worn
The costly gem is far—far from me—why
Should I disdain the ruby with my tears?

[*Going—a voice in the air.*

Take up the gem my son; its radiant red
The feet of Hema's holy daughter shed
And wondrous virtue gave. Let it adorn
Thy hand, and thou wilt shortly cease to mourn
Thy absent bride—once more by this restored
To bless her sorrowing and lamented lord.

Pur.—What voice is this! Descends some friendly sage
In pity of my griefs, or in some deer

Disguised, directs me thus? Seer, I obey
And thank thy holy counsel; Gem divine,
Restore me to my love, and I will bear thee
High on my diadem, and hold thee over
As dear as Iswara his crescent moon.

[*Takes the gem and proceeds, then pauses.*

What means this strange emotion, as I gaze
Upon this vine? No blossoms deck its boughs;
Nipped by the falling rains, like briny tears,
That wash the ruddy freshness from the lips,
The buds have perished, and the mournful shrub
All unadorned appears to pine in absence;
No bees regale her with their songs; silent
And sad, she lonely shows the image
Of my repentant love, who now laments
Her causeless indignation. I will press
The melancholy likeness to my heart.

Air.

Vine of the wilderness, behold
A lone heart-broken wretch in me,
Who dreams in his embrace to fold
His love, as wild he clings to thee.
And might relenting fate restore
To these fond arms the nymph I mourn.
I'd bear her hence, and never more
To these forbidden haunts return.

[*Goes to embrace the creeper, which is transformed to Urvasi.*

What can this mean! through every fibre spreads
The conscious touch of Urvasi—yet. all
I deemed her charms deceived me—let me wake
And realise the vision or dispel it.
'Tis no deceit—'Tis she; my best beloved.

[FAINTS.

Urv. (In tears.) Revive, my lord.

Pur. (Reviving.) Thy loss, dear love, has
Plunged my sinking spirit
Deep into dreariest gloom; but now thy sight
Arrests my soul, and calls me back to bliss.

Urv.—I knew not of your woe, myself deprived
Of conscious being.

Pur.—How! What mean you? Speak!

Urv.—I will explain; but let me first implore
Forgiveness, that my causeless wrath has wrought
So sad a change in you.

Urv.—Enough, enough;
You mine once more, all else is quite forgotten,
And every thought is ecstasy. But come,
Say how you cheered your time, your lord away?
For me—

Air.

I have said to the starry-plummed bird,
And the *koil* of love-breathing song;
To the lord of the elephant herd,
And the bee as he murmured along;
To the swan, and the loud waterfall,
To the chakwa, the rock, and the roe:

In thy search have I sued to them all,
But none of them lightened my woe.

Urv.—To me, all news of my lamented lord
Came but in fond imaginings.

Pur.—How thus?

Urv.—In ancient days, the warrior god adopted
A cænobite's observance; and for this,
Retiring to the woods that stud the vale
Of Gandhamadana, then called Akalusha,
He framed this law—

Pur.—What law? Proceed!

Urv.—The female that should rashly pass the bounds
Proscribed, and penetrate the forest shades,
Should instant metamorphose undergo,
And to a twining shrub should be transformed,
Alone from such sad change to be redeemed
By the celestial gem, whose ruby glow
Is gleaned from Gauri's foot. This law I broke.
Bewildered by the sage's imprecation,
I thoughtless plunged into the thicket's glooms
Shunned ever by the gods, and in a vine
My form and faculties awhile were lost.

Pur.—'Tis all explained. No ordinary cause
I knew detained thee from me: thee, whose fears
Brooked not my momentary separation,
Even in thy dreams. The virtue of the gem,

As thou hast said, this day effects our meeting.
Behold it here!

Urv.—The ruby of reunion:
This holy gem restores me to my nature.

[*Takes*] *it and puts it respectfully to her forehead.*

Pur.—A moment thus: let me behold thy brow,
Irradiated by this heavenly jewel,
Like the red lotus ere its buds expand.

Urv.—The king delights to flatter me; but now
Let us return to Pratishthana. Long
The city mourns its absent lord, and I,
The cause of his departure, shall incur
The angry censures of the people. Come,
How will it please you travel?

Pur.—Yonder cloud,
Shall be our downy car, to waft us swift
And lightly on our way; the lightnings wave
Its glittering banners, and the bow of Indra
Hangs as its over-arching canopy
Of variegated and resplendent hues.

Air,

The ardent swan his mate recovers,
And all his spirit is delight:
With her aloft in air he hovers,
And homeward wings his joyous flight,

[EXEUNT ON THE CLOUD—MUSIC.

ACT V.

The Palace of Pururavas.

Enter Manavaka.

At last, thank the fates, the king has returned with Madam Urvasi from the groves of Nandana, the pleasant gardens of the Gods. My friend is once more attentive to his royal duties and the cares of state; yet he seems out of spirits. What should be the cause? Except the want of children, he has nothing to grieve her. This is a bustling day. The king and his queen have just performed their royal ablutions where the Yamuna and the Ganges meet: he must be at his toilet by this time, and by joining him I shall secure a share of the flowers and perfumes prepared for him.

(Noise behind.) The ruby! the ruby! A hawk, taking it for a piece of flesh, has borne away the ruby of reunion which had been taken out of its red palm-leaf case, and was being carried to the king for him to wear while absent from the nymph!

Man.—Here's a pretty piece of work! the jewel my friend so highly prized. Ho, here he comes, not yet attired. I will keep aloof.

[*Enter Pnruravas in haste, followed by the Chamberlain, a Hunter, and attendants.*

Pur.—Where is the winged thief that rashly courts
This own destruction, and persumes to violate

The dwelling of his soverign;

Hunter.—Yonder he goes, the golden chain of the jewel hanging from his beak.

Pur.—I see him! As he rapid flies around
In airy rings, the whirling chain appears
To hem him in a fiery circle.
What's to be done?

Man.—(Advancing.) Punish him, to be sure; put the culprit to death.

Pur.—Bring me my bow

[*A female attandant goes out and returns with a bow and arrows, which she gives to the king.*

'Tis now too late—he flies
Far to the south, beyond the arrow's reach.
Red *asoka* flowers, the precious gem
Graces the sky: with sullen fires it glows
Like angry Mars, bursting at intervals
Through the thick clouds that overhang the night.
My good Talavya (to the Chamberlain),
Give command, the bird
Be tracked, and followed to his perch.

Cham.—The king shall be obeyed. [EXIT.

Man.—Now please you sit; the thief will not be able to escape your power.

Pur.—(Sits.) Were it an ordinary gem, its loss
Would move me not; but to lose this would vex me;
To it I owe reunion with my love.

Man.—Well, there is this comfort, as you have the lady, you are no longer in need of the jewel.

[*Enter Chamberlain, with an arrow and the jewel.*

Cham.—Victory to your Grace! The bird, condemned by your Majesty's decree, has fallen, pierced by this shaft; the ruby is recovered. It has been cleansed with water; please you say to whom it shall be entrusted.

Pur.—Ho, forester! replace the gem
Safe in its casket.

Hunter.—As your Majesty commands.

[EXIT THE KIRAT OR FORESTER.

Pur.—Know you to whom the shaft belongs?

Cham.—There is a name inscribed upon it, your Grace, but my eye sight cannot distinguish the characters.

Pur.—Let me see them.

[*Takes the arrow, and oxpresses wonder and delight.*

Cham.—With your Grace's leave I will now attend to other duties. [EXIT.

Man.—What does your Majesty study so intently.

Pur.—Listen—the arrow of the all-subduing Ayus,
The son of Urvasi and Pururavas.

Man.—Joy to your Grace! Fate has crowned your wishes.

Pur.—How should this be? But for the interval
Of the Naimisha sacrificial rite
My Urvasi has always been with me.

I do recall, indeed, a transient period,
When her soft cheek was paler than the leaf.
Cold-nipped and shrivelled, and her eloquent eye
Betrayed unwonted lassitude; aught else
I never noted.

Mau. Oh you must not suppose that the nymphs of heaven manage these matters like those of earth. No, no; they have the power to counteract all such appearances.

Pur.—It may be so. Yet why this mystery?
Why keep from me all knowledge of my child?

Man.—Oh, there's no accounting for the fancies of celestial spirits.

[*Enter Chamberlain.*

Cham.—So please your majesty, a saintly dame and a young lad from the hermitage of Chyavan solicit admittance.

Pur.—Let them enter quick!

[*Enter a Tapasi or Female ascetic, and a Boy, with a bow in his hand.*

Man.—Observe him, sir. That warrior lad must be the owner of the arrow; he is your perfect image:

Pur.—May it prove so! My imperfect sight
Is dimmed with tears; my heart is overcome
With tenderness, and strong emotions crowd
My agitated mind; on all my limbs
A sudden tremor seizes. How I long
To clasp him to my bosom!

Cham.—Here pause, most reverend lady.

Pur.—(Bowing.) Hail, holy dame!

Tap.—May fortune ever wait
The glorious line of Soma, (Apart.) Now, methinks,
The king has inward intimation given him
I bring him here his son. (Aloud.) Boy, pay your homage.

[AYUS BOWS.

Pur.—May your years be many!

Ayus.—(Apart.) If I dared listen to my heart, I should
Believe this were my father, I his son;
For what affection else would give a charm
To the endearments and embrace of age?

Pur.—What brings thee to our presence, saintly dame?

Tap.—Let the king hear. This princely youth, the son
Of Urvasi, was for some cause confined,
Without your knowledge, to my secret care.
The ceremonies of his martial birth
The pious Chyávana has duly ministered,
Taught him the knowledge fitted to his station,
And lastly trained his growing youth to arms!
But now my charge expires, for an act
This day achieved, unfits him to remain
An inmate of the peaceful hermitage.

Pur.—What act?

Tap.—Whilst on his mission with the Rishi's sons,
To gather fuel, flowers, and holy grass
From the adjacent woods, he aimed a shaft

Against a hawk, new perched upon a tree
With his fresh prey, and took his felon life.
This deed of blood excludes him from our haunts,
And by sage's orders I conduct him
Again to Urvasi. I would see the queen.

Pur.—Be seated, and meanwhile, Talavya,
Apprise our queen, that we would see her here.

[EXIT CHAMBERLAIN

Come hither. boy. As the moon's silver ray
Affects the lunar gem, his presence sheds
Spontaneous joy, and through each fibre darts
The consciousness that I behold my son.

Tap.—Obey your sire.

[*The prince advances and prostrates himself. Puruxavas raises and embraces him, and places him on the footstool of his throne.*

Pur.—Salute your father's friend. Boy, fear not.

Man.—What should he fear? He has seen baboons enough in the hermitage.

Ayus.—(Smiling.) Accept my homage, sir.

Mau.—Fortune attend you ever!

[*Enter Urvasi, preceded by the Chamberlain.*

Cham.—This way, your Grace.

Urv.—(Seeing Ayus.) What youth is this, who, in the royal presence,
Armed with the bow and quiver, honoured sits
Upon the golden footstool, whilst the king
Is fondly playing with his twisted tresses!

Ha! Satyavati too! it is my son;
His growth outstrips my memory.

Pur.—Behold your mother, boy; her gaze intent
Is fixed upon you, and her heaving bosom
Has rent its veiling scarf.

Tap.—Haste to embrace her.

[*Ayus rises and goes to his mother, who embraces him, then, after a pause,*

Urv.—Hail, holy mother!

Tap.—Ever may you know
Your lord's affection!

Ayus.—Mother, accept my salutations.

Urv.—(Kisses him.) My dear boy,
Be long your father's happiness and pride.
(Advances.) Glory to the king!

Pur.—To the matron, honour!

[*Hands Urvasi to a seat with him on the throne.*

Be seated all. [THEY SIT.

Tap.—The princely youth is perfectly accomplished
In all the science that becomes his rank,
And is of years and strength to bear the load
Of martial mail. Unfitted to the thoughts
And duties of the tranquil hermitage,
I yield him, therefore, in the royal presence,
Back to his mother's arms.

Urv.—And I receive him
Most willingly: for it is no longer meet

He should disturb the quiet of devotion.
When he is satiate with his father's sight
He may revisit you ; till then, farewell.

Pur.—And bear my reverence to the holy sage.

Ayus.—Will you not take me with you, Satyavati ?

Tap.—No my dear child : the labours of the student
Are all performed ; 'tis time you enter now
On loftier duties.

Ayus.—Well, if it must be so,
Farewell ; but send me here my favourite peacock.

Tap.—I will ; and boy, remember that you heed
Your father ever. Peace be unto all !

[EXIT.

Pur.—Thus blessed, my love, with thee and with my son,
I envy not the happiness of Indra.

[*Weeps violently.*

Urv.—Ah, me !

Pur.—What means this sudden grief ?
Why, when I contemplate with ecstasy
The proud perpetuation of my race,
Should these dear drops in swift succession spread
A pearly fillet on thy heaving bosom ?

Urv.—Alas, my lord ! the name of Swarga's king
Brings to my memory dread decree
By him denounced, which, in thy sight
Of this loved boy, I had a while forgotten.
When for your love I gladly left the courts
Of heaven, the monarch thus declared his will

"Go, and be happy with the prince, my friend:
But when he views the son that thou shalt bear him,
Then hitherward direct thy prompt return."
'Twas fear of this that bade me keep concealed
My infant's birth, and instant I conveyed him
To Chyavana's retreat, entrusting him
To yonder pious dame to be instructed;
Such my pretext, in our most sacred lore.
The fated term expires, and to console
This father for my loss, he is restored.—
I may no longer tarry.

Pur.—Adverse fate
Is still intent to mar my perfect joy,
Scarce have I known the blessing of a son,
When my fair bride is snatched from my embrace.
The tree that languished in the summer's blaze,
Puts forth reviving, as young descends,
Its leafy shoots, when lo! the lightning bursts
Fierce on its top and fells it to the ground.

Man.—I see nothing left for this but to abandon the throne, assume the the coat of bark, and betake yourself to the forests.

Urv.—But what remains for me, my task on earth
Fulfilled? Once gone, the king will soon forget me.

Pur—Dearest, not so. It is no grateful task
To tear our memory from those we love.

But we must bow to power supreme; do you
Obey your lord; for me, I will resign
My throne to this our son, and with the deer
Will henceforth mourn amidst the lonely woods.

Ayus.—Excuse me, sire; my tears are all unfit
For such a burthen; one so long upheld
By such exalted merits.

Pur.—Fear it not.
The elephant cub soon tames the forest herds;
The snake scarce hatched concocts the deadly poison;
Kings are in boyhood monarchs, and endowed
With powers inborn to rule the race of man:
Nature, not age, gives fitness. (*To the Chamberlain.*) Talavya, bid
Our ministers and priests be all prepared
For this our son's inauguration—speed!

Cham.—I obey.

[*Exit sorrowfully, and all on the scene express grief.*

Pur.—What sudden splendour breaks! whence are these flashes
Of lightning in a cloudless sky?

Urv.—'Tis Narada.

Pur.—His braided curls are of a golden dye;
His sacred cord, bright as the silver moon;
Around his neck are strings of heavenly pearls;
Like a celestial tree with glittering stem
He moves. Prepare we to receive him.

Urv.—Here,
His offering of respect, gathered in haste,
Present the sage.
[*Gives the king some flowers*

NARADA DESCENDS.

Par.—Triumph attend
The brave defender of this middle sphere!

Pur.—(Presenting the oblation.) Reverence to the sage!

Urv.—Accept my homage. [Bows.

Nar.—Never be wife and husband disunited.

Pur.—(Apart.) Oh might this be! (Aloud.)
Advance, my son, and pay
Your adoration to the holy seer.

Ayus.—Ayus, the son of Urvasi, presumes
To pay you homage. [Bows to Narada.

Nar.—May your days be many! King attend;
The mighty Indra, to whom all is known,
By me thus intimates his high commands:—
Forego your purpose of ascetic sorrow.
The sages, to whose wisdom past and future
Are as the present, have foretold at hand
Hostilities in heaven, and the gods will need
Your prowess: then relinquish not your arms
And Urvasi shall be through life united
With thee in holy bonds.

Urv.—These happy words
Extract a barbed arrow from my bosom.

Pur.—Whatever Indra wills, I shall obey.

Nar.—'Tis wisely said: he will not be unthankful.

The fiery element sustains the sun;
The sun returns his rays to nourish fire.

[*Looking upwards.*

Rambha, appear, and bring the holy wave
Consigned by Indra to your charge, to consecrate
The prince's elevation to the throne,
As partner of the empire.

[*Rambha and other nymphs descend with a golden vase containing the water of the heavenly Ganges, throne and other paraphernalia, which they arrange.*

Ram.—All is prepared.

Nar.—Prince, to your seat.

[*Narada leads Ayus to the throne of Inauguration, takes the golden ewer from Rambha, and pours water on the head of the prince.*

Rambha, complete the rite.

[*Rambha and the Apsarasas perform the rest of the ceremony.*

Ram.—Now, prince, salute your parents and the sage.

[*As Ayus bows to them respectively, they reply.*

Nar.—Unvarying fortune wait upon thy reign!

Pur.—My son, sustain the honour of your lineage.

Urv.—My son, be still obedient to thy sire.

[CHORUS OF BARDS WITHOUT.

Glory, all glory, Ayus attending,
Still in the son may the father we trace;
Justice and valour together extending
The sway of his sceptre and fame of his race.
Son of the monarch the universe filling,
Son of the God of the mist-shedding night,
Son of the sage, whom the great Brahma willing,
Called with creation to life and to light.

SECOND CHORUS.

Now bright o'er the regions the glories are gleaming
The sceptre and sway of the father have won,
And brighter than ever the radiance is streaming,
Enhanced and confirmed by the fame of the son.
So Ganga descends from the peaks of the mountain
That shine with the light of unperishing snows,
And mighty meandering far from their fountain,
In the breast of the ocean the waters repose.

Ram.—(To Urvasi.) No ordinary fate, dear sister, blesses you
With such a son and lord.

Urv.—I own my happiness.
Come, my dear child, and offer to the queen,
Your elder mother, filial homage.

Pur.—Hold,
One moment; we will presently together.

Nar.—The splendours of your son's inauguration
Bring to my memory the glorious time

When Mahasena was anointed chief.
Of all the heavenly hosts.

Pur.—To you I owe.
Such honour.

Nar.—Is there ought else Indra can do
To serve his friend,

Pur.—To hold me in esteem
Is all I covet. Yet haply may this chance :—
May learning and prosperity oppose
No more each other, as their wont, as foes,
But in a friendly bond together twined,
Ensure the real welfare of mankind

[EXEUNT OMNES.

MEGHADUTA;

OR

CLOUD MESSENGER.

BY

KALIDASA.

TRANSLATED INTO ENGLISH VERSE WITH ANNOTATIONS BY

H. H. WILSON.

PUBLISHED BY

THE SOCIETY FOR THE RESUSCITATION OF INDIAN LITERATURE.

CALCUTTA:

PRINTED BY H. C. DAS, ELYSIUM PRESS,

1901.

THE

MEGHA DUTA

OR

CLOUD MESSENGER.

WHERE *Ramagiri's* shadowy woods extends
And those pure streams where *Sita* bathed, descend,
Spoiled of his glories, severed from his wife,
A vanished *Yaksha* passed his lonely life;
Doomed by KUVERA'S anger to sustain,
Twelve tedious months of solitude and pain.

To these drear hills through circling days confined,
In dull unvaried grief, the God repined;
And sorrow withering every youthful charm,
Had slipped the golden bracelet from his arm,

When with *Askarha's* blooms the air was hung,
And one dark *Cloud* around the mountain clung;

In form some elephant, whose sportive rage,
Ramparts, scarce equal to his might, engage.

Long on the mass of mead-reviewing dew,
The heavenly exile fixed his eager view ;
And still the melancholy tear suppressed,
Though bitterest sorrow wrung his heaving
breast ;

Reflection told what promise of delight,
Sprang from such gathering shades to happier
sight,
Where the worn traveller is joyed to trace,
His home approaching, and a wife's embrace :

What hope alas was his ! yet fancy found,
Some solace in the glooms that deepened round,
And bade him hail amidst the labouring air,
A friendly envoy to his distant fair :

Who charged with grateful tidings might impart,
New life and pleasure to her drooping heart.
Cheered with the thought he culled each
budding flower,
And wildly wooed the fertilizing power ;

(For who ! a prey to agonizing grief,
Explores not idlest sources for relief ?
And as to creatures sensible of pain,
To lifeless nature, loves not to complain ?)

Due homage offered, and oblations made,
The *Yaksha* thus the *Cloud* majestic prayed.
Hail! friend of INDRA, counsellor divine,
Illustrious offspring of a glorious line.

Wearer of shapes at will, thy worth I know,
And bold entrust thee with my fated woe;
For better far solicitations fail,
With high desert, than with the base prevail.

Thou art the wretch's aid, affliction's friend!
To me, unfortunate, thy succour lend;
My lonely state compassionate behold,
Who mourn the vengeance of the God of gold;
Condemed amidst these dreary rocks to pine,
And all I wish, and all I love resign.

Where dwell the *Yakshas* in their sparkling fields,
And SIVA's crescent groves surrounding gilds,

Direct thy licensed journey, and relate,
To her who mourns in *Aloka* my fate;
There shalt thou find, the partner of my woes,
True to her faith, and stranger to repose;
Her task to weep our destiny severe,
And count the moments of the lingering year;

A painful life she leads, but still she lives,
While hope its aid invigorating gives;
For female hearts, though fragile as the flower,

Are firm, when closed by hope's investing power.
Still as thou ridest on the friendly gale,
Shall widowed wives thy march advancing hail;
And all whom no tyrannic laws control,
Shall bless thy shadows deepening as they roll:
The gentle breeze shall fan thy stately way,
In sportive wreathes the *Cranes* around thee play;
Pleased on thy left the *Chataka* along,
Pursues thy path, and cheers it with his song;
And when thy thunders soothe the parching earth,
And showers expected, raise her mushroom birth;
The *Swans* for mount *Kailasa* shall prepare,
And track thy course attendant through the air.
Sport be thy greeting to this hill addressed,
This hill with RAMA's holy feet imprest;
Thy ancient friend, whose scorching sorrows mourn,
Thy frequent absence, and delayed return.
Yet ere thy ear can drink what love inspires,
The lengthened way my guiding aid requires;
Oft on whose path, full many a lofty hill,
Shall ease thy toils, and many a cooling rill;
Rise from these streams and seek the upper sky;
Then to the north with daring pinions fly:
The beauteous *Sylphs* shall mark thee with amaze,
As backward bent thou strik'st their upward gaze,

In doubt if by the gale abruptly torn,
Some mountain peak along the air is borne:
The ponderous *Elephants* who prop the skies,
Shall view thy form expansive with surprise;
Now first their arrogance exchanged for shame,
Lost in thy bulk their long unrivalled fame.
Eastward where various gems with blending ray,
In INDRA's bow o'er yonder hillock play,
And on thy shadowy form such radiance shed,
As *Peacock's* plumes around, a KRISHNA spread,
Direct thy course to *Mala* smiling ground,
Where fragrant tillage breathes the fields around;
Thy fertile gifts, which looks of love reward,
Where bright-eyed Peasants tread the verdant sward.
Thence sailing north and veering to the west,
On *Amrakutas* lofty ridges rest;
Oft have thy showers the mountain's flames allayed
Then fear not wearied to demand its aid;
Not e'en the vilest, when a falling friend,
Solicits help it once was his to lend,
The aid that gratitude exacts denies;
Much less the virtuous shall the claim despise.
When o'er the wooded mountain's towering head,
They hovering shades like flowing tresses spread;
Its form shall shine with charms unknown before,

That heavenly hosts may gaze at and adore ;
This earth's round breast; bright swelling from the ground,
And with thy orb as with a nipple crowned.
Next bending down-wards from thy lofty flight,
On *Chitrakuta's* humbler peak alight ;
O'er the tall hill thy weariness forego,
And quenching rain-drops on its flames bestow ;
For speedy fruits are certain to await,
Assistance yielded to the good and great.
Thence journeying onwards *Vind'hya's* ridgy chain,
And *Reva's* rill that bathes its foot attain ;
Where amidst rocks whose variegated glow,
The royal elephant's rich trappings show,
Arduous she winds, and next through beds of flowers,
She wins her way, and washes *Jumbu* bowers ;
Here the soft dews thy path has lost resume,
And sip the gelid current's rich perfume,
Where the wild Elephant delights to shed,
The juice exuding fragrant from his head ;
Then swift proceed, nor shall the blast have force,
To check with empty gusts thy ponderous course.
Reviving nature bounteous shall dispense,
To cheer thy journey, every charm of sense ;

Blossoms with blended green and russet hue,
And opening buds shall smile upon thy view;
Earth's blazing woods in incense shall arise,
And warbling birds with music fiill the skies.
Respectful Demigods shall curious count,
The chattering Storks in lengthening order mount;
Shall mark the *Chatakas* who in thy train,
Expect impatiently the dropping rain:
And when thy muttering thunders speak thee near,
Shall clasp their brides half ecstasy, half fear.
Ah! much I dread the long protracted way,
Where charms so numerous spring to tempt delay;
Will not the frequent hill retard thy flight,
Nor flowery plain persuade prolonged delight?
Or can the Peacock's animated hail,
The bird with lucid eyes, to lure the fail?
Lo! where awhile the Swans reluctant cower,
Dasarnas field await the coming shower:
Then shall their groves diffuse profounder gloom,
And brighter buds the deepening shade illume:
Then shall the ancient tree whose branches wear,
The marks of village reverence and care,
Shake through each leaf, as birds profanely wrest,
The venerend boughs to form the rising nest.
Where royal *Vidisa* confers renown;
Thy warmest wish shall fruit delightful crown;

There *Vetraveti's* stream ambrosial laves,
A gentle bank with mildly murmuring waves,
And there her rippling brow and polished face,
Invite thy smiles, and sue for thy embrace,
Next o'er the lesser hills thy flights suspend.
And growth erect to drooping flowrets lend;
While sweeter fragrance breathes from each recess,
Than rich perfumes the hireling wantons dress.
On *Naga Nadi's* banks thy waters shed,
And raise the feeble jasmin's languid head;
Grant for a while thy interposing shroud,
To where those damsels woo the friendly Cloud,
As while the garlands flowery stores they seek,
The scorching sun beams singe the tender cheek;
The ear-hung lotus fades, and vain they chase,
Fatigued and faint, the drops that dew the face.
What though to northern climes the journey lay,
Consent to track a shortly devious way;
To fair *Ujaini's* palaces and pride,
And beauteous daughters, turn awhile aside:
Those glancing eyes, those lightning looks unseen,
Dark are thy days, and thou in vain hast been.
Diverging thither now the road proceeds,
Where eddying waters fair *Nirvindhya* leads,
Who speaks the language amorous maids devise.

The lore of signs, the eloquence of eyes,
And seeks with lavish beauty to arrest,
Thy course and woo thee to her bridal breast.
The torrent passed behold the Sindhu glide,
As though the hair band bound the slender tide;
Bleached with the withered folliage that the breeze,
Has showered rude from overhanging trees;
To thee she looks for succour to restore,
Her lagging waters, and her leafy shore.
Behold the city whose immortal fame,
Glows in *Avanti's* or *visala's* name?
Renowned for deeds that worth and love inspire
And bards to paint them with poetic fire:
The fairest portion of celestial birth,
Of INDRA's paradise transferred to earth,
The last reward to acts austerest given;
The only recompense then left to heaven.
Here as the early Zephyrs waft along,
In swelling harmony the woodland song,
They scatter sweetness from the fragrant flower,
That joyful opens to the morning hour;
With friendly zeal they sport around the maid,
Who early courts their vivifying aid,
And cool from *Sipras* gelid waves embrace,
Each languid limb, and enervated grace.

Here should thy spirit with thy toils decay,
Rest from the labors of the wearying way,
Round every house the flowery fragrance spreads;
Oe'r every floor the painted footstep treads;
Breathed through each casement, swell the
scented air
Soft odors shaken from dishevelled hair;
Pleased on each terrace dancing with delight,
The friendly Peacock hails thy grateful flight:
Delay then, certain in *Ujayin* to find,
All that restores the frame, or cheers the mind.
Hence with new zeal to SIVA homage pay,
The God whom earth, and hell, and heaven obey;
The choir who tend his holy fame shall view,
With awe, in thee his neck's celestial blue;
Soft through the rustling grove the fragrant gale,
Shall sweets from *Gandhavati's* fount exhale;
Where with rich dust the lotus blossoms esteem,
And youthful beauties frolic in stream.
Here, till the sun has vanished in the west,
Till evening brings its sacred ritual, rest;
Then reap the recompense of holy prayer,
Like drums thy thunders echoing in the air.
They who with burning feet, and aching arms,
With wanton gestures, and emblazoned charms,
In MAHÁDEVA's fame the measure tread,

Or wave the gorgeous chowrie o'er his head;
Shall turn on thee the grateful-speaking eye,
Whose glances glean like bees along the sky,
As from thy presence, showers benign and sweet,
Cool the parched earth, and soothe their tender
feet.
Nay more BHAVANI shall herself approve,
And pay thy services with looks of love;
When as her SIVA'S twilight rites begin,
And he would clothe him in the reeking skin,
He deems thy form the sanguinary hide,
And casts his elephant attire aside;
For at his shoulders like a dusky robe,
Mantling impends thy vast and shadowy globe:
Where ample forests, stretched it's skirts below,
Projecting trees like dangling limbs bestow;
And vermil roses fiercely blooming shed,
Their rich reflected glow, their blood-resembling
red.
Amidst the darkness palpable that shrouds,
Deep as the touch stone's gloom, the night with
clouds,
With glittering lines of yellow lightning break,
And frequent trace in heaven the golden streak:
To those fond fair who tread the royal way,
The path their doubtful feet explore betray,

Those thunders hushed, whose shower-foreboding
sound,
Would check their ardour, and their hopes con-
found.
On some cool terrace, where the turtle dove.
In gentlest accents breathes connubial love,
Repose awhile, or plead your amorous vows.
Through the long night, the lightning for your
spouse;
Your path retraced, resumed your promised flight
When in the east the Sun restores the light;
And shun his course; for with the dawning sky,
The sorrowing wife dispels the tearful eye,
Her Lord returned; so comes the sun to chase,
The dewy tears that stain the *Padma's* face,
And ill his eager penitence will bear,
That thou shoulds't check his progress thro'
the air.
Now to *Gambhira's* wave thy shadow flies,
And on the stream's pellucid surface lies,
Like some loved image faithfully imprest,
Deep in the maiden's pure unsullied breast:
And vain thy struggles to escape her wiles,
Or disappoint those stweetly treacherous smiles,
Which glistening *Saphara's* insidious dart,
Bright as the lotus, at thy vanquished heart:

What breast so firm unmoved by female charms?
Not thine my friend; for now her waving arms,
O'er hanging *Bayas*, in thy grasp enclosed,
Rent her cœrulean vest, and charms exposed,
Prove how successfully she tempts delay,
And wins thee loitering from the lengthening
way.
Thence satiate lead along the gentle breeze,
That bows the lofty summits of the trees,
And pure with fragrance that the earth in flowers,
Repays profuse to fertilizing showers,
Vocal with sounds the elephants excite,
To *Deragiri* wings its welcome flight;
There change thy form, and showering roses shed,
Bathed in the dews of heaven, on SKANDA's head;
Son of the Crescent's God, whom holy ire,
Called from the flame of all devouring fire,
To snatch the Lord of *Swerga* from despair,
And timely save the trembling hosts of air.
Next bid thy thunders o'er the mountain float,
And echoing caves repeat the pealing note;
Fit music for the bird whose lucid eye,
Gleams like the horned beauty of the sky,
Whose moulting plumes to love maternal dear,
Lend brilliant pendants to BHAVANI's ear.
To him whose youth in *Sara* thickets strayed,

Reared by the nymphs, thy adoration paid,
Resume thy road, and to the world proclaim,
The glorious tale of RANTIDEVA's fame.
Sprung from the blood of countless oxen shed,
And a fair river through the regions spread.
Each lute-armed spirit from thy path retires,
Lest drops ungenial damp the tuneful wires;
Celestial couples bending from the skies,
Turn on thy distant course their downward, eyes,
And watch thee lessening in thy long descent;
To rob the river's scanty stores intent;
As clothed in sacred darkness not thine own,
Thine is the azure of the costly stone;
A central sapphire, in the loosened girth,
Of scattering pearls, that strung the blooming earth.

The streamlet traversed, to the eager sight,
Of *Dasapura's* fair impart delight;
Welcomed with looks that sparkling eyes bestow,
Whose arching brows like graceful creepers glow,
Whose upturned lashes, to thy lofty way,
The pearly ball, and pupil dark display;
Such contrast as the lovely *Cunda* shews,
When the black bee sits pleased amidst her snows.
Hence to the land of BRAHMA's favored sons,
O'er *Kuru's* fatal field thy journey runs;

With deepest glooms hang o'er the deadly plain,
Dewed with the blood of mighty warriors slain;
There ARJUN's wrath opposing armies felt,
And countless arrows strong *Gandiva* dealt,
Thick as thy drops, that in the pelting shower,
Incessant hurtle round the shrinking flower.
O'er *Saraswati's* waters wing your course,
And inward prove their purifying force;
Most holy, since oppressed with heaviest grief,
The ploughshare's mighty Lord, here sought relief;
From kindred strife, and REVATI withdrew,
And to these banks, and holy musing flew.
Thy journey next o'er *Canac'hala* bends,
Where JAHNU's daughter from the hills descends,
Whose lengthening stream, to SAGAR's virtue given,
Conducts his numerous progeny to heaven;
She who with smiling waves disportive strayed,
Through SAMBHU's locks, and with his tresses played;
Unheeding as she flowed delighted down,
The gathering storm of GOURI's jealous frown.
Should her clear current tempt thy thirsty lip,
And thou inclining bend the stream to sip,
Thy form like INDRA's Elephant displayed,

Shall clothe the crystal waves with deepest shade,
With sacred glooms the darkening waves
shall glide.
As where the *Jumna* mixes with the tide.
As SIVA's *Bull* upon his sacred neck,
Amidst his ermine, owns some sable speck,
So shall thy shade upon the mountain show,
Whose sides are silvered with eternal snow;
Where GUNGA leades her purifying waves,
And the Musk Deer spring frequent from the
caves,
From writhing boughs should forest flames arise,
Whose breath the air, and brand the *Yac*
supplies,
Instant afford the aid 'tis thine to lend,
And with a thousand friendly streams descend;
For still on earth prosperity proceeds,
From acts of love, and charitable deeds.
Shame is the fruit of actions indiscreet,
And vain presumption ends but in defeat;
So shall the *Sarabhas* who thee oppose,
Themselves to pain, and infamy expose;
When round their heads, amidst the lowering sky
White as a brilliant smile, thy hail stones fly.
Next to the mountain with the foot imprest,
Of him who wears the crescent for his crest,

Devoutly pass, and with religious glow,
Around the spot in pious circles go;
For there have saints the sacred altar raised.
And their eternal offerings have blazed;
And blest the faithful worshippers, for they,
The stain of sin, with life shall cast away;
And after death a glad admittance gain.
To SIVA's glorious, and immortal train
Here wake the chorus; bid the thunder's sound,
Deep and reiterated roll around,
Loud as a hundred drums; while softer strains,
The swelling gale breathes sweetly through the canes;
And from the lovely songsters of the skies,
Hymns to the victor of TRIPURA, rise.
Thence to the snow clad hills thy course direct,
And *Krouncha's* celebrated pass select;
That pass the swans in annual flight explore;
And erst a Hero's mighty arrows tore.
Winding thy way, due north through the defile,
Thy form compressed, with borrowed grace shall smile;
The sable foot that BALI marked with dread,
A god triumphant o'er creation spread.
Ascended thence a transcient period rest;
Renowned *Kailasā's* venerated guest;

That mount whose sides with brightest lustre shine,
A polished mirror, worthy charms divine;
Whose base a RAVAN from its centre wrung,
Shaken not sundered, stable though unstrung;
Whose lofty peaks to distant realms in sight,
Present a SIVA's smile, lotus white;
And lo! those peaks than ivory more clear,
When yet unstained the parted tusks appear,
Beam with new lustre, as around their head,
Thy glossy glooms metallic darkness spread;
As shews a HALABHRITA's sable vest,
More fair the pallid beauty of his breast.
Haply accross thy long and mountain way,
In sport may GOURI with her SIVA stray,
Her serpent bracelet from her wrist displaced,
And in her arms, the mighty God embraced.
Should thus it fortune, be it thine to lend,
A path their holy footsteps may ascend;
Close in thy hollow form thy stores comprest,
While by the touch of feet celestial blest.
Next let each maid of heaven, each blooming girl,
Thy graceful form in sportive mischief whirl,
While lightning gems around each wrist that wind,

Release the treasures in thy breast confined:
Nor fear their aim thy progress to delay;
A grateful succour in the sultry day;
For soon thy thunders shall disperse a train,
Of heart as timid, as of purpose vain.
Where bright the mountain's crystal glories break,
Explore the golden lotus-covered lake:
Imbibe the dews of *Manasa*, and spread,
A friendly veil round *Airavâta's* head;
Or life dispensing with the *Zephyrs* go,
Where heavenly trees, with fainting blossoms blow.
Now on the mountain's side like some dear friend,
Behold the city of Gods impend;
Thy goal behold, where *Ganga's* winding rill,
Skirts like a costly train the sacred hill;
Where brilliant pearls descend in lucid showers;
And Clouds like tresses, clothe her lofty towers.
There every palace with thy glory vies.
Whose soaring summits kiss the lofty skies;
Whose beauteous inmates bright as lightning glare,
And tabors mock the thunders of the air;
The rainbow flickering gleams along the walls,
And glittering rain, in sparkling diamonds falls.

There lovely triflers wanton through the day,
Dress all their care, and their labour play,
One while the fluttering lotus fans the fair,
Or *Kunda* top knots crown the jetty hair;
Now o'er the cheek the Lod'h's pale pollen shines,
Now'midst their curls the Amaranth entwines;
These graces varying with the varying year,
Sirisha blossoms deck the tender ear;
Or new *Kadambas* with thy coming born,
The parted locks, and polished front adorn.
Thus graced they woo the *Yakshas* to their arms,
And gems, and wine, and music, aid their charms
The strains divine with art celestial thrill,
And wines from grapes of heavenly growth distill,
The gems bestrew each terrace of delight,
Like stars that glitter through the shades of night.
There when the sun restores the rising day,
What deeds of love his tell-tale beams display;
The withered garlands on the pathway found,
The faded lotus prostrate on the ground.
The pearls that bursting zones have taught to roam,
Speak of fond maids and wanderers from home.
High on its costly stem with diamonds bright,
The splendid lamp glows vivid through the night;
Or the soft glories of the lunar beam,

In gems condensed, diffuse their graceful gleam;
What though while SIVA with the God of gold,
Delights a friendly intercourse to hold;
The *Lord* of *Love* remembering former woe,
Wields not in *Alaca* his bee-strung bow:
Yet still he triumphs, for each maid supplies,
The fatal bow; with love-inspiring eyes,
And wanton glances emulate the dart,
That speeds unerring to the beating heart.
The gale that blows eternally their guide,
High over *Alaca* the Clouds divide,
Scattered they lie, as if dispersed by fear,
And conscious crime spoke retribution near:
Some just award, for showers that lately soiled,
The painted floor, or gilded roof dispoiled.
North-wards from where KUVERA holds his state,
Where INDRA's bow surmounts the arching gate;
Where on rich boughs, the clustering flower depends,
And low to earth, the tall Mandara bends:
Pride of the grove, whose wants my fair supplies,
And nurtures like a child; my dwelling lies.
There is the fountain emerald steps denote,
Where golden buds, on stalks of coral float,
And for whose limpid waves the Swans forsake,
Pleased at thy sight, the mount encircled lake.
Soft from the pool ascends a shelving ground;

Where shades devoted to delight abound;
Where the cœrulean summit towers above,
The golden circle of a plantain grove:
Lamented haunts whom now in thee I view,
As glittering lightning girt thy base of blue.
See where the clustering *Mad'havi* entwines,
And bright *Curuvaca* the wreath confines;
Profuse, *Asoca* sheds it radiant flower,
And budding *Cesara* adorns the bower;
These are my rivals; for the one would greet,
As I would willingly, my charmer's feet,
And with my fondness, would the other sip,
The grateful nectar of her honied lip.
A golden column on a crystal base,
Begirt with jewels rises o'er the place;
Here when the evening twilight shades the skies,
The blue necked Peacock to the summit flies,
And moves in graceful circles to tone,
My fair awakens from her tinkling zone.
These be thy guides; and faithfully preserve,
The marks I give thee; or e'en move, observe,
Where painted emblems holy wealth design,
KUVERA's treasures; that abode is mine:
Haply its honors are not now to boast,
Dimmed by my fate, and in my exile lost;
For when the sun withdraws his cheering rays,
Faint are the charms the *Kamala* displays.

To those loved scenes repaired, that awful size,
Like a young Elephant, in haste disguise;
Lest terror seize my fair one, as thy form
Hangs o'er the hillock, and portends the storm.
Thence to the inner mansion bend thy sight,
Diffusing round a mild and quivering light,
As when through evening shades, soft flashes play,
Where the bright fire-fly wings his glittering way.
There in the fane a beauteous creature stands,
The first best work of the Creator's hands;
Whose slender limbs inadequately bear,
A full orbed bosom, and a weight of care;
Whose teeth like pearls, whose lips like *Bimbas* show
And fawn like eyes still tremble as they glow.
Lone as the widow *Chaeravaci* mourns,
Her faithful memory to her husband turns,
And sad, and silent, shalt thou find my wife,
Half of my soul, and partner of my life,
Nipped by chill sorrow, as the flower enfold,
Their shrinking petals, for the withering cold.
I view her now! long weeping swells her eyes,
And those dear lips are dried by parching sighs;
Sad on her hand her pallid cheek declines,
And half unseen through veiling tresses shines;
As when a darkling night the moon enshrouds,

A few faint rays break struggling through the
clouds.
Now at thy sight I mark fresh sorrows flow,
And sacred sacrifice augments her woe;
I mark her now, with fancy's aid retrace,
This wasted figure, and this haggard face.
Now from her favorite bird she seeks relief,
And tells the tuneful *Sarica* her grief,
Mourns o'er the feathered prisoner's kindred fate
And fondly questions of it's absent mate.
In vain the lute for harmony is strung,
And round the robe-neglected shoulder slung;
And faltering accents strive to catch in vain,
Our race's old commemorative strain:
The falling tear that from reflection springs,
Corrodes incessantly the silvery strings;
Recurring woe still pressing on the heart,
The skilful hand forgets its grateful art,
And idly wandering strikes no measured tone,
But wakes a sad wild warbling of its own.
At times such solace animates her mind,
As widowed wives in cheerless absence find;
She counts the flowers now faded on the floor,
That graced with monthly piety the door.
Thence reckons up the period since from home,
And far from her, was I compelled to roam;
And deeming fond my term of exile run,

Conceives my homeward journey is begun.
Lightened by tasks like these the day proceeds,
But much I dread a bitterer night succeeds:
When thou shalt view her on the earth's cold breast,
On lonely couch of separation rest,
Disturbed by tears those pallid cheeks that burn,
And visions of her dearer half's return.
Now seeking sleep, a husband to restore,
And waking now, his absence to deplore;
Deprived of slumber by returning woes,
Or mocked by idle phantoms of repose;
Till her slight form, consumed by ceaseless pain,
Shews like the moon, fast hastening to it's wane.
Crisp from the purifying wave her hair
Conceals the charms, no more her pleasing care;
And with neglected nails her fingers chase,
Fatigued, the tresses wandering o'er her face,
Firm winds the fillet, as it first was wove,
When fate relentless force me from my love;
And never flowery wreathes, nor costly pearls,
Must hope to decorate the fettered curls;
Loosed by no hand, until the law divine,
Accomplished, that delighted hand is mine.
Dull as the flower when clouds through other sweep,
Not wholly waking, nor resigned to sleep;

Her heavy eyelids languidly unclose,
To where the moon its silvery radiance throws
Mild through the chamber; once a welcome light,
Avoided now, and hateful to her sight.
Those charms that glittering ornaments oppress,
Those restless slumbers that proclaim distress,
That slender figure worn by grief severe,
Shall surely gain thy sympathizing tear;
For the soft breast is swift to overflow,
In moist compassion, at the claims of woe.
The same fond wife as when compelled to part,
Her love was mine, I still possess her heart;
Her well known faith this confidence affords.
Nor vain conceit suggests unmeaning words;
No boaster I! and time shall quickly teach,
With observation joined, how just my speech.
O'er her left limbs shall glad pulsations play,
And signs auspicious indicate thy way;
And like the lotus trembling on the tide,
While its deep roots the sportive fish divide,
So tremulous throbs the eye's enchanting ball
Loose o'er whose lids neglected tresses fall.
Soothed by expected bliss should gentle sleep,
O'er her soft limbs and frame exhausted creep,
Delay thy tidings, and suspend thy flight,
And watch in silent patience through the night;

Withhold thy thunders, lest the awful sound,
Her slumber banish and her dreams confound,
Where her fond arms, like winding shrubs she flings,
Around my neck, and to my bosom clings.
Behold her rising with the early morn,
Fair as the flower that opening buds adorn;
And strive to animate her drooping mind,
With cooling rain drops, and refreshing wind;
Restrain thy lightnings, as her timid gaze,
Shrinks from the bright intolerable blaze;
And murmuring softly, gentle sounds prepare,
With words like these to raise her from despair.
'Oh wife adored! whose lord still lives for thee;
'Behold his friend, and messenger in me;
'Who now approach thy beautious presence fraught,
'With many a tender, and consoling thought;
'Such tasks are mine: where absent lovers stray,
'I speed the wanderer lightly on his way;
'And with my thunders teach his lagging mind,
'New hopes the braid of absence to unbind.'
As beautious MAIT'HILI with glad surprise,
Bent on the Son of air her opening eyes;
So my fair partner's pleased uplifted gaze,
Thy friendly presence with delight surveys;
She smiles, she speaks, her misery foregoes,

And deep attention on thy words bestows;
For such dear tidings happiness impart,
Scarce less than mutual meeting to the heart.
Being, of years protracted, aid thy friend,
And with my words thine own suggestions blend;
Say thus; 'Thy lord o'er RAMA'S mountain strays,
'Nor cares but those of absence blight his days;
'His only wish by me his friend to know,
'If he is blest with health, that thou art so;
'For still this fear especially must wait,
'On every creature of our passing state.
'What though to distance driven by wrath divine
'Imagination joins his form with thine;
'Such as I view is his emaciate frame,
'Such his regrets, his scorching pangs the same;
'To every sigh of thine, his sigh replies,
'And tears responsive trickle from his eyes.
'By thee unheard, by those bright eyes unseen,
'Since fate resists and regions intervene,
'To me the message of his love consigned,
'Pourtrays the sufferings of his constant mind;
'Oh, were he present, fondly would he seek,
'In secret whisper that inviting check;
'Woo thee in close approach his words to hear,
'And breathe these tender accents in thine ear.'
"Goddess beloved, how vainly I explore,

"The world to trace the semblance I adore;
"Thy graceful form the flexile tendril shews;
"And like thy locks the peacock's plumage glows;
"Mild as thy cheeks, the moon's new beams appear,
"And mild those soft eyes adorn the timid deer;
"In rippling brooks thy curling brows I see,
"But only view combined these charms in thee.
"E'en in these wilds our unrelenting fate,
"Proscribes the union, love and art create;
"When with the colors that the rock supplies,
"O'er the rude stone thy pictured beauties rise,
"Fain would I think, once more we fondly meet;
"And seek to fall in homage at thy feet;
"In vain; for envious tears my purpose blight,
"And veil the lovely image from my sight.
"Why should the God who wields the five-fold dart,
"Direct his shafts at this afflicted heart;
"Nor spare to agonize an aching breast,
"By sultry suns, and banishment oppressed;
"Oh! that these heavy hours would swiftly fly,
"And lead a happier fate, and milder sky.
"Believe me Dearest that my doom severe,
"Obtains from heavenly eyes the frequent tear;
"And where the spirits of these groves attend,

"The pitying drops in pearly showers descend;
"As oft in sleep they mark my outstretched arms,
"That clasp in blissful dreams thy fancied charms,
"Play through the air, and fold in fond embrace,
"Impassive matter, and etherial space.
"Soft and delightful to my senses blows,
"The breeze that south-ward wafts *Himala's* snows,
"And rich impregnated with gums divine,
"Exuding fragrant from the shattered pine,
"Diffuses sweets to all, but most to me.
"Has it not touched, does it not breathe of thee?
"What are my tasks: to speed the lagging night,
"And urge impatiently the rising light;
"The light returned, I sicken at the ray,
"And shun as eagerly the shining day:
"Vain are my labors in this lonely state,
"But fate proscribes, and we must bow to fate.
"Let then my firmness save thee from despair,
"Who trust myself, nor sink beneath my care.
"Trust to futurity, for still we view;
"The always wretched, always blest are few;
"Life like a wheel's revolving orb turns round;
"Now whirled in air, now dragged along the ground.

"When from his serpent couch that swims the deep,
"*Sarangí* rises from celestial sleep;
"When four more months unmarked have run their course;
"To us all gloom; the curse has lost its force:
"The grief from separation born expires,
"And Autumn's nights reward our chaste desires.
"Once more I view thee as mine eyes unclose,
"Laid by my side, and lulled by soft repose;
"And now I mark thee startle from thy sleep,
"Loose thy enfolding arms, and wake to weep;
"My anxious love long vainly seeks reply;
"Till, as the smile relumes that lucid eye,
"Thy arch avowal owns, that jealous fear,
"Affrighted slumber, and aroused the tear.
"While thus, Oh Goddess, with the dark black eyes,
"My fond assurance confidence supplies;
"Let not the tales that idle tatlers bear,
"Subvert thy faith, nor teach thee to despair;
"True love no time nor distance can destroy,
"And independant of all present joy,
"It grows in absence
"Some dear memorials, some loved lines excite."
Such, vast Dispenser of the dews of heaven,
Such is my suit, and such thy promise given;

Fearless upon thy friendship I rely,
Nor ask that promise, nor expect reply;
To thee the thirsty *Chatacas* complain:
Thy only answer is the falling rain;
And still such answer from the God proceeds,
Who grant our wishes, not in words, but deeds.
Thy task performed, consoled the mourner's mind;
Haste thy return these solitudes to find;
Soar from the mountain, whose exalted brow,
The horns of SIVA'S bull majestic plough,
And hither speeding, to my sorrowing heart,
Shrunk like the bud at dawn, relief impart.
With welcome news my woes tumultuous still,
And all my wishes tenderly fulfil.
Then to whatever scenes invite thy way,
Waft thy rich stores, and grateful glooms convey;
And ne'er may destiny like mine divide,
Thy brilliant spouse, the lightning, from thy side."
This said he ceased: the messenger of air,
Conveyed to Alaca his wild despair;
The God of wealth relenting learnt his state,
And swift curtailed the limit of his fate;
Removed the curse, restored him to his wife,
And blest with ceaseless joy their everlasting life.

THE END.

KUMAR SHAMBHAVAM

OR

THE BIRTH OF WAR-GOD.

[*TRANSLATED INTO ENGLISH*]

A POEM BY

KALIDASA.

—:0:—

PUBLISHED BY

THE SOCIETY FOR THE RESUSCITATION
OF INDIAN LITERATURE.

CALCUTTA:

PRINTED BY H. C. DASS, ELYSIUM PRESS,
Kashi Ghose's Lane, Beadon Street.

1901.

KUMARA SAMBHAVAM.

CANTO I.

There is in the Northern Quarter, the great king of mountains the Himalnya animated by deity, standing as the measuring rod of the earth and having entered the eastern and western seas.

Having turned him into a calf and the mount Meru standing as the milker competent for milking all the mountains caused the earth to milk out glittering jewels and great herbs instructed by Prithu.

It was the source of endless jewels. The snow did not become the destroyer of its beauty. For one fault becomes lost in a multitude of virtues as the stain on the lunar disc becomes lost in the rays of the moon.

It bears on its peak red mineralledness inducing the coquetry and decorations of Apsaras under a mistaken idea of its being evening and by which divisions of clouds were tinged of a red hue. When troubled by rains the Siddhas, after having previously sought the shade on the lower peaks of clouds moving up to the middle part of the mountain, betake themselves to its sunny summits.

In this mountain the hunters track the way of the maned lions by whom elephants had been killed by means of pearls dropped from the concavity of of their claws even without seeing their foot-steps whose bloody stains had been washed off by the melting down of the snow.

In this mountain the barks of the *Bhurja*-tree with characters written on them with red mineral fluid like the red marks on the elephant's trunk become a useful instrument of Vidyadhara fairies in the way of amatory correspondence.

This mountain, filling the hollow parts of rattling bamboos with the wind rising from the mouths of caves, wishes to obtain as it were the position of the supplier of musical tunes of the Kinnaras about to sing high.

In this mountain the scent, by the issue of milk of Sarala trees rubbed against by elephants for assuaging the itching of their temples, perfumes the peaks.

This mountain protects from the sun the darkness adhering to its caves afraid as it were of the day for great persons consider inferior persons taking refuge as their own proteges.

The chamari deer make significant his tittle "king of mountains" by the fan of their hair and handsome by the waving of their tails fair as moonlight.

The air of this mountain, charged with particles of the water-fall of the Ganges by which Devadaru is shaken and by which the peacock's feathers used by the hunters as girdles are agitated, is enjoyed by hunters by whom the deer are sought.

The sun revolving below causes to open or flourish by rays shooting upward the lotuses growing in the lakes over this mountain the residue of which had been plucked by the hands of the seven Rishis.

Observing the productiveness of sacrificial requisites as also its strength capable of supporting the earth the lord of creation himself conferred on it the kingdom of mountains to which were allotted shares in sacrifices.

Himalaya, the friend of Meru, understanding the limits of authority, married for the perpetuation of his family, by the prescribed ceremonial Mena the mental daughter of the Pitris equal to himself and reverenced even by the Munis.

She gave birth to Mainaka who was to marry (afterwards) a serpent damsel and who had formed a friendly tie with the ocean though Vitra's foe Indra the clipper of wings was angry unconscious of the pain of wounds by the thunder-bolt.

On account of her father Daksha insulting her husband the former wife of Bhava, the chaste Sati, having given up her body by means of Yoga, betook herself to the wife of the mountain for a fresh birth.

That blessed Sati was begotten by the king of mountains on her Menaka intent on holy devotion and undefiled by reason of entire application to sacred observances as success is produced in morals by virtue of enterprise.

Her birth-day, on which all the quarters were clear with the wind clear of dust and a shower of flowers following the blowing of konches, came to pass for the comfort of embodied persons or organic living creatures, moveable or immoveable.

The mother, by means of her daughter resplendent with a halo of light, shone as lands by the side of Mount Vidura shining by means of jewel ribs springing up from the roaring of fresh clouds.

Having received birth she grew up in handsome limbs like the lunar line with other increments of the moon contained in the moon-light itself.

By the patronymic Parvati derived from the mountain, her father, her relations called her who was dear to them. Being forbidden by the mother to practise austerities by means of the words "U má" *oh dont* the hand-some faced girl afterwards got the additional name Umâ.

The eye of the mountain, though having a son in that child, did not get satiety as in mango blossoms of the spring with endless flowers a collection of black bees has great attachment.

As a lamp by a very luminous flame, as the way of heaven by the three-coursed Mandakini, as a scholar by refined or gramatically rectified speech so he was by her, both purified and adored.

With altars of Mandakini's sand, with balls, with artificial pet sons *i.e.* dolls she often played. Being in the midst of her maids a taste for sports grew up as it were in childhood.

As rows of swans come to the Ganges in the autumn, as its own light comes at night to the great orb, so on her, of stable education at the time of education all the intellectual acquisitions of a former existence came.

She adorned with unartificial ornament got into the age following infancy *i.e.* youth, the instrument of hilarity without what is called intoxicating liquor and the weapon of Káma without flowers.

Her body, symmetrically developed by fresh youth, became handsome in all parts like a painting touched up by a fresh brush.

By the lustre of the raised toe and nail and from setting the feet her two feet, emitting as it were redness, assumed the splendour of the land lotus moving about.

With the body somewhat stooping in gait affected by sportive gestures she was instructed by swans coveting instruction in turn and desirous of receiving the beautiful sound of anklets.

Having a waist like the middle of an altar the

young lady held three beautiful streaks placed in a ladder.

This is my inference that her two arms, more tender than the *Sirisha* flower, though worsted by Kamadeva whose symbal was a fish, were like cords for encircling the neck of Hara.

The unstable goddess of Fortune and beauty when got to the moon does not enjoy the excellences of the lotus [which is supposed to close at night] and again when she gets to the lotus she does not obtain lunar splendour. But getting to Uma's face she received the two fold delight both of the moon and the lotus. If a flower could have been contained in a fresh leaf, if a pearl could have been in a transparent coral then it might have imitated her fair smile beautified with red lips.

To her speaking with a voice distilling nectar even a *kokila*, nurtured by strange birds, appears hoarse-sounding to the hearer like a discordant instrument being struck.

The unstable look, not different from a blue lotus affected by a strong breeze, was received by her, the large-eyed, from female deer or was it received from her by the female deer.

Seeing the beauty of her two long-curved eye-brows as if produced by a pencil with black paint and expert in action Kamadeva gave up pride of beauty for his own bow.

If in the mind of the irrational animals there were or could be a feeling of shame then doubtless the Chamari deer, seeing the collection of hair of the daughter of the mountain king, would make slack their fondness for hair.

By the whole collection of examplar substances, each in its own respective place, having been placed assiduously by the creator of the universe she was made as if from a desire on the part of the creator of seeing beauty concentrated in one place.

Narada, rambling at pleasure, having seen that damsel near her father, declared that she would be the one wife, possessing half the body, by love, of Siva.

Though her age was mature yet the father remained averse from the desire of having any other bride-groom than Siva for his daughter, for excepting fire other heats do not deserve the ghee consecrated by Mantras.

The mountain was not able to make or ask the God Siva himself not suing, to receive his daughter for fear of the request failing. A noble person takes to indifference even in a wished-for object.

From the very time when in her former birth the fine-teethed damsel gave up her body because of Daksha's anger, the lord of brutes Siva, forsaking all attachments, remained unmarried.

The skin-clothed Siva, of a restrained spirit, dwelt for ascetic meditation, on a certain peak of the Himalaya mountain wherein the Devadaru trees were washed by the streams of the Ganga and where the musk-scented Kinnaras sang.

Siva's followers, having Nameru flowers in their vests, clothed in the bark of the Bhurja, tender to the feet, ornamented with red arsenic, sat on the surface of rocks abounding in fragrant resin.

The humped bull, proudly bellowing but with an agreeable voice and bruising by the points of his hoofs solid rocks of snow seen with difficulty by the terrified Gavaya deer and unable to endure the lion's roar, bellowed.

The eight-formed Siva, having there set up a fire lighted by sacrificial wood, another of his own forms, himself the dispenser of the fruits of asceticism, practised asceticism actuated by some desire which none could guess.

Having worshipped the price-less who was worshipped of the dwellers of heaven with offerings the lord of mountains directed his devoted daughter accompanied by her maids to serve him.

Siva permitted her to serve him though her attractions were calculated to be an impediment to mental abstraction. They alone are firm whose minds are not perturbed on there being a cause of perturbation.

The fine-haired damsel Parvati, plucking flowers for offering, expert in cleaning the altar, and bringing waters for the daily rites and kusa grass, worshipped him, her labor alleviated by the rays of the moon on Siva's head.

CANTO II.

Oppressed by the Asura Tara, the dwellers of heaven, with Indra at their head, went to the residence of Brahma.

Brahma manifested himself to them the beauty of whose faces had faded like the sun appearing in the morning over lakes whose lotuses were closed.

They all, having bowed, addressed the creator of all who had heads on four sides, the lord of speech, with significant words.

"Salutation to thee, three-formed, existing as one spirit before creation but afterwards betaking to distinctive forms for the separation of three qualities Sattwa, Rajas and Tamas.

O thou uncreate, the seed sown by thee in the midst of waters is not fruitless for therein is produced the universe, moveable and immoveable. Thou, its cause, art sung.

Manifesting thy glory by three forms thou alone holdest the causeship of destruction, conservation and creation. Male and female are but parts of thy body who wert divided in two forms by desire of creation. They themselves are held as parents of the creation.

Of thee whose night and day are divided by the

measure of thy own time, sleeping and walking are but the destruction and creation of all creatures.

Thou art the cause of the universe, thyself causeless——thou the end of the universe theyself endless——thou the beginning of the universe, thyself without beginning——thou the lord of the universe, thyself lordless.

Thou knowest thyself by thy own act, thou createst thy form in thyself by thy own act, dost thou absorb thyself in thyself.

Thou art liquid, thou also solid hard, thou art gross, thou also subtle, thou art light and thou art heavy; thou art also perfectly developed and thou undeveloped, according to thy own desire in the atomic and other forms at thy command.

Of those sentences whose first syllable is *Om*, whose pronounciation is by the three accents, whose ordinance is sacrifice and whose ritualistic fruit is heaven thou art the cause.

They call thee Prakriti or nature engaging in the act of creation for the purposes of *Purusha* or soul. They know theyself also to be the *Puruska* or soul, sitting apart and looking on Prakriti.

Thou art father even of the fathers, God even of Gods. Thou art superior even of superiors, creater even of Prajapatis.

Thyself art even the sacrificial offering ghee, also the sacrifice, the object enjoyed and the enjoyer—the everlasting. Thou art the object of knowledge and also the knower, the meditator and the supreme object of meditation "

Having heard these laudatory expressions from them, true and agreeable the creator, being inclined to grace the Gods, replied

Uttered by the four mouths of that primeval poet the four fold utterance of sounds was successful

" O ye great powers, welcome to you who having by your authority held your own rights have at once taken possession by your long arms

What is this? Why your faces do not possess as before your own light like stars whose light has been enfeebled by frost

By the extinction of the flame the thunderbolt of the destroyer of Vitra, not emitting the divine weapon, appears contracted in the corners

Irresistable by the enemy the noose in the hand of Varuna has betaken to the miserable plight of a serpent bereft of its energy by incantations

Kuvera's arm, destitute of its club, like a tree whose branches have broken down, declares as it were his defeat like a javelin sticking in his heart Yama also marking the ground by his staff, its spendour gone to ruin, imparts the smallness of an exinguished fire brand to this his staff though at one time never failing

Why these Adityas, cold by the destruction of their fiery energy like paintings, have got to the condition of being gazed upon at pleasure,

From the revolving instability of the winds their stoppage of onward velocity is inferred like the stoppage of a stream of water from the incursion of an opposite stream.

The heads of the Rudras too having the Innar curves pendent on the downcast crests of clotted hair are declaring the loss of hunkara.

Having once gained place, have you been made to turn back by stronger enemies as in jurisprudence, eithics, grammar &c a general rule or law is made to submit to special legislation or exception.

O my sons, what do you all so earnestly ask for from myself having come in a body? In me is the office of the creation of the worlds and in you is placed the office of their preservation.

Indra, with his thousand eyes beautiful like the lotus shaken by the gentle breeze, moved Vrihaspati, the preceptor of Gods.

Vrihaspati, the lord of speech, who though only two-eyed was wiser than the thousand and two-eyed Indra, with palms joined said this to the lotus-seated Brahma.

"True what you say, our rights have been overturned by enemies. Yourself inhering in every person how O Lord, thou knowest it not.

Elated with the boon obtained from you the great Asura, by name Taraka, has got up like a comet for the oppression of the worlds.

The sun spreads only so much heat in his town

by which alone the opening of the lotus in his tank is accomplished.

The moon serves him always with all his digits. He does not take only that line which has become the crest jem of Hara or Siva.

The wind, desisting from its course in his garden from fear of the consequences of theft or blowing off of any flowers, does not blow more than the air excited by the fan by his side.

The six seasons having given up attendance in gradation serve him each in its turn like gardeners bent on collecting flowers.

The lord of rivers with great labour watches jewels fit for presents within the waters until maturity.

The serpents with Vasuki as their leader, with crest jems glittering on their hoods, having got at night the state of fixed lamps serve him around.

Indra also, looking for acts of grace from him, propitiates him with the ornaments of the desire-fulfilling tree presented by means of ambassadors.

Though he is thus served yet he opposes the three worlds for the wicked can only be moderated by injuries in return not by benefits.

The trees of Indra's Nandana gardens whose leaves were gently plucked by the hands of the celestial women are being felled by him.

He is fanned when asleep by chouries exciting wind only like breaths, showering drops of tears of captive goddesses.

Having plucked off peaks of Meru beaten by the troops of the sun's horses hills for amusement have been formed by him in his own mansions.

Of Mandakini the waters soiled by the temporal juice of the quarters are the only residuum; of the golden lotuses their produce his tanks are now the only repository.

Pleasure on surveying the worlds is not felt by the gods, the way of their chariots having become waste from fear of his incursion.

The enchanter snatches away the ghee afforded by priests in sacrifices that are held. We see it in our very sight from fire's mouth.

The great Uchchaisrava of Indra, that jewel of a horse, has been siezed by him like the glory acquired from a long time set in Indra's person.

All our measures against the murderous Asura have been baffled in their effects like powerful medicines in a malignant congestive fever.

Our hope of victory by Hari's quoit, its lustre rising by the re-action of the stroke, lies as a breast plate fixed to his neck.

His elephants by which the Airavata (cloud-elephant) was defeated now lie in clouds swollen with abundant water and repeat strokes on the surface.

O Lord, we desire to create a General for his destruction as persons desirous of emancipation seek, for the cessation of the world, the righteousness which cuts assunder the bondage of works, having placed in front which defender of the divine troops the cutter of mountains, Indra, shall bring back from the enemy the Fortune of victory like a captive."

On the termination of that speech the self-existent Brahma made a speech which excelled by its felicitousness the rain which succeeds thunder.

"This your desire shall be accomplished. Have a little patience. But in the matter of this General I shall not engage personally in the business of his creation.

From myself that demon has become possessed of Fortune and therefore from myself he ought not to have destruction again. Even one should not cut off himself a poisonous tree after having reared it.

This itself was asked by him of yore and it was promised by me. For by means of a boon his ascetic meditation which was able to consume the world was destroyed by me.

Who can withstand him engaged in war himself a war-like person except a portion of Siva's substance?

That god is the supreme luminary, beyond the quality of Tamas. He is not comprehensible in his dignity and greatness by me or by Vishnu.

Do you, that seek a remedy, labour to attract the mind of Sambhu absorbed in ascetic contemplation by the beauty of Uma like iron by a magnet.

The two alone are able to bear the energy of us

two, Sambhu's and mine. Either she, Uma to bear Sambhu's or his watery form to bear mine.

Having obtained your General from black-necked Siva he shall liberate the branded locks of the captive Goddesses by the amplitude of his energy or power."

Having thus addressed the gods the cause of the universe Brahma vanished. The gods too, fixed in mind about what they should do, went to heaven.

Having fixed on Kamdeva as the proper agent the chastiser of the demon Paka Indra remembered him with a mind doubly swift from his haste in the accomplishment of the object.

The flower-bowed Kamdeva, whose weapon the mango-blossom was deposited in the hands of his companion the spring, having attached his bow the beautiful extremeties of which were set with eye-brow creepers of handsome female,to his neck marked by the bracelet of his wife Rati, attended on him.

——:o:——

CANTO III.

HAVING left the gods thousand eyes of Indra fell simultaneously on Kamadeva because of its dependance on an object; the regard of masters is generally unstable in their dependants.

Being allowed room near the throne by Vasava and having acknowledged his master's grace by bowing his head he began to speak thus secretly to him.

"O thou that knowest the excellences of all men, command us what thou wouldst to be done in these worlds. I wish thy favour excited by thy remembrance of me be extended into a command.

By what person ambitious of dignity by means of excessively long asceticisms thy jealousy has been begotten? For he shall soon become subject to the influence of this my bow to which the arrow is set.

Let him, who from fear of repeated existence but against thy will has betaken to the way of emancipation, remain long bound by glances of women with amorous movements of the eye-brows.

Say, the wealth and virtue of which thy foe though taught morals by Sukra himself shall the agent of infused morality injure like rapid currents the two shores of a river.

Say what female austerely following out her bow of having one husband only but because of her beauty entered into thy unstable mind thou desirest to have released from modesty and of her own accord taking hold of thee with her arm around thy neck?

Be propitous O hero, let thy thunder-bolt rest. By means of my arrows any foe of the gods whoever he be, the power of his arm being rendered futile, shall fear even women with their under lips swelling with rage.

By thy grace though I am armed only with

flowers, having got only one helper in the spring I shall make a failure of patience even of Hara who has the pinaka bow in hand; what are other bowmen in comparison."

Having taken down his foot from his thigh and honouring the footstool by resting on it Indra thus spoke to Kama who had asserted his power in the designed object that is of attracting the heart of Siva.

"Oh friend, all this is accomplished in thee; both are my weapons the thunder-bolt and yourself. The thunder-bolt is ineffectual in those who are powerful by force of asceticism, but you as a weapon can both go on all sides and are also affective.

I know thy strength. I shall employ thee equal to myself in a heavy work. Having observed his habit of sustaining the earth the chief of serpents is appointed by Krishna for holding his body.

By thee declaring the course of arrow to reach Siva whose mark is a bull our work is almost accomplished already. Understand this itself is the desired object of Gods enjoying shares in sacrifices but now having enemies.

These gods wish for a General begotten of Siva's energy for their victory. Siva too can be managed only by the cast of thy one arrow for he, the repository of the members of mantras, being now fixed in spirit in his own essence.

By the direction of her father the daughter of the

king of mountains is serving Siva practicing asceticism on a high land. This has been heard by me from the mouth of Apsaras for that class are my emissaries. Therefore go for the accomplishment of this business of the gods. This object to be encompassed by another cause that is the presence of Parvati, requires thee as its ultimate cause as the seed and the sprout requires water before production.

Thine is the use of the weapons in that means for the victory of the gods for thou art the successful agent. Even a work of no note which requires one peculiar talent is for the glory of men.

These gods are the petitioners, the business is of the three worlds, and the work to be done by thy bow is not very hurtful. Oh thou art of a wonderful and enviable power.

The spring too, Oh destroyer of the spirit, from his companionship with you though not spoken to is thy helper. Charge the wind saying become the exciter of fire.

Saying "so be it" Kama having received his master's command as a holy residuum went away. Indra touched his body by his hand rendered rough by driving the Airavat.

Followed by the spring his dear friend and by his wife Rati and determined to accomplish the requested business even at the loss of his body Kama went with fear to the hermitage of Siva in the Himalaya.

Having assumed his own form the source of pride unto Kama, the spring, hostile to fixed austere contemplation of the ascetic Munis, appeared in that forest.

The sun being bent on going unseasonably to the quarter in the keeping of Kuvera, the North the Southern quarter, by its face, discharged air like a sigh of sorrow.

The Asoka tree produced at once flowers with leaves commencing from the trunk itself and did not wait for a stroke of the feet of females sounding with anklets.

The spring set black bees, the characters as it were of Kama's name, on arrow-like fresh mango blossoms with young leaves produced at once as feathers getting completion.

Notwithstanding the excellence of colour the Karnikara flower, distresed, offended the mind by its unscentedness. The inclination of the Creator of the universe becomes generally averse to the collection of all virtues in one subject.

The excessively red Palasa flowers, curved like a young moon because of being unblown, appeared like wounds from nails just inflicted on the forest sites coming together with the spring.

The beauty of the spring having put forth at the outset the Tilaka flower as a mark of beauty variegated by adhering black bees as a black paint, adorned by the orient sun as a red tincture and with young mango blossoms for her lips.

Being obstructed in their view by particles of dust of the flower stalk of Piyala trees the deer, buoyant with hilarity, ranged about against the winds over the forest plains resounding with the fall of old leaves.

The sounds which the male Kokila, with the neck red from the taste of the mango sprouts, gave out sweetly became the speech of Kama able to counteract the sensitiveness of virtuous women.

The rise of perspiration of Kinnara women, with clear nether lips and the color of the face slightly yellowish because of the decline of cold, made a footing on the painted writings of the body.

On seeing the untimely rise of spring the ascetics dwelling in Siva's forest became with difficulty controllers of their minds and prevented with labor their perterbation.

Madana, with his flower-bow stringed and Rati for his companion, having reached that region, both orders of creatures indicated by their acts a state pervaded by the sentiment of attachment having reached its maximum. In one flower vessel the black-bee drank honey following his own beloved mate. The black deer stratched by his born the female deer, her eyse closed by his touch.

The female elephant gave out of love to the male elephant a mouthful of warte scented with the lotus dust. The Chakrabaka, named after the part of a carriage *viz.*, wheel, treated his wife with a lotus stalk half-devoured.

In the intervals of singing the Kinnara kissed his wife's face the painting on which was a little washed off by drops of perspiration and bedecked by eyes rolling a little by the effect of liquors.

Even the trees received, from their wives the creepers, having large clusters of flowers and beautified with resplendant young red leaves as their lips, the entwining embrace of their bending branch-arms.

Though hearing the songs of Apsaras at that time Siva became bent on spiritual contemplation for obstructions can never interrupt the fixed devotion of those who can keep under control their minds.

Going to the door of the creeper-house Nandi, with a golden rod placed in his left hand, directed by the sign of the fore-finger placed on the mouth, Siva's troops not to disturb.

By Nandi's command the whole forest, with trees unshaken, black bees still, the birds silent and the deer stopped ranging, remained like an effort transferred to painting *i.e.* like a landscape.

Avoiding the range of his sight like a place with Venus in front on setting out on a journey Kama entered by sides the place of meditation of Siva covered by the branches of Nameru trees.

He, whose body was on the verge of destruction, saw the self-controlled three-eyed Siva sitting on an altar of Devadaru tree with a tiger-skin laid over it.

He was sitting in the *Virasana* posture with the fore half of his body still, perpendicular and large, with both shoulders bent and because of the two hands being placed with the concave of the palms upward like a full blown lotus in the bosom.

His clotted hair was tied up with snakes; double strings of rosaries were fixed to his ears and he wore a hide of black deer darkened still more by the reflection of his black throat.

He had three eyes almost closed in meditation, not frowning, untwinkling, looking downward and observing the nose.

He was sitting like a cloud without an effort of rain, like a reservoir of waters in which there was no wave upheaving from the stoppage of inward vital airs, like an unshaken flame in a place where there is no wind.

By means of the rays of light getting a way through the third eye in the cranium and issuing from the crown of the head was obscured the beauty, more tender than the fibres of the lotus stalk, of the crescent on Siva's head.

Having fixed in the heart the mind controlled by meditation restricted from action through nine doors *i.e.* having no communication with external world he was beholding the spirit in himself whom persons conversant with knowledge subjective know.

Seeing from a short distance the three eyed Siva in that state beyond the ken of thought Kama, his head trembling through fear, did not perceive that the bow and arrow dropped from his own hand.

As if restoring his power which was on the verge of destruction by the beauty of her body there appeared the daughter the king of mountains followed by two forest-goddesses.

She was carrying ornaments of spring flowers which by means of Asoka flower left in the shade the ruby, wherein the Karnikar flowers had appropriated the splendour of gold and in which the Sindhuvara had become like a collection of pearls.

Wearing an orient-red garment she was stooping a little by the weight of her rising breast like a walking creeper with leaves bent down by clusters of flowers.

With eyes unstable from fear she was warding off every moment by a toy lotus a black bee, whose thirst was excited by her perfumed sweet breath, flying near her nether lip red as *Vimb*.

Seeing her unblemished in all her limbs and more handsome than Rati the flower-bannered Kama again expected the success of his undertaking in the self-restrained spear-holder Siva.

Uma too approached the site of the door of her future husband Sambhu. He was absorbed in delight by seeing within by meditation the chief light styled supreme spirit.

The lord, whose site was with difficulty held below by the extremeties of the hood of the king of serpents, having gradually set the vital airs at liberty, slackened the hard meditative posture in which he had sat.

Having bowed down Nandi announced to him that the daughter of the mountain had come for doing service and admitted her whose admission was allowed by a mere sign of the eye-brow.

The collection of spring flowers plucked by her own hands mixed with parts of stalks were scattered by her two companions over the feet of Siva.

Uma too, dropping the fresh Karnikara flower which was resplendent amid her dark locks, made a bow with her head whereof leaves dropped from the ear by the very act of bowing to Siva whose emblem was a bull.

Siva's benediction on Uma's bowing down before him was "obtain a husband not having another wife." She was indeed told a truth by Siva. The sayings of great personages never cherish an unreal signification.

Kama, watching the fit time for his arrow, desirous of entering like a grasshopper the mouth of the fire, fixing his aim at Hara in the presence of Uma, touched the bow string.

Gouri then offered to the mountain dweller Siva, by a hand red as copper, a wreath of the seeds of the lotus of the river Mandakini dried by the rays of the sun.

As soon as out of the respect to the offerer the three-eyed Siva was about to accept the wreath the flower-bannered applied a never-failing arrow by name Fascination to his bow.

His firmness a little lost like the ocean at the commencement of the moon's rise fixed his three eyes on the face of Uma with lips like the fruit vimb.

Betraying sentiment by her limbs resplendent like a young Kadamva the daughter of the mountain stood bending and flushing with a very handsome face, the eyes cast down through bashfulness.

Having again strongly restrained the distraction of his senses by virtue of his self-control and desiring to discover the cause of the perturbation of his mind he cast his sight at the corners of the four quarters.

Siva saw Kama with his fist clenched at the corner of the right eye, his shoulder bent, his left leg contracted and his handsome bow stretched circularly attempting to strike.

From the third eye of him increased in rage at the attack against his devotion and having a face difficult to look at owing to the contraction of his brows a flaming fire suddenly issued out.

"O lord, refrain, refrain thy anger." While these words of the gods were passing in the sky that ire, produced from Siva's eyes, turned Kama into a residuum of ashes.

The operation of the senses being stopped by a delusion produced by a sharp discomfiture and gnorant of her husband's destruction Rati was benefitted as it were, by being for a moment stunned.

Having quickly destroyed him, the obstruction of asceticism as the thunder-bolt breaks a tree, the ascetic Siva, desiring to avoid the vicinity of women, vanished with his troops.

Considering that the desire of her father that she should be Siva's wife had become futile and with her handsome body becoming more bashful in the presence of two companions she went on with dejected face homeward.

Immediately having received by his two arms his pitiable daughter her eyes closed by fear of Rudra's rage like the celestial elephant, supporting the lotus adhering to his tusk the mountain became one that follows way wherever it might lead having his form enlarged by his haste.

——:o:——

CANTO IV.

The wife of Kama, being in a fainting feet and motionless, was restored to sense by Providenee willing to make her feel her new state of widow-hood which was intolerable to the feeling.

She made her two eyes which had opened at the end of her fit intent on observing things around her. She did not know that the darling object of those two never satiated eyes had become utterly lost to sight.

Saying "O thou lord of my life, art thou living?" and getting up she saw before her on the ground a human figure turned into ashes by the fire of Siva's rage. Again distracted, her bosom becoming of a brown hue by rolling on the ground and her hairs scattered she bewailed making the forest site as it were equally distressed with herself.

"This that thy body which was the sampler by its beautifulness of gay persons has fallen into such a state yet I am not not lacireted. Oh women are hard.

Having cast aside me whose life is dependent on thee, having in a moment broken through thy friendship where art thou fled like a collection of water with embankments broken down rushing out leaving behind the lotus whose life is dependent on itself.

Thou hast not ever done anything displeasing to me nor has anything adverse to thee been done by me. Why then is not thy sight granted without any cause to Rati who is bewailing thee.

Is it, oh Smara, that thou rememberest my binding thee with the waist band on names of some rival dropping from thy lips in unconscious moments or my beating thee with the ornament lotus by which thine eyes would be injured from the dropping pollen of the flower.

To please me thou wouldst say "thou dwellest in my heart." I perceive it now to be a pretext. If this were not a mere complementary saying how is it that thou art destitute of body and Rati is uninjured.

I shall on my part take to thy way who art a new sojourner in the other world. But this world is defrauded by fate for happineess of embodied beings is indeed dependent on thee.

The roads of the city being veiled by the darkness of the night who, oh dear, except thee is able to make the females distracted by the roar of clouds to reach the residence of their friends.

Thou being non-existent the intoxication of wine turning the eyes red and causing words to slip at every step is now but a mere farce on the part of jolly women.

Oh thou bodyless, having learnt that his dear friend's body is turned into a mere word the moon whose rise will now be fruitless on the dark fortnight passing away will give up his waning with regret.

Say whose arrow shall the fresh mango blossoms with beautiful yellow and red petiole brought to notice by the melodious voice of the male Kokila become.

This row of black bees employed many times by thee to do duty as a bow string now condoles with me heavily afflicted by means of humming in piteous tones.

O thou versed in love, this ornament of the flowers of season set by thee on my limbs is still held but that handsome body of thine is not seen.

Before the decoration (dying) of my left foot was finished thou wert called away by the cruel God. Do thou make my left foot now red.

By voluntarily burning myself as a Sati I will again become a refugee in your bosom while, O dear, you are not coveted in heaven by the artful females of the Gods.

Even though I may follow thee my lasting shame will be that I have lived one moment after thee.

Thyself being separated from me in the other world how could I finish the last decoration ? Thou hast incurred an unexpected condition at once with thy body and thy life.

I remember thy smiling discourse with the spring and the glance in the corner of thy eye whilst thou wert making thy arrow straight and the bow was being attached to thy arrow.

Where is thy bosom friend the spring who had prepared thy bow with flowers ; he has not been made to incur by the fierce holder of pinaka the condition."

Having been wounded in his heart by those bewailing expressions of Rati as it were by arrows besmeared with poison the spring appeared before her to condole with her in her affliction.

Seeing him she cried exceedingly and pressing her breasts struck her chest for sorrow increases before an intimate friend or relative.

Afflicted she addressed him thus " See, O Spring, what is the state of your friend. This heap of ashes variegated like a pigeon in small particles is scattered by the winds.

O Kama, grant now a sight of yourself. This spring wishes to see you. The love of men is indeed unstable in their wives but it is not certainly in their friend.

Was not the universe including gods and demons made by this thy friend to do the command of thy bow whose string was lotus stalk fibres and whose arrows were delicate flowers.

Thy friend is gone. He will not return like a amp struck out by the wind. I am like his wick. See me smoking by intolerable distress.

In the murder of Kama by fate leaving me is not a half-murder done? On the secure refuge-tree being broken down by an elephant the creeper must drop down.

Therefore do this service immediately to a friend. By applying fire make me reach the vicinity of my husband.

The moon-light goes with the moon, the lightning is dissolved with the cloud. That women go the way of their husbands is understood even by those of little sense.

Having painted my breasts by this auspicious heaps of ashes of my beloved husband's body as in bed of new leaves I shall place my body in the fire.

O excellent friend, in the flower-bed you have often been a companion to us both. Make now soon likewise my funeral pile being petitioned by my bowing with palms joined,

After that question set the fire to me by blowing the south wind. It is certainly known to thee how my husband Kama is not for one moment cheered without me.

Having done this, offer, to us two, one doubled palmful of water. Without dividing it in the other world thy friend will drink it with me.

O spring, in ceremonies for the other world, offer clusters of mango blossoms with tender leaves for thy friend for he is fond of them."

A voice from the sky tenderly addressed Rati thus determined in giving up her body as a first shower shows pity on the fish Saphari distressed by the drying up of the pond.

"O thou wife of the flower-armed, thy husband will not long remain unattainable to thee. Hear by what work he got into the condition of a moth in the flame of Siva's eye.

Prompted by his senses, the lord of creation Brahma felt a desire for her own daughter. Then having suppressed his mental perversion he cursed

Kama who in consequence thereof has experienced this.

When Siva shall marry Parvati being inclined to her by virtue of her asceticism then obtaining happiness he shall join Kama to his body.

Asked by Dharma Brahma spoke thus the word setting limit to the malediction against Kama. For the self restrained and clouds are productive causes both of lightning and of nectar.

O thou of beautiful face, preserve this body in which there will be a reunion with thy husband for the river whose waters have been drunk off by the sun at the close of summer is again joined by streams.

In this manner some creature of an invisible form prevented Rati's thought of bringing on death. And by faith in that voice the friend of the flower bannered the Spring comforted her by words well-composed.

Then thinned by sorrow the wife of Kama remained expecting the termination of her misfortune as the curve of the diurnal moon obscured by the fading of its rays expects the evening.

CANTO V.

Kama being burnt in her presence by Siva, Parvati, being baffled in her wishes, reproached her beauty in her mind for hadsomeness is only a desirable accomplishment as productive of graciousness in husbands.

She wished to render beauty fruitful by practising fixed devotion by means of asceticisms. How else can these two be obtained *viz.*, such love as she subsequently found in Siva and such a husband too?

Having heard of her daughter prepared for asceticism, whose mind was set on Siva, the lord of mountains, Mena, embracing her by the chest and dissuading her from the great vow fit only for a Muni, spoke to her.

Worship at home the deities desired by the mind. Where O child is asceticism and where is thy body? The tender Sirisha flower may endure the footsteps of the black bee but not of a bird.

Thus exhorting her daughter of firm purpose Mena was not able to restrain her from her undertaking. Who can oppose the mind resolutely set on its desired object or water inclining downwards?

At a certain time, she, fixed as she was by the mouth of a competent intimate maid, asked of her father permission to retire from home into the forests for ascetic devotion to last until the issue of its object.

Permitted by her revered father who was pleased with her suitable determination Gauri went to a peak full of peacocks, which was among the people afterwards called after her Gauri-peak.

Having cast aside her wreath of pearls by the waiving of whose string the sandal-paste had been wiped off she, fixed in her resolve, wore a waist coat of barks of trees twany like a young sun.

As her face had been lovely by her decorated hair so it became by her clotted hair, as a lotus becomes resplendent not only by rows of black bees, but also by contact with moss or weeds.

The votaress was tied with zone of grass which reddened the fair form it girdled round. Never before the Lady's waist had felt the ceaseless pain of such a rough belt.

Her hand, not employed in the decoration of her lower lip now giving up its red hue and not requiring hand to apply ornamenting lip salve and from the ball reddened by the painting of the bosom of which the fingers were bruised by contact with Kusa grass, was made by her a companion of the rosary.

She, who was troubled even by the flowers in her tresses dropped by her turning on a costly bed, now slept making an arm her pillow and sitting down on the bare ground.

Two things were deposited by her engaged in ascetic exercises with two parties with a view to take them back; one was lovely motion in tender creepers, the other was rolling look in the female deer.

Herself unsleeping she nourished the small trees with the liqtuid issue of her jar-breasts her first-born maternal affection for whom even Kartikeya would not be able to counteract.

Even the deer, nourished by grants of handfuls

of wild grain, had such confidence in her as that by their eyes she measured the eyes of her maids in front of herself.

Even the Munis went to see her, having gone through ablutions, made the fire offering and put on the garment of barks. In those who have grown up in religion age is not taken into account.

And that hermitage became sanctifying in which the injurious animals had given up their former noxiousness, in which guests were served by trees with their desired fruits and in which the sacred fire was collected in the new leaf huts.

When by the exercise of asceticism at first undertaken she considered the desired fruit unattainable then not reckoning the tenderness of her body she commenced to practise severe asceticism.

She, who got fatigued even by playing with dolls, entered into severe asceticism. Surely her body was made of golden lotus by nature both tender as lotus and strong as gold.

Having got into the midst of four blazing fires and having overcome the solar light dazzling to the eyes the fine-waisted damsel, smiling delightedly, used to gaze at the sun in summer looking at nothing else.

Her face, thus heated by the rays of the Sun, got the splendour of the lotus which opens when the sun shines. Only at the large eye corners a site was gradually obtained by blackness.

Rain and nectareous moon was her ordained sustenance, a livelihood not otherwise than that of a tree which lives on light, air and rain.

Excessively heated by a five-fold fire, one from the sky *i.e.* the sun and four others on her four sides from the burning fuel and having been washed with fresh waters *i.e.* the rain at the close of the summer she let off heat together with the heated earth.

The first drops of water, standing for a moment on the eye-lashes, striking the lower lip, then dashing on the swollen bosom and then dropping by sides, got after a long time to the navel.

The nights, with lightning looks, saw her sleeping on a rock, unhoused and in the midst of uninterrupted rain and storm, remaining as it were the witness of her great asceticism.

Remaining in the water and taking pity on the couple of Chakravakas seperated before her and crying to one another she passed the nights of Pous in which the winds were producing excessive frosts.

By a mouth lotus-scented at night and the lower lips quaking from cold and exhibiting the beauty of lotus leaf she made as it were a furnishing of lotus for the waters deprived of their supply of lotuses by showers of frost.

Living on leaves of trees dropped off themselves is of itself the highest degree of asceticism. But by her even that nourishment was refused.

Afflicting day and night by such vows her own

body tender as lotus fibres she greatly excelled the asceticism of ascetics acquired by bodies capable of enduring trouble.

Then a certain person, with clotted hair, clad in deer skin, holding a staff, bold in speech and shining as it were with Vedic light, entered the hermitage, the first stage of Brahmanical life endued as it were with a body.

With very respectful adoration the hospitable Parvati advanced to receive him. Even where there is equality the great persons become excessively attentive in acts of homage and civility.

Having accepted the adoration offered according to rule and rested a while he, looking at Uma with upright eyes, began to speak incoherently.

Are wood and Kusa grass for sacrificial acts easily obtainable and waters fit for thy ablution? Dost thou engage in asceticism in adaptation to thy own strength? Forsooth the body is the first requisite for religious works.

Are the clusters of creepers grown by waters supplied by thee thriving? They rise to equality with thy lower lip, which though long bereft of red-dying is still red.

Is thy mind at ease with the deer which seize from attachment the sacrificial grass in thy hands and which, O lotus-eyed, by their rolling eyes claim equality with thy eyes.

Men say, O Parvati, that a handsome appearance

does not tend to sin. That saying is true for thy virtue, O thou with large eyes, has got to the position of instructing regular Munis.

This mountain with his race was not so sanctified by the waters of the Ganges fallen from the sky smiling with the showered offering of the seven Rishis as by thine unstained acts.

Hereby virtue appears, more especially now to me, the most excellent of the three objects *viz.*, virtue, wealth and desire, since it is, O thou of excellent thoughts, served by thee of whose mind wealth and desire are no objects.

You ought not to consider me a stranger thus highly honoured by yourself since O thou that stoopest with thy body, the meeting of good persons is itself described by the wise as friendship contracted by the utterance of seven words.

From the very nature of a Brahmin being disposed to loquacity this person is desirous of asking something of you, so forbearing. O thou lady ascetic, if it be not a secret thou oughtest to answer me.

Your birth is in the race of the Primival Brahma. Your body is the concentration of the beauty of the three worlds. You have every enjoyment already and are youthful. Then what better fruit of asceticism can there be?

From some intolerable grievance there may possibly be such an ascetic disposition in high-minded ladies. But on reflection I see that such a case does not appear in you, O thou of a slender frame.

This thy frame is incapable of incurring grief or disregard. How, O thou with beautiful eye-brows, could there be any disrespect in thy father's house? There can be no stranger's attack on you. Who could extend his hand for taking the jem on a serpent's hood?

Why it is that in youth having cast away ornaments, barks of trees suitable for old age are worn by thee? Say, if the night, with the moon and stars shining, is intended for Aruna, the sun's charioteer.

If thou desirest heaven thy labor is uselesss for thy father's territories are divine sites. And if thou desire a bride-groom away with ascetic devotion for a jewel does not seek an acceptor. It is sought by the would-be recipient.

Your desire for a bridegroom is made known by a warm breath or sigh. But still my mind falls into doubt for no one appears worthy of your desire. How can there be a desired person who is unattainable?

Oh there is some stern youth desired by thee who disregards thy clotted hair hanging loosely on thy cheeks, long destitute of ear lotuses and twany like the extremeties of paddy.

What sentient man's mind is not afflicted who sees thee exceedingly emaciated by ascetic vows fit only for Munis with thy limbs sun-burnt like the unar carve by day ?

Thy beloved one is self-defrauded by his pride of beauty since he does not come within the sight of thy eye which has an agreeable glance with curved eye-lashes. O Gouri, thou hast been toiling for some time and there is the merit of my asceticism too collected during my primary stage. Therefore by the half of that merit recieve your desired boon of a bride-groom and I wish to know him well.

Thus addressed by the Brahmin penetrating into her inmost thought she was not able to declare her bridegroom's name. She looked, with averted eyes having the black paint defaced, upon her companion remaining at her side.

Her companion said to him :—" Hear, O Brahmacharin, for whom Uma has made her body a means of ascetic practice turning as it were a lotus leaf into a parasol.

Disregarding the highly rich Indra and others, the lords of the four quarters, this lady wishes, with high aspirations, to obtain for her husband the Pinaka-handed Siva who is not subject to personal attractions from the overthrow of Kama.

Turned back by his intolerable fury, the arrow of the flower-bowed Kama, whose body was destroyed, its points not reaching the enemy of the three cities, afflicted this lady with a deep stroke.

Thenceforward remaining love-stricken in her

father's house her curls have become grey by the sandal mark on the forehead'; the young lady never obtained any rest not even on the surface of rocks of solid snow.

On the acts of Siva commencing to be sung by means of words dropped from a sobbing throat this lady repeatedly caused the daughters of the king of Kinnaras, her companions in singing, to weep at the extremity of the forest.

Having for a moment closed her two eyes at night of which a third part was yet remaining she would suddenly awake speaking incoherently "O Nilkantha, where are you going?" and throwing her clasped arms on an imaginary neck.

Drawing a picture of the moon-crested Siva in her own hand she would in secret reprove him saying "Since you are by the wise called all-pervading how do you not know this person in a state of love to you?"

When after seeking she did not see any other means of getting the lord of universe, she, by the permission of her father, betook herself to the hermitage in our company for asceticism.

Fruits have appeared in these trees which had been grown by her and have witnessed her asceticism but her desire, having the moon-crested Siva for its object, appears as far from fulfillment as ever. I do not know when that desired but unattainable person will have pity on this our friend, looked on by companions with tears, emaciated by asceticism, like Indra taking pity on ploughed ground afflicted by drought?

Thus addressed manifestly in good will by Parvati's companion acquainted with her inmost purpose the stranger, whose signs of joy were not manifested, asked Uma thus:—" Dear lady, is this so? or is it a joke?"

Then depositing the wreath of crystal beds drawn inward with the fingers in the fore-parts of her hand the daughter of the mountain, her speech long suppressed, spoke in measured syllables with great difficulty.

''O thou superior adept in the Veda, as it has been heard by you, I am ambitious of getting up to high dignity. And this asceticism is but a miserable means of attaining it. But there is nothing to which a desire and hope will not resort through delusion.

The Brahmacharin said:—" Siva is known to me and you again are desirous of him. Considering him to delight in evil habits I cannot serve your purpose in such an evil choice,

O thou whose determination is set on a despicable object as Siva, how this thy hand, with the marriage string set on it, shall endure the very first encounter with Siva's hand braceletted with snakes.

Consider yourself if these two things befit each other, the bridal silk dress on which are pictures of the beatiful swan and Siva's skin-clothing showering drops of blood.

Even thy ill-wishing enemies cannot imagine such a misfortune of thine that the red-tinged steps of thy two feet set on clusters of flowers in a beautiful room will be on the cemetries with dead bodies scattered on them.

Say what can be more incongruous that Siva's embrace being easily attainable, on this thy bosom the site of yellow sandal wood the dusty ashes of funeral pyres will form a seat.

It is again a misfortune that great people seeing an old bull ridden by you, who when married, will be carried by a great elephant, will laugh and ridicule you.

By the desire of association with Siva two should be grieved for, namely, the luminous digit of the moon which is already on Siva's head and thou too equally luminous and each being the joy of the eye of this world.

His body is deformed with eyes ; his birth and race are unknown ; he must be extremely poor not having a rag to put on. O thou, with eyes like a deer, has he a single recommendation as bridegroom, namely the possession of beauty, wealth and dignity?

Divert your mind from such an evil desire ; where such a person so low and vile and where thou who art so happy and fortunate? There is great inequality between an impaling stick at the cemetry, for execution of felons and the holy sacrificial stake consecrated by the Vedic ritual.

The Brahmin having thus spoken against her wishes she manifested anger by the quaking of her nether lips and drawing obliquely her two eyes with red corners.

She spoke to him :—Forsooth thou dost not know Siva since thou speakest thus to me. The ignorant cannot understand the character of great men which is not the same as of the world and the motives of which are incomprehensible to them.

Good things are used by persons but on remedying some evil or by one desirous of wealth and dignity. Of what use are these things by which through hope the state of mind is disturbcd to Siva who is the refuge of the universe without any desire?

Being poor he is the source of all wealth. Roving about in cemetries he is the lord of the three worlds. Being terrific in appearance he is called Siva or felicitous. There are none that understand the essential nature of Siva.

Whether it glitters with ornaments or be endued with snakes, whether an elephant skin hangs on it or it be dressed in silk, whether it has a scull on it or the moon for its crest the body of him whose form is the universe cannot be determined.

Indra, riding on the elephant of the quarter with temporal juice distilling, touches with his crown the feet of Siva though a poor man riding a bull and makes his toe red with the pollen of full blown flowers of the celestial tree.

Even while desiring to find fault one thing has been well spoken with reference to the Lord whom the Vedas declare to be the cause even of the self-begotten Brahma. How can he be of a known origin ?

Now do away with the altercation. Let him be as has been heard by thee, so entirely and without exception. But my mind is fixed in love on him. One who acts from his own desires regards not what may be said against him.

O dear companion, this Brahmin, whose lips are quivering, is going to say something again. Don't allow him to speak for not only he who reviles a great person but he too who hears him is also a partaker of the sin.

Otherwise I shall go away from hence." Saying this the young lady was going away when Siva, whose emblem was the great bull, assuming his own form and smiling took hold of her. Seeing him, quaking, her body perspiring and taking a step the daughter of the king of mountains neither went nor stood still like a river stopped in its course by the obstruction of a mountain.

" O thou stooping in thy limbs, henceforward I am thy slave bought by asceticisms." On the moon-crested Siva saying this she immediately forgot the exhaustion produced by austerity for fatigue becomes refreshed by success.

CANTO VI.

GAURI secretly deputed her maid with a communication to Siva, the soul of the universe, saying, "The lord of the mountains is my giver, I cannot marry without his order or leave."

As the singing bird parched on the Mango branch does duty as a mouth of the tree, so the maid acted as Parvati's mouth.

Having promised "even so" and let go with difficulty Uma to her father the chastiser of Kama, called to mind the seven luminous Rishis.

Illumining the sky by their encircling lights those ascetics, having asceticism for their wealth, with Arundhuti in their company immediately arrived before the lord.

They had bathed in the streams of the etherial Ganges whose waves were throwing up the flowers of the celestial trees on the banks which were perumed with the temporal juice of the elephants of the quarters.

They wore sacrificial threads set with pearls, were clad in bark-garm ents set with gold, had rosaries of jewelled beads like desire fulfilling celestial trees and had retired from the world.

Driving his horses below and lowering his standard even the thousand-rayed sun paid obeisance to them.

At the general dissolution, they, taking hold of the earth which had been raised up, by the arms rested on the tusk of the great bear.

Because of their forming the remains of creation after Brahma sung by the archælogists they are called ancient creators.

Though enjoying the fruits of untainted asceticisms of a former birth they are still ascetics.

Being in the midst of them and her eyes cast on the feet of her husband Vasishtha, the chaste Arundhati shone much like the success of asceticism personally present.

The Lord Siva looked upon her and the Munis without distinction of dignity. That this is female and this is male is not to be regarded, the character of the good is to be honored. From seeing her Siva's desire for a wife became greater, for good wives are certainly the fundamental cause of righteous acts

For the sake of righteousness, Siva having been caused to form a regard for Parvati the mind of Kama, who was in fear for his previous transgression, again breathed in hope.

After worshipping the parent of the universe all those Munis, who could repeat all the Vedas and Vedangas with hair standing on end said.

Our prescribed study of the Veda, our offering in the fire according to rule, our practical asceticism have borne fruit to-day, since we have been made to become an object of the Spirit's mind thou having remembered and looked for us, an object which was beyond our expectation.

He is the highest of all successful persons in whose mind thou remainest, how much greater still he who remains in thy mind or in that of Brahma.

True it is we inhabit a higher station than both the sun and the moon; but today by thy kind remembrance of us we have attained a still higher place than they.

Being honoured by thee we think highly of ourselves. Thy regard of high persons in respect of his virtues begets general credit.

That delight of ours, O thou having three eyes, which is produced from thy thinking of us cannot be related to thee who art the indwelling spirit of all embodied persons.

Thou art seen visibly but we do not know thee in thy real presence. Be favourable. Relate thyself. Thou art not within the range of natural intellects.

Is this thy form the same by which thou createst the developed universe? Or is it that by which thou preservest it? or is it the portion which destroys it? which of the three is it?

Or rather, O god, let this our high desire remain

aside. But command us who have thus presented ourselves, being thought of by thee, what we shall do.

Then the Supreme lord Siva, increasing the feeble light, by the rays of his white teeth, of the moon in his crest, replied.

As it is known to you none of my efforts is for purpose of self. By eight forms becoming thus am I not known?

I am requested to beget a son by the gods oppressed by foes as clouds are asked by Chatakas oppressed by thirst.

Therefore I wish to get Parvati for the purpose of begetting a son as the sacrificer desires to have wood or flint for the production of fire.

On my behalf you are to ask the Himalaya for her, for matrimonial alliances formed by the intervention of the good do not tend to reverses.

Having been joined in alliance with him, lofty, having stability and bearing the weight of the earth know me also not to be defrauded.

You are teachers of morals and you do not require to be taught how the Himalaya is to be addressed for his daughter.

The noble Arundhuti is also fit to render good offices in this matter; generally in such affairs there is great dexterity in matron ladies.

Therefore proceed to Oshadhiprastha (herb-peak), the capital of the Himalaya, for the accomplishment of this business. I shall expect you at this cataract of the river Mahakoshi.

On his, the chief of ascetics, becoming inclined to marriage, the ascetics, sons of Brahma, gave up their shame for having wives.

Having assented by the utterance of Om the collection of ascetics departed. The lord Siva also got to the place first pointed out.

Having got up to the sky, dark as iron, those great Rishis too, as swift as meditation, came to Oshadhiprastha.

As if Alaka (the city of Kuvera) the seat of wealth and plenty were transplanted there. Or it was built to accomodate the excess of the heavenly dwellers.

It was surrounded by Ganga's streams with herbs glittering within the ramparts and with large jewelled stone walls handsome even in its fortifications.

There elephants were stronger than lions, the horses were of the breed of Vila, one of Indra's stud, the citizens were Yakshas and Kinnaras and the women were fairies.

There the sound of drums of houses whose tops were in contact with clouds was imagined to be but the echo of the cloud's roar but was distinguished as such by the tunes.

There the beauty of flags on houses, formed without the labour of the citizens, was secured by means of celestial trees themselves with wet clothes hanging to dry on their moving branches.

At night on drinking sites of crystal palaces the reflections of celestial luminaries get the position of decorative presents of honour.

Being shown the way in inclement weather by the light of glittering herbs the rambling women do not feel that it is dark.

The inhabitants of this city were ever youthful and never fell into decrepitude. There was no other lord of death than the flower-armed god of love and no loss of sensation save the sleep after sexual intercourse.

There young men sought to propitiate the anger of women only in which their brows were contracted, their lips quaked and they threatened them with their soft fingers.

Their pleasure-garden was the fragrant Gandha-madana in which the Vidyadhara ramblers used to sleep in the shade of the celestial Samantaka trees.

Having seen the capital of the Himalaya the heavenly ascetics considered their penances in quest of heaven as useless privations.

When they alighted quickly on the mountain's house, their clotted locks, as still as painted flames, attracted the notice of the porters below.

Alighting from the sky according to seniority that row of ascetics shone like a row of suns reflected in the water.

Taking offerings and bending the earth with his heavy foot steps the mountain advanced to meet them.

With lips ruddy like red mineral, tall, having large arms like the Devadaru tree and rock-chested by nature he was at once recognized as the Himálaya.

Having paid them honours according to rule and himself the shower he introduced them into the seraglio.

The seven Rishis being seated there on seats of reed, the lord of mountains, having also taken a seat, said.

Your unexpected appearance appears like a shower without the rise of clouds or like fruits whose blossoms had never appeared.

I consider myself, by your favour, like a fool turned wise, like iron turned into gold and as if ascended to heaven from the earth.

Henceforward for the purification of creatures I shall be sought. That which has been inhabited by the adorable is called a place of pilgrimage.

I know myself to be sanctified by two things, O excellent Brahmins, by the stream of the heavenly Ganga over my head and by the washing of your feet.

I consider my body as enjoying your favour in both forms, moving about in your service and as a mountain impressed by your feet.

Though extending to the extremities of the regions my limbs cannot contain the excessive delight produced by your condescending to honor me with a visit.

By the sight of you luminaries not only is the darkness lurking in my caves dispelled, but also the greater darkness which is within myself appertaining to the quality of Rajas.

You are desireless what can I do for you. I consider your advent here to be solely for my sanctification.

Still you ought to give me a command in some little matter for servants, in respect of their lords, are favoured by appointment to some service.

Here is myself, here is my wife and this is my daughter, the life of the family; say by which of us can any thing be done for you here. I do not say any thing about gold or silver because I regard them as no substance.

Himalaya, thus speaking by means of the echo resounding from the mouths of caverns, spoke like two persons to the same effect.

Then moved by the Rishis, Angiras, the foremost in matters of speech, replied to the mountain.

All that you have offered is in your power, but greater than all this is the loftiness of thy mind which is equal to thy summits.

It is fitting that they call thee the mount Himalaya Vishnu for thy bosom has become a receptacle, like that of Vishnu himself, of all creatures moveable and immoveable.

How could the serpent have held the earth, with hoods as tender as lotus fibres if thou hast not supported it from the bottom of the lower regions.

Thy glories and thy rivers, extending uninterrupted, untainted and unrestrained by the waves of the sea, purify the worlds because of their purity.

Even as Ganga is magnified by the foot of the Supreme one, Vishnu, from which the river was produced, so also by thee, of lofty summit, its second source.

The extension of Hari's glory upward, downward and horizontally curved was at a fixed time when he took the corresponding three steps and covered all space——but thine is everlasting——thou coveredest space without any commencement.

By thee holding a place among the eaters of sacrifices the eminent golden summit of Sumeru is rendered futile.

All hardness has been made over by thee to thy fixed form but this, thy body, by which you pay honor to the good, is lowly by devotion.

Then hear the purpose of our coming. We also share in the labour, O mountain king, since we carry to thee the message. He who holds, with the half moon, the high title of Ishwara endowed with the eight attributes, which is not shared by any other person, by whom this universe is held by his eight forms calculated to assist one another by their respective powers as a carriage is held on the road by horses, whom situated with the body the yogis seeks, whose site is free from the fear of revolving, he Sambhu, the observer of the world's doings, himself the giver of boons, asks for thy daughter through us.

Thou art fit to unite him as the sense with thy daughter as the word, for a daughter given to a good husband is not to be regretted by the father. Let all the creatures, fixed and moveable, turn Uma into their mother for the Lord Siva is the father of the universe.

Let the gods, having bowed to the blue necked, illumine her two feet with the light of their crest jems.

Uma is the bride, you are the giver, ourselves the petitioners for Siva and Sambhu is the bridegroom. Indeed this ceremonial is sufficient for the exaltation of thy race.

By means of alliance through thy daughter you become the father-in-law of the father of the universe who is a lauder of none, but is lauded, who is adored by all, but himself adores none.

The divine ascetic thus speaking Parvati, remaining by her father's side with the head downwards, was counting the petals of her lotus.

Although fully desirous the mountain looked up to the face of Mena for advice. In matters concerning daughters generally the heads of families follow the leading of wives.

Mena too assented to the desired business of her

husband. Chaste and devoted wives never oppose the wishes of their husband.

Having considered well the proposal and given a well-thought-out reply to the Rishi the mountain took hold of her daughter auspiciously and said—

"Come, O chlld, thou art destined an alms-giving to the soul of the universe. The sages are themselves the petitioners and the fruit of married life is obtained by me."

Having thus addressed his daughter the mountain spoke to the ascetics :—"Parvati bows to you all as the bride of the three-eyed Siva."

Having cheered the speech of the mountain which became important by the accomplishment of their desired object, they magnified Ambica by benedictions whose fruition was at hand.

Arundhati took her up in her arms whose two golden ear-rings dropped off by her eagerness to make a bow and blushing.

Arundhati also removed the grief of her mother whose face was full of tears at the prospect of parting with her daughter and who was overcome by her affection to her daughter by relating the virtues of the bride-groom who had no other consort before.

Having been asked by Siva's future relation for an auspicious wedding day the bark-clothed Munis fixed one after three days and went away.

Bidding good bye to Himalaya, meeting Siva

again and communicating to him the success of their business, they dismissed by him went up to the sky.

Impatiently anxious for the company of the mount's daughter, the lord of brutes, too, Siva passed three days with difficulty. Why would not love disturb other weak creatures, subject to the senses, since it touches even the master of his senses.

CANTO VII.

In the light fortnight and on the day endowed with the virtues of the auspicious Jamitra (the seventh) the Himalaya, with his relations, celebrated the scarament of matrimony of his daughter.

By the celebration of ceremonial festivities for matrimony from house to house in consequence of the people's regard the whole city of the mountain in which the matrons were eagerly engaged as well as seraglio resembled one large household.

That city, with its high-ways strewn with flowers of heavenly trees, with its waving flags made of China silken cloth, by the brilliance of gate ways of shining gold, shone like a second heaven.

Though there were other sons and daughters Uma, because her hand was about to be received by a bride-groom, became peculiarly dear as life of her parents as if she was an only child as if she were found after being lost and as if she had been dead and had risen again.

Having benedictions pronounced on her she went from bosom to bosom and every relative presented her jewels. The affection of the mountain's race though shared by other relatives was now centred in in her as its one repository.

At the sacred hour to Mitra, the asterism posterior Phalguni having got into conjunction with the moon, the female relatives, who had husbands and sons living, made decorations on her body.

She was adorned with *durva* grass sprouts mixed with white mustard seeds. The decoration of the annointment was beautiful all through. She was clad in a silken raiment reaching up to the middle and furnished with an arrow according to the Kshatrya custom.

The girl, having got possession of a new sacramental arrow, shone like the lunar curve, at the close of the dark fortnight increasing by the rays of the sun.

The women conducted her, the oil on whose body was absorbed by *lodhra* powders, whose body had been coloured by a dry yellow fragrant drug and who was clothed in a raiment adapted to the ablution, towards the quadrangular bath room.

In that room paved with emerald stones, beautified with rows of pearls set in it they bathed her with water from golden pots inclined to pour their contents amid the sound of trumpets.

Parvati, being purified in the body by the holy ceremonial bath and being clothed in fresh clothing for meeting the bride-groom, shone like the earth supplied with a good water-wash from thunder-clouds.

She was then conducted by women devoted to their husbands from the bathing place to the middle of the auspicious altar on which was prepared a seat with canopy over it and joined with four pillars of jems.

Having set there the slender one with her face towards the east the women tarried for a moment, their eyes attracted by her natural beauty though the articles of decoration were near.

A woman tied the extremety of her hair, which had been dried by the heat of incense, with flowers in it, as a fine knot, by means of a wreath of the yellow Madhuka intermingled with Durva grass.

They decorated her body, already perfumed with Aguru perfume, with saffron paint. She stood there excelling the beauty of the three-streamed Ganga whose sand banks were set off by the yellow Chakravakas.

Having excelled in beauty the lotus with black bees sticking to it and the moon's disc with streaks of clouds about it her beauty, by means of her decorated tresses, abolished the use of their names as exemplars of beauty.

On account of the acquisition of excellency of color, the stalk of barley, which was placed on her ears, fixed the eyes of spectators on her checks, whitened by the application of Lodhra powders and rendered excessively orient by the application of saffron.

The fruition of Parvati's beauty, who had a body symmetrical in its parts, whose under-lip was marked by a line the redness of which was refined by a little wax, was near at hand.

Having been blessed by a maid jocosely after being decorated by the same maid in her feet with red dyes saying "touch the lunar digit on thy husband's head with this thy foot", she, as a return for such a blessing, struck her silently with a flower wreath.

The black dye was applied to her two eyes, beautiful as a full blown lotus, not from an idea of its increasing the beauty of the eye but because it was auspicious as a protection from evil influences.

On being endued with ornaments she shone like a creeper by means of flowers springing up, like the night by means of rising luminaries and like a river by means of birds adhering to its banks.

And having looked at, in the reflection of a mirror, her beautiful body with her large eyes she became eager for the reception of Hara for the decoration of women has for its fruit the oservance of their husbands.

Having taken with two fingers yellow orpiment and red arsenic, as an auspicious mixture dye, and having raised her head, on the two ears of which were attached two splendid ear-rings, her mother,

Mena, being over come with tears of joy, performed with difficulty *tilaka* of her daughter's matrimonial ceremony, in whose mind after the commencement of youth, a strong desire had taken place for the first time.

With eyes agitated by tears she also tied the auspicious matrimonial arm-band of wool on Uma's hand also as an amulet which was, by her agitation, fixed to a wrong place but which was set right by the nurse's fingers.

Clad in fresh silk or linen and holding a new mirror she repeatedly shone like the shore of the milk-ocean streaken with foam flakes, and an autumnal night with full moon.

Knowing what ceremonies were necessary the mother assisted her, the perpetuator of the family, to make obeisance to the adorable family-gods and made her touch the feet of the chaste women according to grades.

Uma, bowing down, was addressed by them, " Acquire the undivided love of thy husband." But she having possession of half his body her happiness, on marrying Siva, exceeded their best wishes.

Having completed the initial ceremony of her marriage with a magnificence equal to his wishes, his joyous interest and wealth, the happy mountain, himself courteous, remained in the assembly of his relations expecting the advent of the bull-sigued Siva.

Meanwhile on Kailasha ornaments corresponding to the former marriage ornaments were plaoed in front of Siva, the chastiser of the city Tripura by the seven regardful divine mothers.

Out of reverence for them the Beauty of those auspicious ornaments was only touched by the Lord Siva who himself underwent an alteration suitable for a wedding.

The ashes did duty for scented ointment, the skulls, which Siva carried about him, put forth the beauty of the pure crest jem and on the borders of the elephant hide itself became the appearance of silken dress with pictures of swans.

The third eye, which was shining in the middle of the frontal bone within which was situated a pure twany pupil, served the purpose of the yellow arsenic painting on the fore-heed.

The snakes disappeared as such but their jems did duty for ornaments of Siva's body.

Siva having the moon for his crest jem required no other ornament for his head.

Thus the only generative cause of miracles, Siva, the creator of perfect decoration by his own power, looked at himself attached to the reflection in the sword blade brought by the troops near him.

Leaning on Nandi's arm and mounted on his great bull whose large back was covered by a tiger skin and which through reverence for him had contracted his huge stature like Mount Kailasha, he set out for his marriage procession.

Following him, the seven divine mothers; whose ear-rings were waving by the shaking of their vehicles, turned the sky like unto a reservoir of lotuses reddened by the dust of their haloes of splendour.

And after them whose splendour was that of gold appeared the goddess Kali ornamented with skulls like a range of black clouds attended by cranes and casting lightings far in front.

Then the sound of the auspicious trumpet caused by the troops of Siva, going in advance, declared to the goods the oppurtunity of worshipping Siva.

The sun of a thousand rays held his umbrella made fresh by the divine artist Vishwakarma. Having his head not far from its silk Siva appeared as one on whose head the Ganges was falling.

Though in form different from rivers yet recognised as it were by being accompanied by flights of swans, Ganga and Jamuna too, in embodied forms, served the god with chowries.

Magnifying his glory by the expressions "Prosper like fire magnified by clarified butter" the first creator Brahma and Vishnu, the soul, bearing the mystic mark of Srivatsa, came to him.

The one only form was divided three fold. Sometimes Hara or Siva was senior to Vishnu and Hari or Vishnu to him and Brahma to both; and they too Vishnu and Siva were sometimes prior to Brahma.

Humbly attired by laying aside their parapharnalia of state Indra and other divine rulers of several worlds applied to Nandi for introduction to Siva's presence. And being presented by him they prostrated themselves with joined palms.

Siva returned the complements to Brahma by a nod, to Hari by conversation, to Indra, the killer of Vitra, by a smile, and to all other gods by the sight itself according to seniority.

The seven Rishis blessed him saying "Prosper" and he spoke to them with a smile:—"In the matrimonial sacrifice here celebrated you have been chosen by me as priests."

Saying it Siva, who had a lunar digit in his crest, went on whose exploits at Tripura were being sung by expert Gandharvas with Viswavasu as their leader, himself being perfectly dispassionate.

The bull going beautifully with golden bells resounding, constantly shaking his two horns, and dipped in the clouds as from strokes on the surface when fixed in the mind, carried him in the sky.

The bull reached in a moment the city which had never encountered an enemy's attack and defended by the chief of mountains, being drawn in by the rays shot from his eyes as by strings of gold.

Being looked at by the citizens with upward faces from curiosity and having descended from the etherial way marked by his own arrows when discharged against Tripura Siva, whose throat was cloud black, reached the vicinity of the earth's surface.

Pleased at Siva's coming, the emperor of the mountains advanced to recieve him with troops of elephants mounted on by relations, having rich ornaments as with his own mountain sides with trees rich with flowers.

On the gates of the city door being opened two companies of the followers of the god and the mountain went together whose clangor went a long way like two streams breaking through the same sluice gate.

The mountain shrank on being bowed to by Hara adored by the three worlds for he did not notice that his own head at first had been lowly bent by Siva's majesty.

Going before his future son-in-law the Himalaya, the splendour of his face glowing with joy, made him enter his wealthy city in which flowers were strewn ankle deep in the ways of the shops.

Giving up all other business the beauteous females of the city tried in rows of palaces only to look at Ishana.

Suddenly starting up to the lattices one female will not stay to bind her long black tresses dropping down save by the hand.

Another took her foot away from her maiden on which the dye was wet and streaming and rushed in haste to the chamber. And wherever she went she impressed it with a crimson foot-print.

Another having adorned the right eye with collyrium the left eye still destitute of that decoration went hurriedly to the window with pencil in the hand.

The waist band, of another female, rising up in haste, half stringed with diamonds and therefore dropping them at every step, had at that time the string as the residuum sticking to the tip of the great toe.

The bull-eyed windows, their holes filled with the faces in which was the perfume of wines and in which the rolling eyes of the ladies excited deeply by curiosity were like flying black bees, were ornamented as it were by lotuses.

Then the moon-crested Siva passed into the high road abounding in flags and high gate-ways, making the domes of palaces even in the day doubly splendid by the effusion of moon-light from his crest.

The women were so absorbed in the sight of Siva that they did not notice any thing else for the functions of their other senses had, as it were by universal identity, all entered the eye.

Rightly did Uma, though so tender, practise such difficult asceticism for such a husband. Most fortunate are the women who may obtain even the state of a slave to him, what then must be said of her who obtains repose on his bosom.

If the creator had not united this conple of a beauty to be coveted by all surely the labour of his creating such a beauty would have been fruitless.

Forsooth the body of the flower-bannered Kama was not burnt by Siva possessed by wrath. I think on seeing this god Kama, of his own accord, gave up his body from shame.

Having obtained alliance with this lord, O fortunate, which had long been the desire of his heart, the king of mountains, shall hold, O dear companion, his head already lofty from his supporting the earth, still higher.

Thus hearing the words, of the women of Oshadhiprastha pleasing to the ear the three-eyed Siva came into the abode of the Himalya where handfuls of parched grain were in their downward course by the bracelets of the crowded women.

Siva leaning on Vishnu's arm, having alighted there like the sun, from his Bull white like the autumnal cloud, entered the other courtyard of the lord of mountains which had been entered before by the lotus-seated Brahma.

Following him, the gods too with Indra as their leader and the great Rishis with the seven Rishis as their leaders and his hosts came to the abode of the mountain like the most excellent objects coming after unfailing undertakings.

Having got a seat the lord Siva fittingly accepted the offering of honor with jems, and curds with honey or wine and a pair of new silk dresses all presented by the mountain the mantras not being neglected.

Clad in silk he was next conducted near to the bride by respectful persons familiar with the seraglio, as the sea, with its line of froth manifest, is led near to the coast by the new lunar rays.

The appearance of Uma elated the heart of Siva just as the moon does the water lily kumuda, and then Siva's heart became as cheerful as the waters are by the full blown Kumuda, as the whole world is by the autumn with its clear moon.

Becoming unstable on their encountering each other the eyes of the two were a litttle fixed for the ceremonious exchange of looks. Then turning back and coveting each other they felt the torment of shame.

The eight-formed Siva took hold of her hand with red fingers presented by the chief of mountains as the first shoot of Kama, who, afraid of him, had concealed his body in that of Uma.

Uma's horripilation manifested itself and the bull-signed Siva too became perspiring in the fingers. By the joining of their hands the operation of Kama was as it were equally divided.

Other ordinary couples, whose reception of hands is brought about, sustain first rate beauty by the vicinity of these two. How is to be described then the beauty of that couple?

By their going round and keeping on the right a fire blazing upward that couple shone like the day and night revolving at the lateral extremities of the mount Meru, joined together.

Having conducted that couple with closed eyes by contact with each other, thrice around the fire the priest caused the bride to cast the parched grain in that blazing flame.

Under the priest's instruction the bride brought doubled palm-fuls of the parched grain smoke of an agreeable scent to her facc, which was spiring over the cheeks and serving for the time as the ear-lotus for her.

By the reception of the ritual smoke the bride's face, whose ear ornamens of barley were withered, became a little moist and ruddy on the cheeks tinged with the black collyrium issuing out of the two eyes.

The priest said to the bride :—" O child, this fire is witness to the fact of your marriage with Siva. Abandoning controversy you should pay implicit obedience to your husband."

That saying of the priest having entered into the ears to the extremety of the eyes was recieved into the inmost mind by Bhavani as the first rain is drunk by the earth excessively heated in the summer season.

Having been directed by the everlasting one the husband, lovely to behold, to look at the polar star, she, having lifted her face and growing nervous, said with difficulty "it has been looked at."

Having been made to go through the ceremony of marriage by the priest learned in the ritual, these two, the parents of all creatures, bowed to Brahma sitting on the lotus seat.

The bride was saluted on return by the Creator with the benedictory words:—"O beauteous one, be thou a mother of heroes." Though eloquent he could not say anything to Siva for what could possibly be an object of desire to him?

Afterwards having come to a quandrangular altar strewn with ritual substances and sitting on golden seats the husband and wife experienced the sprinkling of moist grain customary among people and therefore not to be disregarded.

The goddess Lakshmi held on them a lotus umbrella having a large lotus stalk stick which had got the splendour of strings of pearls by means of multitudes of water-drops adhering to the extremities of leaves.

By a language uttered in a two-fold manner, Sanskrit and Prakrita the goddess Saraswati praised the husband in Sanskrit and the bride in Prakrit which was easily comprehensible.

They saw for a while the first scene of the Apsaras in which varying actions were manifested according to the five different articulation, in which different modes were set answering the different sentiments of love, satire, pity and in which were exhibited their graceful gestures.

Afterwards having prostrated themselves with doubled palms on their crests the gods asked of Hara who has just married a wife to accept some service from the five arrowed Kama who at the termination of the curse had resumed his form.

Free from anger the lord now permitted in himself even the operation of his arrows. Certainly a representation made in the proper season by men conversant with business, to their lords, becomes sucessful.

Having dismissed the gods and taking the daughter of the mountain by the hand the moon-crested Siva came to the sleeping house having golden pots full of water endued with the beauty of flowery decoration and on the floor of which were spread beddings.

There the lord made Gauri laugh secretly by the funny actions of his follower's faces. Gauri, who was ornamented with the modest shame of a recent marriage, drew her face lifted by him and spoke with difficulty even to maids that used to sleep with her.

CANTO VIII.

After Siva's marriage with the daughter of the mountain-chief she was afraid of having a free sexual intercourse with him, still his desire was satisfied. In the beginning the daughter of the mountain used to give no reply to the words of Mahadeva. On his holding her cloth she wished to free herself and go away and used to lie with her face against him still the newly-wedded Parvati conduced to his satisfaction.

When the Lord out of curiosity used to close his eye-lids as if in sleep Parvati used confidently to fix her eyes on him. Afterwards smiling a little he used to open his eyes and she, as if struck by a lightning, used to close her own.

When her beloved consort used to place his hands on her navel she used to obstruct him but the cloth round her waist used to be loosened of itself. Her friends used to instruct Parvati saying "friend, without the least fear, satisfy Sankara secretly." But when she used to come before her beloved she forgot every thing. When Shankara used to vouchsafe proposals of intercourse Parvati used to accept them by her looks and to reply by the shaking of her head.

When in a solitary place Sankara used to take away her raiment Parvati used to shut up his eyes with her hands. But she found no means to obstruct the vision of the eye situate on his forehead, and so all her efforts were futile.

She used to take away her lips when kissed by him and her hands used to give way when embraced ruthlessly. Although the husband is pained at heart still rare is the attempt of the newly married brides to prevent the delightful endeavour of the husbands to hold sexual intercourse.

None else but Parvati could bear the intercourse of Siva in which he used to kiss her without cutting her lips and place his nails (on the breast) without wounding her. When her friends used to press her to describe the incidents of the night she could not do so out of shame.

When taking up a mirror Parvati used to mark the signs of intercourse her beloved consort used to go stealthily behind her back. Seeing the reflection of her beloved behind her own, she used to feel abashed and exclaim " What is this ? What is this ?"

Seeing that Mahadeva was enjoying the youthfulness of Parvati her mother was exceedingly happy; when daughter becomes a favourite of her hausband the mother feels no other misery. Maheshwara having spent thus a few days in her company Parvati gradually perceived the pleasure of sexual intercourse and felt no more any pain in conseqnence thereof. Then she used to return the embrace of her husband, and did not take away her face when solicited for a kiss. And when her husband used to] hold the ornament on her waist she used to hold his hands lightly. Within a short time from gestures it could be perceived, that they were mutually] attached to each other. They used to flatter each other and feel pangs even for a short separation. The wife used to please her husband in the same way as the latter used to do the former. As the river Janhavi does not go elsewhere leaving the ocean and the ocean too does not go anywhere leaving her so their love prospered without experiencing the least separation.

Maheshwara instructed Parvati secretly in the art of sexual intercourse and made her a disciple. She, too learning that dexterous art of youthful women, made a *Dakshina* (preceptor's present) of all delightful contrivances of intercourse.

When she used to feel pain on accouut of her love biting her lips she used to move about her fingers, and afterwards when let loose she used to remove the pain by the cool rays of the moon. When Shankara's eye on the forehead was besmeared with the scented powders from Parvati's tresses at the time of kissing he used to clear it up by the lotus scented wind of her mouth. Thus engaged in sexual intercourse and showing favour towards Manmatha, Shankara spent a month in Uma's company, at the residence of the Mountain-chief.

Then with the permission of the Himalaya and Menaka stricken with grief consequent upon the separation from their daughter, Shankara, being within his own self, riding his own bull of unmitigated course, roamed at large happily.

Having placed Uma first on that bull, swift as the wind, the Lord Shankara sat behind her and therefore taking before Uma's rising breasts he came to the mount Sumeru. And there making a house of golden creepers he enjoyed the pleasure of pressing the breasts and sexual intercourse. He lived a few days on the mount Mandara resorted to, by the black-bee, drinking the honey of Parvati's lotus-face, and made of rocks impressed with the foot-prints of the lotus-navelled deity.

The Lord of mountains and the preceptor of the universe went to a twane-coloured mountain. There terrified at the terrific roars of the elephants Parvati threw her tender arms around his neck. And removing her anxiety he enjoyed beautiful moon-light there. Once on a time he went to the mount Malaya and enjoyed sexual intercourse with his wife. Shaking the sandal forest and carrying the filaments of Lavanga creepers, light southern wind removed the exhaustion of his wife consequent upon the sexual intercourse. There while bathing in a stream, Parvati, finding fault with her husband, struck him with a golden lily. Mahadeva took up water in his palms and threw it at Parvati's eyes which, thereat, were immediately closed. While thus sporting Sapharis moved about Uma's waist and her tongue appeared two-fold in the water. Thereupon they repaired to the garden of Nandana where he performed her decoration with Sachi's favourite Parijata flowers and was seen by Apsaras.

Thus did enjoy Shankara heavenly and earthly joy in Parvati's company. Afterwards when the sun's rays became very fierce they repaired to the mount Gandhamadana. There seated on a golden rock and seeing the Sun, capable of being seen, the Lord said to his wife, reclining on his left arm.

" Dear! look, the Sun, applying the beauty of the lotus to its two extremeties, bright like your eyes, is destroying the day like the lord of subjects destroying the universe at the final dissolution. Behold, the sun declining, the fountains, of your father, deprived of its rays, have been divorced from the rain-bows. Having feasted on the filaments of lotus in the lake the pair of Chakravas have left each other's neck and are being painfully separated from eaeh other. Having left their sweet scented habitations of the day the elephants are going to live in the water abounding in black bees living inside the closed lotuses. Look, O dear, the sun, by his long reflection. in the west, has made a golden bridge in the lake. Having spent the day in the lake the leaders of the boar-herd are coming out with lily stalks in their tusks. See, O thou having pointed breasts, the peococks, waiting under trees and spreading a circle of white are as if drinking the declining sun. Darkness appearing in the east, a portion of the sky, the water of which being drunk up by the sun, is looking like a lake full of lotuses almost dried up. Look, O dear, the deer are entering into hermitages; the trees, with their roots well watered, are appearing beautiful with growing leaves. The sacrificial cows are entering into hermitages, and the sacrificial fire of the evening is being lighted up. By these the hermitages have put on a most beautiful appearance.

The lotuses out of love have not been closed as yet so that the black-bees may soon occupy their residences. By the sun of limited rays the western quarter is appearing like a maiden decorated with Bandhujiva flowers. Reciting the Sama Vedas in a sweet voice thousands of Rishis, living on the sun's rays, are chanting the glories of the sun transfering its own heat to the fire. Having placed the day within the great ocean, the lord of the day is setting with his horses, with their manes down. The setting of the sun illustrates a great truth, *viz.*, the greater rises a luminous body the more is its depression at the time of the setting. Though the feet of the sun followed the twilight, his heat was deposited in the setting hill for why would not he, whom he had rewarded at the time of rising, follow him in this hour of danger ?

Look, O thou of curling locks, how crimson, yellow and red clouds are looking beautiful. Perhaps the evening has decoratted them so that you will see them. Look the mountain is dividing the evening heat amongst the manes of the lions, creeper-producing trees and its summits covered with minerals. Look, O dear, the ascetics, conversant with rituals, rising up from the earth are making oblations of sacred water, and after performing all the evening rites they are reciting the sweet Vedic mantras. O thou of sweet speech, the time for my evening rites has also come. Permit me therefore to perform them. These thy companious, of the same age with thee, will please you.

Thereupon showing disregard at the words of her husband by the gesture of her lips Parvati began to converse with Vijaya who was near her. Even the Iswara himself went to perform the evening rites by reciting mantras. Beholding that Parvati did not reply to him out of jealousy Maheswara again appeared before her and smiling a little said "Useless is thy wrath, O Parvati, cast it off therefore. I have been governed by Sandhya and not by any other female. I enjoy thy company always—the only separation is in the evening for performing Sandhya rites. Our union is like that of the pair of Chakravakas. Do you not know it? O thou of beautiful limbs! O sensitive lady, the body which was cast off by the sensitive lady, the body, which was cast off by the self-sprung after creating the progenitors, is serving the rising and setting. For that reason I attach so much importance to this matter. For that reason like unto the well-fixed earth she is assailed by darkness. Look how she appears beautiful like a river issuing out of molten minerals with forests of Tamala on one of its banks. With the red circular disc of the sun in the evening rising obliquely the western quarter has assumed crimson hue like a field of battle.

O thou of large-eyes, when the light, begotten by the union of day and night, will be possessed by Sumeru all the ten quarters will be enveloped by pitch darkness. In the night vision proceeds no where, up, down, behind and before. The universe lies in darkness like an embryo in the womb. Look O dear, darkness is putting all on the same level, pure or impure, fixed or moveable, straight or curve. The distinction between the good and evil has been done away with. Oh! fie on darkness. O thou having a lotus face, forsooth the moon is rising for destroying the darkness of the night. Look the quarters appear to have been covered with the filaments of Ketaka flowers. Hiding himself behind the Mandara mountain the moon is seeing the night full of stars. O dear, you have come to me with your companions. He has appeared behind us as if to hear what conversation passes between us.

The moon-like smiles of the formerly-seen body were kept obscured from view, but urged by the night the quarters are throwing them out like a deep secret. As if displaying water by means of the rays of the moon like Pryangu flowers, the sky is troubling the pair of Chakravakas. The moon has appeared for furnishing you with ear-ornaments. You can with yours nails, pointed as needless, cut off the new barley stalks. Holding the darkness like tresses with finger-like rays the moon is kissing the closed lotus like face of the night.

O Parvati, the rays of the newly risen sun piercing the thick darkness of the sky it is looking like the Manasa lake spoiled by the elephants. Having cast off his crimson hue the moon assumed a circular form of pure white; occasional defects of persons, who are by nature pure, are never permanent. By the water trickling from moon jems watered by the rays of the moon the mountains are awaking in proper time the peacocks sleeping on their waist. O thou of unblemished beauty, spreading his rays on the top of desire-fulfilling trees, the moon is as if coming to count their gifts. According to the height and depression of the mountain, this moon-light, accompanied with darkness, is appearing like a painting painted on the bodies of the elephants inebriated with the trickling of temporal juice. As if being unable to bear this yellow light of the moon's rays, the lilies, devoid of the humming of black-bees, are unfolding themselves quickly.

O Chandi, the wind blowing, the cloth, tied to the desire-fulfilling tree, bathed with the pure rays, but shaken by the wind, is appearing as fickle. With the drops of the lunar rays, tender like flowers dropped at the foot of a tree, and sticking on the leaves taken up by fingers, your tresses may be beautifully decorated. As the newly married bride, trembling in fear, to approach her husband, is united with him in proper time so the stars, of feeble light, are being united with the moon.

O thou having eyes in which lunar rays are settled, pure lunar rays are as if coming out from thy cheeks, which are pale white by digestion, mill-white like Shara reeds & delighted by the delightful Nature.

The presiding Goddess of this mount Gandhamadana, has brought for you the honey of celestial tree in a crimson-coloured vessel made of moon-stone.

Your mouth is by nature sweet-scented by raw ilaments ; your eyes are by nature dark ; if wine is placed here can it change the natural quality? or let your companions, ever respectful and devoted to you, drink this wine which excites sexual desire.

Saying these noble words Mahadeva caused Ambika to drink the wine. Parvati felt sweet intoxication. She then followed him like a person humbled by unquestionable laws. Then with growing desire, devoid of shame and anxious to go to bed, the beautiful-faced Parvati placed herself between wine and Mahadeva.

Then Iswara began to drink, not by his mouth, but by his eyes, the face of Parvati, furnished with rolling eyes, faltering speech, drops of perspiration and sweet smile in consequence of intoxication. Then carrying Parvati, with hanging golden Mekhala, heavy on account of her heavy waist Siva entered the room of Manistones, covered with ashes, constructed for his meditation.

As the moon lies down on the autumnal clouds so Siva too, with his dear wife, laid himself down on a bed beautiful like the banks of the Ganges and spread with a cover white like a swan. There he held sexual intercourse with Parvati, in which her locks were scattered, sandal pastes were dissipated, cuts were made on her person with nails and her waist band was torn. Still Shankara was not satiated with Parvati. When the luminious bodies began to decline she pressed Mahadeva on her breast and closed her eyes sportively. After the termination of the night Kinnaras began to sing benedietory songs by playing Murchana on their respective flutes. Parvati then aroused him and he opened his eyes along with the Sun. Then they released themselves from each other's embrace. The wind coming from the forest skirt of the mount Gandhamadana, which creates waves in the Manasa lake, began to serve them.

Mahadeva was then marking the marks of nails on Parvati's thighs. She began to draw her loosened cloth but Mahadeva prevented her. Parvati's eys were reddened with night-keeping; her lips were cut deeply; her paint on the forehead was washed off and her tresses were scattered. Mahadeva lost himself on seeing Parvati's countenance.

Light set in after the termination of the night. Still Maheshwara could not leave the bed the cover of which was raised some where and depressed elsewhere, on which the Mekhala was heaped, and which was tinged with the dye of the foot.

Shankara began to drink day and night the nectar of his dear's mouth capable of enhancing his delight. When any visitor used to come Vijaya brought the news to him and he recieved him.

As the fire inside the ocean is not satiated with drinking its water so Shambhu, enjoying in the company of Parvati, spent a hundred seasons like one night. Still his desire for sexual enjoyment was not satiated.

CANTO IX.

ONCE while entering the house of pleasure, Shankara, the black-bee of the lotus face of his dear consort and ever engaged in conversation of love, saw a pigeon speaking on love. That pigeon was swelling his throat and rolling his red eyes and moving his tail. His wings were set disorderly and he was showing signs of joy caused by inward lust. His fore feet were covered with small feathers and white. He was moving about in circles. Beholding that peacock coming out like a messenger of foam from the lake of nectar where Rati and Manmatha were sporting the moon-crested Siva experienced delight for a short time.

Beholding that beautiful celestial pigeon and understanding that he was Agni under the guise of a bird, he, in anger, with his eye-brows contracted, appeared dreadful.

Thereupon trembling in fear the fire, with clasped hands, said to the destroyer of Cupid.

"O lord, thou art the only lord of the universe, and dost destroy the dangers of the dwellers of heaven. O lord of asceticism, assailed by the Daityas, Indra and other deities are adoring thee. Enjoying thy dear wife's love thou hast spent a hundred seasons. Thou art living in a solitary place. And therefore not being able to see thee the celestials and their lord have been overpowered with misfortune. O thou Omniscient! Solicited by the Devas, waiting for an opportunity to serve thee, I, assuming the form of a bird have come here in search of thee. Thus, O lord, thinking all this in thy mind, do thou pardon us. All the celestials seek refuge with thee. We have been defeated by our enemies and cannot bear any more delay. O lord, be propitiated and and procreate a son. Making him his General, the king of gods may regain the prosperity of heaven and govern the three worlds by thy favour."

Hearing that sensible prayer of fire Shankara was pleased and the dwellers of mountains propitiated him with many panegyric verses.

Shankara, the destroyer of Madana, ever pleased at heart began to think of creating the destroyer of Taraka and the success of Indra's General.

Then the sexual intercourse of Mahadeva, who

could control the discharge of seminal fluid, being obstructed, he began to discharge the same fluid unbearable like the fire of dissolution. He threw it into fire of golden semen. The unbearable semen of the destroyer of Smara being thrown into him the mirror-like, pure body of fire, all on a sudden spoiled by steam and air, assumed a disfigured hue. The pleasure of her sexual intercourse being obstructed the daughter of the mountain imprecated angrily a terrible curse on fire.

"Highly wicked is your action. Therefore you will eat every thing, be visited by leprosy and other diseases and there will be smoke in your womb." Like the moon visited by consumption on account of Daksha's imprecation, like a lotus petal disfiguired by frost the fire, assuming a disfigured body, departed.

Beholding fire in that plight Maheshwara, with various sweet words relating to the art of sexual intercourse, began to enliven the mind of the daughter of the mountain, who was smiling a little out of shame and whose mind was humbled.

With the corner of his cloth Mahadeva rubbed the mark of collyrium extended by the incessant drops of perspiration on the stain-less and moon-like countenance, of his dear wife. With his trembling hand, with fingers perspiring he gently rubbed the perspiration of the lotus-like countenance of Parvati and fanning her he soon made her comfortable.

The moon-crested Siva tied with garlands of Parijata flowers the tresses of Parvati unloosened and fallen on her with flowers dropping on account of her enjoying with him. The moon-faced destroyer of Smara painted Parvati's palm with musk as if writing the world enchanting letters of Smara there. Thereupon Mahadeva put *Tathanka* on her which became as it were the wheels of the car of the flower-bannered Kama desirous of conquering the world, by which he would get on his car, her face, and conquer the world. He put a necklace of pearls around her neck spreading on her breasts. It looked like two streams of the Ganges on the summit of the mount Sumeru.

The destroyer of Smara decorated, with Rasana garlands, the waist of Parvati bearing in rows marks of nails. It appeared like the noose of Manmatha for binding his deer-like mind. Making collyrium in the fire on his fore-head he put it into her eyes like two new lotuses. Embraced by her in delight he rubbed his finger on his own blue throat. Shankara put red dye on the tip of the lotus foot of that lotus-eyed goddess and then washed off his hand with the water of the Ganges on his head. Then rubbing the mirror against his own body covered with ashes and cleansing it thereby he held it before his wife, dear as his life, so that she might mark the beauty of decoration. Seeing the marks of sexunl intercourse on her own body reflected in the mirror held up by her dear husband she felt herself abashed. Her deep attachment manifested itself in the shape of the stirring of hairs.

Casting off shame and looking in the mirror with a little smile at the decoration made by her husband Parvati considered herself the foremost of all lucky women.

In the meantime, her beloved companions Jaya and Vijaya intervening began to serve Parvati lying at a distance from the moon-crested Siva. Then the Vaitalikas began to sing auspicious songs outside on the beautifully painted altar. For pleasing the trident-handed deity the Gandharvas began to sing in accompaniment with the blowing of conchs.

Then at the time proper for the deities to look upon Mahadeva Nandi came there and bowing with folded hands communicated to him their desire for service.

Holding the daughter of the mountain by the hand, after sexual intercourse and moving slowly like swans in the lake of Manasa Siva set out towards the celestials.

Thereupon Indra and other Gods, in order, came and bowed with placing their hands on their heads unto Maheswara and the Himalaya's daughter Uma, the mother of the three worlds.

Having welcomed and dismissed the gods the bull-signed deity, leaning on Nandi's arms, got upon his bull and went away with Parvati. Then going by the ethereal way on his bull, quick-coursing like the mind he began to enjoy the breeze accompanied with the smell of Parijata flowers grown on the mountain.

Thereupon the trident-handed Siva arrived at the crystal mountain Kailasha, touching the sky, holding cresent and containing serpents and riches.

Their husbands bowing to them, the sensitive Siddha damsels, seeing their reflection on the crystal, look towards others by mistake. The marks of the moon reflected on the crystal and beautified by its lustre, display beauty at musk-deer set to play by Gouri. Seeing the reflection of their own forms on the crystal and mistaking them for other elephants, the chiefs of the herds strike them fiercely with their tusks and move about with wounds on their faces and tusks.

Seeing the reflection of stars in night on crystal palaces the Siddha damsels are about to catch them mistaking them for pearls dropped at the time of sexul intercourse. The sky-ranging, mirror-like moon is ranging on the summit as the abode of Siva and the price-less crest jem of the mountain-chief. The celestials, assailed by Cupid, meeting their loves in secret, display their forms as many, although one, on being reflected on the crystal.

On the summit of the crystal mountain the moon-crested Siva spent many days, in sportive amusement in Gouris' company. Holding the hand of the destroyer of Smara, the charmingly sportive Gouri went in ways making a beautiful sound, instructed by Nandi preceding with a cane in hand.

Hinted by Mahadeva by the contraction of his eye-brows Bhringi began to dance, by moving his horns and making various hideous gestures, for pleasing Parvati. Commanded by his own lord the Maheshawara in delight Kali, for pleasing Siva's consort, began to dance shaking the garlands of skulls around his neck and making various gestures with his hideous teeth. When Bhringi and Kali thus danced hideously, the damsel, stricken with fear and losing all control over her limbs, sat on Mahadeva's lap and embraced him fiercely. When Parvati, with her rising breasts, pressed him in embrace Maheshwara was filled with unknown delight and worked up with desire. Thus pleased by the daughter of the mountain by various means the moon-crested Siva lived happily on the mount Kailasa with his own followers,

CANTO X.

Thereupon carrying that fierce and great energy of Maheshwara the fire arrived at the court of the king of celestials encircled by the gods. Then Indra, the king of gods, looked respectfully with his thousand eyes at the fire, incapable of being seen, with a smoke-coloured burning circle, Seeing Agni in that plight Indra thought for a long time that he might have caused anger to the enemy of Kandarpa. Seeing Agni, water came out of the mouths of the gods. They looked at him every moment. Then with the welcome order of the king of the gods he took his seat. Accosted by the king of gods, saying "O Carrier of sacrificial offerings, how have you come by this highly distressful condition?" He sighing heavily replied.

"O King of gods, by thy command, which cannot be transgressed I went to Maheswara, engaged in sexual enjoyment with Gouri. Assuming the form of a pigeon and trembling greatly in fear, I approached the enemy of Smara. Knowing me under the false guise of a bird the omniscient Purusha, in great anger, thought of makihg a Homa with the fire burning on his fore-head. With great humility and pregnant words I eulogised him. He was pleased and propitiated with me. For who is not pleased when he is lauded?

Shankara, the Saviour of the refugees, saved me from the great fear of being devoured by the fire of anger. Then renouncing the embrace of the daughter of mountain in shame he desisted from the enjoyments of sexual intercourse. Immediately the mother of the universe, angered for the obstruction of her sexual pleasure, imprecated a curse on me. Being consumed by the energy thereof I could not bear the unbearable weight of the body. I am being consumed by that great and terrific energy. O Vasava, save my life and do me a good office."

Hearing those piteous words of Agni the king of gods was greatly sorry at heart and began to think of measures to avert the present evil. Then touching the body, of the Fire consumed by energy, with his fingers the lord of immortals said:—

"O Carrier of Havya, you yourself are a deity and the mouth of the Pitris and men. You please them with Swaha, Swadha & Vashatkar. Offering clarified butter to you the sacrificers, freed from sins, enjoy eternal heaven. O hutashana, offering Havi, sanctified with mantras to you, the ascetics attain Siddhi. Forsooth, you are the lord of asceticism. You carry many articles to the sun. They, converted into clouds, pour down rain which creates food stuff. Therefore you are protector of the world. You range the heart of the elements. They gain strength by you, they acquire longevity through you and therefore you give vitality to the world. For benefitting this celestial host you have been visited by this calamity. This danger is an object of pride to you since that wicked demon is injuring our cause. The goddess Bhagirathi has been pleased with our devotion. If you plunge your body into her water this your burning pain will be removed. O carrier of havya, be not depressed. Go to the Ganges. Speediness conduces to the success of necessary actions. That celestial stream is the watery form of Shambhu. She will transfer from you to herself the unbearable energy of Sambhu."

Saying it the king of gods stopped. Taking leave from him the Fire proceeded to the celestial stream. After going a little distance he reached the goddess Ganga, destroying the mass of sins. That celestial stream, like unto the stairs of heaven, is the presiding goddess of the celestial road. She destroys sins and saves the creatures from dangers. Virtue is stationed in the Ganges only, living in the matted locks of Mahesha, destructive of sins, and conferring emancipation to the race of Sagara. She has sprung from the lotus-foot of Vishnu and descended from the region of Brahma. With three streams she is continually purifying the three worlds.

Beholding Agni, from a distance, to approach, the ever delighted Surudhani with rising waves for her hands welcomed him for the accomplishment of his work. Swans swimming in her waters were emitting sweet notes. As if in those words she spoke to fire "I will remove your pain and do you good," With her heaving roars rising towards the bank the celestial Ganga went in advance to receive Agni. Thereupon stricken with burning pain Agni speedily plunged himself into the water of Bhagirathi. Do the persons, overpowered by dangers, delay in averting them? Plunging his body into the water of the exhaustion-removing, purifying, virtue-giving Ganga ever doing good, Agni was pacified. The Hutashana transferred to the water of Ganga the energy of Maheswara, the cause of his internal burning sensation. Bathed in that sacred water like unto nectarine streams the fire-god, highly pleased, departed for his own quarter. Bearing the unbearable seminal fluid of the destroyer of Smara, the etherial and sin-destroying Ganga began to suffer terribly. Assailed by thousands of scintillations of the fire of dissolution the acquatic animals, leaving that hot water, went elsewhere. By Rudra's energy the water of the Ganges became highly heated and swollen. With great difficulty she bore it. When the hot rays, the eyes of the world as it were, were about to rise in the month of Magha, the six Kirtikas came to the Ganges for bathing. Bathing in her thousands of white and sky-touching waves and performing their ablutions there the pious men attain heaven. She was as if declaring this. Strewn with Durva grass, Akshata and flowers, intended for the offerings of the adorations of well-bathed Munis, her banks assumed a great beauty. On her banks were seated yogis in Padma postures, engaged in the meditation of Brahma, fallen into yoga sleep and having serpents tied around their persons.

In some places of her banks, the Rishis, standing on thir toes and looking towards the solar disc, were engaged in the meditation of Brahma. Beholding the sacred streams of Ganga the six Kirtikas were highly pleased. What person is there to whose delight this river of nectarine streams does not conduce?

Thinking that a sight of her, whom the god of of gods carries on his crown is productive of virtue the six Kirtikas cherished a great reverence in their hearts. Bowing to her who gives emancipation and who flows from the foot of Vishnu, and shorn of sins they with delight and devotion chanted her glories. The six Kirtikas, with great devotion, began to serve Ganga who saves the three worlds, whom they have obtained by their good fortune, the very representative as it were of the emancipation of pious sages.

Having their sins washed off by her pure water, been well bathed, the six ascetic Kirtikas bathed there. Having bathed in that charming Mandakini on account of the fruition of their good luck they considered themselves highly pious and were greatly pleased.

As soon as they entered into the water of the Ganges, the seminal fluid of Mahadeva entered into their bodies. Bearing that unbearable and burning semem of Rudra they began to suffer greatly like unto persons sunk into an ocean of poison. Rising up from the Ganges they felt great exhaustion. And being unable to bear that semen they were as if being consumed by an internal fire. That semen of Siva entering into their womb from the river they soon conceived. When they perceived full well that they had concieved they were greatly sorry in fear of their husbands. On account of this incident they thought "Against our will this shameful and death-like misfortune has overtaken us." They all together began thus to bewail and lament. Thereupon, for fear of curse they threw that conception in a forest of reeds and went home. When they threw up in the sky that embryo, tender and lustrious like the rays of the moon, it, assuming an effulgence, defying hundreds of suns and setting at naugh the head of the moon-crested deity, was born with six faces.

CANTO XI.

Thereupon on being bowed to and solicited by Indra and other celestials the celestial stream nursed that baby by giving it milk from her own breasts. Sucking every moment her breasts full of nectar that baby grew up like the digit of the moon. When the six Kirtikas began to serve him he acquired a form of indescribable beauty. The eyes of the Ganges, the Fire and the six Kirtikas were full of tears of joy. They began to quarrel amongst themselves to come by the celestial boy. In the meantime, ranging at will with Parvati, Shankara came there in a car swift like the mind. Beholding the boy of six faces, the daughter of the mountain and the lord of mountains cherished natural affection for him and their eyes were full of tears of joy. Thereupon the goddess Gouri said to the moon-crested Siva:—

"O lord, who is this celestial infant before us? Of what most fortunate man is he the son? What woman, the luckiest of her race, is his mother? This celestial Ganges, this fire and the six Kirtakas are shamelessly quarrelling amongst themselves, each of them saying "This is my son! This is my son." Whose, amongst them or amongst the Devas, Daityas, Gandharvas, Siddhas, Uragas and Rakshasas, son is this infant, the concentrated beauty of the universe? Tell me this, O lord!".

Being thus accosted smilingly by his consort, dear like his life unto him out of curiosity, Maheshwara, knowing that an occasion for great felicity had arrived, gave vent to words conducive to pleasure.

"O mother of a heroe, this son, a great heroe and the delight of thee worlds, is yours. O auspicious lady, this son will do good unto the celestials. Who else but you can mother this most excellent, highly heroic, accomplished and most beautiful son? O worshipful lady, you are the source of auspiciousness to the world. It is really true. Consider well that ocean is the birth place of jems. Therefore listen attentively to his history. In great anger I discharged my irrepressible energy at Agni. By bathing in the Ganges he transferred it to her. Afterwards when the six Kirtikas went to bathe in the Ganges the seminal fluid passed into their body and they concieved. They threw the embryo in the forest of reed; from it is born this boy, as if the festivity of the entire universe, mobile and immobile.

O daughter of the mountain-chief, by this son, the most beautiful in the universe, you have been made the foremost of all good mothers. Do not delay; fill up your lap with this boy."

Hearing these words of Mahadeva, the creator of the three worlds, the plump-bodied Parvati, the protectress of the entire universe, in great delight got down from the car, saluted by the gods with hands on their crowns, stationed in the sky and became very anxious to recieve her son. Although Ganga, the six Kirtikas and fire bowed unto her with folded hands, still not noticing them, she affectionately took up the son on her lap, for people are maddened with joy on the birth of a son. Although the boy was sitting before her Parvati could not see him for her eyes were filled with tears of joy. But touching him with her fingers she experienced indescribable joy. With her body filled with surprise and joy and bathed in tears of joy she, on account of growing affection, cast her eyes on that beautiful boy, effulgent like the moon, who had come within her view. Seeing that boy for a short time she was, as if, desiring to have a thousand eyes for whose mind is not delighted after seeing a beautiful son? Holding those two tender hands which touch the backs of the submissive gods and demons Parvati took up that boy, beautiful like the rising full moon, on her lap.

Taking her son on her lap, the source of nectar, the lotus-faced goddess Parvati, adorable to the universe, became the foremost of all women having sons. When filled with affection and delight Parvati, the only mother of the universe, took him on her lap, milk began to ooze out from her breasts. Looked at by Surudhani and the six Kartikas, Shadanana, having six mothers, began to suck the breasts of Parvati, the mother of the entire universe. With her one mouth bathed in tears of joy Parvati, the consort of the moon-crested Siva, kissed his six faces, appearing like six lotuses on one stalk. As the golden mountain shines, holding the new moon in the east like unto fruit of a creeper, or a lotus of the heavenly stream, so Parvati with the boy on her lap appeared highly beautiful. The moon-crested Siva delightedly and carefully holding her hand, Parvati with her son on her lap, got upon the car touching the sky.

With his hairs stirring up in delight Maheshwara too, out of affection for his son, took him from the lap of the daughter of the mountain. Handing over that holy son, the only receptacle of joy, to her husband, the daughter of the mountain stood embracing her husband. Then in the quick-coursing car the moon-crested Siva returned home within a short time.

Thereupon stationed in his most beautiful mansion situate on the summit of the crystal mountain Mahadeva ordered all his ghosts to make festivities conducive to his own pleasure. The followers of Siva celebrated with great delight the birth of the son of the daughter of the mountain chief. The ghosts set up moveable golden gateways covered with Santanaka flowers in crystal palaces. On the occasion of that festival Gandharva and Vidyadhara women came to the palace of Parvati and ordered by her began to sing auspicious songs. With auspicious articles in their hands the Matris came there like mothers. And putting Durva grass and *akshata* on the head of the son of the daughter of the mountain they took him in their lap. Plunged into joy the Apsaras, when the trumpets were sounded, began to dance embracing the boy, in accompaniment with the music of Vina, displaying various gestures. Delightful wind blew on the occasion of that festival, the waters were clean and the quarters put on a delightful appearance. Bugles were then sounded in heaven accompanied with the blowing of conchs. And the cars of celestials pouring torrents of flowers, moved about in the sky. Thus the festival on the birth of the son of Maheswara and the daughter of the mountain was celebrated over the entire universe; only the goddess of Taraka's prosperity trembled.

With various childish sports conducive to their pleasure the Kumara stole the minds of the mountain-god and mountain-daughter. To whose pleasure the play of a child does not conduce? With a single mouth Maheshwara and Parvati respectively kissed the six faces of this son in which teeth were not grown. Sometimes slipping and again walking firm, sometimes trembling and again walking straight the boy increased the joy of his parents. Covered with dust while playing in the court-yard, smiling without any cause and uttering incoherent words the boy used to go to the lap of his parents and increase their joy. The boy used sometimes to hold the horns of Siva's carrier, the clotted hairs of his father and sharp horns of Shringi and thus conduce to the pleasure of Hara and Parvati. On a certain occasion going to the lap of his father the infant son of Mahesha used to count the teeth of the serpents around his neck, saying, one, nine, two, ten, five and seven. Sometimes, the boy putting his finger into the mouth of the skulls engarlanding Siva and catch the teeth resembling pearl-drops. Again he used to plunge his limbs into the water of the stream flowing on Siva's head; and when his hands were cold he used to warm them in the fire kept on the fore-head of his sire. Again putting obliquely on his neck the moon hanging on the crown of Shambhu wearing matted locks he used to kiss it. Thus did Hara and Parvati spend day and night with great delight witnessing the childish sports of their son. Increasing the deep joy of his parents with various lovely childish sports the boy attained youth within six days and learnt from Mahadeva all the scriptures and the use of all weapons.

CANTO XII.

Thereupon oppressed by the wily Asuras, and accordingly stricken with great anxiety Sachi's lord, along with all the celestials, approached the enemy of Andhaka as a thirsty chataka begs water from a cloud. In fear of the haughty Asuras the king of gods could not range all over the etherial way. Still imperceptibly and with great adieu he ascended from the cloud on the mount Kailasha painted with the foot-steps of Hara and Gouri. Leaning on Matali's hand Indra got down from his cloudy car and proceeded towards the abode of the trident-handed deity like unto a thirsty person approaching a stream in summer. Although going alone still he saw a multiplicity of his own forms being reflected on the crystal aud thus reached the house of the Lord. The king of gods arrived at the gate of Shankara, constructed artistically with various jems. Highly terrific Nandi was standing there with a golden rod in hand. Seeing the king of gods all on a sudden Nandi, with a golden rod hanging from his waist, welcomed him and conducted him to the court of Maheshwara.

Thereupon commanded by the Lord with the contraction of his eye-brows Nandi preceded the gods and their king and conducted them to the abode of the three-eyed deity. Thereupon the thousand-eyed deity saw Mahadeva in that assembly-hall adorned with various jems and occupied by

Chanda, Bhringi and other leading goblins having diverse forms. Lighted with jems of serpents hanging on his head and wearing matted locks he shone there like the highly elevated peak of the mount Sumeru filled with burning metals. A garland of skulls was shining on his neck. Parvati was seated on his lap. And situate on his matted locks the goddess Ganga was as if smiling with her white foams. He held on his head the moon which shed lustre on the Ganga bearing its reflection, the serpents and the quarters with its snow-white and trembling rays.

Overpowering the sun and his other two moon-like eyes, the fire like unto that of the universal dissolution which reduced Madana into ashes was shining in the eye that was on his forehead. With the great lustre of his blue throat, as if a necklace of blue jems has been sportively put there by Gouri Shankara was shining there. Stationed on his two ears and lighting up all around with rays set with valuable jems, the sun and the moon were as if serving him in the shape of two ear-rings. His limbs, covered with a thick skin, like that of a huge elephant, covered with ashes of gods and Asuras at the time of universal dissolution were appearing there like the mount Himalaya. He had as if in his hand the skull vessel of Brahma, on his limbs the garland of Vishnu's bones and that of the bones of the celestials on his neck and held the trident destructive of wars. He wore a garland of skulls, revived with hope, round his neck. And reviving by the nectarine currents coming down from his head those skulls were reciting the Vedas. The daughter of the mountain chief, of the hue of molten gold, was seated on his lap and for which he looked like an autumnal cloud accompanied with lightning. He held by two fingers the unbearable trident Pinaka which consumed the Asura Pura who made the wives of the demon Gaya widowed. He was seated on a excellent seat with a golden foot stool set with various precious jems. Two Ganas where fanning him on two sides with chowries. Other Ganas, devotedly learning the use of weapons, were looking at him. Amvika, with the corner of her cloth, was fanning the Kumara. And casting his looks on him Mahadeva was experiencing great delight.

Beholding thus the lord of the daughter of the mountain there the lord of Sachi stood stupified for some time, for whose mind is not agitated on seeing the repositary of effulgence? With his thousand beautiful eyes resembling full blown lotuses the king of gods began to look at Mahadeva for some time. Thereat it appeared that there stood a tree covered with blossoming flowers. Seeing Shankara with his thousand eyes the king of gods regarded himself fortunate and thought within himself :—These my thousand eyes used only to look at my dear Sachi formerly. Now looking at Mahadeva they have justified their existence. Therefore beholding Kumara armed with powerful weapons, seated by Mahadeva like a mount of gold Purandera began to hope for victory. Placing the golden rod on his breast and folding his hands Nandi said :—"O thou having a blue throat! O thou having three eyes, O Maheshwara! the thousand-eyed king of celestials is standing before thee seeking an opportunity for bowing unto thee. Be thou propitiated with him. The object of thy grace stands before thee, do thou extend thy grace unto him."

Thereupon with love and delight the destroyer of Tripura favoured Indra, the destroyer of Asuras and adored of the celestials, with his nectarine looks. Then taking down in humble devotion his head with Parijata flowers dropping from his crown, the foremost of gods, the deity of thousand eyes, the only adorable one in heaven, bowed unto Mahadeva, the only god of the universe. Having bowed respectfully unto Mahadeva, worthy of the adoration of all the worlds, the king of heaven and gods was crowned with consummate success. Thereupon lowering down their respective heads with delighted eyes the other celestials, endued with reverential faith, one by one appeared before his foot-stool and bowed unto the enemy of Smara. Afterwards on a golden seat being brought before by the Ganas at the command of their Lord the king of celestials sat on it and experienced great delight. Who is not pleased in receiving a recognition from his master? Thereupon with a slight smile Maheshwara looked at other celestials and honored them. Then seated all together within his view they attained to great delight.

Seeing the pale countenance with pity of Indra and other gods seated with folded hands before him, who were being oppressed by the Asuras and whose wives had been ravished by them Mahadeva said:—"O heroes! O deities dwelling in heaven! great is the power of your arms. Why then are your countenances pale like a lotus stricken with frost? Despite great piety the dwellers of heaven have been divorced from their regions. Have you all relinguished your respective superiority? Casting off their honor, wealth and celestial homes why the great gods are ranging on earth like ordinary mortals? Like unto virtue declining with the increase of sin why Yama and other gods have left their beautiful celestial homes which other creatures cannot acquire? O celestials! why do you look pale like distressed persons in the presence of the destroyer of Pura. The Demon Taraka has conquered the three worlds. Have you been greatly assailed by him? Relate every thing clearly to me. I alone am able to avert the defeat inflicted by that great Asura. What else save clouds can quench the forest-fire?

Hearing those words of the great god Mahadeva, the destroyer of Manmatha, the deities headed by

Indra were greatly relieved and delighted. Signs of joy appeared on their smiling countenances. Thereupon after the termination of Siva's speech the king of the celestials began his own in that advantageous moment. For if words are said in a proper time they yeild fruits.

" O lord, thou art the effulgent lamp of knowledge destructive of the quality of darkness. Present, past and future and all that is is within the ken of thy knowledge. O lord, dost thou not know that we have been dislodged from our respective stations by the terrible and the highly powerful Asura Taraka always oppressing the immortals? Having obtained an infalliable boon from the Creator the terrific and the highly powerful demon Taraka is regarding Indra, the enemy of Jambhu and other gods as straw. When I lauded the Grand father with verses he said that the son of the enemy of Smara would go out to the field as general and destroy the Asuras. Now the gods, residing in heaven, are suffering great pain, like that caused by a mace cutting to the quick, caused by the commands and oppressions of that irrepressible demon. Here is present before us the heroe who will remove the misery of the gods after destroying in battle that great Asura like unto a mace stuck to the heart of the Prosperity of three worlds. O lord, let the quarters resound with the cries of the wives of the great Asura, on his head being cut off by the sharpened arrows of thy son discharged in battle. Having that great Asura as food to the beasts of prey in the battle-field may thy son loosen the tresses of celestial damsels kept captives in heaven."

Hearing the words of the king of celestials and filled with anger caused by the atrocities of that demon the destroyer of Smara, showing favour unto the gods, again said :—

"Hear my words, O king of gods and deities. Well armed for the work of gods Kumara will in no time try to do you good. Although I was controlling my passion still I espoused the hand of the daughter of the mountain. The only cause of it is that a heroic son, begotten by me, will kill that Asura in the battle-field. Therefore appoint him as your genetnal for killing your enemy. May the king of gods along with deties again sanctify the celestial region." Then the divine lord of Bhavani blessed his son who was anxious for a battle saying "Achieve victory in the war of gods." It is a great virtue to persons devoted to their father. The lord of gods and brutes having said thus about the war, the daughter of the mountain was greatly pleased on hearing of the prowess of her son. Women, giving birth to heroes, enjoy great pleasure on witnessing the prowess of their sons in battle. Having obtained Kartikeya, the powerful son of Uma's lord, the destroyer of the collyrium in the eyes of the enemy's wives, and the saviour of the world, the king of gods was highly pleased. Who is not elated with joy when his desire is crowned with success ?

CANTO XIII.

Thereupon having put on a dress for journey and about to be followed by the celestials Kumar touched with his hand the feet of Mahadeva the preserver of the three worlds. Maheshwara welcomed him by blessing. "O heroe ! O child ! reinstate in battle the gods in their respective positions." Then bowing humbly his head he saluted the feet of his mother. With the tears of joy of his mother the auspicious sprinkling ceremony of the great heroe was performed. Embracing her son warmly and smelling his head the daughter of the mountain, ever fond of her son, said " Defeating the enemies make good my name "*the mother of heroes.*" Having saluted Siva and Uma with a reverent heart the General Kumar Kartikeya, the source of misery to proud Danavas, set out for the celestial region. Then having bowed unto Uma and Mahadeva and circumambulated them the leading celestials followed Kumara. The deities endued with burning effulgence going in anger, the sky, even in day time, appeared to have been covered with luminous stars. The beautiful Kumar proceeded in their midst like the moon amongst stars and other luminous bodies. Passing over the starry way in a moment Indra and other deities arrived with Kumara at the region of the seven Rishis. Being unable to enter immediately into heaven, seen after a long time, for fear of the great Asura, the gods tarried outside for some time. They quarrelled amongst themselves about their entering into heaven occupied by their enemy, saying "You go first. I wfll not go before." Kumar was sportively marking the haste of the gods and his eyes were expanded with joy. The celestials, stricken with the fear of the enemy, fixed their eyes on him. With his moon-like countenance lighted up with the rays of smile that heroe, preceding them all and awaiting the arrival of Taraka, addressed the celestials saying.

"O ye immortals! do not fear. Enter fearlessly into heaven. Let that great Asura, the enemy of the celestials, seen by Death himself, appear in my view. Let my arrows immediately make a feast of his blood, whose two arms have been elated with pride for drawing the hairs of the goddess of prosperity of heaven. May this my unmitigated power cut off the head of the enemy and conduce to your happiness."

These words of the son of the enemy of Andhaka whose mind was bent upon killing the enemy greatly gladdened the king of the celestials. And after a long time their lotus-like countenances were expanded with joy. Then greatly delighted the thousand-eyed deity rubbed him with his raiment.

Filled with great joy, Brahma, assailed by the Asuras, kissed his six faces with his four mouths having eyes filled with tears of joy. Narada and other celestial Saints approved highly of his speeah bearing a most excellent signification. In order to encourage that hero of great energy the Devas, with Gandharvas, Vidyadharas and Siddhas, cast off their fear and pleased him with saying "O heroe, be thou crowned with success." Then eulogising the son of the killer of Tripura with exclamations of "Well said," they with their golden raiments touched his person. Thereupon the gods followed the son of the daughter of the mountain who was desirous of defeating Purandara's enemy as the ghosts follow the enemy of Smara. Thereupon they reached the celestial river the water of which was rendered twany by the washing of the dyes of the celestial damsels. Some going before began to describe with pleasure the watery sports of boars wounded by the trunks of the elephants of quarters.

Preceding Kartikeya saw the ethereal river of heaven watering again and again the canals dug around the trees grown on its bank. Her banks were covered with altars having pillows set with jems by the celestial damsels sportively ranging in the sky and sweet-speeched like golden geese. Covered with black bees drawn by the perfume of her water, and filaments of golden lotuses loosened by the movements of golden geese her water appeared red.

On her waves were reflected the forms of the celestials collected on her bank out of curiosity. And seeing them the passers-by experienced great delight.

Beholding that celestial stream after a long time as if not seen before the king of gods had his eyes expanded with surprise. Approaching that Mandakini adored of the celestials, Kumara, placing his folded hands on his crown, lauded and saluted her. Shaking the full blown lotuses and embracing the waves the wind served the Kumara after removing the drops of perspiration from his forehead. While passing on Kartikaya, the son of the enemy of Smara, saw before him Indra's pleasure-garden Nandana, containing various trees the branches of which were broken. When Kartikeya saw that garden the beauty of which was despoiled by the wicked Danavas his face put on a grim visage and his eyes became reddened.

Thereupon Kumara beheld Amaravati, the essence of the entire universe. At that time the celestial cars were not moving about there—all the pleasures thereof were spoiled and that city, the cream of the entire universe, was in a pitiable condition. The prosperity of the city was pilfered,, by the enemies and she looked poorly on every side. Seeing her like a helpless woman Kumara was stricken with pity. Seeing in that city the atrocities of the enemy of gods he was filled with anger, and mortification. Anxious or battle and looking at Amaravati in that wretched plight he entered there along with the celestials. Seeing the crystal palaces, standing on the expanded fangs of huge serpents, the pillars of which were broken down by the teeth of the kings of demons he was filled with great mortification. The golden lotuses, engraved in that city, were spoiled with the temporal juice of the elephants of quarters——the sappire altars were filled with golden geese and the lakes were covered with reeds. Witnessing these oppressions of the enemies Kumara was worked up with sorrow and shame. Preceding the king of gods took him to his own palace Vaijayanta, the pillars of which were broken by the tusks of the elephants, and jems were covered with cobwebs. The king of gods himself showing the way Kumara, followed by other gods, entered there by stairs set with jems. Thereupon having benedictory ceremonies performed by the Munis, Kumara entered inside the palace decorated with garlands of Parijata flowers and gate-ways beautified with natural desire-fullfilling trees.

Having circumambulated the great saint Kashyapa, the originator of gods and demons, Kartikeya saluted him by bending low his six heads. Afterwards he touched with his head the feet of the wife of that great Rishi, Aditi, adorable unto the world. Thereupon Kashyapa and Aditi, the mother of Suras, blessed him who was desirous of defeating Taraka saying " Defeat the Asura Taraka in battle."

8

Then Kumar saluted the deities, living under the protection of Aditi, who had come there to see him. The gods welcomed him with blessings. Then Kumara saluted Indra's queen Sachi, the daughter of Puloma. She too received him with blessings. Then approaching the seven Mothers, Aditi and others Kumara saluted them with reverence. They also blessed him. Here Indra and other gods assembled and filled with joy appointed him as their Generalissimo. While having accepted the command of the celestial army Kumara, the son of Hara of endless enegies, inspired the gods with the hope of victory over their enemy, they finding an apportunity for battle cast off all sorrow.

CANTO XIV.

Thereupon Kartikeya, the son of the enemy of Andhaka, ever anxious to enter into battle and desirous of victory, began to make preparations for war along with the celestials for destroying the great Asura Taraka in battle by force. Then the great bowman Kartikeya ascended a huge car by name *Vijitwar*, swift like the mind, and irrepressible like victory hard to acquire. Some one held at that time over his head the beautiful and well-built golden umbrella which saved the prosperity of heaven from dangers and assailed that of the Asuras. Some fanned him with chowries beautiful like the rays of the autumnal moon. And preceding Kinnaras, and Charanas chanted aloud the glories of Kartikeya anxious to fight. Putting on a war-dress, holding his infalliable thunder-bolt which had cut off the wings of the mountains, and riding his elephant Airavata like unto a huge crystal mountain the king of heaven followed him. Riding his infuriated lamb, huge like a mountain summit, blazing the more in anger begotten by hatered and inspired with greater energy the fire-god followed him. Holding a dreadful rod and riding an infureated bull, huge-bodied like a black mountain and capable of piercing rocks with its horns Yama, desirous of fighting, followed the celestial General. Riding a goblin Nairita, worked up with terrific anger on account of hatered and elated with pride, followed for battle the son of Andhaka' enemy. Riding a Makara huge like a gate and dreadful, Varuna, endued with youthful zeal and holding his noose followed Kumara, mad after fighting. Riding his deer which can pass over Kailasha and other mounts in a moment and going like wind, the fierce and great warrior Kuvera followed Kumara. Holding a huge mace which was desirous of drinking the blood of the enemies, and riding a conveyance carried by men he followed the Lord's son who was about to plunge himself into the ocean of war. Riding huge bulls white like snow-clad mountains the Pinakis, who bind their clotted locks with huge serpents and hold blazing tridents in the battle-field, followed Kumara. Other dwellers of heaven too, out of reverence for the battle, riding their most excellent carriers and having countenances beaming with joy, followed Kumara.

Thereupon Kartikeya, son of Trident-handed Siva, led the great celestial army to the battle-field. It consisted of lofty golden standards, moving umbrellas of variegated colours, clatter of car-wheels and the sound of bells around the necks of elephants. The lustre of this army lighted up the quarters. The quarters, sky and earth were filled with their war-cries, and thick-set flags. The quarters and the sky were filled with the sound of drums at which the prosperity of the Asuras trembled. Resounding with the sound of drums like unto the roaring of the ocean and capable of causing abortion of Asura women, the sky, assailed with the dust raised by the soldiers, was as if making a dreadful noise. Dust of golden mountains was raised by horse hoops, spread by cars and the ears of the elephants, caught by clouds and dispersed by the wind. And gradually the sky was filled with it. Dust of gold was raised in the valley by the hoops of horses and scattered over all the quarters by the gusts of wind made it impossible to discern the directions. Being all over the army, beneath, upwards, before, in the rear and on all sides the dust of gold defeated the rays of the newly-risen sun. Dust of gold raised by the soldiers shone brilliantly in the sky. It appeared thereat that twany clouds had risen in the red dye of the untimely evening. Seeing their own reflections on the golden ground and mistaking them for others rising from the nether region the elephants began to strike them fiercely with their tusks. Rendered tawny with golden dusts and going slowly the celestial elephants going to the mount of pure gold saw their own reflections before. Shaking the forest skirts with their noise the army, of the king of immortals anxious to fight a great battle, descended from the golden mountain. The loud cries of the war-elephants increased by the trinkling of their bells could not arouse the lions sleeping at ease in the caves of the mount. Are the lions called kings of beasts because they are not terrified by the sound of bugles and its echo in the caves as well as by the sound of huge cars? The war-cries of the soldiers rending even the mountains maddened the lions. In fear of being struck by the celestial host the deer fled away but the lions came out of the caves and stood fearlessly at their mouth. Filled with curiosity people delightedly looked at Amaravati. The army did not extend all over the vast and extensive foot of the mount of celestials. The huge army marched covering the earth. It was not measured anywhere and proceeded towards heaven. It appeared like the extensive and moving city of Gandharvas. When he roar of the army entered into ears it appeared that a great sound extending all over the world had arisen on account of the churning of the ocean of milk. The ears were covered with noise of elephants, neighings of horses and the rattle of car-wheels. The dust raised by the soldiers stuck for some time to the hairs, eyes, eye-lashes and breasts of women kept in prison by the Asuras, and to their flags, horses, cars and elephants. The dust of the army covered the sky and the sun. When the dust assumed the form of new clouds the golden standards rising up to sky, looked like lightning. The vast interstice between the heaven and earth being covered with dust people began to think that it was coming either from up or down. But no body could ascertain the cause. On account of the spreading of the dust, so thick that even a needle's point could not pierce it, the vision of creatures could not extend on any side. On account of the roars of the elephants of quarters being resounded on cars and of the neighing of horses it appeared that the sky was roaring. Not even finding time to breathe on account of the roars of infuriated elephants, neighs of tall horses, and the rattle of the wheels of moving cars decorated with standards the sky was as if greatly assailed. The quarters as if became talkative by the terrific roars of elephants, tinkling of bells and cries of heroes. A river was immediately created by the temporal juice trickling from the infuriated elephants. It was converted into mud by the dust raised by the hoofs of the horses; and when the cars passed over it it became solid earth. The movements of the horses lowered some places and elevated others. But the cars and elephants levelled them all. The sound of bugles capable of rending the huge mountains which was resounded in the sky and the extremities of the quarters terrified the world as if with the roaring of the ocean. The flags obstructing the sky and quarters on being shaken by the wind, and the golden bells making a tinkling sound were plunged into the ocean of dust. The incessant ringing of the bells and the roars of the infuriated elephants were clouded by the sound of drums. When the clothes of the women of the quarters in menses dropped down by the terrific cries of the soldiers all the quarters were clouded with dust and the sun disappeared. Attacking by force the women of quarters and soiling them with dust the soldiers set up a terrible roar by the echo of the sound of bugles. When the elephants like unto moving mountains, covered the sky it appeared that thick clouds were bent down on earth by the weight of water of the illimitable oceans, roaring terribly at the time of the universal dissolution and poured their contents on mountains filling up the space between the sky and earth.

CANTO XV.

THE rumour that Indra, the destroyer of Bala, is coming out with Kartikeya, the son of Andhaka's enemy, at the head of his army, shook the heart of the Asuras. Hearing that the son of Manmatha's enemy shining in victoroy, was coming out with victorious army of gods the minds of the leading Asuras were greatly agitated. Placing their hands on their crests the guards said to the king of Daityas :—

"O king of Asuras, himself desirous of battle, Jambha's enemy Indra is coming with the son of Smara's enemy."

The king of Asuras began to laugh tauntingly saying "I have made slaves of the three worlds. Sachi's lord has defeated me many times and he will vanquish me this time with the help of Girisha's son."

With his lips trembling that proud and fiercely powerful Asura, Taraka, ordered his Generals to get ready for battle, with a view to conquer the three worlds. Armed for battle the Generals began to wait outside the gate of the courtyard filled with submissive kings. Many commanders, elated with the pride of churning the ocean, were waiting there on horse-back. When pointed out by the warder they saluted the king of Daityas at which he was highly pleased. Thereupon the Asura Taraka proceeded towards the battle-field in his terrible and huge car, the rattle of whose wheels caused the temporal juice of the elephants of quarters to ooze, which could destroy the strength of Indra and was capable of being obstructed by the great ocean and mountain only. Then a huge army followed the king of Daityas. It set up a roar terrible like that of the ocean agitated at the time of universal dissolution. Its flags obstructed the rays of the sun. And the dust raised by it covered the sun and the extremeties of the quarters. The dust raised by the soldiers of the Asura king while proceeding towards the celestials, increased the whiteness of the teeth of the elephants of quarters and created mud in jars full of sacred water.

The mountain caves of the great Asura and the sky were agitated with sound of drums. Rising at the roars of the huge army of the enemy of gods the celestial river washed the houses of heaven with numberless waves. The evil omens, as if the standards of Death himself, appeared before the Asuras who were about to march for the battle-field. Flying above the army of the Asura-chief, dreadful-looking celestial birds began to obstruct the rays of the sun. It presaged the sure destruction of the Daityas. Then the wind, blowing high, broke into pieces the umbrella rods and disturbed great men, horses, elephants, and huge cars. Then went before them huge serpents, dark like collyrium and of dreadful forms, vomitting poisonous fire and presaging evil. United with the huge serpents the sun began to shed fierce rays, as if out of his enmity towards his enemy, the great Asura, he was going with his mouth wide open. Assembled together and looking towards the solar disc the jackals began to cry hideously being desirous of drinking blood, after the termination of the war of the king of celestials. Dropped down during the day stars began to fall around the army of Asuras. Thereat people thought that a great disaster, destructive of the lives of Asuras, was present. Rising up with their rays, lighting up the sky up to the extremities of the quarters, and rending them with fierce sound fere-brands began to drop down from the cloudless sky. The sky began to pour down burning embers, blood and bones. And displaying smoky flames it showed brownish dust in the quarters. Terrible gusts of winds, setting up sounds like unto those at the time of universal dissolution and capable of piercing the ear-holes, and striking down the summits of mountains filled up with the dust the earth, sky and interstices between the quarters. There took place such a terrible earth-quake rending the mountains and agitating the oceans so that huge elephants shook before the army of the enemies of the celestial, horses dropped down and people fell embracing one another. Collected together and looking up to the solar disc the dogs began to yell hideously before the Asuras.

Even beholding these evil omens presaging a terrible result, the wily king of Asuras Taraka, influenced by an evil destiny, did not, in anger, desist from setting out for the battle. Although he was prevented by many Asuras on seeing these evil omens still he went on. For useless is the advice of the good unto him blindly following evil ways. The umbrella of the great Asura was struck down on the ground. It so appeared then that the drinking bowl of death, made of silver, was placed on the ground. His crown was torn knowing as if that the severing of his head was certain. And by the continuous dropping of pearls it was, as it were, weeping pouring drops of tears. Anticipating the certain death of the Asura-chief although prevented by his followers on all sides the vultures came near his head as if being desirous of taking it. People saw a huge serpent, dark as collyrium, spreading lustre of the jem on his hood, hiss as if desirous of vomitting venom. Dreadful fire, originating from the axles of his car, consumed the hair cowries and quivers. Although repeatedly visited by these evil omens, still the king of Asuras, worked up with pride, did not desist from setting out for war. Then an etherial voice of the Maruts was heard.

"O Asura, maddened with pride, do not vaunt of the strength of thy arms in a combat with the son of Shankara and ever victorious Indra. As nocturnal darkness cannot overpower the sun so the great Asuras will not be able to defeat Kartikeya born six days before. So thy quarrel with him will do thee injury. Dost thou expect victory over him in battle who has made holes in the great mountain Kroucha which stands clouding the sky with hundreds of summits and obstructing the way of the guardians of the quarters. In sooth it is an imppossibility. It is impossible for thee to fight with that lion-like heroe, the glory of the three worlds, with whom even Jamadagnya does not wish to fight,—Jamadagnya the night of death unto the Kshatryas, who having learnt the science of war from Siva sprinkled himself with the blood of the thighs of kings for twenty one times."

Hearing this most important ethereal speech that great Asura was beside himself with anger and possessed by pride did not hear. Shaking the three worlds with the weight of his army he proceeded towards heaven. Then the sky-ranging deities said :—

"O proud Asura, do not show your pride before the great prowess of Mahadeva's son. Seeking refuge with this only heroe of the universe live at ease for a tong time."

Thereupon the king of Daityas replied :—"O ye deities ranging in the sky, what do you say, taking the opposite side of the Asuras. Alas, immediately forgetting the pain inflicted by my arrows you will take to your heels. Stationed in the sky and depending upon the strength of a boy, six days old, what are you speaking harshly like wicked dogs in the night of a Kartika month? This infant son of the ascetic will surely meet with destruction. As even an innocent man is killed by keeping company with a thief, so after destroying you all first I will afterwards kill that innocent boy."

The king of Asuras after having said this the sky-ranging gods, holding huge daggers, fled away in fear, each striking the other with his knee-joints.

Thereupon laughing hideously in pride and placing his shining sword in the sheath the king of Asuras said to his charioteer "Do you soon drive the car where the king of gods is."

Thus commanded he drove the car swift as the mind and the Asura Taraka reached the fore-part of the dreadful celestial army. Beholding that vast celestial army and being anxious to play with his huge arms the king of Asuras was filled with great delight. Worked up with a desire to fight the followers of the Daitya went on as swiftly as the mind. Do the heroes ever make delay in battle?

Plunging themselves into the ocean of soldiers, throwing up their arms the soldiers of the Asura began to recite their own names. Beholding before the army of the Asura like a vast ocean all the gods were worked up with anxiety. But the result of the future battle was perceptible in the corner of the eye of the son of Smara's enemy the commander-in-chief of the celestial army. Seeing the celestial solders stricken with anxiety on beholding the enemy's army the General Kartikeya looked with graceful eyes at them inorder to ascertain his own strength. Seeing that great heroe in battle Indra and other gods exclaimed "I will defeat the enemy in battle," and began to display great zeal. Who is there who does not display his power on being united with the foremost of heroes. The car-warriors respectfully reciting their names the soldiers of the holder of thunder-bolt as well as those of his enemy took up their arms.

There arose a great tumult from the two armies of the gods and demons, extending far and wide and worked up with anger like unto that of the two oceans heaving and going beyond their banks at the time of dissolution. If appeared that inorder to make profuse presents unto death a great tumult, capable of rending the mountains, filled the belly of the universe.

CANTO XVI.

Thereupon displaying their respective arms the celestial and Asura hosts began to fight a terrible battle. The foot soldiers confronted the foot, the car-warriors fought with the car-warriors, the infantry with the infantry, the elephant-warriors with other elephant-warriors. The panegyrists began to sing the history of the heroes. Worked up with eulogy the the heroes, without spending a moment, began to fight. When the heroes began to fight with one another their bodies increased with the joy of war and thereat their coats of mail dropped down from their persons. With coats of mail sundered mercilessly the sky and the quarters were rendered brown as if with cotton. Covered with blood, the swords of the heroes effulgent like the rays of the sun, appeared like so many lightnings. Arrows shot by clever warriors, emitting flames from their mouths like dreadful serpents covered the sky. Piercing deeply the body the arrows of the bowmen, without blood in their mouths, dropped down at a distance on the ground. The arrows first struck down the elephants piercing their body and then dropped down amongst the hostile warriors: the sky being strewn with thick and blazing arrows the car-warriors amongst the gods went elsewhere. Struck with the arrows of the warriors and being bewildered the sky began to make a hoarse sound in the shape of the war-cries of the Generals. Tempted to drink the blood of the warriors, engaged in the action, the arrows, shot off bows drawn to ears, dropped down at a distance. The heroes holding the unsheathed swords in their hands, they, appearing as the so many mouths of the battle by their lustre, began to laugh. The swords, bathed in blood, dancing in the palms of the warriors it appeared that lightnings manifested themselves in the vast battle-field clouded with dust. The burning effulgence of the persons of the leading car-warriors moved in the sky of battle like the rays of the sun. At the terrible war-cries of the assembled warriors some dropped down from the horses and others became insensible. Encountering their hostile combatants some heroes taking pleasure in battle were filled with joy. The cowards fled from the battle-field in dismay. Moving about and fighting with other heroes and calling them by names some warriors said "I have settled to fight you first." Some warriors struck at the arms of others coming towards them from all sides with hairs standing on end. The pearls dropped from the trappings of elephants and looked like seeds sown in the battle-field.

Terrified at the war-cries of the heroes, the elephants, not even controlled by the strokes of the hook began to fly away to the end of the quarter. Running in the battle-field, the huge-elephants, with bodies wounded with shafts, scattered the warriors and threw them into the ocean of blood. Confronting the enemies, some warriors, standing on huge cars in the rivers of blood, began to discharge arrows. The horses, having their heads severed with swords, dropped down not before having struck down the enemies whose heads were cut off with daggers. Falling down the heads of heroes, cut off by arrows, ran towards the enemies biting their lips with teeth. Holding the heads, of the leading warriors cut off with crescent-shaped arrows with their teeth the hawks began to fly away, covering all the quarters. Although the elephant-riders were wounded with arrows still the elephants began to move about; and it appeared thereat that the mountains were being shaken by the wind of dissolution. When the elephant-riders, in anger came between the infantry and cavalry the latter began to slaughter the former with Prashas. The fire, originating from the clashing of the tusks of the elephants began to consume all on a sudden the elephant-warriors killed by the weapons of the enemies. When the elephants, in anger, threw up the foot-soldiers with their trunks, their master, seated on them killed the enemies, thus thrown up, by cutting them in twain with their swords. The elephants caught the warriors and threw them at a distance. As soon as they were dead their souls held the celestial damsels by the neck. Weapons stole away the trunks which the infantry had cut off with their sharp swords. When the foot-soldiers were thrown up towards heaven by the elephants with their trunks crimson-hued celestial damsels came and covered the welkin. When the elephants thus began to fight the combatants killed one another with their weapons. Seeing the elephant riders swoon away the bowmen and horse-soldiers began to wait for sometime in expectation of an engagement. Desirous of cutting off the trunks of the wicked elephants with their swords the infantry began to get upon them piercing their tusks. Cutting the four legs of the elephants although the foot soldiers went under them they quickly came out before they dropped down.

Although caught by infuriated elephants the heroes killed them with their swords and remained themselves unhurt. One horse-soldier striking another such with his weapon, could not know before he was wounded that he was cut on his breast by the Prasa of the falling combatant. The huge horse, with his eyes dilated in fear, did not leave the body of the warrior covered with wounds even after he had dropped down dead. By the huge Pasa which he had formerly in his hand, the heroe, seated firm on horse back, although killed by his enemy, seemed alive and moving about in the battle-field with Prasa in his hand. Although severed with a sharp sword, the horse-soldier, before he swooned away, tried to kill his combatant in anger. When striking each other in anger both the heroes dropped down on earth they began to fight with knives or closed one another with arms or by holding one another's hairs. Setting formerly arrows to their bows, car-warriors, firmly seated, appeared alive although killed by other car-warriors. One car-warrior, seeing another fallen in swoon, desisted from striking him but waited in expectation of an engagement till he regained conscious ness. Two car-warriors, holding most excellent weapons, killed by each other, went to heaven and began to fight again for one Apsara. When the heads of the two heroes were chopped off with crescent-shaped arrows the sky-rangers saw their bodies dancing on earth. When trumpets were struck in the battle-field rendered slippery with blood goblin women and trunkless demons began to dance with great difficulty. Thus when the encounter between the gods and demons began a stream of blood flowed in the battle-field in which the elephants were like banks. With his eyes reddened in anger and frowning the king of Asuras came before the guardians of the quarters with a desire to fight with them.

CANTO XVII.

When worked with a desire to sport in the battle-field Kartikeya, the commander-in-chief of the celestial army came before the guardians of the quarters, maddened with the fury of battle, assembled in the sky and quarters darkened with arrows. Then laughing hideously, the Asura-chief Taraka covered all the quarters with a down pour of arrows by which it appeared that clouds covered a huge mountain with incessant showers. As Garudas tear into pieces the serpents so the sharp arrows discharged by Indra and other guardian deities of quarters in the battle-field sundered into atoms the shafts of the king of Asuras. Like unto fire covering the quarters and sky the king of Asuras too, with burning arrows, with his name written thereon with grass, cut off the shafts of the celestial soldiers. The arrows, which were discharged by the Asura chief moving about and burning in anger in the battle-field, assuming terrific forms like raging serpents, fettered the leading celestials. Bound by the Asura in serpentine nooses and sighing heavily they desisted from fighting. In order to avert the evil the guardians of the quarters approached Kartikeya. Released from the calamity of being fettered by serpentine nooses by favourable looks of the son of Tripura's enemy they began to serve Kumara desirous of achieving a great victory.

Thereupon burning like the fire of anger the large-armed celestial enemy Taraka said to his charioteer :—" The gods headed by Indra bound by me with serpentine nooses have been released by the looks of the infant son of Mahesha. Leaving them I will offer sacrifice of beasts to the battle-field. Therefore drive my car to the Shambhu's son. I will see how much strength that proud Kurmar holds on his arms."

The charioteer drove his car making a rattle deep like the muttering of clouds. It proceeded slowly on the mud caused by flesh, bones and blood. Seeing that car of the celestial enemy come with a terrific form at the time of grinding the enemies like a huge mountain shaken by the wind at the time of universal dissolution the celestial soldiers began to tremble in fear. Seeing the soldiers of the deities of the quarters thus terrified approach Kartikeya anxious to sport in battle the terrific lord of Daityas Taraka, who held a bow with great prowess, said :—

"O weaver son of Sambhu, desist soon from this work which causes uneasiness unto the king of celestials. Am I afraid of the attack of your arms tender like new lotuses and unused to victories? You are the only and best son of Girisha and Gouri. Why will you die a premature death in the net of my arrows? Therefore no use of a battle. Flying from the battle-field in my fear fill up the tender laps of thy parents. O son of Girisha, considering it well in your mind give up the party of Jambhu's enemy. This Indra himself will sink in deep water, but forsooth before that he will drown you like a heavy boat."

Hearing those words of the Asura Taraka in the battle-field Kartikeya, the son of the three-eyed Siva, with his lips trembling in anger and eyes reddened like a full-blown lotus, cast his looks on his bow and replied :—Yes it becomes you to give vent to such words in pride. I will examine your superior strength of arms; string your bow and take up arrows."

On Kartikeya saying it the Asura, with his lips expanded in anger said :—"If you wish battle being elated with the pride of your strength then bear my arrows bathed in blood." Saying it the king of Asuras immediately stringed his bow, dreadful-looking unto his enemies. Then in anger Kumara set a dreadful looking arrow to his bow resembling a huge serpent. Then stretching his bow to his ears the Daitya-chief discharged arrows. They spread on all sides of his bow. It appeared that the painter of the sky (the sun) was painting arrows on all sides of a mountain with his rays. Covering the celestial army with his shining arrows the Daitya-chief whose shafts strike terror unto heroes was not seen there himself. The various arrows, discharged in battle by the son of Manmatha's enemy drawing his bow to his ear, cut all on a sudden into pieces the shafts of the enemy of gods. Assailing the body of the numerous sky-rangers, and making the day rendered inclement by arrows of the king of Asuras fair he stood there lighting up the world by the irrepressible effulgence of his own person like unto the lord of gods. Then the great Asura-king, Taraka, of fierce energy, in battle more patient, and expert in spreading illusions, began to fight an illusive battle hard to stand. Thereupon when Kumara became victorious in that illusive battle, that highly irrepresible Asura, the flag of victory in the world, seeing his illusion baffled and worked up with anger, laughing hideously put an airy arrow to his bow. As soon as that arrow was shot a terrible wind blew there, causing whirl-winds as at the time of universal dissolution, making a dreadful and hoarse sound raising up dust and covering the middle of the sky and the sun of fierce rays. The wind blew up the umbrellas of the gods white like

Kunda flowers, which flew irregularly in the sky darkened with dust like swans. It also blew up huge flags white like new Mallika flowers at which it appeared that the etherial Ganga was making a thousand of movements. The cars of the celestial host were thrown out of way by that terrible wind. The horses dropped down trembling and the charioteers fled away on all sides in dismay. Trembling, wandering away into wrong tracks and falling down on earth the huge elephants of the army looked like mountains whose wings were cut off by Vasava. When the horses of the celestial host were struck down by that terrible storm, the distressed warriors, throwing off their arms, dropped down on earth as if wounded with weapons. Assailed with that terrific storm the infantry of the gods began to cry distressfully and fearfully. Weapons came out of their hands and fell down on earth at some distance. Thus when the soldiers of the gods were greatly agitated by the king of Daityas with the strokes of his weapons that foremost of gods, Kartikeya, for regaining the prosperity of heaven, began to display a celestial effulgence.

Thereupon united with Kumara and accordingly comforted the soldiers again began to fight. Seeing it the king of Asuras, burning like fire in great anger, discharged a flaming fiery weapon. Thereat obstructing the vision of the gods thick smokes, darkening the ten quarters, black like clouds and shining like lotuses, began to move about in the sky. Seeing the sky covered with darkness setting thick like clouds at the extremities of the quarters as well as with smokes the swans immediately became anxious to go to the lake of Manasa. Then a fire, dreadful like that at the universal dissolution, was ablaze on all sides of the celestial host. Thereat the sky and quarters became red with flames. With continual flames of burning fire and smokes the sky appeared like a row of clouds accompanied with lightnings. Scorched greatly with that unbearable flame moving about in the sky and greatly agitated the celestial host approached the son of Sambhu. Beholding the celestial army thus assailed by fire and overwhelmed Kumara, smiling a little, set an arrow to his bow. Then shaking the mountain summits there arose in sky, muttering terribly, thick clouds dark like darkness, accompanied with the smokes of dissolution. Accompanied with clouds muttering terribly, lightnings, like unto dreadful tongues at the time of universal dissolution, appeared in the sky, lighted up the quarters and ,surprized people. With clouds looking like black throats and like night of dissolution with the rows of teeth, lightnings appeared there as if in terrible rage. Covering the sky and quarters, and assailing the minds with terrible roars clouds began to pour torrents of rain on all sides. When the sky was enshrouded with clouds many rivers of blood flowed in the battle-field, the dead bodies of Asuras striking against their banks. Then the fire spreading to the extremeties of quarters and about to devour the universe was extinguished by rain poured by clouds, covering the sky and destroying many an Asura stricken greatly with the roars of Varuna's weapons.

Thereupon worked up with anger the Asura began to strike Kumara with many razor-shaped arrows discharged from his bow drawn up to ears. The celestials began to fly away on all sides in his fear. Like unto a Yogin destroying worldly objects with infallible rules of self-restraint Kumara, engaged in sport in the battle, cut off into pieces with arrows the bow and shafts of the king of Asuras. Thereupon burning in anger and looking dreadful like a serpent Lord Paramount of the Asuras, Taraka got down from his car, and with leathern fences, and sword in his hands confronted Kumara. Seeing that Asura-chief, having strength of arms invincible unto the soldiers of the gods, approach and looking delightful with a face like unto a lotus the Lord's son, Kartikeya, discharged a huge weapon Sakti capable of consuming everything like the fire of dissolution. Lighting up the sky and the quarters, the great Sakti, accompanied with the tears of grief of the Asuras and tears of joy of the regents of quarters, dropped on the breast of the Asura-chief.

Beholding the Asura Taraka struck down by that Sakti like unto a mountain summit by the wind at the end of a cycle Indra and other gods were filled with delight. Deprived of his life Taraka, the king of the offspring of Danu, fell like a mountain struck by a whirl-wind. With his fangs Ananta, the king of serpents, could with difficulty hold the earth sinking down under the weight of his person. At that time the Kalpa tree, served by black-bees drawn there by perfume, began to shower flowers accompanied with water drops of the celestial river on Shambhu's son Kartikeya the enemy of the Asuras. Thereupon with their faces expanded with joy and bodies filled with delight Indra and other gods, together with the leading celestials, welcomed the strength of Taraka's enemy. Thus when did the son of Smara's enemy, ever victorious in battle, destroyed the king of Danavas, the enemy of the three worlds and like unto a mace, to the abode of death, and when Vala's enemy the king of gods, regained his kingdom in heaven, the celestials bowed unto him touching his foot with their jewelled crests. Released from dangers the gods were crowned with sucess.

THE END.

RITU-SAMHARA

OR

AN ACCOUNT OF SEASONS.

[*TRANSLATED INTO ENGLISH*]

A POEM BY

KALIDASA.

PUBLISHED BY

THE SOCIETY FOR THE RESUSCITATION
OF INDIAN LITERATURE.

CALCUTTA:
PRINTED BY H. C. DAS, ELYSIUM PRESS,
Kashi Ghose's Lane, Beadon Street.

1901.

RITU SAMHARA.

A DESCRIPTION OF THE SUMMER.

O DEAR, of late the Summer has set in when the rays of the sun become very fierce, the clear and cool rays of the moon are sought, the watery contents of big ponds become scanty for people continually bathing there and the force of Cupid becomes lessened.

During this season people are fond of moon-lit nights, water houses, various jewels and sandal-paste.

During summer nights seated at ease in sweet-scented and charming mansons men enjoy the nectar of lips shaken by the air of the mouth and sweet music of Vina set in tunes.

With waists decorated with chains, breasts pasted with sandal and bedecked with necklace, and tresses perfumed with charming scents beautiful damsels remove the summer sufferings of the males.

Dying their feet with deep red-dyes the beautiful waisted damsels beautify the Nupuras making sound sweet to the ears like swans. Their every foot-step increases the passion of men. Look, O dear, whose calm mind is not agitated with sentiments of love on seeing the rising breasts of damsels pasted with sandal, their breasts adorned with necklaces and their waists bedecked with golden chains?

Always perspiring heavily the youthful damsels, with pointed breasts, cast off thick-set clothes and cover their breasts with thin ones.

By means of the wind of fans soaked with sandal water, by means of touching the breasts, covered with necklaces of women and by the sweet music of Vina, even the sleeping sentiment of love in men's minds is excited.

Seeing the faces of women lying asleep in night at white mansions and chastising his own beauty, the moon, filled with shame, becomes pale in the morning.

The earth is stricken with the fierce heat of the sun, the dust is raised by the terrible wind. Even persons, living in strange countries and having their minds consumed by the fire of separation from their loves, cannot look at it.

Greatly assailed by the heat of the sun and with tongues dried up by thirst the deer are looking up to the blue sky mistaking it for a pond. The glances of sportive women, accompanied with smiles like unto the moon-lit night were creating desire in the minds of men living apart from their wives.

Assailed with excessive heat and scorched with the heated dust ; the [serpents, sighing heavily, and with their hoods bent, are taking shelter under the shade of the peacock's feathers.

The lions have become weak and shorn of energy with thirst. They are breathing hard and lying on earth with their mouths wide open. Their tongues are shaking with thirst. Their manes are trembling. And even seeing the elephants near they are not rising up to kill them.

With their throats dried up with thirst, stricken with thirst and heat not getting even a drop of water they are running about hither and thither in search of it and are not terrified at seeing a lion.

The body and the mind of the peacocks have been greatly assailed with the fierce rays of the sun like unto fire increased by sacrificial offerings. Though the serpents are taking shelter under their tails they are not killing them.

Greatly assailed with heat the boars with their long mouths are digging the dried mud of the tanks as if they are seeking shelter in the nether region in search of cold water.

Assailed with heat the frogs are leaping up from heated and muddy water and are waiting under the fangs of snakes stricken with thirst.

Assailing one another and quarrelling amongst themselves the elephants are uprooting lotuses from the lake, killing the distressed fishes, driving away the terrified Sarasas and drying up the mud of the tank.

The jem, set on the hood of the serpents, is being lighted up with the rays of the sun. They are drinking air with their tongues. And distressed with the fire of their vemon, the heat of the sun and thirst they are not killing even the frogs.

From the trembling mouth of the buffaloes reddened tongues, covered with foams, are coming out. And stricken with thirst and seeking water with their faces turned up they are coming out of the mountain caves.

The green grass of the forest has been scorched by the forest-fire, dried leaves are being carried away by strong winds, the tanks are being dried up by the heat of the sun. To look to any side of the forest inspires one with fear.

Although a greater portion of leaves has fallen down from trees still sitting somehow on them the birds are breathing. Tired the monkeys are seeking the groves of the mountains. The Sarabhas with great difficulty are taking up water from the wells.

Increased by the wind, fire, red like red lead or new blown Kusuma flowers, is consuming the earth as if being anxious to embrace the tops of trees and creepers.

Forest-fire is being lighted and increased in mountain caves by the fierce wind, is with great sound entering into the forest of dried bamboos, is spreading on all sids in the midst of the heap of cotton and touching the hairs of the deer is killing them. Collected in a mass in the forest of Salmali trees, the fire, spreading its golden rays, is blowing in the cavity of trees. It is spreading up to its top on getting dried leaves and is moving about on all sides of the forest with the help of the wind.

Assailed with the forest-fire, elephants, Gavayas, and lions, forgetting their enmity and behaving towards one another as friends, are going out of the forest scorched with the fire and taking shelter on the banks of the rivers are entering into them.

Lotuses being unfolded in the lakes have put on a beautiful appearance and all the quarters have been perfumed with the smell of Patala flowers. At this time, plunging into cool water and clear rays of the moon are welcome unto people. The women and to listen to sweet songs in summer are objects of great enjoyment.

A DESCRIPTION OF THE RAINY SEASON.

O dear, with the infuriated elephants in the shape of clouds surcharged with water, with flags in the form of lightings and musical instruments in the shape of thunder, all favourite unto pleasure-seekers, the beautiful rainy season has appeared like a king.

Appearing somewhere like red lotus, somewhere

like ground collyrium and somewhere like breasts of pregnant women the clouds have covered the sky.

Pouring rain in torrents at the request of the thirst-stricken Chatakas and emitting slow mutterings pleasing to the ears, clouds, bent down by the weight of their watery contents, are slowly moving on.

Making sounds of music with thunder, taking rainbow with the string of lightning set to it and with the strokes of sharpened arrows in the shape of torrents the clouds are agitating the minds of people.

With green grass which have grown like Vaidurya jems riving the earth, leaves of Kandali creepers and Indragopa insects the earth has been filled up. It appears as if prostitutes, bedecked with red jems, are sitting there.

Maddened with joy the peacocks are emitting sweet notes. Sometimes they are unfolding their tails, sometimes showing anxiety to kiss and embrace their mates and are again dancing.

The rivers being filled up with the muddy water of the rains their force is increased. Therefore felling down the trees on both the banks, they, like unchaste women, are going quickly towards the ocean.

With tender green grass, remnants, after the deer have grazed on them, and with trees clothed with new leaves and branches the forests on the mount Vindhya are pilfering the minds of men.

The deer, endued with eyes like trembling Kuvalaya flowers are seeing the beauty of the forest with terror-stricken looks, and are exciting curiosity in the mind.

The clouds are always muttering dreadfully and have enshrouded the night with thick darkness. Still finding their way by the light of the lightning the unchaste women are going to their lovers.

Surprised at the deep muttering of clouds and flashes of lightning the women are embracing again and again their offending husbands on the bed.

Sprinkling their lips with the water from their Kuvalaya-like eyes, and casting aside garlands, ornaments, scents etc., objects of enjoyments, the wives of absentee husbands are spending the night in despair.

Terrified at seeing the new water spoiled with insects, grass and other refuges the frogs are going down obliquely like snakes.

Leaving the full-blown lotuses, anxious to give honey, in expectation of new ones the insensible black-bees, humming sweetly, are sitting on the feathers of dancing peacoks mistaking them for lotuses.

The infuriated wild elephants are crying again and again at the muttering of new clouds. The black-bees are covering their temples for temporal juice.

Clouds, bent down by the weight of water, are overing all the sides of the mountain. The fountains are filled with water and the peacocks are dancing in delight. With these objects of beauty the mountains are filling the minds if men with curiosity.

Whose mind is not being maddened by the breeze cooled by coming in contact with clouds surcharged with water, shaking the Kadamva, Sarja, Arjuna, Neepa and Ketaki trees and spreading the perfume of their flowers?

Spreading their tresses up to their waist and decorating their ears with sweet-scented flowers, the women, showing their breasts adorned with necklaces and faces smelling liquor, are exciting lust in the mind of lustful men.

The clouds, bent down by the weight of water and accompanied with lightings and rain-bows and the women, adorned with jewelled waist-bands and ear-rings, are simultaneously agitating the minds of men living apart from their wives.

Making garlands of sweet scented Ketaki, Kadamva and Keshara flowers and making ear-rings with the filaments of Arjuna flowers the pleasure-seeking women are decorating their heads and ears.

Perfuming their person with black Aguru sandal, putting on ear-rings of flowers and binding their tresses, the women, on hearing the muttering of clouds in the evening, are quickly leaving the apartments of their elders for their own bed-rooms.

Shaken slowly by the breeze, the clouds, black like red lotuses, huge, bent down by water and adorned with lightnings and rain-bows, are peltering the minds of women having travelling husbands.

The heat of the forest has been removed by the sprinkling of new water and the Kadamva flowers have blossomed. It appears that the forest is experiencing horripillation out of joy. On the branches of trees being shaken by the wind it appears that the entire forest is dancing in delight. On the blossoming of Ketaka flowers it appears that the forest is smiling.

Like unto a husband this rainy season has put on the heads of women garlands of Malati, Yuthika Vakula and other full blown wild flowers, and ear-rings of Kadamva flowers on their ears.

During this season the women carry chains on their rising breasts, thick clothes on their waists, and tresses of hairs accompanied with drops of perspiration caused by their watering the plants, on the middle part of their body.

Beholding the beauty of trees pressed down by flowers soaked with drops of new rain in this season and with the scent of Ketaki flowers the women are worked up with joy.

Thinking "He is our refuge when we are bent down by the weight of water" the clouds are enliveing with torrents the mount Vindhya assailed with fierce heat (of the summer.)

O dear, may the rainy season, the pilferer of the heart of many a beautiful women, the sincere friend of trees and creepers and the life of creatures, do you good ever and anon.

A DESCRIPTION OF THE AUTUMN.

Clothed in a raiment of kasa flowers, and making a sound of *nupuras* in the shape of the cries of maddened geese, the lotus-faced and the highly beautiful autumn has appeared like a newly wedded bride. Ripe paddies on all sides are appearing like her beautiful limbs.

In this season the earth has been whitened with kasa flowers, the night with the moon, the river with the swans and the lakes with Malati flowers.

Having fckle and beautiful Shaphari fishes for their tongues, the rows of swans sitting on their banks for neck-chains and the extensive banks for their waists the rivers are flowing slowly like inebriete women.

Some where white like a conch or a lotus and fanned by cloud-like chowries, passing in hundred parts on being thinned by the pouring of water and shaken by the wind the sky is shining like a king.

What youth is there whose mind is not attracted by this autumn in which the sky is beautiful like a mass of ground collyruim, the earth is sunny with Banduka flowers and the waters are covered with beautiful lotuses ?

The maddened black-bees are drinking the honey of kovidar trees, whose charming branches are being slowly shaken by the soft breeze and covered with tender leaves abounding in profuse flowers. Who is there, whose mind is not rent asunder by this spectacle?

Clad in a raiment of clear rays and adorned with ornaments of stars, the moon-faced night, setting aside the veil of clouds is increasing day by day like a girl.

The waves of the rivers are being broken by Karandavas. The banks are being covered with swans and Sarasas and the filaments of lotuses and the swans are emitting notes hither and hither. Whose mind is not delighted with seeing these beautiful sights?

Adorned with rays giving joy to the eyes and stealing away minds, the dew-powing moon, ever producing delight of the mind, is assailing the persons of women assailed with the poisonous shafts of the death of their husbands.

Shaking the paddy creepers bent down with the weight of fruits, making the Karuvaka trees pressed down with the weight of flowers dance and shaking the full blown lotuses the wind is by force agitating the mind of young men.

Adorned with the pairs of maddened swans, pure and full blown lotuses and lillies, the lakes, in which waves have been caused by the soft morning breeze, are agitating suddenly the mind of all.

The rainbow has disappeared in the clouds, the lightnings do not appear on the flag of the sky, the cranes do not shake the sky with the wind of their wings and the peacocks do not look up to the sky.

Leaving the peacocks who have desisted from dancing Kamadeva is approaching the swans emitting sweet notes, and leaving aside the kadamva, Surja, Arjuna and Neepa trees is going to Saptachada trees.

The gardens have been beautified with Shephetika flowers. Residing there the birds are emiting sweet notes with great glee. The eyes of the she-deer, living in the forest skirts, are looking like lotuses. Seeing these sights the minds of men are being greatly agitated.

Trembling the forests of kalhara, lotus and lillies, becoming cooler in their contact and carrying dews placed on leaves the morning breeze is creating great agitation.

Covered with ripe paddy, beautified with kine grazing at ease and echoing with the notes of swans and Sarasas, the fields, situate on the village skirts, are gladdening the people.

The swans are imitating the charming gait of women, the full blown lotuses the beauty of their face, the red lotuses their beautiful glances and the waves the charming gestures of their eye-brows.

The leaves of Shyama creepers, bent down by the weight of flowers, are imitating the beauty of the adorned gems of women and the garlands of Asoka flowers that of their smiles beautifying their lips.

The women are decorating their dark-blue tresses with new Malati flowers and putting on various red lotuses on their ears adorned with most excellent golden ear-rings.

Filled with great delight the women are decorating their breasts with chain soaked in Sandal paste, their capacious waists with Rasana chains and their feet with Nupuras making sweet sound.

During this autumn the moon, freed from clouds, the sky bespangled with stars and the lakes covered with full blown lillies, adorned with swans and water clear like emerald are appearing highly beautiful. Cooled by coming in contact with flowers the breeze blows in autumn. The quarters are freed of clouds and delightful. The earth is freed of mud. The sky is adorned with clear rays of the moon and garland of stars.

In the morning of this season, the lotuses, unfolded by the rays of the sun, put on the beauty of the most youthful damsel. When the rays of the moon disappear the lillies fade away like the smiles of women whose husbands are away.

Seeing the beauty of their wives' eyes in red lotuses, the beauty of their sounding gold ornaments in mad swans, the beauty of their cheeks in Banduka flowers, the travellers weep with their minds greatly agitated.

Transferring the beauty of the moon to the countenances of women, the notes of the geese to the Nupuras, the beauty of Badhuka flowers to the lips the beautiful autumn is as if disappering.

May this season autumn, with a countenance like a full blown lotus, with eyes like red lotuses, clothed in blossoming Kasa flowers like unto a white raiment, and smiling like lillies, give in profusion joy to your minds like an inebriete damsel.

A DESCRIPTION OF HEMANTA OR THE DEWY SEASON.

O dear, the Hemanta has set in. In this season the herbs have become beautiful with the growth of new leaves, the Lodhra trees have blossomed, the paddy has rippened, the lotus is being blown up and heavy dews are falling.

The breasts of women, having beautiful breasts, are not being dyed with red arsenic and the snow is not being decorated with Kunda flowers and moon-like garlands of pearls.

Bangles and ornaments are not finding room on the hands and arms of women and thin cloth is not finding room on their waist and breasts.

The damsels are not decorating their waists with

chains of gold set with jems and their lotus feet with Nupuras.

For celebrating the festival of sexual intercourse the women are dying their bodies with turmeric, decorating their lotus-like countenances with leaves and perfuming their heads with black Aguru and incense.

The countenances of women have become weak and pale with the toil of sexual intercourse; on account of growing joy they are not laughing aloud on seeing lips wounded with teeth.

The winter has occupied the breasts and thighs of women. And being weakened by their oppressions they are weeping in the morning with tears falling in the shape of dews from leaves.

The boundary lines, being covered with profuse paddy beautified with the she-deer and resonant with cries of beautiful Krounchas moving about on all sides, are gladdening the minds of the people.

Adorned with full blown red lotuses, maddened geese and clear water, the cool lakes are pilfering the hearts of men.

O dear, the Priyangu creepers are being continually shaken by the breeze, cooled by snow, riping and looking pale like women stricken with the absence of their husbands.

The mouths of men are being perfumed by drinking the honey of flowers and their persons are being scented with breaths. Desirous of holding sexual intercourse they are lying down embracing each other.

The merciless sexual intercourse of youthful damsels has manifested itself in the lips marked with cuts of teeth and breasts wounded with nails.

Some women, holding up mirrors, are decorating their lotus faces in the new beams of the sun and biting their lips already bitten by their lovers.

Some woman has been greatly exhausted with the toil of sexual intercourse. Her eyes have become reddened with night-keeping. And keeping her scattered hairs on the end of the bed and being heated by the mild rays of the sun she is sleeping.

Another woman, looking beautiful with her black tresses, and pressed down with the weight of her rising breasts, is dressing her hairs, removing therefrom the garlands used before the sweet scent whereof has disappeared.

Seeing her own person enjoyed by her lover and accordingly filled with delight another youthful damsel is increasing the beauty of her lips. Drawing her hairs for binding them into tresses she is contracting a little her eye-brows. And she is putting on a new cloth. Some beautiful damsels have been greatly worn out with the toil of sexual intercourse. Their limbs have been exhausted and their capacious thighs and breasts have swollen. They are rubbing their persons with sweet-scented oil and turmeric.

The boundaries of the villages have been covered

with ripe paddies. May this Hemanta, the mine of many virtues, the pilferers of the hearts of charming women and reasonant with the notes of kraunchas, conduce to your happiness.

A DESCRIPTION OF THE WINTER.

O thou of most excellent thighs, listen to an account of the winter when the earth is covered with paddy and sugar-candy, when the Krounchas emit notes at their sweet pleasure and when all sorts of enjoyments attain to their consummation—the winter which is favourite unto women.

In this season, rooms with windows closed, fire, the rays of the sun and women clad in thick clothes are the objects of enjoyment unto men.

Sandal, cool like the rays of the moon, the roof of mansions, clear like the autumnal moon, breeze cooled by snow cannot attract the mind of men in this season.

In this season people do not like places cool with the fall of dews and the night cooled with the rays of the moon and adorned with stars.

Eating betel leaves in great anxiety, wearing pastes and garlands and perfuming their faces with the honey of flowers the women are entering into bed rooms sufficiently perfumed with black Aguru.

Beholding their husbands, offending, trembling and scolded the women, inebriete with drinking honey, are forgetting their previous offences being desirous of holding sexual intercourse. Being kept up till late hours by cruel youths engaged in sexual intercourse these youthful damsels, with their breasts perspiring, walk slowly in the morning.

With their breasts adorned with beautiful filaments, waists clad in silken raiments and tresses bedecked with flowers the damsels are beautifying the, more the winter.

Rendered twany by the red arsenic dyes of women and pressed and protected by their enjoyable breasts the source of heat the lustful persons are sleeping at ease after defeating the winter.

In winter nights filled with delight women drink, in the company of their husbands, most excellent wines, shaken by the sweet-scented breath and capable of creating exhilaration and desire.

Seeing, after the intoxication is over, her own person enjoyed by her lover some one amongst women, with breasts pressed down by the embrace of her dearest, is leaving smilingly her sleeping apartment for another room.

With fading garlands sweet-scented with Aguru and dishevelled curling locks some one, having capacious waist, deep navel and of a middle stature, is leaving in the morning her bed-chamber for another room. Adorned with eyes beautiful like golden lotuses, extending up to ears, washed immediately with water and having their extremities reddened, as well as with countenances with tresses hanging on the shoulders, some women are appearing highly beautiful in their rooms in the morning.

Pained with the weight of their capacious backs and as well as with that of their rising breasts some women are going slowly; and casting off their night dresses they are putting on those fit to be worn during the day.

Marking the disfigurement of their breasts caused by the hands and nails of their lovers, and paleness of their lips, cheeks and faces caused by kisses and teeth, during sexual intercourse in the night some women are hiding themselves in the room out of shame.

During this season molasses, Shaly padies and sugar canes are produced in abundance. Desire for enjoyments and luxuries increases and therefore the minds of those whose lovers are away are greatly agitated. O dear, may this winter conduce to your well being always.

A DESCRIPTION OF THE SPRING.

O dear, having mangoe blossoms for his sharp arrows and black bees for the string of his bow, the foremost of heroes Basanta (Spring) has come for rending the hearts of pleasure-seeking persons.

Now the trees are covered with flowers, the lakes are full of lotuses, the women are anxious for enjoyments, the wind is full of perfume, the winds are delightful and the days are beautiful. O dear, everything is beautiful during the spring.

This highly charming spring multiplies the beauty of the water of the lakes, of the jewelled girdle, of the lunar rays, of women and of mangoe trees bent down by blossoms.

During the spring the pleasure-seeking women, increase the beauty of their waists, with their raiments colored with Kusamba flowers and that of their breasts with those colored with red arsenic.

The beauty of full blown Mallika flowers is manifest in new Karnikara flowers serving for the ear-rings of women and in Asoka flowers decorating their black and curling locks.

They have put on their breasts chains pasted with white sandal, on their arms armlets, on their hands bracelets and on their waists girdles.

Drops of perspiration on the breasts and faces of women, resembling golden lotuses and adorned with sandal marks, are appearing like pearls born on their limbs.

Raiments are dropping down from their limbs assailed by the lovers with their enjoyments. And when they are approaching them the women are anxious to embrace them.

The limbs of the women have become weak and pale with sexual intercourse, anxious thoughts and night-keeping. They are sighing again and again in idleness. Ananga (Cupid) is making women (even in this plight) anxious to decorate their bodies and engage in enjoyments.

Kama is living in may forms on the persons of women—in their eyes worn out with intoxication, in their fickleness, in paleness of their breasts, in the depth of their navels, and spaciousness of their backs.

Ananga has made the limbs of women exhausted with night-keeping, has caused faltering in their speech with the drinking of wine and brought about the contraction of their eye-brows.

The damsels, exhausted with intoxication, are pasting their limbs and breasts with Pryangu, black aguru, red arsenic and sandal scented with musk.

Casting off thick raiments, men, pierced by the shafts of Kandarpa, are putting on dyed clothes perfumed with black Aguru.

The male coels, maddened with drinking the honey of mangoe blossoms, are kissing with joy their mates. Humming sweetly the black-bees, intent on drinking the honey of lotuses, are enlivening their dear ones.

The mango trees have been bent down a little with the weight of new red leaves. And blossoming their branches have put on a beautiful appearance. Shaken by the wind these mango trees are agitating the minds of women.

Covered up to roots with flowers dark-blue like lotus the blossoming Asoka trees are exciting the sorrow of separation in the minds of women.

Seeing the maddened black-bees kiss the beautiful flowers of the Madhavi creepers adorned with tender leaves shaken slowly by the breeze the minds of pleasure-seeking men are worked up with desire.

Who is there a conscious man whose mind is not pained with the arrows of Kandarpa on seeing the grace of the new grown blossoms of Kuruvaka trees pilfering the beauty of the faces of their dear wives.

With the advent of the spring the trees are being slowly shaken by the breeze. Adorned all over with the forests of Asoka trees bent down with flowers resembling burning fire the earth is looking like a forest damsel clad in a crimson coloured raiment.

Are not the hearts of young men and women rent asunder by the blossoming Kinsuka flowers crooked like the eyes of Shuka birds? Are they not scorched by the Karnikara flowers? Again the coels are killing them completely with their sweet notes.

Even the minds of bashful and gentle women of good families are being agitated in the spring by the notes of joyous coels and the humming of black-bees.

In the spring, with the termination of the winter, the slow and sweet breeze, shaking the blossoming branches of mango trees, spreading on all sides the notes of coels, is blowing pilfering the hearts of men.

Beautiful gardens, adorned with Kunda flowers white like the smiles of damsels, are stealing away even the minds of the ascetics shorn of the desire for enjoyment. They have already pilfered the minds of young men, stained with the desire for worldly enjoyments.

With golden girdles hanging on their waists and necklaces adorning their rising breasts the pleasure-seeking women, with the help of the notes of coels and black-bees, are pilfering the minds of men in the month of Chaitra.

Beholding the mountains, adorned with various blossoming trees and resonant with the notes of coels men are experiencing great delight.

Seeing the blossoming mango trees the traveller, with his mind stricken with separation from his dear wife, is opening his eyes, weeping, expressing sorrow, covering his nose with his hand and exclaiming cries of despair.

With the humming of black-bees inebriete with honey, notes of Kokilas, mango blossoms and charming Karnikara-like arrows the spring is continually wounding the hearts of sensitive women.

With beautiful mango blossoms for his arrows, Kingsuka flowers for his bow, black-bees for his bow-string, the moon for his umbrella, the southern wind for his infuriated elephant and the coels for his panegyrists may the god Kama, with his companion Spring, do good unto all.

In the spring the women perfume even the palaces cooled a little with frost with beautiful flowers and decorate their breasts with various flower garlands.

Seeing on the road mango trees like unto gold shaken by the breeze, pouring flowers, the travellers, whose weak body is not worthy of being struck, are swooning away being wounded with the shafts of Madana.

The spring is mocking at the sweet words of women by the sweet notes of the Kokilas, at their smiling teeth by the beauty of Kunda flowers and at their palms by new grown leaves.

With their charming, pale and lotus-like countenances resembling golden lotuses, with breasts pasted with sandal and decorated with necklace, and with inebriete glances the women are creating desire even in the minds of self-controlled Munis.

Of the lotus-like countenances perfumed with honey, of women, their eyes reddened a little like Lodhra flowers, beautiful tresses like Kuruvaka flowers, rising breasts and waists which is it that does not excite desire in the spring?

In this season even the firm-minded women are being worked up by the breeze perfumed with mango blossoms, and assailed by the notes of Kokilas and the humming of black-bees.

The charming evening, clear lunar rays, notes of male coels, the sweet scented breeze, the humming of maddened black-bees, and drinking in the night—all these excite the desire.

In this season men love shade of the trees in the day and the rays of the moon in the night. They lie down in cool mansions and embrace their lady loves.

THE END.

RAGHU VAMSHA

OR

AN ACCOUNT OF THE FAMILY OF RAGHU.

BY

KALIDASA.

[*TRANSLATED INTO ENGLISH PROSE.*]

PUBLISHED BY

THE SOCIETY FOR THE RESUSCITATION
OF INDIAN LITERATURE.

CALCUTTA:

PRINTED BY H. C. DAS, ELYSIUM PRESS,
Kashi Ghose's Lane, Beadon Street.

1901.

RAGHU VAMSHA

OR

AN ACCOUNT OF THE FAMILY OF RAGHU.

I wish to write about this family for many sages had done so before ; just as a thread may pass through parts bored with a diamond.

Though I am not rich in words yet I wish to write the history of the kings of Raghu's family who led pure lives from their birth, who were persevering in all their undertakings till they were successful, whose empires extended up to the Sea, whose cars went up to the celestial region, who duly offered oblations to the sacred fire, who gave to every one what he prayed for, who administered punishment to the offenders proportionate to their crimes, who always worked in proper hours, who amassed wealth only to be given to the poor, who spoke very little from the fear of deviating from the truth, who made wars only to acquire fame, who took wives only to beget children, who acquired learning in boyhood, who managed worldly affairs in youth, who retired into woods in old age, and who died engaged in religious meditation. Their accomplishments being present in my ears have induced me to undertake this bold work.

Those who can discriminate good and evil are qualified to read my work. It is fire alone that can testify the purity and impurity of gold.

In the days of yore there flourished a son of the sun by name Manu. He was respected of the learned. As Om is the first letter of the Vedas so he was the first progenitor of all kings.

As the moon originated from the ocean of milk so the pure-souled Dilipa was born in the pious family of Manu.

He had a broad chest and a bull-like neck. He was long-armed and tall like a *Sala* tree. He was as if the Kshatriya virtue incarnate on earth to do its duty.

He was like the lofty mount Meru extending over the earth excelling all in the hardness of its essence and brightness of its colour.

His wisdom was like his stature and his knowledge of Scriptures was like his intellect. His actions were in consonance with his knowledge of Shastras and his success was in keeping with his actions.

By his dreadful form and royal qualities he was unto his dependants like an ocean by its jems and aquatic animals.

As driven by an expert charioteer the after-wheel of a car does not transgress the track of the fore-wheel, so his subjects did not deviate from the moral laws observed since the time of Manu.

The sun draws moisture from the earth to pay her a thousand-fold in return. So did he collect tributes from his subjects for their well-being.

His army was like the umbrella, chowri and other parapharnalia of royalty. For achieving his end he depended upon his ability to understand Scripture properly and his skill in drawing his bow.

Like unto pristine impressions his actions, who was of close counsels, and whose gestures never betrayed his mind, were judged only by the result.

Fear never urged him on to defend himself, misfortune never made him pious, avarice did not tempt him to collect money, love of pleasure never prompted him to seek it.

He observed silence in a secret confided to him, forgave an offender even when able to punish him and never praised himself in good works. All these qualities were in him in unision.

He was not addicted to sexual pleasures, was a master of every department of knowledge and led a pious life. He had every advantage of old age without decrepitude.

He made arrangements for the education, maintenance and safety of his people. He was a father to them all, their own fathers giving them birth only.

He was learned. He married for the sake of children and punished the guilty for the behoof of his subjects. Thus virtue led him to acquire wealth and objects of enjoyment.

He milched the earth for performing sacrifices (for Indra) who in return milched the sky for his crops. Thus they governed both the worlds exchanging their good things.

No other king could acquire so much fame as he, for theft was entirely unknown in his territories, people knowing only the term.

An honourable enemy was to him like medicine to a patient. But he could cast a friend, proved bad, as a finger bit by a serpent.

Forsooth God created him with the ingredients of five elements for like them his qualities were employed for the good of others.

The sea-coast was the wall and the ocean itself the entrenchment of his empire. There was no other ruler of the earth and he governed it like his own household. He had a wife by name Sudakshina born in the family of Magadha. As becoming her name she was kind and benevolent. She was to the king what *Dakshina* is to sacrifice.

Though he had other wives he considered Sudakshina and Lakshmi as his true wives.

He was anxious to have a son by his favourite consort Sudakshina and was impatient to see the day when his desire would be satisfied.

In order to perform certain ceremonies for begetting a son he handed over the administration to his minister.

Having worshipped Brahma the self-controlled pair set out for the hermitage of their preceptor Vasistha with a view to have a son.

They went on a car making a soft and deep sound and looked like lightning and Airavata riding the clouds of the rainy season.

To avoid disturbing the hermitage they took a few retainers with them. But their natural dignity inspired the on-lookers with such an awe as if they had an army with them.

Gently shaking the forest trees and carrying the fragrance of sal and filaments of flowers pleasant breeze comforted them on the way.

Mistaking the deep rattle of the car-wheel for the rumbling of clouds the peacock and pea-hen emitted sweet notes. And the cries of the male and female birds, resembling the first note of the music, delighted their ears.

The male and female deer gazed on the passing car and the king and queen, as they passed on, compared their eyes with theirs.

Sometimes they cast their looks upwards on rows of cranes emitting sweet notes and resembling garlands suspended on gates without any support.

As if fore-boding the fulfillment of their object auspicious wind blew from behind so that the dust raised by the horse's hoof could not touch the crown of the king or the curling locks of the queen.

They smelt the sweet odour of the full blown lotus resembling their own breath in fragrance, which was cooled by the contact of the waves of the lake.

As they passed through villages gifted away by them in which there were pillars commemorating the same they received offerings of honour and blessings from the Brahmanas who were in possession thereof.

They met with milkmen carrying fresh butter and asked them to describe the names of the wild trees that had grown on the road side.

Thus while putting on pure dress and both seated on the same seat the king with his queen went on they looked beautiful like the moon of pure rays emerging from midst with the planet Chitra by his side.

The learned and the beautiful king was busy in pointing various objects on the road side to his wife so that he could not perceive the distance they had traversed.

He, of renown hard to acquire, and whose horses were fatigued, reached, along with his queen, the hermitage of the great self-controlled Rishi in the evening.

It was being filled with ascetics returned from woods, with fuel, flowers and fruits and welcomed by fire invisible to ordinary observers.

There the deer, accustomed to feed on *niba* rice,

given them by the female anchorites, obstructed the doors as if they were their children.

There having watered the plants the ascetic girls went away in great haste lest they might frighten birds come for drinking the water.

In the yards of the hermitages in the evening grass and paddy dried by the sun were collected in heaps and the deer lay down at ease and chewed the cud.

There smoke, fragrant with the perfume of burnt offerings and indicating a burning fire raised by the wind, purified the hearts of guests coming to that sacred place.

Having ordered the charioteer to look after the horses the king helped the queen to descend and then himself got down from the car.

The polite ascetics, whose senses had been controlled, received with due honor their wise protector, the king and his royal wife.

The king saw the ascetic Vasistha who had just finished his evening rites, seated on the same seat with his wife Arundhuti. They looked like Agni and his wife Swaha seated side by side.

The king and the queen, the princess of Magadha saluted the preceptor and his wife; they too welcomed them with blessings.

After offering them the rites of hospitality and removing their exhaustion the ascetic enquired about the welfare of his kingdom.

Then the King, the best of speakers and the conqueror of enemy's cities, addressed Vasistha, who was well versed in the Astharva Veda, in words fraught with noble sense.

"While thou art my protector against calamities caused by men and gods it is certain that every thing is well in my seven members.

Thy mystic formulæ subdue unseen foes whereas my arrows pierce visible objects only. So by the power of thy mantras my arrows have been made useless.

The offerings, thrown by thee duly into the sacred fire, are converted into rain and revive the withered crops of my empire.

It is owing to thy Brahminic influence my subjects live long, spend their days fearlessly and are never visited by calamities of drought and excessive rain.

When my spiritual guide, Brahma's son, is anxious on my account, what wonder is that I am secure from dangers and shall enjoy perpetual happiness.

But as I have got no children by this thy daughter-in-law, the world, with all the islands, although abounding in many precious things, cannot conduce to my happiness.

My departed manes cannot enjoy to their full satisfaction the offerings I present to them at the Sraddha but keep a portion of them in reserve fearing that such offerings will terminate after my death.

They drink the oblations of water, offered by me,

heated with their sighs thinking that they shall no longer have them after my death.

By celebrating sacrifices I have paid my debts to the celestials, but having so sons I have not been able to satisfy my debts to my ancestral manes. I am like the Lokaloka mountain, half lighted by the Sun and half enshrouded in darkness.

The fruits of devotion and charity make as happy in the after life but children of good lineage conduce to happiness both here and hereafter.

Dost thou not feel as much pain on seeing me childless as thou experiencest on finding the tree of the asylum, carefully reared by thy own hands, bearing no fruits ?

My debt to my departed manes pains me as much as the stake does a newly caught elephant tied to it.

O Father, do for me that by which I may satisfy that debt. Thou art alone able to gratify the wishes of the Ikshwakus when they themselves fail to do so."

Hearing the king's prayer Vasistha engaged in meditation with closed eyes for some time and remained as calm as a lake undisturbed by fishes. By the power of coneentration the self-controlled (Rishi) could find out what stood in the way of the king's getting a son and said.

"O king, once on a time in the days of yore, while you were returning to earth after having served the king of celestials the worshipful cow Surabhi was lying down on the road side under the shade of the desire-fulfilling tree. Fearing lest you might fail in your duty by Sudakshina who had just bathed after menses, you forgot to pay her due honors.

She imprecated therefore a curse on you, saying " For thus dishonoring me you will not got a son till you worship my child."

Owing to the noise of the waters of the etherial Ganges disturbed by the sportive elephants of the quarters neither yourself nor your charioter could hear the curse.

For thus dishonoring the cow your heart's desire has not been fulfilled for our welfare is injured when we fail to honor them to whom honor is due.

Guarded by serpents she is now in the nether world for giving butter and milk to the regent of water, necessary for the celebration of a sacrifice in which he is engaged.

Being purified, yourself and your queen worship her child and representative Nandini; when she will be propitiated your desire will be crowned with success."

While Vasistha was giving him this advice the fault-less cow Nandini, which enabled him to feed the sacred fire, returned from the forest.

She was of the reddish colour like a new leaf and there was a white curve line on her fore-head. She resembled evening crowned with the crescent.

As she saw her calf she sprinkled the earth with lukewarm milk, holier than the sacred ablution, from her plump teats.

The dust raised by her feet covered the king's body who stood hard by and sanctified it as if he had bathed in the sacred stream. The ascetic, conversant with the prognostications of good and evil; seeing the holy Nandini approach the hermitage, said to the king whose desire was about to be fulfilled.

" O king, when the blessed Nandini has just arrived with the mention of her name the time is not far off when your object will be accom plished.

Living on roots and fruits you should propitiate her by constantly following her as one should please the goddess of learning by study.

You should walk when she walks, stand when she stands, and sit and drink when she does so.

My daughter-in-law too, being self-controlled, should follow her reverentially to the end of the hermitage in the morning and advance thither in the evening to receive her.

Thus serve her till she is pleased. May no mishap stand in your way and may you be the happiest of fathers as your father was on obtaining you as his son."

The disciple, conversant with the knowledge of time and place, along with his wife, accepted the command of their preceptor by bending low their heads and saying " So be it."

The night approaching the truthful and polite Vasistha, the son of Brahma, asked the king, whose happiness was about to down, to retire.

Vasistha, conversant with the knowledge of ceremonies, gave him fruits, roots and a bed of straw in consideration of what he was to perform, though he could procure him all the things of the world through his power of devotion.

In pursuance of the set rules the royal pair passed the night on the straw bed given them by that prince of hermits and rose in the morning hearing Vasistha's disciples chant the Vedas.

CANTO II.

In the morning after the queen had presented to Rishi's cow perfume and garlands and after the calf had been tied after milking, the king, having glory for his wealth, set her free for going to the forest.

Like Smriti following the Sruti, the queen, the foremost of the chaste women, followed closely the track of the cow, sanctified by the dust of her hoofs.

Having sent back his queen to the hermitage the illustrious and the kind-hearted king began to protcct Nandini who could give more milk than the water of the four oceans and who resembled the earth in the shape of a cow having four seas for four teats.

For celebrating the vow he sent away his remaining followers though they wanted to follow him. He stood in need of no external help for his protection for the descendants of Vaivaswata could protect themselves by their own prowess.

The king tended the cow by collecting sweet grass, brushing his body, driving away flies and permitting her to graze at large.

He stopped when the cow stopped, walked when she walked, stood up when she stood up and drank when she drank. He followed her as her own shadow.

Though there was no insignia of royalty on his person still he had such an effulgence that people could know him as a king. He was like an young elephant full of native wildness not yet sufficiently known.

While traversing the forest ways the trees on both the sides, with the sweet notes of the birds, used to sing the glories of the Varuna-like energetic king who had no followers by him.

When that king, effulgent like the fire, used to approach the creepers, they, shaken by the breeze, dropped flowers on him, like women of the city who used to welcome him with a downpour of fried grain.

The native mildness of his nature shining through his countenance begat so much confidence in the female deer, that though he had a bow in hand they used to gratify their large eyes by gazing at him without any fear.

He heard the presiding gooddess of the forest sing aloud his praise while the wind, passing through the holes in the bamboos, made a music similar to that of the flutes.

Cooled by the water of the mountain-spring, carrying the perfume of the gently shaken flowers the wind refreshed the pious king who was without any umbrella and therefore stricken with heat.

When he entered the woods, the forest fire was put out without rain; fruits and flowers grew in profusion and stronger animals did not prey on the weaker.

In the evening the sun, red as the new leaves, and the hermit's cow used to walk homeward sanctifying the quarters.

The King followed Nandini who used to help the ascetic in worshipping the gods, in performing annual Sraddhas of his ancestors and in treating his his guests. Followed by Dilipa, adored of the sages, she shone like faith followed by action. As he went on he saw the woodland strewn with swine just risen from muddy pools, the peacocks going to their sheltering trees and flocks of antelopes lying on the grass.

Being pained by the weight of her udders the cow, that had given birth to one calf only, went on slowly. The king too, on account of the heaviness of her person, went on slowly. Their view was indeed very charming.

Nandini, followed by the king, and welcomed by

the queen by coming in advance looked like twilight between day and night.

Having circumambulated and bowed to her with a vessel of offerings in her hand Sudakshina respectfully poured them on the part of her head intervening between her two beautiful horns, which was like the gate of success.

Although impatient to see her calf yet Nandini stood still and accepted the offerings. The king and the queen were really pleased to see this, for signs of gratification displayed by great men indicate the fullfilment of the object of their proteges.

Having prostrated himself at the feet of his spiritual guide and his wife and performed the evening rites, Dilipa 'again began to serve the calf of Suravi lying at ease after being milked.

The royal pair put offerings and a light near Nandini, they slept after she had fallen asleep and got up in the morning as soon as she was awake.

Thus observing the vow for a son, the king, who was well known for relieving the poor of their sufferings, passed twenty-one days along with his queen.

On the twenty-second day being desirous of testing the sincerity of her follower, the asceti's cow entered into a grassy cave of the Himalaya near the falls of the Ganges.

Knowing well that beasts of prey would never think of attacking her far from doing it actually the unsuspecting king feasted on the grandeur of the mountain when suddenly a lion sprang on her.

The cries of the cow, growing louder by the echoe, drew, as it were by the pulling of reins, the eyes of the king, the helper of the distressed, fixed on the mountain.

Then the king, with bow in hand, saw the reddish yellow cow with a long mained lion on her like the blossoming Lodhra tree growing on the mountain side filled with red earth.

Considering himself insulted the king, quick-coursing like a lion, the refuge of those seeking shelter, and the conqueror of the enemy's city, took out an arrow from his quiver to kill the lion that richly deserved to be killed.

As being anxious to kill the lion he was about to take up the arrow the fingers of his right hand remained fixed on the feather, as if in a picture, beautifying his nails.

His right hand being thus rendered immoveable and incapable of punishing the offender he raged like a serpent rendered inert by drugs and incantations.

The king, who was lion-like in prowess and a friend of the pious, was surprised on seeing his limbs paralysed. It was intensified, when the lion, that caught the cow, began to speak like a human being.

"O king, useless is thy attempt. Even if thou couldst discharge thy weapons they would prove futile. The force of the wind can upreot trees but it cannot stand before the mountain.

I am the servant of Siva. He sanctifies my back by placing his feet on it whenever he rides his bull white like the mount Kailasha. My name is Kumbhodara and I am a friend of Nikumbha.

Look at the yo fire tree. It has been adopted by the bull-ensigned Siva as his son. It has been nursed by Skanda's mother by pouring water from golden pots.

One day a wild elephant tore its bark by rubbing his cheek against it. Thereat the Himalay's' daughter was as much stricken with grief as she was when she saw Kartika wounded by the arrows of the Asuras.

Since then the trident-handed deity has appointed me a guard to drive away the elephants; and at his behest I live upon animals that approach this spot.

Mahadeva has been pleased to send this cow at the hour when I take my food. Her blood shall satisfy me as the moon's ambrosia gratifies Rahoo.

Thou art helpless. Desist casting off shame. Thou hast shown sufficient devotion to thy preceptor as a disciple. The reputration of a warrior does not suffer the least if he cannot, by the use of his weapons, save the object he seeks to protect."

Hearing these prouds words of the lion the King was convinced that his weapon was nullified by the power of the lord of Kailasha and therefore his contempt towards himself was decreased.

As Indra, while he was about to hurl his thunder-bolt, was stupified by the glances of Virupaksha, so was the king who for the first time failed to discharge the weapon. He answered the lion saying."

" O king of animals, while my attempt to kill you has become futile, surely what I will say will create redicule. But as thou canst go through the hearts of men I shall do so.

I submit to the command of Mahadeva the creator, preserver and destroyer of all living and inanimats objects. But I cannot neglect this precious cow of my preceptor that is about to be killed before me.

Please therefore feast on my flesh and release my preceptor's cow. As the day is disappearing her calf is impatient to see her."

Smiling a little and lighting up the cave with the brightness of his teeth, the lion said :—

"O King, you are indiscreet enough in wishing to sacrifice the sovereignty of the world, youth and beautiful body for such an insignificant object.

It is true you have compassion for all living creatures—but consider your death will benefit this cow only whereas your life will protect your subjects against constant danger.

Your fear that your preceptor will be worked with anger like fire at the loss of his only cow; but you may appease his anger by presenting him with crores of cows with large udders.

Protect your strong and youthful body used to many luxuries. Your empire is like that of Indra, the only difference being that it is situate on earth."

When the king of animals stopped after saying this the mountain too, with the echo in his cave, said the same thing to the king.

Hearing the words of the lion, the follower of the god, and being looked at with pitiable eyes by the cow under his clutches the kind-hearted king again said.

"The great word Kshatra is universally known to signify *one who saves from danger*. If I act against that tradition of what use is a kingdom or a contaminated life to me?

O lion, how can I pacify the rage of the ascetic by presenting him with other cows in the place of Nandini who is not different from Surabhi. You have been able to attack her only by the power of Rudra.

It is my duty therefore to release her even at the cost of life. It will appease your hunger and the Homa ceremony of the ascetic will not be stopped.

You are devoted to your master. It is proved by your care of this fir tree. You know therefore a servant cannot appear before his master, without himself being wounded and losing the object of his care.

If you think that you should not kill me then spare my body of reputation instead of my corporeal frame. I consider this body of five elements as useless.

The wise say that conversation begets friendship. I have seen you in this forest and already a friendship has sprung up on account of the conversation. O servant of the lord of goblins, you should not disregard the request of a friend."

When the lion accepted his proposal by saying 'So be it' the king threw drown his arms and contracting his body presented a lump of flesh to the lion to be devoured by him.

As the king sat on the ground with his face bent down, looking at intervals towards the lion and expecting that it would jump on his shoulders the celestials showered flowers on him.

Then hearing the nectarine words "Rise up my son." the king stood up and saw that there was no lion. Filled with affection like his own mother the cow stood before him and milk flowed from her udders.

The cow said to the king, who was filled with surprise ;—"It is an illusion spread by me for testing your sincerety. What to speak of other animals even Yama, for the influence of the Rishi, cannot assail me.

Son, I am pleased to see your devotion to your preceptor and your compassion for me. Pray for a boon from me. Do not think me a cow that gives milk only. I can gratify people's wishes also when I am pleased."

Thus commanded, the king who granted the prayer of the supplicants, and who by the strength of his arms, had attained to the dignity of a heroe, with folded hands, prayed for a son, the perpetuator of his race, by his wife Sudakshina.

Having granted the boon of the king who was anxious to have a son the cow said :—"O son, hold my milk in a vessel of leaves and drink it."

The king replied :—" Mother, after your calf had drunk the milk and a portion had been reserved for Homa then with the permission of the Rishi, I will drink the remnant like the sixth part of the produce of the earth."

More pleased at these words than she had been before the cow proceeded happily from the mouun-tain cave towards the hermitage, the king following her.

Marking signs of joy on the king's face bright as the clear moon Vasistha and the queen inferred that Nandini had been pleased. So the king's narration of the subject was a mere repetition.

After Nandini's calf had drunk her milk and a portion had been reserved for Homa, the king, with his preceptor's permission, drank the remnant eagerly which was white and the very personification of fame.

With the termination of the vow the self-restrained

Vasistha blessed the royal pair in the following morning and permitted them to return to their capital.

Having circumambulated in order the sacred fire, Vasistha and his wife Arundhati and the cow with the calf by her side, the king left the hermitage with an air of dignity increased by the performance of auspicious ceremonies.

The king, ever untiring in his labour, with his religiously wedded wife, got upon his car which was like that of his own wishes and which being driven along an easy path, produced a sweet noise.

Gladdened at his return after a long absence his subjects repeatedly looked at the king, emaciated by the observance of a vow for getting a son but were not satiated for he was like the new moon to them after the expiration of the dark fortnight.

The king entered the capital, decorated with flags, amidst the çheers of the citizens, and took upon himself the burden af the world like the king of serpents.

As the damsels of the quarters held the lunar disc coming out of the eyes of the sage Atri, as the celestial stream Ganga held the semen of Siva discharged by the Fire-God so the queen Sudakshina conceived a child destined to perpetuate the Ikshaku race which was endued with the effulgence of the eight guardians deities of the quarters.

CANTO III.

Thereupon the Queen Sudakshina bore signs of pregnancy which was like her husband's desire about to fructify and a moon to her companions and indicated the continuity of the Ikshwaka family.

Being emaciated she could not decorate her person with ornaments and her complexion was pale like the Lodhra flower. She was like night verging on the dawn with a pale moon and a few stars.

As an elephant is not satiated with smelling the earthy scent of the new water of the pool in the forest soaked with rain at the termination of the summer so the king was not satiated with the earthy fragrance of her mouth when he met her in private.

The queen did not like any food except earth, perhaps because her son would be the sole ruler of the world as Indra is of the celestial region.

Dilipa, the king of North Kosala, used always to enquire kindly of the maids of the queen, saying "the princess of Magadha cannot out of shame ask for any thing she wishes to have. Can you tell me what she likes."

No sooner Sudakshina, stricken with a desire for articles of food but never relishing them, asked for any thing than, she was immediately supplied with them.

When her misery consequent on distaste was gone queen Sudakshina regained her health and looked beautiful like a creeper that, after leaving off old, leaves, has put forth new ones of greater beauty.

Owing to her nipples becoming dark in time, her large breasts excelled in beauty the full grown lotus buds with black-bees sitting on them.

The pregnant queen appeared to the eyes of the king like the earth abounding in jems, the Sami tree with fire lying inside and the Saraswati flowing through sand.

The king Dilipa performed *Punsavana* and other rites necessary for the pregnancy with grandeur proportionate to his love for her, to the wealth collected by the strength of his arms from the various quarters and the joy he experienced in expectation of a son.

Whenever the king went to her quarters the queen Sudakshina, having fickle eyes, rose up with difficulty from her seat in consequence of the weight of her womb containing the parts of the various presiding deities of the quarters and welcomed him with hands languidly joined together. This sight gave him great pleasure.

Trustworthy physicians, expert in the treatment of infants, nourished the embryo with great care and as the time of delivery was drawing nigh the queen appeared to her husband as the clouded welkin about to pour down showers.

As the energy manifesting itself in three forms, namely power, good counsel and readiness, gives birth to inexhaustible riches, so Sudakshina, like unto

Sachi herself, gave birth to a son in due time. Five of the planets were in ascendant and at a distance from the sun at the time and this indicated his future greatness.

At the time of the prince's birth the sky was clear, a delightful breeze was blowing, and the sacrificial fire, with its flame directed towards the south, received offerings of clarified butter. In fact every thing indicated good for the birth of such a man is intended for the behoof of the world.

The lying-in-room being lighted up on all sides with natural effulgance of the boy of auspicious birth the feeble mid-night lamps were put into shade and appeared like painted pictures.

Except the white um brella, bright as the rays of the moon and the two chowries the king gave away all his valuables to his attendant of the seraglio who conveyed to him the nectarine intelligence of the son's birth.

When the king saw the lovely face of his son with eyes motionless like the lotus in a lake where there is no wind his heart overflowed with delight like ocean on seeing the moon. The family priest Vasistha came from his hermitage and celebrated the birth-rites of Dilipa's son who shone like a diamond after it has been cleaned.

The birth-ceremony of the child was solemnized by the sweet music and dance of the courtezans in the king's palace and also by the sound of Dundhavi in the celestial region.

No one had been in prison in the kingdom of Dilipa, a great and skilful adminstrator so on this occasion he had none to set at liberty except his own-self whom he released from the fetters of indebtedness to his departed manes.

Knowing that this boy would go to the other end of the ocean of scriptures and enemies, the king Dilipa, who was a master of roots of verbs, gave him the name of Raghu which is derived from the verb *lagh* meaning to go.

Under the fostering care of his immensely rich sire the prince Raghu grew up, as the moon, parmeated by the rays of the sun, increases in size after the period of conjunction.

Like unto Parvati and Mahadeva on the birth of the six-headed deity, like unto Sachi and Purandara on that of Jayanta, the queen Sudakshina and Dilipa who were like Uma and her husband, or Sachi and her lord, experienced great joy on obtaining a son equal to Kumara or Jayanta.

The mutual love of the royal pair like that of a couple of Chakravakas was increased rather than decreased on being shared by their only child.

Great was the delight of Dilipa when the nurse, taught the child to walk with the help of her fingers and bow down imitating her.

When the king placed him on his lap, the pleasure

caused by the the touch of his person, poured nectar on his body. With closed eyes he used to enjoyt that fong-sought-for pleasure.

As Brahma, the Creator of the world, regarded it stable through Vishnu, in whom the quality of Sattwa or goodness predominated, and who was but his another form, so the king, the protector of the world, regarded the perpetuity of his race secure through his son of most excellent birth.

After the celebration of his *Chuda* ceremony, the princes, along with the minister's sons of the same age, having flowing locks, entered into the ocean of words through his acquaintance with the fifty lettered alphabet.

In due time he was invested with sacrificial thread and placed under the tuition of learned teachers whose labors were crowned with success for instructions given to a worthy pupil always yeild fruits.

As the sun, by means of a horse swifter than the wind, rides from one end of the welkin to the other so Raghu, greatly endowed with intellectual powers, crossed the four oceans of knowledge.

Gradually going beyond boy-hood Raghu arrived at youth. And like the calf changed into a bull and the young of an elephant into a powerful animal his person displayed a beauty shorn of the fickleness of the boy-hood.

Dilipa then made him perform the rite of the cutting of the hair and had him married. The princesses bound to Ragh in the wedlock chain, appeared beautiful like the daughters of Daksha when united with the moon.

The arms of the highly powerful and the youthful Raghu were long ;like yokes, his breast was spacious like a door cover and his neck was thick. Though he surpassed his old father in size still he looked small by his humility.

At length desirous of lighting the heavy burden of governing the subjects which he had so long borne king Dilipa, who was gentle by nature and culture, installed Raghu as the heir-apparent of the throne.

As beauty gradually passes from a fading lotus to a new one, so the goddess of empire, appreciating merit, moved by degrees, from her principal residence the king Dilipa, to her new seat, lying nigh, the crown prince. Like the fire aided by the wind, like the sun in the autumn, like an elephant by the temporal juice the power of Dilipa became formidable by the help of his son Raghu.

Like the king of gods Dilipa celebrated ninety-nine horse sacrifices without any obstrution Raghu, with bow in hand, and his companions, guarded the sacrificial horse.

At last Indra, in his invisible form, pilfered the horse, even before the very eyes of its guards armed with bows, let loose by Dilipa to wander at ease.

Raghu's soldiers were surprised at this sudden incident and knew not what to do. Just in the nick of time, Vasistha's cow, Nandini, of whose power the prince Raghu had heard before, came there roving at large.

Having washed his eyes with the sacred urine of Nandini, Dilipa's son, honored of the good, began to see objects beyond the ken of the senses.

The Prince espied Purandara, the cutter of the wings of mountains, fly eastward, with sacrificial horse tied to the car with a rope and repeatedly struck by the charioteer into quietness.

By his thousand winkless eyes and green horse he took him for Indra; and impeding him in the way he said, his voice touching the sky.

"O King of gods, the wise assign to thee the first place amongst the partakers of sacrificial offerings. Why dost thou obstruct the celebration of a sacrifice undertaken by my father who is always engaged in such sacrifices?

Thou art the lord of the three worlds and canst see objects imperciptible to the senses. It is proper for thee to punish them who hinder the celebration of sacrifices. If thou thyself standst in the way of good men performing good works there will be an end of it ere long.

Therefore, O Maghavan, thou shouldst return the horse which is the *sine quanon* of the sacrifice. Those who point out good ways never wend evil ways."

Hearing those bold words of Raghu the king of the celestials stopped his car and said.

"O Kshatrya boy, what you have said is true. But those who value fame should protect it from their enemies. Your father is about to excell my world-wide reputation by sacrifices.

The word "Purusottama or the best of male beings" designates Vishnu only; the word Maheswara or Great God" signifies the three-eyed Mahadeva only; similarly by the expression "the performer of a hundred sacrefices" the ascetics know me. All these three words have only one signification and not two.

Following in the wake of Kapila I have siezed this horse. Trying in vain to release do not attain yourself to the condition of the offspring of Sagara."

Again, Raghu, the guard of the sacrificial horse, spoke fearlessly to Purandara:—"If this is your firm resolve, take up your weapons. Know, you cannot achieve your end so long Raghu remains unconquered."

Saying this he raised up his head to set an arrow to his bow. He slightly advanced his right foot and threw back his left looking like Siva while he attempted to burn the celestial city of the Asura Tripura.

Waxing wroth at the hostile attitude of Raghu Indra set an inffallible shaft to his bow which is seen for a short time on the new clouds.

The arrow, which was ever used to drink the blood of the dreadful Asuras, pierced the broad chest of Dilip's son and began to drink human blood never tasted by it before.

The prince, who was like unto Kumara in prowess, shot an arrow with his own name engraven on it at the arm of Indra whose palm was hardened by goading the celestial elephant Airavata and was dyed with the paintings on Sachi's cheeks.

With a peacock-feathered arrow Raghu struck down the top of Indra's car with the figure of a thunder-bolt placed on it. At this the king of celestials was so much worked up with anger as if the hairs of the celestial goddess of fortune had been forcibly plucked.

There tock place a terrible encounter between the two warriors, each hoping for victory. Innumerable, dreadful feathered arrows went up and down. Filled with surprise the Siddhas stood by Indra and the troops of Raghu by him.

As with rain water a cloud cannot extinguish the fire of lightning begotten by itself so Indra could not defeat Raghu who had a portion of his unbearable essence in him.

Then Raghu shot a crescent shaped arrow, which soundig deep like the churning of the ocean, cut off the string of the bow held by Indra in his hand besmeared with scented sandal.

Burning in anger Indra cast off his bow and

bent upon killing his powerful enemy took up his burning thunder that had clipped off the wings of the mountains.

Struck at the breast by that powerful weapon Raghu dropped down on the ground along with the tears of his soldiers and recovering in a moment he rose up in the midst of their joyous exclamations.

Seeing Raghu unscathed even by that ruthless weapon the destroyer of Vitra was highly pleased with his great power for merit is honored everywhere.

Then Vasava spoke distinctly :—" This weapon of mine, well tempered, is invincible even when discharged againt the mountains. None but you has been able to withstand it. I am pleased with you. Tell me what you wish to have except this horse."

The Prince Raghu put into his quiver the half-raised arrow feathered in gold which had lightened his fingers and gently said to the king of the celestials.

" O lord, if thou art not willing to part with this horse do that by which my father, always engaged in the celebration of sacrifices, may reap the fruits of a fully performed horse sacrifice.

Holding an imperial assemblage for the horse sacrifice my father has assumed one of the forms of the eight-formed Siva and is therefore inaccessible to the common people. Send one of thy messengers to communicate to that best of kings what has happened.

Indra, having Matali for his charioteer, granted Raghu's prayer saying ' So be it" and drove towards his heavenly mansion. Raghu, with an indifferent heart, returned to the imperial assemblage.

Before his return to the palace king Dilipa had learnt every thing from Indra's emissary. So he received his son by touching his body, which bore the wound inflicted by the thunderbolt, with his hand, cooled with joy.

Desirous of having a station in the celestial region, thus did the king Dilipa perform in his old age ninety-nine horse-sacrifices which were as it were the so many steps for ascending the heaven.

In pursuance of the practice of the kings of the Ikshaku dynasty, who in old age retired from the world and engaged in meditative contemplation, the king, giving up all desires for worldly objects, made over duly the royal umbrella to his son, and adopted the *Vanaprastha* life along with his queen.

CANTO IV.

After the termination of the day, as the fire shines more brilliantly on receiving the light of the sun so acquiring the kingdom given by his Sire Raghu became more powerful than before.

On hearing of the establishment of Raghu on the throne of Dilipa the fire of grief that had been smoking in the hearts of conquered kings became as if ablaze.

As men eagerly look up to the rain-flag hoisted over the gate of a palace so the subjects of Raghu and their children were filled up with joy on seeing his elevation.

Raghu, of elephantine gait, simultaneously occupied his father's throne and his enemies' territories.

Hiding herself Lakshmi (the goddess of fortune) served the newly installed Raghu with her umbrella of the hundred petalled lotus.

Permeating the bodies of the panegyrists at the time of their singing his glories, the goddess of learning served that king, worthy of being lauded, with encomiums pregnant with meaning.

Though the earth had been enjoyed before by the adorable Manu and other kings yet she served Raghu devotedly like a wife who had no other husband.

By meting out punishment proportionate to the crimes he pleased his subjects like the south wind, neither too hot nor too cold.

As the fruits of the mangoe tree do not lead men to grieve for the flowers, so Raghu, by the excess of qualities, gave no occasion to his people to feel the loss of his sire.

Ministers, well versed in polity, pointed out to him what is good and what is bad and he adopted the former and discarded the latter.

On Raghu's accession to the throne, the five elements, earth etc, were greatly improved in quality so that every thing in his regeme appeared new.

As the appellation *chandra* of the moon is true for its giving delight and the name *Tapan* of the sun is so for imparting heat so Raghu made immense justice to his appellation *Raja* for he pleased his subjects.

True it is that he had eyes extending to the ears, but properly speaking his eyes were the Shastras by which he could see even the minutest duties. When Raghu was comfortable after establishing peace all through his kingdom, the autumn, having the lotus for its ensign, appeared before like the goddess of empire.

The light of the sun, whose course was unobstructed on account of the termination of the rain and the lightness of the clouds, and the irrepressible power of Raghu spread all over the quarters.

Indra, the king of the celestials, laid aside his rain-bow and Raghu took up his bow of victory. Thus the two, one after another, took up their respective bows, for the behoof of their subjects.

Having the lotus as if for his umbrella and the blossoming Kasa flowers for his chowries the autumn resembled Raghu but he could never equal the king in splendour.

With his gracious face the king and with pure rays, the moon, equally delighted the eyes of the spectators.

The brightness of Raghu's fame reflected itself in the flocks of geese, in the stars and in the water adorned with lilies. The wives of husbandmen, who guarded the corn-fields, sat in the shade of sugarcane plants and sang the glory of Raghu, begotten by his accomplishments, beginning with the incidents of his youth.

With the rising on one hand, of the very powerful Agastya (the star canopus) water became clean, and with Raghu's accession on the other hand to the throne, the hearts of his enemies became muddy with the fear of defeat.

Excited with the exhurberance of their strength humped bulls digged up the banks of rivers and thus imitated the prowess of Raghu.

Smelling the intoxicating odour of *Saptaparna* flowers the elephants exuded temporal juice, as if in emulation, from seven different parts of their bodies.

Making rivers fordable and drying up roads, the autumn urged on Raghu to set out for conquest before he was excited by the love of enterprise to do so.

The fire, lighted on the holy occasion of consecrating war-horses and fed duly with offerings, directing its flame towards the south, granted him victory as it were with its own hand.

Having made arrangements for defending his capital and out-lying forts against any foreign invasion, safe-guarding his army from any attack from behind and seeing favourable omens the king set out for conquest with six-fold forces.

As the drops of water, thrown up by the waves of the milk-ocean caused by the dashing of the churning rod, the mount Mandara, sprinkled the person of Vishnu so the aged ladies of the capital poured handfuls of fried grain on the person of the king when he started on the expedition of conquest.

The king, who was like unto Indra, first started towards the East with his flag shaken by the favourable wind, which as it were frowned upon his enemies.

The dust, raised the car-wheels and elephants by resembling so many clouds made the sky look like the earth, and the earth like the clouded sky.

First went his prowess, then the noise of his soldiers, then clouds of dust and last of all his four-fold forces. Thus, as if divided into four divisions, the army of Raghu marched on.

The king Raghu, of vast resources as he was, dug tanks in waterless tracts, bridged the navigable rivers and felled down the trees of the forest.

Commanding his own army the king shone like Bhagiratha taking the Ganga out of the matted locks of Hara and leading her to the East.

As the huge-tusked elephants went on uprooting the trees that fell in their way or breaking their branches or spoiling their fruits and flowers so did Raghu march dethroning, humiliating and despoiling the kings who opposed him.

Thus having conquered all the Eastern kingdoms, the victorious Raghu reached the shore of the great ocean, darkened with palm trees.

As a cane plant saves itself by following the current of a river so the kings saved themselves by submitting to Raghu who destroyed the aggressive kings.

By his power he vanquished the kings of Bengal possessing fleets and placed monuments of victory in the islands of the river Ganges.

As the Kalam pady yields a harvest after being first rooted out and then transplanted, so the kings of Bengal, who laid themselves down at the lotus-feet of Raghu, being first dethroned and then re-instated honoured him by paying immense riches.

Having crossed the river Kapisa by means of a bridge of elephants he proceeded towards Kalinga the road to which was pointed out by the inhabitants of Utkala.

As a driver strikes the head of a restive elephant with a sharp goad so Raghu made vigorous attack against the mount Mahendra.

As the mountains pelted stones at Indra when he came to lop off their wings so the king of Kalinga, who had a strong elephant force, obstructed Raghu with various weapons.

Raghu, a descendent of the Kakustha family, bore patiently the discharge of Narachas made by his enemies of the Mahendra mount, and assumed the beauty of victory as if on being bathed duly with sanctified water.

His soldiers prepared there a drinking site and in cups of betel leaves drank as if the glory of the enemies in the shape of cocoanut tody.

The king Raghu, who always gained victory by a fair battle, deprived the king of the Mahendra mountain who was first taken a captive and then set at liberty.

Then marching along the Sea-coast adorned with rows of pam trees laden with fruits, Raghu, to whom victory came of itself, entered the Southern country situate under the star Agastya.

The temporal juice of the elephants, and the sweet-scented unguents of his soldiers while bathing in the river Kaveri, lent to her waters sweet perfume and thus created in the mind of her husband the the ocean, doubts about her fidelity.

After doing a little distance the soldiers of the victory-seeking Raghu spent some time at the foot of the Malaya mountain full of Harita birds that frequent forests of pepper.

There the fruits of cardamum plants being ground into dust by the horses' hoofs, flew up and settled in the temples of elephants emitting fragrant temporal juice.

The ropes tied round the necks of elephants, which were tearing off the shackles of their feet, being bound to the grooves made on the trunks of the Sandal trees by the serpents winding round them did not become loosened.

The heat of the sun is diminished when he is in the south, but the Pandya kings of that quarter could not stand before the power of Raghu.

They saluted the feet of Raghu and presenting him with costly pearls found at the conjunction of the river Tamraparni and the great ocean appeared to give them their amassed glory.

Having enjoyed the mount Malaya covered with Sandal trees as well as the mount Durdur, both constituting as it were the breasts of the South, the irrepressible king crossed the mount Sahya which looked like the waist of a damsel shorn of the cloth on account of the receding of the ocean.

When his four-fold army went out to conquer the kings of the West, the great sea, which had been made to retire from the mount Sahya by the arms of Purasurama, appeared once more to touch it.

Disregarding personal decorations the terrified Kerala women fled away before him. And as at times they looked behind, the dust deposited on their locks, looked like powder of red arsenic. Carried by the cool breeze of the river Murala, the dust of the Ketaki flowers, falling on the weapons of Raghu's soldiers, acted as unsolicited perfume.

The sound of the trappings of horses, when on speed, defeated the murmuring noise of *Rajtals* trees shaken by the wind.

Leaving the Punnaga flowers, swarms of black bees sat on the temples of elephants, perfumed with temporal juice, tied to the trunks of the date trees.

At the request of Jamadagni's son the ocean had gone to a great distance, but it now paid its tribute through the western kings.

Being cut and covered with inscriptions by the tusks of the maddened elephants the Trikuta mountain formed as it were a high monument of victory in that quarter.

As a Yogin follows the path of divine knowledge to vanquish his enemies the senses so Raghu proceeded by an inland route to defeat the Persians.

As untimely clouds cannot bear the heat of the new sun which gives red tint to the lotus so he could not bear the crimson colour, caused by the drinking of wine, of the lotus countenances of Yavana women.

A great encounter took place between him and the Yavanas having cavalry. And the field being enshrouded in darkness the two armies marked their respective positions from the twang of their bows.

Being cut off by his spears the bearded heads of of the Yavanas covered the earth like so many bee-hives.

Taking off their head-gears the remaining Yavana soldiers prayed for mercy which was shown to them for anger of the great is appeas ed by submission.

Having spread excellent seats of skin on a site

surrounded with vine his soldiers removed the fatigue of victory with wine.

Raghu then proceeded to the North to vanquish the northern princes by the power of his arms like the sun, who during the northern solistice, draws by his rays the moisture of the earth.

His horses removed their fatigue by rolling on the banks of the Indus flowing through Cashmere and shook their manes reddened with powder of Kumkuma, grown on its banks.

Raghu displayed so great a power in killing the Hunas of the north that their wives reddened their white checks by striking them with their hands.

Unable to bear the power of Raghu the Kambhoja kings prostrated themselves before him like Akshata tree bruised by his elephants tied to them.

He constantly received tributes in the shape of the most excellent horses and heaps of gold ; but they could not come before him.

Then Raghu, escorted by his cavalry, got upon the mount Himalaya. The dust of red earth and other minerals raised by his horses' hoofs seemed to increase the bulk of their summits.

The lions lying in caves, that were equally powerful like the king, did not get up on hearing the shouts of the soldiers but simply looked on fearlessly.

The breeze, causing sound of bamboos, the murmering noise of Bhurja leaves, and carrying the spray of the Ganges, served him on the way.

His troopers enjoyed rest under the shade of Nameru trees on rocks perfumed with the musk of deer that had lain on it before.

Reflecting their effulgence on the neck-chains of the elephants tied to Sarala trees, the herbs, growing on the Himalaya, served the purpose of oil-lamps to Raghu in the night.

At stages left by him, the fir-trees, bruised by the neck-chains of elephants, described to the Kinnars the size of those animals.

There a great encounter took plaee between Raghu and the Ganas of the mountains in which *naraches*, *vindipalas* and stones caused fire by striking against one another.

Having compelled by arrows the *Utsavsanketas*, to terminate their festivities he made the Kinnaras sing the glories of his victorious arms.

From the presents brought for him by the mountaineers he formed an estimate of Himalaya's wealth and who also formed an idea of the king's power.

Having established his own undecaying fame there the king got down from the Himalaya without attacking, out of contempt, the mount Kailasha which was once shaken by Pulasta's son Ravana and thus making it ashamed.

He then crossed the Lauhitya and the king of Pragyotish began to tremble as well as the black Aguru trees to which the elephants of that victorious king were tied.

What to speak of bearing the attack of the soldiers he could not even withstand the sight of the dust which was raised by Raghu's car-wheels and which resembled an inclement day with the sun enshrouded in clouds but with no rain.

On the arrival of the king Raghu who had excelled even the power of Indra the king of Kamrupa sought refuge with him by presenting him those infuriated eiephants with which he used to attack other kings.

With offerings of jems for flowers the king of Kamrupa worshipped the shadow of his feet as the presiding deity of his golden foot-stool.

Having thus finished the conquest of all the quarters and covered the crowns of the kings, unprotected by umbrellas, with the dust of his car-wheels the victorious Raghu returned to his own kingdom.

Like clouds, riches, acquired by the pious, are given away in charities. With the immense wealth which he had amassed after subduing all the quarters Raghu performed the sacrifice of *Vishwajit* in which one has to give away all his belongings.

After the termination of the sacrifice, Raghu, whose ministers were his friends, having removed from the minds of the subdued kings the sorrow of defeat by honoring them with suitable presents, allowed them to return to their own kindoms and wives.

When all these kings prostrated themselves before Raghu at the time of their departure the dust of the floral chaplets reddened his toes which were attainable by his favour and bore the marks of flags, thunderbolts and umbrellas.

CANTO V.

After the Emporor Raghu had given away all his riches in the *Vishwajita* sacrifice there came Koutsa, the pupil of the ascetic Varatantu, after finishing his education, with the object of securing a present of honor for his preceptor.

The king, of extraordinary character, hospitable and highly illustrious went out and received his Veda-knowing guest with offerings in an earthen vase instead of that of gold which he had not.

The king, well-versed in duties and rules of action, who was the foremost of those who value honor as wealth, honored his guest duly and making him seated near him, addressed him with folded hands, saying:

"O thou of sharp intellect, is thy preceptor, the foremost of ascetics, and the creator of mantras, from whom thou hast acquired thy unlimited knowledge as the animate creatures derive their animation from the sun, well?

I hope his three fold penance in which he has engaged his body, speech and mind, and which has made Indra lose his patience has not suffered any extinction from obstacles.

I hope the fatigue-removing trees which you have reared with a father's care and around which you have made water pits have not suffered from storm or forest fire.

Are little fawns, whom the ascetics from affection do not prevent from eating the long sacrificial grass and whose umbilical cords, dropping off, fall on their laps, quite well ?

Are the sacred streams, in which you daily bathe and whose water you offer to the departed manes and on whose bank you throw the sixth part of the gathered paddy, well ?

I hope cows, buffaloes and other household cattle have not entered the hermitage and eaten up the wild paddy with which the guests are entertained and Rishis themselves are supported.

Having trained you properly has the ascetic granted you permission to return home to enter the second stage where one can be of immense service to the community ?

I am not satisfied only with the arrival of such an honorable man as yourself at my court. I wish to satisfy some behest. Have you come here at your preceptor's command or of your own accord to honor me ?"

From the very vessel of offerings the pupil of Baratantu had inferred that Raghu had nothing in hand. Still worked up with a feeble hope at the noble words of the king he replied.

"It is all well with us, O king. No evil can overtake the people when you are their king. Can darkness enshroud the earth when the sun is in the sky?

It is an everlasting practice in your family to honor those to whom honor is due. But O great king, you have surpassed your fore-fathers in this respect. But I am sorry I have come at a bad time as a supplicant to you.

Having given away all your riches to worthy persons, you have nothing left but your body like the bare stalks of paddy after corn is taken away by the foreters.

The poverty that you have brought upon yourself by celebrating this sacrifice has led to your glory. The waning of the moon when the gods drink its ambrosia gives him greater glory than his increase.

Having nothing else to do, I shall secure my teacher's fee from some ene else. May it fare well with you. Even a chataka bird does not pray for water of the autumnal cloud shorn of its watery content."

Saying it the disciple of Varatantu was about to go away but the king entreating him not to do so, said, "O learned man! what present do you wish to make to your preceptor and what is its extent?"

The wise Brahmacharin Koutsa described every

thing truly to the king who had duly performed the sacrifice, was shorn of pride and regulated the four castes and the four *Asramas* of the Brahmanas.

"Having finished my education I expressed a desire of making a present to my preceptor; but at first he considered my unflinching devotion to him as tantamount to a present.

Being angry at my importunity and not thinking that I was poor he said " For the fourteen Sastras I taught you bring me fourteen crores of gold coin."

O King, I have been convinced that you have nothing left but the tittle of the king. It is not proper for me therefore to request you to pay the heavy amount demanded by my preceptor as his fee."

Thus addressed by the Veda-knowing Brahman, the sole king of the earth, who was beautiful like the king of Brahmanas (the moon) and who had never wended evil ways, once more said.

" Let not the new stigma visit me that a Brahman's son, well read in the Vedas, having prayed to Raghu for help in making a present to his preceptor, went back disappointed to another liberal man.

O worshipful sir, please remain in this sacred house of three fires as the fourth for two or three days. I shall in the meantime try to satisfy your demand."

With a delighted heart the Brahmana accepted the unfailing promise of the King saying 'So be it." The king knew that there was no wealth available on earth and he therefore determined to procure it from Kuvera.

By the power of Vasistha's mantras with which his coronation ceremony was performed the king could direct his car, like clouds driven by the wind, to the heavens, mountains, oceans and every where.

Desirous of vanquishing Kuvera like an ordinary feudatory chief Raghu enjoyed rest in the evening of the day previous to his departure in his chariot well equipped and with a controlled mind full of pure feelings.

In the morning, on the eve of his departure his treasury keepers astonishingly informed him of the fall of a shower of gold from sky into the treasury.

Having obtained from Kevera, against whom he was about to march, a heap of shining gold resembling a rock detached from the mount Sameru, the king gave it all to Koutsa.

The desire-less Koutsa reluctant to take more than what was due to his preceptor and the king determined to give him more than what he wanted were both highly admired by the people of Ayodhya.

Then having sent that treasury carried by hundreds of camels and mares the king bent down his head for saluting him. The Muni, touching his body before his departure, said.

" No wonder it is O king, that the earth satisfies the desire of the kings who strictly observe their royal duties. But your power is beyond comprehension since you have milked from heaven your desired object.

You have got all the blessings of life. May you like your father who was blessed with an illutrious son like your self, have a son after you. No other blessing can I pour on you for it will be entirely superfluous."

Having thus blessed the king the Brahmana went to his preceptor. As the creatures receive light from the sun so the king soon got a son by the hermit's blessings.

At the Brahma hour his queen gave birth to a son like Kumara. Seeing that his son was born at the Brahma hour the king named him Aja *i. e* unborn after the god Brahma.

He was strongly built, energetic and spirited and naturally tall in appearance like his sire. He resembled his father like a lamp rusembling another from which it is lighted.

When the education of the prince was completed and he was in the bloom of youth, the goddess of fortune enamoured of him only waited for Raghu's permission, as a modest girl, after choosing a husband after her mind, awaits her father's consent to marry him.

In the meantime Bhoj king of Vidarbha sent a trustworthy emissary to Raghu's court to bring Aja on the occasion of his sister's Swayamvara.

Regarding a matrimonial alliance with the Bhoja king desirable and thinking of the marriageable age of his son Raghu despatched him escorted by troops to the rich city of Vidarbha.

Wherever the prince halted on his way to Vidharbha the villagers presented him with tents, bedding, furniture and other necessary articles and therefore he was not the least inconvenienced on his journey through the forest and his halting stages were like pleasure gardens.

Proceeding in this wise on their journey the prince and his soldiers, with their banners turned grey with dust, halted on the banks of Nermuda, decorated with Karanj trees, gently shaken by the cool breeze surcharged with the watery drops of the river.

At this time a wild elephant came out of the river. His cheeks were washed clean of the temporal juice and before he came out of the water, black-bees hovering over the surface of the water indicated his presence there.

Although the red earth had been washed off his tusks yet the blue lines, extending upwards, clearly indicated that he had been busy with the sport of digging up the foot of the Rikshavan mountain.

Contracting and extending his trunk again and again the elephant broke through the high waves as if breaking the bolts of his stable and reached the shore with a great noise.

Having first thrown up the water with his breast

and along with it many water plants on the river bank the mountain-like elephant reached the shore.

The maddening juice which was for the time being stopped by his immersion in water, again flowed down the temples of that incomparable elephant when he met the tame elephants of Aja.

Smelling the bitter and unbearable smell of that elephat and resembling the milky juice of the Saptachhada tree the war-elephants fled in wrong ways despite the attempts of the drivers to control them.

The steeds broke their reins and fled away quickly; the chariots, with their axles broken, fell on the ground and the soldiers grew anxious to protect their females. Thus in a monent the whole camp was thrown into utter confusion.

Knowing that wild elephants are unslayable by the kings Aja gently drew his bow and struck the forehead of the impetuous animal with a shaft in order to check its course.

No sooner the elephant was struck by the prince's arrow than he was transformed into a beautiful ærial being encircled with rays of light.

Then having showered on the head of Aja flowers from the Kalpa tree by his power, the etherial being, who was an adept in the art of speech, said, enhancing the lustre of the pearl necklace hanging on his breast by the sheen of his teeth.

" Know me to be the son of Pryadarshana, the king of the Gandharvas. My name is Pryamvada.

By the curse of the ascetic Matanga who was displeased with my arrogance I was transformed into an elephant.

Water is by nature cool but is heated only by fire and the rays of the sun. I fell at his feet. His anger was gone and his native equanimity returned again.

He said :—When your temple wlll be struck by the iron arrow of Aja of the Ikshaku race you will regain your own beautiful form.

I have been freed from the curse by you who are powerful and whom I have so long sought to see. But if I do not do you any good in return of what use is my restoration to my own form ?

Friend, I have a weapon by name *Sanmohan* (fascitation). It is drawn and discharged by different mantras. Take from me this Gandharva weapon which secures victory but does not kill an enemy.

You should not be ashamed of what you have done. It was kind of you to have struck me thus. You should not refuse to take this weapon which I offer you of my own accord."

Aja, who was the foremost of men and a master of arms, replied "be it so." Then washing his hands and mouths with the sacred water of the Narmuda, sprung of the moon, and turning his face to the north he learnt the mantra of the weapon from the Gandharva prince freed from the curse.

Then the Gandharva prince and Aja, who had

been made friends by an unforeseen circumstance, parted with each other, one proceding to the garden of Kuvera and the other to the well governed and charming country Vidarbha.

As the ocean rises to receive the moon, so the Vidarbha king, with his heart full of joy, advanced to receive the prince who had arrived at the boundary of his capital.

Going before him humbly king Bhoja conducted him into the city and presented him with his own servants and articles of use so that the spectators regarded Aja to be the host and the king of Vidarbha to be the guest.

With the termination of boyhood Cupid takes possession of the youth. So the prince representing Raghu occupied Bhoja's palace pointed out by his servants humbly before which, on raised altars, vessels, full of water, were placed.

As a damsel, who does not understand the heart of her husband, delays to meet him in the night so did sleep make delay in lighting on the eyes of Aja who was anxious to see the priceless jewel of a damsel at whose Swayamvara so many princes were assembled.

During sleep his broad shoulders were pressed by his ear-rings and the unguents which were on his body were dislodged. In the morning, panegyrists, fo the same age and sweet speech, thus lauded him.

"O foremost of the intelligent, leave thy bed for

the night is gone. The Providence has divided between you two the responsibility of the world. Thy father, aroused from sleep, has put his shoulders to one part do thou now do also the same thing.

Seeing thee under the influence of sleep Lakshmi, disregarding his attachment to thee, passed the night like an unchaste woman, enjoying the beauty of the moon. But the moon has gone down to the extremity of the west, casting off the resemblance between him and thy countenance.

Let thy eyes, with cool pupils rolling inside and and the lotus with black-bees, simultaneously unfold their loveliness and imitate each other.

As if desirous of securing the natural fragrance of thy breath through borrowed sweetness the morning breeze is pilfering the flowers of the trees and coming in contact with the lotus unfolded by the rising sun.

Beautiful, pearl-like, white dew drops are falling on the coppery leaves of the trees, are shining greatly and imitating the playful smiles on thy lips brightened by the sheen of thy teeth.

Before the rising of the sun, the source of light his driver the Aruna has driven away the darkness. O heroe, when thou wilt take the field thy father will feel no necessity of killing his enemies.

Having shaken off sleep by changing sides thy elephants are drawing their chains. Permeated by the rays of the morning sun their tusks, resembling lotus buds, appear to have ploughed the sides of a mountain of red earth.

O lotus-eyed prince, thy Persian horses, tied in spacious tents, are soiling with the warm vapour of their mouth, the rock-salts placed before them.

The flower garlands presented to thee have withered away. The lamps are shedding a pale light and this thy sweet-singing parrot in the cage is emitting the words uttered by us to arouse thee."

As the celestial elephant, Supratika, aroused by the sweet notes of the geese, leaves the sandy side of the Ganges, so the prince Aja left his bed as he heard the well-composed verses of the panegyrists.

Then in pursuance of the rules of Shastras, Aja, with fine eye-lashes, performed the morning rites. And being properly dressed with the help of clever servants he went to the assembly of kings held for the Swayamvara.

CANTO VI.

At the Swayamvara assemblage the prince Aja saw the kings occupying thrones on a richly made *dias* like so many sky-ranging celestials richly dressed.

On seeing Aja, born in the family of Kakustha, beautiful like Kamadeva as if revived into existence by Siva at the earnest prayer of Rati, the kings despaired of obtaining the hand of Indumati.

As a young lion, topping over the rocks, gets at the highest summit of a mountain, so Aja got upon the most elevated *dias* by a flight of beautiful stairs pointed out by the king of Vidarbha.

He sat on a throne set with jems and covered with drapes of diverse colours and looked like Kartikeya seated on the back of a peacock.

Like a lightning appearing as many and playing on the clouds the goddess of beauty dividing herself into many in the persons of the kings was invested with such effulgence that it was difficult to look at her.

Seated on a precious throne in the midst of richly dressed kings, Raghu's son Aja looked as beautiful as the Parijat tree in the midst of Kalpa trees. Leaving the other kings the eyes of the citizens were now turned on Raghu's son as black-bees, seated on flowers, fly off to the temples of wild elephants scented with temporal juice.

Then the panegyrists began to sing the glories of the solar and lunar kings, the smoke of Aguru rose up to the flags decorating the place and the sound of conchs filled the air making the peacocks dance in glee in the gardens hard by. In the meantime the bride Indumati, looking beautiful in her wedding dress and ornaments carried by men in a palanquin and surrounded by her attendants, appeared in the splendid portico leading to the dias.

The minds of the kings were now drawn to the

bride, the cynosure of the hundred eyes, a maiden specially created by the Creator, their bodies only remaining on the seats.

Their growing attachment for the maiden was like the first emissary of their love and their amorous gestures were like the fresh green leaves of the trees.

One king, holding the stem of a lotus, began to whirl it sportively so that the trembling petals struck against the bees sitting on them and the filaments of the inside, thrown up, formed a circle in the air.

Another gallant king, taking up the garland that had dropped off his neck and was hanging being tied to an end of his bracelet set with diamonds, put it back in its proper place by slightly bending his head.

Another king, casting down slightly his beautiful eyes and contracting his principal toe exhibiting the brightness of its nail, scribbled on the golden foot-stool.

Another king, resting his hand on the throne, and raising up his shoulder, began to converse with a friend. For his thus turning his face the necklace, which beautified his breast, touched the upper part of his loins.

Another young prince tore into pieces the white petals of a Ketaki flower, an ornament befitting an amorous damsel's ear, with his finger nails which would have otherwise been placed on his love's waist.

With his palm resembling a red lotus and marked with the sign of flag another king cast his dice resplendent with the lustre of the jems of his finger-rings.

Thinking that his crown was falling off his head though it remained in its proper place another king held it firmly by his hand. And thereat the interstices between the fingers were shining with the lustre of the diamonds thereon.

Then the female gate-keeper Sunanda, who was eloquent and well familiar with the deeds and lineage of each soverign present at the assemblage, conducted the princess first of all to the king of Magadha and spoke eloquently like a male.

This king protects those who seek refuge with him. He is grave by nature and pleases his subjects. He rules in Magadha and is justly named *Parantapa* the aggressor of the enemies.

Athough there are thousands of other kings still by him the Earth is recognised as having a king. There are hosts of stars and planents in the sky but the night is illumined by the moon only.

This king always celebrates sacrifices which the king of celestials attends by invitation. Therefore on account of the long separation from her lord the goddess Sachi has for a long time ceased to decorate her tresses falling on her pale cheeks with Mandara flowers. If you select this king as your husband you will gratify the eyes of the women of Pushapura looking through windows when you enter that city.

When Sunanda spoke thus the thin-built princess eyed the king of Magadha. Without uttering a word she drew aside her garland of Madhuka flowers intersetrung with Durvas and made a cold bow, thus rejecting his offer.

As the waves raised by the wind carry the swans in the lake Manasa from one lotus to another so Sunanda conducted the princess to another king and said to her:—"This is the king of Anga, who although living on earth enjoys the prosperity of Indra. [When he went to the celestial region) for vanquishing the Asuras the celestial damsels also expressed an eager desire for enjoying his youthful beauty. The Rishis, expert in the art of elephant training, trained his elephants.

Having caused heavy drops of tears to fall on the breasts of the wives of his enemies he, as it were, put a stringless chain around their necks instead of pearl necklaces.

Although naturally living in different places, Lakshmi and Saraswati are living unitedly in him. For his beauty and sweet speech, O fair princess, you are worth of this king and therefore make yourself the third (of qualities).

Hearing those words and taking away her eyes from the king Indumati spoke to her friend's mother Sunanda "let us go." It was not owing to the fact that the king was not beautiful or that the princess could not discriminate virtues and demerits well but that the tastes of persons always vary.

The guard Sunanda pointed out to Indumati another king who, although lovely to look at like the newly risen moon, was umbearable to his enemies.

This long-armed, broad chested and slender-waisted king of Avanti is shining like the sun carefully polished bright on the grinding wheel by Vishwakarman.

The dust, raised by the horses when this king of three-fold power namely courage, energy and policy sets out on expedition, casts into shade the lustre of the jewels on the crowns of the neighbouring princes.

Living near Mahakala where dwells the moon-crested Mahadeva this king enjoys with his consorts moon-lit nights even in the dark fort-night.

O you having thighs like the trunk of a plaintain tree, do you wish to live with this youthful king of Avanti in the gardens fanned by breezes cooled with the waves of the Sipra river?

As the lily does not cherish any love for the sun who unfolds the lotus and dries up the mud by his heat so the extraordinarily beautiful Indumai did not feel attachment for the king of Avanti who was the joy of his friends and the death of his enemies.

Then taking her, whose body was lustrous like the inside of a lotus, who had fine teeth and endless accomplishments, the charming creation of the Creator just in the bloom her youth, before another king Sunada spoke.

In the days of yore there flourished a king, ever engaged in yoga, by name Kartavirya, who used to set forth thousand arms at the time of fight, who had erected sacrificial stakes at the eighteen insular contiments of the world and had been more than worthy of the little king. Whenever any one of his subjects used to think of a misdeed even in his mind that chastiser, with bow in his hand, came before him and put down his mental transgression.

The king of Ceylon who had defeated Indra, lived in his prison sighing heavily, with his hands bound fast with the string of his bow, till the king's pleasure.

This king, whose name is Pratipa, who strictly follows scriptures and the advice of the old and experienced men, is born in his family. He has removed the blame of Fortune that she is fickle caused by the faults of her subjects.

The Fire-god helps him at the time of battle and therefore he considers the sharp edge of Parasu Rama's axe who was like the night of death to the Kshatryas harmless as a lotus petal.

If you wish to feast upon the sight of Reva, through the palace-widow, which flows beautifully even in winter, which looks like the girdle of the walls of the city of Mhaismati, be the consort of this long-armed king.

As a lotus does not like the full moon, freed from clouds in the autumn so Indumati did not like that highly beautiful and charming king.

Sunanda, the guard of the seraglio, thus spoke to the princess about Sushena, the king of Surashena, whose glories were widely known even in the celestial region, and who was like a lamp both to his maternal and paternal famlies endued with pure manners.

This king who celebrates sacrifices duly is born in Neep family. Virtues, naturally hostile, have cast off their mutual conflict in him like beasts when they come to the peaceful abode of a hermit.

The moon-like effulgence of his person which gives pleasure to the eyes, falls in his own house and his heroic power falls on the house of his enemy and covers its top with a net of arrows.

Whitened by the sandal pastes decorating the breasts of the women of his seraglio while sporting in the water, the river of black water, although flowing from Mathura, appears to have received the water of the Ganges.

With the jewel which sheds its lustre on his breast and which was given him by the serpent Kalya living in Jamuna when frightened by Garuda he over-clouds even Krishna with his costly Koustava jem.

O fair princess, selecting this prince as your husband spend your days happily in Vrindavana where beds are made of tender leaves, strewn with flowers and which is in no wise inferior to the garden of Kuvera.

Sitting on a rock cooled with water and scented with mountainous herbs in the charming valley of Govardhana hill do you enjoy the pleasure of seeing the peacocks dance in the rainy season.

Indumati, possessing a navel beautiful like an eddy, who was destined to be another's wife, passed by that king, like an ocean-going river with a beautiful eddy changing its course on coming across a hill.

When the maiden princess, having a full-moon-like countenance, came to Hemangada, the king of Kalinga, whose arms were decorated with bracelets and who had rooted out his foes, the maid-servant said.

This king, whose strength is impregnable like the mount Mahendra, is the master of the Mahendra mountain and the great sea. When he goes out on an expedition the mount Mahendra, with its fountains as if precedes him like an elephant exuding juice.

This king, possessed of beautiful arms, the foremost of bowmen, bears on his two arms two black lines caused by the constant rubbing of bow strings, like two torrents of the tears of the damsels of the enemies taken captives mixed with collyrium.

When lying asleep in his palace, the ocean adjacent to it, awakens him, the waves of which can be seen from the palace window and whose deep sound dispensed with the necessity of ringing bells to announce different hours.

The drops of perspiration being removed from your body by the winds which carry away flowers of Lavanga trees from other islands, sport you with this king on the sea-shore which is filled with the sound of the Tati trees.

The youngest sister of the Bhoja Raj, who is attracted by real beauty, went away from the king though she was tempted by the maid, like the goddess of prosperity from a person whose luck s bad, drawn near by manliness.

Then approaching the king of Nagpur, beautiful like a celestial the female door-keeper Sunada said to the daughter of the Bhojaraj :—" O you having eyes like those of Chakora, look at this king.

He is the king of the Pandu kingdom. With pearl chains hanging on his shoulders, and breast pasted with gold coloured sandal he is shining like the king of mountains abounding in springs and stricken with the rays of the new sun.

Agastya, who had obstructed the growing height of the Vindhya mountain, who had, with one pamful, drunk up the great sea and vomitted out it again, affectionately enquires of this king when he stands with body wet after the celebration of the horse sacrifice, if the bathing ceremony had been properly done.

Having made a treaty with him lest he might devastate the province of Janasthana the proud king of Lanka set out for defeating Indra. This king obtained from Hara the rare weapon Brahmasira

This king is born in a good family, O fair damsel, if he formally marries you, you will be a co-wife with the southern quarter abounding in gems and girt by the ocean as her waist chain.

O you having good sense, sport happily in the valleys of Malaya Hills where arecanuts are entwined by the betel creepers, the sandal trees are clasped by cardamum and the beds are covered with Tamala leaves.

The body of this king is dark like a blue lotus and your colour is fair like Gorochana. Your union therefore will increase your mutual beauty as that between the cloud and lightning.

The advice of Sunada did not find room in the heart of the sister of the Vidarbha chief as the rays of the moon do not penetrate a lotus folded in the absence of the sun.

Every king, whom Indumati passed by while choosing her husband, assumed a pale look as the houses on a high way are covered with darkness in the absence of lamps.

When she appeared before Raghu's son he doubted whether she would choose him or not but the throbbing of his right hand, adorned with a bracelet, removed his mis-givings.

On appearing before that prince who was perfectly handsome she stopped from going elsewhere. The bees, after getting a blossoming mangoe tree, do not seek another.

Sunanda, who knew full well how to begin or end a conversation, began to say, on finding Indumati, fair like the moon, fixing her attention on him.

There was a king born in the race of Ikshaku, by name Kakutstha, who was Lord Paramount of all kings and from whom the great kings of Northern Kosala inherited the illustrious tittle of Kakusthya.

Riding on the humb of Indra assuming the form of a bull this king appeared like the trident-handed Siva and caused the paintings on the cheeks of Asura women to be removed by his arrows.

When after casting off his bull form the king of gods assumed his most excellent form he sat with him on the same throne touching with his own armlet that of Indra loosened by his driving the elephant Airavata.

In his family was born the king Dilipa who was like a lamp of the house. After celebrating ninety-nine horse sacrifices he did not stop for his inability but for the jealousy of Indra.

During his regeme not even the wind dared shake the mantles of the dancing girls fallen asleep on the road half way from the place of performance, what to speak of others attempting to rob them.

That king's son Raghu is now governing the kingdom. In performing the *Vishwajit* sacrifice he has given away all the riches accumulated by him from the four quarters of the globe and has only an earthen vessel left to him.

It is impossible to gauge the world-wide reputation of Raghu which has travelled over the mountain, gone across the seas, extended to nether region and gone up to the sky.

This prince is born of him like Jayanta of the lord of the celestials. This young prince, although an apprentice, bears with his able father the heavy burden of the earth.

Marry this prince therefore who is your match in lineage, beauty, youth and accomplishments the foremost of which is modesty and let the jem be unite w gold. After Sunanda's speech the princess Indumati looked favourably at him as if receiving him with the wedding garland.

Out of bashfulness the princess could not describe her attachment in words. But it did not remain hidden, but manifested itself by breaking through the person of the damsel of curling tresses in the shape of horripillation.

Indumati thus fixing her attachment on Aja, Sunanda, in a joke, said "Shall I proceed to others." But the bride looked angrily at her.

The damsel, whose thighs were beautiful like the trunk of an elephant, caused the made servant Sunanda, to place the garland, reddened with auspicious powder round the neck of Raghu's son like her love incarnate.

By that garland of auspicious flowers which was hanging down on his broad chest the worthy prince thought as if the sister of Vidarbha has thrown her her arms round his neck.

Pleased at the union of the bride and bridegroom equally qualified the citizens spoke with one voice though it was unpleasant to the ears of the other kings that Indumati was like the light of the moon freed from clouds or the Ganges united with the ocean becoming her.

That assembly, in which the party of the bridegroom were filled with delight and that of the rejected kings were filled with dejection, appeared like a lake in the morning crowded with new blown lotuses on one side and sleeping lilies on the other.

CANTO VII.

Then taking his sister, who, on being united with a worthy bride-groom, looked like the very incarnation of Devasena when united with Kartikeya, the king of Vidarbha went towards his palace.

The kings who were rejected by Indumati became pale like planets in the morning. And speaking ill of their own beauty and dress they returned to their respective camps.

The goddess Sachi appears herself at a Swayamvara assemblage (for destroying those who put in obstacles there). And therefore the kings, though they cherished hostility against Aja, suppressed their anger.

The bride-groom with the bride reached the royal road, which, from begining to end, was strewn with auspicious articles and flowers, decorated with rainbow and where the heat was destroyed by the shade of the flags.

Leaving off the works taken in hand, the ladies of the seraglio, stricken with curiosity to see them, displayed the following gestures on the houses furnished with golden lattices.

Some one, in a hurry to get at the window, forgot to bind her tresses though held by the hand, from which flowers were dropping for the loosening of the knot.

Another, snatching away her feet from the hands of the maid before the dye was dried up, and giving up her slow motion, dyed the entire road leading to the window with red lac.

Another, who had decorated her right eye with collyrium and had not done the left, ran to the window with the brush in her hand.

Another, in a hurry to go, could not tie the loosened waist cloth but held it with her hand and looked through the window, the lustre of the ornaments of fingers brightening up her navel.

The jewelled beads of the half-strung girdle of another woman when she rose up in a hurry and took up and put down her foot steps in difficulty, dropped down; the string only remained attached to the end of her toe.

The loopholes of the windows being covered with curiosity-stricken faces of women having mouths smelling wine and fickle eyes it appeared as if black-bees have sat upon full blown lotuses.

They could not perceive any thing else when they feasted upon him with their eyes, as if the functions of the other senses had been wholly centred in the eye.

It was well that Indumati, after having been sued by other kings not seen by her, preferred the free choice of a husband as conducive to her well-being; or else how could she obtain a husband equal to herself as Lakshi got Narayana.

If this couple of enviable beauty had not been united with each other then the attempt of the Creator in giving them such beauty would have been useless.

Perhaps Rati and her consort have been born as the bride and bride-groom. Otherwise how could the maiden choose such a becoming husband out of many thousand kings? Mind remembers the pristine unions.

Hearing these sweet and agreeable words given vent to by women the prince Aja reached the palace of his brother-in-law adorned with all sorts of auspicious articles.

Thereupon getting down from the back of the she-elephant the prince shook hands with the king of Kamarupa and then entered into the hearts of women and the quadrangle of four walls pointed out to him by the king of Vidarbha.

Seated on a throne set with variegated jems in that quadrangle the prince received, together with the side-long books of the females, a mixture of honey and a pair of silk raiments offered by the Bhoja Raj.

Dressed in a silk raiment he was conducted by the polite female guards into the seraglio like the white-foamed sea taken to its shore by the rays of the newly risen moon.

Offering oblations of clarified butter and other articles to the sacred fire, and making him the witness, the family priest, like unto fire itself, of the Bhojaraja, united the bride and the bride-groom.

Taking the bride's hand into his own the prince shone like a mango tree entwined by a neighbouring Asoka creeper.

The hairs of the fore-arm of the bride-groom stood erect and the fingers of the bride were wetted with perspiration as if the god of love divided attachment in two equal parts in that pair.

Their eyes, which were anxious to see each other and were casting oblique looks but which were turned away as soon as they met, were suffering from a sort of indescribable modesty.

While circumambulating the fire with rising flames the couple shone like the day and night moving round the golden mount Sumera. Instructed by the divine priest that bride, having a capacious waist and eyes like inebriete *Chakoras*, threw parched grain into the fire, with her face bending low in modesty.

Sacred smokes, perfumed with the smell of clarified butter, Sami leaves and parched grain, rose up from the fire, and touching the cheeks of the bride appeared for a short time like two lotuses pending on her ears.

By the inhalation of that smoke as is the practice the cheeks of the bride became reddened, her eyes were full of tears, mixed with collyrium, and the barley stalks on her ears were withered.

Seated on a golden throne the bride and the bridegroom held on their heads wet rice offered duly by the priest, their friends, the king Bhoja and the ladies whose husbands and children were alive.

The king, the glory of the Bhoja race, having thus performed the wedding ceremony of his sister ordered his servents to distribute presents to the kings according to their rank.

The kings, whose anger was concealed under the cover of external expressions of joy and who accordingly looked like calm smiling lakes harbouring crocodiles inside them, took their departure after bidding farewell to Bhoj and returning back his presents as tokens of friendship.

Determined that that they would take away perforce that beautiful and lovely damsel on Aja's return journey home the kings waited there intercepting his way.

Having finished the wedding ceremony of his youngest sister the king, of Krath Kaisika, sent Aja to his own country, with presents proportionate to his means and becoming the excitement of the hour and accompanied him to some distance.

Having passed three nights with Aja who was known all over the three worlds the king of Kundina came back like the moon turning away from the sun after the conjunction.

The kings had already been enraged with Raghu for having been dispossessed by him of their wealth and now they could not bear the acquisition of the beautiful damsel by his son.

They obstructed Aja in the way while he was taking the daughter of Bhojaraj Indumati as Pralhada had stopped the leg of the three footed Dwarf when it was occupying the space offered by Bali.

Having kept one of the trustworthy ministers of his father's with a large force in charge of Indumati prince Aja encounted the army of the kings as Sona, with rising waves, meets the Ganges.

The infantry fought with the infantry, the car-warriors with the car-warriors, the cavalry with the cavalry and the elephant warriors with elephant warriors. So the encounter took place between equally matched combatants.

Unable to hear each other's words on account of the beating of drums the bowmen did not declare the history of their family but announced their names by letters engraven on the arrows.

In the battle-field the dust, raised by the horse's hoofs, thickened by the car-whels and scattered in the firmanent by the flapping of the ears of the elephants, obstructed the sun like a canopy.

The figures of the fishes painted on the flags of some kings, coming in contact with the dust extended by the wind, appeared like living fishes drinking the muddy water of a newly swollen river.

The clouds of dust growing thick the cars could be known by the clatter of their wheels and elephants by the ringing of the bells round their necks and the friend and foe by the announcement of the name of each other's masters.

When the dust, scattered all over the battle-field, obstructed the eye-sight of the people, the stream of blood issuing from the wounds inflected on men, horses and elephants, served the purpose of the sudden rising of the sun.

The cloud of dust, having its connecting link with the ground cut off by the blood and driven about by the wind in the air, appeared like the smokes that had risen from the fire before it was reduced to red-hot charcoals.

Regaining their consciousness from the swoon caused by blows, the car-warriors reprimanded their drivers who had turned away their steeds and furiously attacked the enemies recognizing them by their flags.

The arrows, of the light-handed bowmen, though cut in twain in their way, reached by their own force their aims with that half that was furnished with arrow heads.

In the encounter between the elephants, the heads, of the elephant warriors having been sundered by razor-like sharp discuses, dropped down on earth after some delay on account of their hairs caught by Sena birds with their talons.

The horse man, who struck the first blow, did not strike again his antagonist lying unconscious on the back of his horse but waited untill he revived. The elephants put out, in fear with the water of their trunks, the fire caused by the unsheathed swords struck by warriors, in mail, against their tusks.

Being strewn, as if with fruits, with the heads of the heroes cut off by shafts, filled as if with cups by the scattered helments of the warriors, and flooded as if with wine by the streams of blood the battle-field appeared like the drinking site of Death.

A female fox, snatching off from the birds a portion of hand the flesh of which was all eaten up by them, threw it off, although fond of flesh having her palate wounded by the armlet.

A heroe, whose head was cut off by the sword of his enemy, immediately attained to the dignity of a celestial seated on a celestial ear with a celestial damsel by his left and he saw his headless trunk dance in the battle-field.

Two heroes, on their drivers being slain, acted both as fighters and drivers. Losing their horses they closed with clubs, and when the latter broke they began to fight, hand to hand.

Two heroes who had been fighting with each other and who died simultaneously, quarrelled over the same celestial damsel when gone to heaven.

The two hosts alternately met with defeat and victory like the two waves of the great ocean alternately raised by two opposite winds.

On his army being routed by the enemy the powerful Aja rushed upon his foes as the fire remains where the fuel is, no matter where the smoke is carried by the wind.

As the great boar, at the end of the cycle, threw back the rising waves, so the heroic Aja, having none to help him, riding on his car and equipped with his armour, bow and quiver, withstood the attack of the kings.

The people saw him place his right hand calmly in the mouth of the quiver. Then the bowstring that warrior, drawn once to his ears, poured forth arrows destructive of enemies.

He covered the earth with the heads of the enemies in which the lips were excessively red for being bitten in anger, which bore distinct and ascending marks of the contraction of eye brows, cut off by him with loud roars with *bhallas*.

Concentrating their physical and mental strength, and collecting their fourfold forces the kings simultaneously attacked him with their mail-piercing weapons.

Just as a dawn covered with mist is known by the faintly visible sun, so his car, enshrouded with the arrows of the enemy was visible by the flags at its top.

The energetic son of the Lord Paramount, beautiful like Kandarpa, discharged at the kings the *Sanmohana* weapon received by him from the Gandharva Pryamvada.

The armies of the kings were at once possessed by deep sleep, their bodies resting motionless against flag-staffs, their head gears slipping down and their hands inert in drawing bows.

Then putting the conch to his lip which would be kissed by his wife the prince blew it. While blowing it the heroe of heroes, seemed to be drinking the living fame acquired by his own self.

Aja's soldiers, when they returned to the field, recognised that blaze and saw him among the stupilied enemies shining like the image of the moon in the midst of the folded lotuses.

Aja caused the following words to be written on the flags of the kings with arrow heads dipped in blood :—The son of Raghu has robbed you of your glory but not of your life through mercy.

With one of his arms resting on an end of the bow, with hairs dishevelled by the pulling off of his helmet, and his brows covered with drops of perspiration Aja spoke to his terrified consort.

"O princess of Vidarbha, look at the enemies who can be robbed of their arms even by boys. I order you to do so. They wanted to take you from me by such-like war feats.

Shorn of the gloom cast by the enemy her countenance shone like a mirror which regains its brightness when the dimness caused by breath is gone.

Though highly pleased she congratulated her lover through her maids and not by herself as she felt abashed, just as the earth, soaked by the drops of the new rains, expresses her joy to the clouds by the cries of peacocks.

Having thus trampled the kings under his left foot and been freed from shame Aja took his accomplished wife home. With her hairs covered with dust raised by the horses of the car she looked like his goddess of victory.

Raghu, who had been informed before of all this, congratulated his son who came back victorious with his praiseworthy wife. And transmitting the charge of his people to his care he became anxious to follow the paths of peace and emancipation. When their sons became able to take the burden of the family the kings of the solar dynasty never remained in their homes.

CANTO VIII.

Before the wedding thread was removed from the hand of the beautiful prince Aja the king Raghu handed over to him the earth like the second Indumati herself.

The other princes, by administering poison and taking recourse to other sinful practices, attempt to get by their kingdoms, but Aja took charge of it, only because he was ordered by his father to do so and not for enjoying pleasures.

Being sprinkled with sacred water by the great Rishi Vasistha the earth and the queen, after going through the ceremony of being sprinkled along with Aja, by their joy so clearly seen, expressed their success of having a becoming husband.

According to the rules laid down in the Atharva Veda the family priest Vasistha performed the Abhiseka ceremony of the heir-apparent. He gradually grew irrepressible to his enemies, for when Kshatriya prowess is united with the Brahma energy it becomes like the union of fire and wind.

Having obtained the youthful Aja as their king the subjects thought that they had got Raghu, with youth returned to him, as their king, for the prince not only inherited the prosperity of his sire but all his accomplishments too.

At that time two auspicious objects, being united with another two auspicious objects, assumed greater beauty. As passing into the hands of Aja his highly prosperous ancestral kingdom appeared beautiful so his youthfulness, united with his humble character, appeared graceful.

The king Aja, endued with incomparable strength of arms, began to enjoy mildly the newly acquired earth like unto a newly married wife lest a least oppression might upset her.

As hundreds of rivers are not insulted by a great ocean so no one met with insult from the king Aja. Therefore all his subjects were, day and night, engaged in works conducive to his well-being and pleasure.

He was neither very hot-tempered nor very excessively mild. In sooth adopting a middle course he gradually brought the kings to his submission without ruining them entirely, as the wind, without either breaking down or uprooting the trees, bends them down only.

Thereupon seeing his son devoid of avarice, self-controlled and encircled by his subjects, the king

Raghu gave up his attachment for the transient objects of the world.

The kings, born in the race of Dilipa, used to hand over the charge of the kingdom, in their old age, to their sons and controlling their minds led the lives of ascetics clad in bark.

But beholding his sire Raghu about to retire into the forest, and saluting his feet with his head adorned with a head-gear the prince Aja prayed to him, saying "Do not repair to the forest leaving me behind."

Thereat moved by the piteous accents and tears of the prince, Raghu, fond of his son, agreed to satisfy his desire. But as a serpent does not take back the cast off slough so he did not take back the prosperous kingdom handed over to his son.

Adopting the final stage of life and controlling his senses he began to live in a solitary site at the outskirt of the city. And the goddess of fortune, enjoyed by his son, began to serve him like a daughter-in-law.

The old king Raghu began to wend the path of beatitude and the new king Aja began to travel by the road of advancement. So like the sky assuming a wonderful appearance when the moon sets and the sun rises the royal family looked highly beautiful.

People regarded Raghu, bearing marks of a king and an ascetic and his son as the two divisions of religion, *viz.*, *Nivritti* (inaction) productive of emancipation and *Pravritti* (action) productive of great advancement, incarnated on earth.

In order to make fresh conquests of territories never conquered before the king Aja became united with ministers, expert in political counsels. King Raghu too, in order to attain emancipation, lived in the company of ascetics conversant with the knowledge of Brahma.

For governing his subjects the youthful king sat on his seat of judgment and the old king Raghu sat on a seat of Kuca grass in a solitary place for practising concentration of mind.

One high-souled king, by the prowess of his wealth and arms, began to subdue the external kings and the other great man (Raghu) by means of devout meditation began to suppress the five vital airs.

The youthful king Aja baffled all the works undertaken by the other kings of the world ; the old king too, by the fire of his divine knowledge, reduced into ashes all his Karma, the cause of repeated births in this world.

Considering the result of his action the youthful king made use of six means, treaty etc ; the old king, looking impartialiy on gold and a clod of earth and controlling his mind continually, conquered the three *gunas*, Sattwa, Rajas and Tamas.

The new king never refrained from vigorously carrying on a work undertaken by him till he obtained the fruits thereof. The old king, of fixed mind, did not abstain from Yoga practices till he saw the *Paramatman.*

Having thus suppressed the selfish actions of the senses and enemies they both engaged their minds in the matters of emancipation and worldly advancement and obtained three-fold Siddhis.

Afterwards Raghu, looking impartially on all, spent a few years at Aja's request and then attained by Yoga to the station of the Eternal Great Purusha standing above the cosmic illusion.

Hearing of the demise of his sire and shedding tears continually Raghu's son, who kept sacred fire, interred his dead body with the ascetics and did no perform the cremation ceremony which was against the practice of the Sanyasins.

Such great souls, [following the path of emancipation, do not long for *Pindas* offered by their sons. Although informed of it, Aja, conversant with the rites of the Sraddha ceremony, performed his obsequial rites out of his respectful love for his father.

After having been consoled by persons, conversant with divine knowledge saying "It is not proper for one to grieve for his father who has attained emancipation" Aja cast off a little his sorrow for his father. And putting arrow to his bow he established his sole sovereignty all over the world and governed it in great happiness.

Having obtained the highly powerful king Aja

as their lord the earth abounded in jems and Indumati gave birth to a heroic son.

This son was Dasharatha. He was effulgent like the sun of thousand rays and his fame travelled all over the ten quarters. The learned recognised him as the father of Rama, the slayer of the ten-headed Ravana.

Being freed severally from the debts to the Rishis, gods and departed manes by means of Vedic studies, sacrifices and a son he shone greatly like the sun freed from the halo around it.

His manliness was devoted to the relief of the distressed and to the proper rewarding of persons well read in scriptural literature. It was not his wealth only that was spent for helping others but all his qualities too were devoted to the same work.

Having looked after the house-hold duties and left the kingdom in charge of his son one day king Aja began to enjoy the company of his queen Indumati in a garden near the city like unto Indra enjoying the company of Sachi in the garden of Nandana.

At that time the great Saint Narada, conversant with three times, was passing by the etherial way for worshipping, with the music of his Vina, the Lord Bholanath, the husband of Bhavani, ever existent, intelligent and blissful, established at the sacred shrine of Gokarna situate on the bank of the southern ocean.

On the top of his Vina was hanging a charming garland of celestial flowers. The powerful wind, as if attracted by its sweet scent, pilfered it.

The black-bees began to follow the flowers of the garland at which it appeared that the *Vina*, of the great Rishi, insulted by the wind, was shedding tears polluted by collyrium.

Having overpowered the beauty of the trees and creepers of that garden, produced by the season, the garland enjoyed ease after dropping on the nipples of the breasts of the beloved queen Indumati.

As soon as she saw that celestial garland which was but the temporary companion of her well-formed breasts the queen became bewildered and shut up her eyes like the moon possesed by Rahu.

Along with the unconscious body of his dearest consort the king also dropped down. It is a well known fact that whenever a drop of oil falls down from the wick of a lamp a part of the burning flame also drops down.

Hearing the piteous cries of the attendants of the royal pair, the geese, Sarasas and other birds, living in that lake, began to cry also out sympathy for them.

Thereupon with water and fanning the fainting fit of the king was a little abated, but the queen remained in that state. Curative measures act successfully only when still lingers there a part of the lease of life.

Then the king Aja, greatly attached to his most

beloved queen, took her up on his own lap ever familiar to her, who was like unto a Vina, before the string is set, for the loss of consciousness.

All the senses being inert the limbs of Indumati had become pale. Therefore by placing her on his lap the king appeared like the morning moon bearing the soiled mark of a hare.

Casting off his natural forbearance in the absence of his dearest consort he began to bewail in accents suppressed by tears.

" What to speak of man composed of flesh and blood, even the hardest iron is heated and melted by fire."

Looking at that garland of flowers the king began to say piteously. " If this tender flower can destroy life as soon as it touches a body then what article of the Destroyer is there which cannot kill a person ?

The destroyer Kritanta destroys a tender article with another tender thing. Herein is the example of a lotus which is killed by the fall of dews.

If this garland of flowers had killed her all on a sudden, why does it not kill me though I have placed it for a long time on my breast ? I understand, by the will of the Providence, some time a poison is changed into ambrosia and again elsewhere ambrosia is changed into poison.

For my ill luck the Creator has created this thunder which, without killing the tree, has destroyed the creeper resting on it."

Thereupon casting his looks upon the dead body of Indumati, the king, ever fond of his wife, said "O dear, you never showed me any disregard although I had comitted a hundred offences but I have committed no offence today. Why dont you welcome me then?

O you of pure smiles, methinks you knew me to be a cheat and dishonest fellow, or else why have you left this world without taking leave of me?

Alas! This cursed life once followed my dearest. Why has it come back again after leaving her? Let it suffer this dreadful pang of separation by its own fault.

O dear, still the drops of perspiration, caused by sexual enjoyment, lie on your lotus face. But where have you gone yourself leaving aside your body? Oh fie on this worthlessness of the body.

O you having a moon-like countenance, formerly I had never in my mind done any thing unpleasant to you. Why have you forsaken me then? In name only I am the lord of the earth, but in sooth my love is firmy fixed on you.

O you having thighs like the trunk of an elephant, the wind shaking your curling tresses black like bees and set with flowers methinks you have revived.

O dearest, as herbs, being lighted up in the night, remove the darkness of the Himalayan caves, so do you, regaining your consciousness in no time, remove my misery. Do not afflict me thus.

The curling locks are being shaken on your countenance but your mouth has desisted from speaking; like unto a lotus of a hundred petals with black bees sleeping in the night it is paining me continually.

Because the night regains the moon and the female Chakravaka its mate and therefore they can withstand the separation. But you have forsaken me for good and this is scorching my body.

Lying down on a tender and delightful bed of new leaves your soft and beautiful body used to suffer pain. How will it suffer today the terrible pang of rising on the funeral pyre?

With the termination of your happy movements, this your first and dearest companion of the sexual intercourse, your tongue is speechless. Finding you engaged in deep slumber from which you will never awake she looks as if also dead with you.

Anxious to go to the celestial region and thinking me hard enough to bear separation you have transferred your sweet speech to the coels, your slow movements to the geese, your fickle eyes to the deer, and your playful gesture to the creepers shaken by the wind. But your separation has become too much for me to bear and therefore these accomplishments are unable to sooth me.

O goddess, you thought of uniting this Sahakara and Priyangu as a couple. It is not proper for you to go for good without uniting them.

By striking it with your feet you performed the *Dohada* ceremoney of this Asoka tree for flowers. She will now give birth to celestial flowers. Instead of decorating your hairs how shall I offer them as a garland for your obsequial rites?

Remembering the favour of the striking of your feet accompanied with the tinkling of Nupuras which others can hardly get, this Asoka tree is shedding tears for you in the shape of flowers. In fact, even this Asoka tree has been overwhelmed with your seperation.

O you sweet-speeched like a Kinnari, without finishing the girdle of Vakula flowers, sweet-scented with your breath, half of which you had strung in my company for your enjoyment, why are you fast asleep?

Your dear companions partake of your joy and misery. This your son, beautiful and prosperous like unto the moon of the first day and myself are greatly devoted to you. It is really cruel of you that still you forsake us all.

My patience is exhausted and my love is gone. The spring and other seasons are shorn of festivities. I stand in no need of ornaments and my bed is forlorn. O dear, you were my minister in household affairs, my friend in sports and my dear disciple in fine arts. What is there mine what the ruthless Death has not stolen by pilfering you?

O you of inebriete eyes, after having drunk the

wine tasted by my lips how will you, after repairing to the next world, drink handfuls of water spoiled with tears?

Know that Aja's happiness terminates to-day although he has immense wealth. No other tempting object will attract my mind. My enjoyment of worldly objects is subject to you."

Having thus bewailed piteously for his dear wife Aja, the king of Koshala, made also the trees sullied with tears in the shape of juice trickling down from their branches.

Having removed from the lap of Aja with difficulty, the all-beautiful Indumati adorned with that death ornament of the celestial garland, his kinsmen consigned her to the fire lighted with Aguru and sandal woods.

Fearing the censure that Aja, although a king, yet followed his wife in death out of grief he did not reduce his body to ashes along with that of his dear wife but he had not the least desire to live.

After ten days the learned king Aja performed with great eclat in that garden near the city the Sraddha ceremony of Indumati whose accomplishments only then remained.

Being pale like the moon in the end of the night on account of the separation of his dearest wife he entered the city seeing his own sorrow in the eyes of the damsels thereof.

Although living in his own hermitage being initiated into a sacrifice the great ascetic Vasistha came to know of the stupifying grief of Aja and communicated to him the following consoling words through one of his disciples.

Approaching the king the disciple said :—O king, Lord Vasistha is engaged in a sacrifice which is not yet finished. Therefore although informed of the cause of your sorrow he has not been able to come here in person.

O you of good temper, he has communicated to you the following short advice. O illustrious king, listen to the message of the great Rishi and bear it in mind.

With the unobstructed eyes of knowledge the great Rishi sees the present, past and future of the three worlds.

O king, formerly terrified at the hard ascetcism carried on by the great saint Trinavindu, the king of gods despatched to him a celestial damsel by name Harini for breaking his devout meditation.

Coming before that ascetic Harini displayed various charming and lustful gestures. Inflamed with anger consequent upon his ascetic observances being obstructed, like unto fire of dissolution in the ocean of peace, he imprecated a curse on her, saying "Go and be born as a woman."

Hearing of that curse Harini prostrated herself at the feet of that great Muni and said with folded palms:—O lord, I am another's servant. Dost thou forgive me if I have acted against thee." Being pleased with her humble words the great saint said. "Seeing celestial flowers you will cast off your human body and repair again to the celestial region."

O king, that Harini was born as Indumati in the family of Krathakaishika and became your consort. And beholding the celestial flowers, the agent for releasing her from the curse, dropped from the sky, she has cast off her body.

It is useless to grieve for her. Death is certain when a person is born. Do you now govern this earth, for the kings have the earth for their wife.

Without being addicted to sensual pleasures you acquired true knowledge in your youth by studying the spiritual science. Taking recourse to patience in this your mental affliction do you display again your accumulated knowledge. If you weep continuously you will not have her. If you follow her it is difficult for you to meet her, for according to their respective Karmas, persons, bound for the next world, proceed by different routes.

Removing now the sorrow for your consort from your heart do you propitiate your wife by offering her *pindas*. The learned say that the tears of kinsmen burn the departed soul.

The learned say death is the natural state of the bodied beings—and birth is merely a disordered state. It is so much an acquisition for creatures as long as they live and breathe in this world. The mistaken people regard the death of their dear ones as an arrow stuck to their hearts but the calm-minded regard it as a door of auspiciousness and accordingly as an arrow uprooted from the heart.

While this union and separation of the body and soul is continually taking place why should the learned grieve for the wife, children and other objects of the world ?

O you the foremost of those who have controlled their senses, you should not yield to grief like an ordinary mortal. If the wind can shake a tree and a mountain, then what is the difference between the two ?"

Having accepted the advice of his preceptor; Vasistha, the highly intelligent Aja dismissed his disciple. But those words of advice, as if obtaining no room in the heart of Aja filled with sorrow, returned to the preceptor Vasistha himself.

Thinking that the prince Dasharatha of tender age was unable to carry on the burden of the kingdom, the sweet-speeched and the truthful king Aja sometimes saw the likeness of his wife in the oil-painting, her resemblance in a particular object and again enjoyed her company temporarily in a dream and thus spent eight years in great distress.

As a fig tree easily passes through a palatial building so that mace of grief forcibly cut through Aja's heart. Thinking that he would in no time follow her dear wife after his death, he regarded that grief, the instrument of death, which it was impossible for the physicians to cure, as highly profitable.

Thereupon having duly installed the prince Dasharata, humble and capable, who had come of age, on the throne, and being unwilling to spend his days in misery with that diseased body he made up his mind to die in hunger.

Thereupon having cast off his body at the sacred shrine of the junction of the rivers Sarayu and Ganges and being recognised as one of the immortals he began to enjoy in the company of his wife, far more beautiful, in a pleasure house in the garden of Nandana.

CANTO IX.

After the demise of his sire, the great car-warrior king Dasharatha, the protector of his dependants, the foremost of self-restrained persons and self-controlled, having obtained the kingdom of North Koshala began to govern it by good laws.

On being governed according to the rules of Shastras the subjects of his ancestral kingdom became greatly attached to their king powerful like Kartikeya.

Vasava, the slayer of Vala, pouring down rain in proper season and the king Dasharatha, born in the race of Manu, spending his money in proper time the learned designated them both as removing the toil of husbandmen.

What to speak of the discomfiture arising from the enemy during the regeme of the god-like, energetic king Dasharatha ever devoted to peace even diseases did not prevail in his kingdom and the Earth abounded in crops.

As the earth looked beautiful during the regeme of Raghu who had conquered the ten quarters and that of his son Aja, so the king Dasharatha, equally powerful like themselves, immitated Yama by adopting the middle course, Kuvera by distributing riches, Varuna by suppressing the wicked and the sun by the beauty of his person.

Neither hunting, dice, wine adorned with the rays of the moon, nor youthful damsels, nor any other sport could attract Dasharatha ever studious of advancement.

He never used humiliating words before Indra although he was the king, and never spoke an untruth even in jest; and he was of such a quiet temperament, shorn of anger that he never used harsh words even towards his enemies.

The kings suffered humiliation and enjoyed advancement at the hands of that scion of Raghu's race. He treated them like friends who obeyed his commands. And he used to show hostility with a heart hard as the iron towards those kings who acted against him.

With his bow always set with a string king Dasharatha, in one car, conquered the earth girt by the ocean; his army, abounding in quick-coursing steeds and elephants, simply announced his victory.

When getting upon a single beautiful chariot and taking up his bow he conquered the world the ocean, with its deep rumbling, acted as the victorious bugle of the king, rich like Kuvera himself.

As Purandara cut off the wings of the mountains with one hundred Kotis of strokes, so king Daṣaratha, having a countenance like a new blown lotus, with a downpour of arrows shot off his sounding bow, destroyed the strength, army and prowess of the enemies.

As the celestials salute their king Indra so hundreds of kings, with the lustre of the jems of their crowns dyed with the lac of fingers, saluted the feet of Dasharatha of unmitigated manliness.

At length, when the children of his enemies, advised by their respective ministers, appeared before the victorious King with folded hands, he, taking compassion on the widowed wives of his enemies, who did not dress their hairs, returned to Ayodhya from the last extremity of the great ocean.

Although he had acquired the sovereignty of twelve empires, still the Lord Paramount Dasharatha, effulgent like the fire and the moon, always remained careful and attentive knowing the goddess of fortune to be fickle at the least loop-hole.

Having forsaken the liberal scion of Raghu's race, king Dasharatha, the protector of the poor, and the ancient Purusha Narayana the chaste goddess Kamala did not serve any other kings.

As the river, born of the mountains, obtains the ocean, so the princesses of Magadha, Koshala and Kekaya obtained the king Dasharatha, the slayer of his enemies, as their husband.

Being united with those three wives king Dasharatha, the destroyer of his enemies and expert in counsels, looked like the king of gods incarnated on earth with the three powers of lordliness, counsel and energy for instructing the subjects.

Having helped the king of gods in battle the great car-warrior king Dasharatha, after removing the fear of celestial damsels by his arrow, made them sing the strength of his arms.

Having collected wealth from the ten quarters by the strength of his arms, King Dasharatha, shorn of the quality of darkness, took off the crown from his head in the horse sacrifice and adorned the sacrificial altars erected on the banks of the rivers Sarayu and Tamasa.

Having assumed the body of Dasharatha, engaged in sacrifice, clad in antelope skin, holding a staff, wearing a silken cloth, observing the vow of silence and carrying a deer horn for itching the eight-formed Lord Mahadeva shone there highly effulgent.

The self controlled king Dasharatha, who had been purified by the sacrificial sprinkling of water, was a fit person to sit in the assemblage of the celestials. He bent his head only before the king of gods.

Preceding the king of gods with a bow in hand the incomparable car-warrior, the king Dasharatha put down the clouds of dust covering the disc of the sun with the blood of the Asuras.

Then the Spring, adorned with new flowers, appeared as if for serving that matchless king Dasharatha who was worshippful and powerful like Yama, Kuvera and Indra in wealth and energy.

When the sun felt a desire for going to the direction protected by Kuvera his charioteer Aruna turned his horses. Afterwards on the wintry frost being removed, he, making the sky clear, left the mount Malaya.

There arose first flowers, then new leaves, then the humming of black bees and then the singing of coels. Thus Spring arrived at the forest adorned with trees and creepers.

As the petitioners used to run after the wealth of the great king Dasharatha, which was increased by his bravery and political strength and was the sole instrument of benifitting good people so the bees and acquatic birds began to run after lotuses unfolded by the spring.

It was not the new grown Asoka flowers only bloosoming in the spring which excited the sexual desire of people, but new buds also, set on the ears of women, which madden the amorous people, did the same.

Drinking the honey of Kuruvaka flowers which were clever enough to yield milk and were like the leafy ornaments, of the presiding goddess of the garden, made by the spring, the bees began to hum.

The Vakula flowers, smelling of wine, all on sudden growing there for drinking the wine of the mouths of beautiful-faced damsels swarms of bees, anxious to drink honey, came there and disturbed the Vakula trees.

With the appearance of the spring the blossoms of the Palasa trees looked like cuts inflicted by the shameless, intoxicated women, with their nails, on the persons of their lovers.

The sun greatly decreased the fall of snow because it caused pain to the lips of women cut with the teeth of their lovers and prevented them from putting on their girdles. But it did not remove it completely.

With her leaves shaken by the waves of the Malaya air, the Sahakara creepers, adorned with buds, as if engaged in the art of dancing, pilfered the minds of men shorn of anger, jealousy and other passions.

The notes of the Kokilas sitting on the blossoming and fragrant trees in the beginning of the spring were audible like the low voice of the coy women.

The creepers of the garden are singing with the sweet humming of black bees and have been adorned with the beautiful teeth of flowers. The new leaves being shaken by the wind it appears as if they are dancing.

United with their respective lovers the women are displaying many beautiful gestures and drinking honey, more fragrant than the Vakula flowers, capable of exciting desire.

With the movements of acquatic birds emitting sweet notes, the tanks, attached to the houses, adorned with full blown lotuses, appeared like women, of smiling faces adorned with girdles.

The night, corrupted by the spring, and growing pale of countenance with the rising of the moon, looked worn out like a woman divorced from the pleasurable company of her lover.

Having spread pure rays capable of removing the exhaustion of sexual intercourse, the moon, after the termination of the winter, excited the five arrows of Cupid.

The women looked highly effulgent like fire inflamed with clarified butter; and they put on their tresses tender Karnikara flowers, constituting as if, the golden ornaments for the presiding goddess of the garden.

Like unto Tilakas adorning the women, the Tilaka trees, engarlanded with bees sitting on beautiful leaves resembling drops of collyrium, increased greatly the beauty of the forest.

Being adorned with bunches of sweet scented flowers the most charming of trees Nava Mallika, began as it were, to steal the minds of the passers by her smiles blooming upon her leaf-like lips.

The soldiers of Cupid, namely, the cloth dyed with Kusuma flowers resembling the newly-risen sun, the barley stalks set on ear-holes and the notes of Kokilas, brought the minds of pleasure-seeking men under the complete control of women.

The *Tilaka Manjaries*, with white filaments remaining, having rows of black-bees seated on them, looked like nets of pearls set on the locks of women.

The bees began to follow the dust of flowers raised by the wind; which was the flag of Madana with bow In his hand, beautified the face of the goddess of spring and resembled the powders of Kumkuma &c.

Although expert in rocking, the women, being anxious to embrace their lovers while experiencing the pleasure of the craddle of the Spring, had their hold of the ropes loosened.

The Kokilas expressing their minds, as if saying" "O Sensitive women, give up your sensitiveness. It is not proper to quarrel for nothing. If your youth when you can enjoy pleasures once goes away it will never return," the sensitive women engaged themselves in sexual pleasures.

Having thus enjoyed the pleasures of vernal festivities in the company of pleasure-seeking women King Dasharatha, resembling the slayer of Madhu, the Spring and Madana, became anxious to go out a-hunting.

By hunting one learns the art of aiming at a moving body and masters the gestures of beasts caused by fear and anger. Besides the body becomes light by endurance and hardships. For this reason obtaining the consent of his ministers the king issued out of the capital.

Dressed in raiments befitting a journey to the forest the king, placing a bow on his capacious shoulders, set out covering the sky with dust raised by the hoops of his horses.

The king had his hairs tied with garlands of wild flowers. He put on a coat of mail green like leaves. The Kundalas on his ears were shaken by the speed of his horses, and he began to range in the sites frequented by the Ruru deer.

Placing their persons on their creepers and transferring their vision to bees the gods of the forest began to behold the beautiful-eyed king who by his laws had pleased the subjects of Koshala.

By his command the hunters, with rods in hand and accompaned by a pack of hounds, entered into the forest. At that time the forest-fire was extinguished, the robbers were suppressed, and the ground, freed from mud, became fit for the running of the horses.

Afterwards the king entered into the forests, abounding in Gavaya and other beasts & various birds and reservoirs of water.

As the month of Bhadra, filled with the mutterings of clouds, holds the rain-bow set with the string of gold-hued lightnings so the joyful king Dasharatha, holding his bow set with string and twanging it worked up the forest-ranging lions with anger.

At that time a herd of deer, musticating Kusa grass, came within his view. Amongst them the young ones, sucking the milk of their mothers, obstructed the movements of the she-deer. And the haughty antelopes went before the herd.

No sooner the king Dasharatha, riding a powerful charger, and taking up an arrow from the quiver, had gone before them than they, straying away from the herd like lotuses shaken by the wind, blackened the forest sites with theirs piteous looks.

When the king Dasharatha, powerful like Indra, aimed with his bow at a deer, his female mate stood by him, Thereat filled with pity the king, on account of his own desire, withdrew the arrow drawn up to ears. Desirous of shooting arrows at others and seeing their beautiful and fear-stricken looks the king, remembering the glances of forward women, loosened his firm grasp placed near his ears.

Then that foremost of kings pursued the track of a herd of boars distinctly marked by their wet footsteps who had all on on a sudden come out of the muddy tanks and fled away quickly.

Bending his body a little on the back of the horse he began to discharge arrows. The boars also attempted to return the attack but they could not perceive that their hips had been fixed on the trees on which they took shelter.

When the wild buffaloes were about to attack him he pierced each of them on the eye with an arrow. The arrows went so very quickly through their bodies, that without being soiled with blood they first struck the buffalloes and then dropped down.

Having cut down the daggers off the heads of the rhinoceros with sharpened razors, the king Dasharatha, the repressor of the wicked, lightened the burden of their heads, but did not destroy their lives. He could not bear the supremacy of his enemies but was not against their living long.

By virtue of his training and lightness of hand the fearless King Dasharatha, in a moment, filled with arrows the mouths of tigers coming out of caves towards him like the branches of a Sarjaru tree broken down by the wind and converted them into so many quivers.

As if envying the tittle of the lions, the king of beasts, and desiring to kill them lying in the centre of the herd the lord of the earth agitated them with the twang of his fearful bow.

Having killed with arrows the lions, the enemies

of the elephants, King Dasharatha, the scion of the Kakuthstha race, discharged his debt to them who were the principal helps in the battle-field.

Somewhere turning the course of his horse the king drove towards the Chamari deer. And having deprived them of white chowries with the stroke of *Bhallas* like unto the hostile kings he enjoyed peace.

Recollecting all on a sudden the looks of his dearest wives adorned with variegated garlands loosened at the time of sexual intercourse the king did no shoot arrows at the peacocks of beautiful feathers flying before his horse.

Passing through the cover of leaves the wind, of the forest, carrying fragments of snow, removed the drops of perspiration caused by toil, lying on the face of the king.

Having made over the adminstration of his kingdom to his minister the Emperor Dasharatha, forgetful of other works, grew attached to hunting. Hunting too, like a clever woman, attracted his mind.

Separated from his kinsmen the king somewhere spent the night on a bed of flowers and leaves with the light of the herbs.

Having his sleep broken in the morning by the flapping of the elephants' ears resembling the sound of drums and hearing the sweet notes of the birds like unto the auspicious songs of the panegyrists he began to range in that charming forest.

Once on a time the king Dasharatha, pursing a

Kuru deer, entered into a deep forest unperceived by his followers and by the help of his steed who was foaming on account of the great exhaustion, arrived at the bank of the river Tamasa filled with ascetics.

A sound like that of the filling up of a pitcher arose all on a sudden from that river. Mistaking that sound for the roar of an elephant he shot an arrow capable of putting a stop to the sound.

Although the wild animals are unslayable by the kings still it was no wonder that the King Dasharatha transgressed this injunction for even the wise, under the influence of Raja guñas, wend evil ways.

Hearing all on a sudden the cries 'O Father !" the king was greatly depressed. Then searching for the cause thereof in the forest of Vetasa he saw a Rishi boy, holding a pitcher, wounded with an arrow. And on account of dreadful repentance he considered himself struck with an arrow.

Getting down immediately from his horse Dasharatha, born in the illustrious family of Raghu, enquired of this Rishi boy of his family. Almost dying with the pain of the mace stuck to his heart the Rishi boy thus expressed his own history :—"O king, I have been begotten by a Vaishya on a Shudra woman. My parents are blind. They are practising penances in this forest. Take me to them." Without taking out the mace from his heart on account of the bewilderment of his senses the king, at the request of the Rishi boy, took him to his parents and communicated to them the miserable condition of their only son and his own misdeed caused by ignorance.

Hearing of that dreadful news the husband and wife bewailed for a long time and ordered the king to take out the mace from the breast of their son. No sooner the king uprooted the mace than the Rishi boy expired.

Thereupon the aged ascetic, with tears in his hand, imprecated a curse on the king, saying " O King, as I, in the old age, die of starvation on account of the sorrowful death of my son so you will in your old age die for your son."

Having been thus cursed by the ascetic Andhaka the king of Koshala, who had committed the offence, communicated to him, who was worked up with anger like a venomous snake struck by the foot.

" O reverend Sir, your curse has proved a blessing to me. I have not as yet seen the lotus-like countenance of a son. As a fire provided by woods, although scorching a cultivable field, increases its productive power, so your curse has proved a boon to me; command, what this cruel and humble servant, worthy of being killed, shall do." The king Dasharatha, having thus prayed to the ascetic, Andhaka Muni and his wife desired to follow their dead son and prayed to the king.

" Collect fuels and light the funeral phyre." The king, at once, with the help of his followers, carried out the order of the ascetic. And having his mind depressed by the sin consequent upon the destruction of a Rishi he retraced his steps back from the forest towards the city. As the Varava fire always burns in the depth of ocean, so the curse of the Rishi, destructive of his ownself, was always present in his mind.

—:0:—

CANTO VII.

Having thus protected the earth the highly prosperous king Dasharatha, like unto Indra in prowess, spent a little less than Ayuta years. But within this long time he could not see the light of a son, the instrument for paying off the debts to the departed manes, and capable of removing the darkness of sorrow.

As the origin of jems was unknown before the ocean was churned so the king spent a long time thinking that the birth of a son was dependant on some cause.

Requested by that king desirous of having a son, the self-controlled Rishis Rishya-shringa and others undertook the celebration of a *Putresthi* sacrifice on his behalf.

As the travellers, distressed by the heat of the sun, run for a shade under a tree so the celestials, oppressed by the Rakshasa king Ravana, appeared before Narayana.

As soon as they arrived at the bank of the ocean the Yoga-sleep of the Lord Prime Purusha was broken. The attention of the person sought for is the sign of success.

The celestials saw the Lord Narayana seated on the snake Ananta. The lustre of jems set on the pangs of the serpents lighted up his person.

Covering her girdle with a raiment the goddess Lakshmi, whose seat is a lotus, had her fingers spread on her lap and the Lord placed his lotus feet thereon.

Clad in a beautiful yellow raiment bright like the new sun, Narayana, whom the Yogins delighted to see and who had eyes like full blown lotuses, looked like a beautiful autumnal day in the very commencement of the season clad in a raiment of the newly risen sun and lotuses.

He bore on his breast the Koustabha jem, the essence of the ocean and the mirror of the goddess Lakshmi which, by its lustre, brightened the mystic mark of Srivatsa.

His four arms, long like branches of a tree, were adorned with celestial ornaments, and it appeared that a second Parijata tree had grown in the ocean.

The living weapons which used to destroy the neck marks of Daitya women, were singing aloud his victory.

Casting off his natural enmity with the king of serpents the king of birds (Garuda), whose body was wounded by thunder bolt, stood before him with folded hands.

After the termination of his Yoga sleep, the lord of the three worlds favoured, with his clear and sacred looks, Bhrigu and other great saints who were anxious to inquire after his good sleep.

Thereupon having saluted Narayana, the slayer of the Asuras, worshipped of the universe and beyond the comprehension of mind and speech the celestials began to chant his glories.

"O lord, thou hast created this universe in the form of Brahma. Thou dost protect it as Vishnu and destroy it as Rudra. Salutation unto thee who art of the forms of Brahma, Vishnu and Maheshwara.

As one sweet taste appears as many with the difference of celestial water and vessels so thou, although freed from changes, dost appear in various forms by the influence of Sattwa and other *gunas*. O lord, no one can measure thee while thou dost measure the universe. Thou dost not require a prayer but thou hast conquered all. Although thou art not manifest in thy subtle form still thou art the cause of this entire universe.

Thou art omnipresent and therefore thou dost reside always in the hearts of all. But no body can see thee. Thou art devoid of any desire still thou dost always practise penances. Thou art kind and shorn of misery for thou art always delightful. Thou art old enough but shorn of decrepitude for thou art above changes. Forsooth thy power is extraordinary.

Thou art omniscient but no body can know thee. Thou art the creator of the entire universe, but art self born. There is no other cause of thy origin. Thou art the lord of all, but no one is thy lord. Thou art without the second but hast the universal form.

O god of gods, the seven Sama Vedas sing thy glories. Thou dost lie in the seven oceans. The seven fires are thy mouth and thou art the stay of the seven regions.

The knowledge of the fourfold objects of life namely religious profit, worldly profit, desire and emancipation, the four yugas, and the four Varnas have originated from thy four mouths.

Having withdrawn the soul from external objects the Yogins, desirous of attaining emancipation, meditate on thy effulgent form in the lotus of their hearts.

Although devoid of birth and death stlll thou wert boon as fish &c. Although motionless thou art destroying the sound and although immersed in Yoga sleep thou art always awake. These contrary actions being present in thee who can ascertain thy true nature ?

Thou dost enjoy the objects of sense and practise hard penances; thou dost protect the subjects and at the same time art perfectly indifferent. Extraordinary are thy deeds.

As the stream of the Ganges, though it flows in various directions, ultimately falls into the great ocean, so all the means of acquiring manliness, though variously described in Scriptures, fall into thee.

Thou art the only refuge of those persons, dissociated from the world, who, for acquiring emancipation, fix their minds on and consign their actions into thee.

As it is not possible to measure the earth, water &c representing thy glory how is it possible to measure thy true nature which can be ascertained by the Vedas and inference.

By remembering thee only people acquire purity. It is impossible to describe the endless fruits acquired by the organs of vision, hearing &c.

It is not possible to calculate the jems of the ocean and the rays of the Sun so the recounting of thy glories who art beyond the comprehension of speech and mouth is not finished even if it is continued for eternity.

There is no wished-for object or aim which thou hast not achieved. That creatures, born on earth, engage in various actions is owing to thy favour only.

That we stop after recounting thy glories is owing to our inability and exhaustion not because we have reached the end of thy accomplishments."

Having thus chanted in various ways his glories the celestials propitiated the Lord who was beyond the ken of senses. That eulogy was the real account of the Lord's glory and not panegyric verses.

The Lord enquiring of their well-being the celestials inferred that He was pleased and said:— "O lord, although the time of dissolution has not come still we have been oppressed by the great ocean of the Rakshasas." Hearing those words, resounding the mountain caves situate near the bank and overcoming the sound of the ocean the Lord, who was without beginning, said in a solemn voice. The goddess of speech emanating from the throat of the ancient poet, the Lord and uttered beautifully and correctly, felt herself satisfied.

That sweet speech, emanating from the lotus mouth of the lord of the universe, being united with the beauty of his teeth appeared like the river Ganges, issued from his lotus feet, flowing upward.

The Lord said:—I have already learnt that the king of the night-rangers has stolen your prowess and energy like unto the quality of ignorance (Tamas) overcoming the Sattwa (goodness) and Rajas (darkness) gunas of creatures.

As the mind of the pious is distressed by iniquitious deeds so my three worlds have been disturbed by the oppressions of that king of Rakshasas. I know this too.

While practising ascetic penances the Ten-necked demon had cut off with his sharp sword his nine heads and reserved his tenth head as a profit for my discus.

As a sandal tree suffers a serpent to get on it so I have borne the dreadful oppression of Ravana grown powerful by the boon of the four-mouthed deity (Brahma).

Having propitiated the Creator with hard penances the wicked Rakshasa, cherishing a contempt for the land of mortals which formed his food, prayed for the boon of not being slain even by the gods.

Therefore having descended on earth as the son of the great king Dasharatha I will offer as food the heads of the Rakshasa-chief, to the battle-field.

You will soon have your respective shares of sacrificial offerings offered by the sacrificers. The illusive Rakshasa will not be able to touch them any more.

The pious men, running in the sky, used to hide themselves in fear, behind the clouds, on seeing the flowery car of Ravana. Let them cast off now that terrible fear; you will soon loosen the tresses of the celestial damsels kept in prison. On account of the imprecation of Nala Kuvera their locks have not been polluted by the touch of the wicked Dashanana.

Having thus poured sweet speech like rain on the

crops of celestials greatly withered by Ravana-like draught Krishna-like clouds disappeared.

As the trees follow the wind by their flowers, so Indra and other gods, by their respective portions, followed Narayana engaged in the work of the celestials.

On the other hand, after the termination of *Putresthi* sacrifice undertaken by the king Dasharatha a celestial being, on account of the presence of Narayana there, came out of the fire, holding a massive cup of gold full of *Charu* with his two hands. Thereat all the priests were filled with surprise.

As the king of the celestials accepted the ambrosia produced by the ocean so king Dasharatha accepted the *Charu* offered by the Prime Purusha despatched by Brahma.

That the king possessed extraordinary qualities was evident from the fact that even the Lord Narayana, the Creator of the three worlds, desired to become his son.

As the sun distributes its early rays between the heaven and earth so the king divided that best of *Churas* full of Vishnu's energy between his two queens Kousalya and Kaikeyi.

The Emperor Dasharatha used to regard highly his first queen Kousalya and was greatly attached to queen Kaikeyi. And hence he was confident that they would give a portion of their respective shares of *Charu* to Sumitra.

Understanding this good object of their husband they each gave a half of their own share to Sumitra.

As a she black bee loves both the lines of temporal juice flowing down the temple of an elephant so Sumitra was attached to both of them, co-wives with her.

As the rays of the sun, called nectar, hold watery conception so the three queens conceived the portions of Narayana for the behoof of mankind.

All conceiving simultaneously the three queens grew pale and looked beautiful like ripened crops.

The queens used to see in dreams that celestial persons holding conch, swords, clubs and maces used to protect them. They used sometimes to see that Garuda, the king of birds, spreading the lustre of his golden wings, was quickly passing in the sky carrying the clouds. Again they saw the goddess Lakshmi, bearing on her breast the Koustava jem given by Narayana, serve them with a lotus in her hand. Sometimes they saw the seven Rishis, after having bathed in the sacred water of Mandakini worship them with reciting the name of Para Brahma. Hearing of those auspicious dreams from the queens the Emperor attained to great delight. And thinking that he would father the father of the universe he regarded himself as the most fortunate and greatest of men. As the one beam of the moon assumes various forms on being reflected in the water of various places and countries, so the Lord

Narayana, without second, began to live in the wombs of those queens dividing himself into many parts. As the herbs acquire in the night light destructive of darkness so the principal queen Kousalya gained in due time a son capable of destroying the darkness of sorrow. Beholding unparalleled beauty of the son the father Dasharatha gave him the name of Rama, the abode of the auspiciousness of the three worlds.

The lustre of Rama's person, the scion of the Raghu family, endued with extraordinary beauty, put into shade the lamps of the lying-in chamber.

As the celestial stream of small breadth shines greatly in the autumn when offerings of lotuses of hundred petals are placed on its banks full of sands the thin-bellied Koushalya looked highly beautiful on giving birth to Rama who lay on the bed.

Kaikeyi gave birth to a highly good-natured son by name Bharata. As humility increases the beauty of wealth so he adorned his own mothers.

As understanding and humility originate from good learning so Sumitra gave birth to the twins Lakshmana and Satrughna.

There was no famine or any other calamity in the entire world. Freedom from diseases and other virtues flourished in the country. Thereat it appeared as if heaven had descended on earth following the Purushottama.

The Lord Narayana having incarnated himself in four parts of Rama &c., the pure wind, freed from dust, blew. It appeared that the four quarters finding their husbands oppressed by Rama to have obtained a refuge, began to breathe.

At that time the fire was freed from smokes, and the sun became delightful. Thereat it was so thought, that they, thinking that their affliction would soon come to an end, had cast off their sorrows.

As soon as Rama was born, the tears of the goddess of prosperity of the Rakshasas, in the shape of jems from the crown of Dashanana, dropped on earth.

The first ceremonial music consequent upon the birth of the Emperor Dasharatha's son was conducted by the celestials by playing on the *Dundubhis.*

The down pour of Parijata flowers made from the heaven in the palace was the first of all auspicious rites performed there.

After going through all the purificatory rites the princes grew up daily sucking the breast milk of the nurses and along with it the joy of Dasharatha consequent upon the birth of sons increased.

As the native vigour of the fire is increased by the oblations of clarified butter poured into it so the natural humility of the princes was increased by good instructions.

By those brothers, attached to one another the unsullied Raghu family shone greatly beautiful like the celestial garden beautified by the seasons.

Although brotherly feelings existed equally amongst them, still the mutual attachment varying Lakshmana was always in the company of Rama and Satrughana was in that of Bharata.

As the attachment between the wind and fire and that between the rays of the moon and the ocean is never slackened so the affection between Rama and Lakshmana and that between Bharata and Satrughna was never shaken.

As the day, covered with blue clouds, after the termination of the summer, attracts the mind of men, so those sons of the king, by their humility and prowess, enchanted the minds of their subjects.

Those four sons of the king shone like four-fold objects of life incarnated on earth.

As the great oceans pleased the king, the master of fourteen quarters, by giving him the entire collection of their jems so the princes, by their accomplishments, satisfied their sire.

As Airavata appears beautiful with his four tusks piercing always the swords of the Asuras, as the Polity shines with four means viz conciliation &c, as Narayana shines with four arms so the king Dasharatha appeared beautiful by his four sons born of the portions of Narayana.

CANTO XI.

Then appearing before the king Dasharatha the great Saint Viswamitra, the scion of the Koushika race, prayed for the young Rama for the destruction of the obstructors of sacrifices for it is useless to examine the age of the powerful.

Although it was a difficult task still the Emperor, who was always at the service of the wise, consigned Rama and Lakshmana to the care of the Rishi, for the kings of Raghu's family even never hesitated to grant the prayer of a person seeking for their life.

At the time of the departure of his sons king Dasharatha ordered for the repairs of the streets of the city. Immediately the wind, with the help of flowers and clouds pouring down water, carried out the order.

Ready to carry out their sire's mandate, the bowmen Rama and Lakshmana saluted his feet. The king too showered tears of joy on the princes about to set out on a journey. Having their crowns wetted with their father's tears the bowmen Rama and Lakshmana followed that foremost of ascetics. The citizens began to behold them with fixed eyes and their looks as if created gates in the highway.

That Muni, having asceticism for his wealth, wanted to take Rama and Lakshmana only with him and for that reason the king did not despatch an army with them but his blessings only which were alone capable of protecting them.

Having saluted their mothers Rama and Lakshmana followed that highly energetic ascetic and shone like months of Chaitra and Vaisakha, brightened for the course of the sun.

As the water swells up and destroys the bank of a river during rains so they moving like the waves shone by their child-like fickle movements.

Although they were used to walk in the courtyards set with jems still by the power of two-fold learning, Vata and Ativata given by the great Rishi they did not feel the least pain in wending the high ways; rather they thought that they were by the sides of their mothers.

Hearing of their past history from the mouth of Viswamitra, the friend of their sire and well versed in Puranas they went on so absent-mindedly that they did not experience the least pain for going on foot although they were used to proceed in vehicles.

The tanks with their sweet water, the birds with notes pleasant to ears, the forest with the dust of sweet-scented flowers and the clouds with shade began to serve them.

The forest-ranging ascetics never experienced that delight on seeing lakes adorned with lotuses and trees capable of removing their toil as they did on beholding the highly beautiful Rama and Lakshmana.

Having arrived with a bow in hand, at the

penance forest of Ananga, reduced into ashes by angry Hara, the son of Dasharatha acted as his representative by the beauty of his person, but could not equal him in work.

Rama and Lakshmana had previously heard from the great Rishi, of Taraka's curse; and now arriving at the unapproachable road shorn of living creatures, by her oppressions they touched the ground with the ends of the bows and easily set strings to it.

Hearing the twang of their bows Tadaka, dark like an Amavasya night and wearing ear-rings of human skulls appeared there like a mass of dense clouds adorned with cranes or Kalika.

Shaking all the trees on the road with great force that Rakshasi, clad in a goblin cloth, attacked Rama with a terrific sound like unto that of the wind rising from the cremation ground.

Beholding Taraka coming, holding a girdle of a man's entrails on her waist and raising up one of her hands Rama discharged his hatered for slaying a woman and an arrow simultaneously.

The hole that was made on Taraka's breast by Rama's arrow hard as a stone, became as if the door, never thought of by Yama, for his entering the country of Rakshasas.

While the Rakshasi, with her heart shattered by Rama's arrow, dropped down, the Prosperity of the king of Lanka, well established by his conquest of the three worlds, trembled.

Assailed with the arrow of Rama-like Capid that Rakshasi, having besmeared her limbs with the sweet sandal of blood, immediately repaired to the region of Yama, her lover.

As the sun-jem receives from the sun its fiery power of consuming fuels so Rama received from the great saint Vishwamitra, who was highly pleased, the infallible weapon along with the mantras for destroying the Rakshasas.

Thereupon he arrived at the sacred hermitage of Vamana, of which he had heard before from the great saint. Although the account of his primitive birth, for the want of an instrument, did not arise in his mind still he became absent-minded.

Thereupon having arrived at his own hermitage along with Rama and Lakshmana the great saint Vishwamitra saw all the articles of adoration collected by his disciples. For welcoming that foremost of anchorites the trees of the hermitage folded their leaf-like hands and the deer stood with their faces up for seeing him.

As spreading their rays in order the sun and the moon protect the three worlds from darkness so Rama and Lakshmana, with their arrows, protected that foremost of ascetics who was engaged in sacrifice.

Thereupon beholding the altar sullied all on a sudden with big drops of blood like unto Vandhujiva flowers, at the time of celebrating the sacrific the priests desisted therefrom in fear. The sacrificial ladles, made of the wood of Vikanto trees, dropped off their hands.

Rama, at once taking up an arrow from his quiver, looked up and saw a Rakshasa host, ever obstructing sacrifices, range fearlessly in the sky. Their flags were being shaken by the wind caused by the wings of the vultures.

Thereupon without aiming at other Rakshasas inimical to sacrifices, Rama shot at their leaders Maricha and Suvahu, for Guruda, the slayer of huge serpents, never displays his power at the Dundubha.

Thereupon shooting off his bow an airy weapon, endued with great velocity, he struck down on earth Taraka's son Maricha, strong like a mountain, like unto a ripe leaf.

Another Rakshasa, by name Suvahu, was also ranging there by virtue of his illusory power. Cutting him into pieces with a razor-shaped arrow, Rama, always expert in killing his enemies, divided them amongst the birds in front of the hermitage.

After Rama and Lakshmana having in their way removed the obstacles of the sacrifice the ascetics, praising their heroic prowess, duly completed the sacrifice of Viswamitra, the head of the family, who was observing the vow of silence.

Bathing after the termination of the sacrifice Vishwamitra blessed the two brothers who saluted him with bending low their crowns and touched their body with palms cut with Kuca reeds.

At that time, the king Janaka, the lord of Mithila, invited the great saint Viswamitra to a sacrifice undertaken by him. While going to Mithila the self-controlled Rishi took with him Rama and Lakshmana who were curiously listening to the story of the snapping of the bow.

After wending the way for a long distance, they arrived in the evening at the hermitage of Goutama who was carrying on penances for a long time. There Goutama's wife Ahalya had acted as the wife of the king of celestials for a short time.

By the favour of the dust of the feet of Rama, capable of destroying sins, Goutama's wife, who was living in the form of rock, regained her own beautiful body.

Hearing that Viswamitra had come with Rama and Lakshmana Janaka, the protector of his subjects, came out with Arghya like unto Dharma incarnate with worldly profit and desire.

The inhabitants of Mithila gazed with eager eyes on two brothers descended on earth from the sky like two Punarvasus. At that time they considered even the fall of eye-lashes as deceiving them.

After the termination of the sacrifices marked with Yupas, the great saint Vishwamitra, the scion of the Koushika race, ever careful about opportune moments, said to the king Janaka :—" Rama has become anxious to see your bow."

Beholding the tender body of the boy Rama born in the illustrious and sacred family and thinking of the difficulty of bending the bow and accordingly pained at heart for the vow of his daughter the king Janaka said :—

" O Lord, I cannot allow the young one of an elephant to engage uselessly in that work which even the huge elephants cannot do.

Many a heroic king and bowman, experiencing shame before this bow, and censuring their arms hardened with the strokes of bow-strings, have fled away."

Then the great saint Vishwamitra said to the king Janaka :—" Witness the prowess of this boy Rama the son of Dasharatha. What is the use of useless words, let this bow, hard as a mountain, witness his strength."

Hearing these confident words of the great saint Vishwamitra, the king Janaka believed that it was not impossible that Rama, bearing a tuft of hair on his head, possessed the necessary strength as there is the burning power in a fire of the dimension of an insect.

As the king of celestials orders the clouds to get ready to receive the fiery bow so the king Janaka ordered his numerous attendants to bring the bow.

As soon as he saw that bow the boy son of

Dasharatha, Rama assumed a dreadful appearance like unto a huge serpent. With that bow the bull-emblemed deity shot infallible arrows at the obstructors of the sacrifice who fled away in the guise of deer.

As cupid strings his tender flowery bow so Rama easily stringed that bow hard as the mountain. All the people present there, with fixed eyes, began to witness the great prowess of Rama in stringing that bow.

With a great stretch Rama snapped the Siva's bow. Thereat the bow sent forth such a sound like unto that of a thunder that it appeared that Purashurama, ever inimical to the Kshastryas, was again getting himself ready to destroy them.

Witnessing the prowess of the prince of Raghu family in snapping that bow and speaking highly of his vow thereabout the truthful king Janaka, the lord of Mithila, making the fire witness before the effulgent ascetic Vishwamitra, gave away that maiden daughter born of no woman, the very personification of Lakshmi, unto Rama. Then he communicated a message through his worshipful priest to the king Dasharatha, saying "making my daughter your daughter-in-law do you make the Nimi family your servants."

The lord of the earth Dasharatha was searching for a fitting bride for his son and in the meantime Janaka's priest came before him, for the desire of a pious man is immediately fulfilled like the fruit of a Kalpa tree.

Having duly honored that Brahmana, the self-controlled Emperor, the companion of the king of gods, learnt every thing from him. And covering the solar disc with the dust raised by his soldiers he started for Mithila.

When king Dasharatha arrived at Mithila his soldiers remained around the city afflicting greatly the trees of the gardens situate at the outskirt; but Janaka's city bore that encompassing of love like a damsel bearing the embraces of her lover.

Those two kings, ever bent on showing good conduct like unto Varuna and Indra, unitedly celebrated the wedding ceremony of their son and daughter.

Rama espoused Sita, the daughter of the earth, Lakshmana Urmila, her youngest sister; and then their two younger brothers married the two daughters of Kushadhwaja, Mandavi and Shrutakirti.

Having newly taken wives the four princes shone like the four-fold means of conciliation, gift, dissension and punishment.

Being united in wed-lock with those princes, the princesses considered themselves fortunate. The union of the bride-groom and bride was like that between confidence and nature.

Having thus celebrated the nuptial ceremony of his sons king Dasharatha, fond of his sons, returned to his capital. King Janaka followed them to the distance of three days' journey. Then taking leave of them he returned to his capital.

As the course of a river transgresses its continent and afflicts the shore so one day in the way a terrible wind, scattering the flags and standards, distressed greatly the soldiers.

Thereupon like unto the jem of the hood of a serpent killed by Garuda the terrible sun shone greatly in its effulgence.

The damsels of the quarters put on tresses of twany color in the shape of the wings of hawks, were clad in crimson raiments in the shape of evening clouds and appeared to have been in menses on being covered with dust.

Taking refuge in the quarter presided over by the sun the jackals began to cry hideously as if to urge on Parasurama who offered oblations of the Kshatrya blood to his departed manes.

Beholding that unfavourable wind and other evil omens the dutiful king Dasharatha requested his family priest Vasistha to take propitiatory steps, He removed the fear of the king saying that they will in the end turn out auspicious.

There arose all on a sudden before the soldiers a bundle of effulgence. After rubbing their eyes they, after a while, saw the figure of a man. Holding sacred thread as the mark of his father, and a bow as the mark of his mother he shone like the sun united with the moon and a serpent.

Following the mandate of his sire, who was dishonored and accordingly had his eyes reddened in anger he cut off the head of his trembling mother. And them subduing hatered he conquered the earth. With the bracelet of beads hanging from the right ear he was as if taking an account of his twenty one massacres of the Kshatryas.

Beholding Parashuram, born in the race of Bhrigu, ever engaged in the destruction of the Kshatryas and considering his weak state and the childhood of his sons king Dasharatha was plunged into a sea of sorrow.

That dreadful enemy and his son both bore the name of Rama; and so it was to him like a serpent and a garland of jems—terrific and pleasant at the same time.

Dasharatha eagerly cried for Arghya. But without looking at that side Jamadagnya cast his eyes, having two dreadful pupils like unto the flames of Kshatrya anger, towards where Bharata's elder brother Rama was.

Placing one hand on the bow and putting an arrow into the hole of the fist of another Bhargava, desirous of fighting, said to Rama, standing before him fearlessly.

"The Kshatryas killed my father and are my enemies. I enjoyed peace after having massacred them for twenty one times. But now hearing of your prowess I have been aroused like a sleeping serpent scotched by a rod.

No other king could before bend that bow of king Janaka. But you have snapped it easily. Methinks, the summit of my prowess has been shattered by you.

Formerly people understood me only by the name "Rama" but it has been divided by you; with your advancement I am really ashamed for it.

My weapon can even rive the mountains. Two enemies are equally sinful to me. First Kartavirya stole away the calf of my cow. But you are ready to suppress my glory.

Unless you are defeated I cannot rejoice at my destruction of the Kshatryas. Fire burns even in the ocean as in dry grass. That is its glory.

Know it for certain that you could break Siva's bow because the Lord Narayana lightened it of its heaviness. When the current of a river loosens the root of a tree planted on its bank even the slightest wind can uproot it.

Now put string to this bow and draw an arrow. There is no need of a battle. If you accomplish this feat I will regard you as strong-armed as myself and admit my defeat before you.

Or if you are afraid at the burning blade of my axe then folding your hands, hardened uselessly by the strokes of the string, pray for my protection.

After the dreadful head of the Bhrigu family had said this Rama, smiling, took up his bow and gave a becoming reply.

Being united with the bow of his another birth he looked highly beautiful. The new cloud is itself beautiful and it becomes wonderfully fine when it is united with the rain-bow.

As the highly powerful Rama placed one end of the bow on the ground and stringed it the Kshatrya enemy Parashurama became divested of his lustre like fire with only smoke remaining.

Then the onlookers saw Dasharatha's son of increasing effulgence and Bhrigu's son of waning prowess, confronting each other like the moon and the sun after the termination of the day.

Beholding Parashurama of weakened prowess and knowing his arrow to be infalliable Rama, merciful like Kumara, said :—" Although you have insulted me I cannot strike you mercilessly because you are a Brahmana. Tell me what shall I obstruct with this arrow—your own movement in the sky or the heaven acquired by your sacrifices ?"

Parashurama said :—" It is not that I did not know thy true form, the ancient Purusha. Thou hast incarnated thyself on earth. With a view to behold thy celestial energy I angered thee.

I have destroyed all my father's enemies and have made over the earth with the oceans to the proper person. Thou art the Eternal Purusha. It is indeed a matter of glorification to me that thou hast defeated me. O foremost of heroes, do thou save my course through the sky for going to the sacred shrine. If the road to the heaven is obstructed I will not experience the slightest afflction for I do not long for enjoyments."

Saying "So be it" Rama, directing his face to the east, discharged the arrow. By that arrow a great obstacle was put in his road to heaven. Saying "forgive me" Rama saluted the feet of Bhrigu Rama. Salutation of the enemy defeated by the prowess of his arms is an object of glorification to a heroe.

The virtuous-souled Parashurama said:—"O foremost of heroes, by thy favour, being freed from Rajagunas inherited from my mother, I have acquired the Sattwa-guna of my father's. So thou hast done me good. It is a great favour for me. O scion of the Raghu race, I now depart. Thou hast descended on earth for accomplishing the work of the gods. May good betide thee." Saying this to Rama and Lakshmana Parashurama disappeared.

After Jamadagnya's departure the king Dasharatha embraced his victorious son and began to think out of affection as if Rama had been born again. After the termination of the temporary sorrow king Dasharatha experienced delight like a tree saved from the forest-fire.

Then spending a few more nights in the way in a tent Siva-like Dasharatha entered the auspicious city of Ayodhya along with his four sons born of the portions of Narayana and the four daughters-in-law incarnations of Lakshmi. With the eyes of women of the city anxious to see Maithili it appeared as if hundreds of Kuvalaya flowers had blossomed on the windows.

CANTO XII.

As in the dawn the inside flame of wick, after having devoured the entire oil of the lamp, is on the verge of being extinguished so king Dasharatha reached the end of his life, and was about to attain emancipation after having desisted from the enjoyment of the objects of life.

Decrepitude, as if afraid of Kaikeyi, reached the ear of Dasharatha in the shape of grey hairs and advised him to hand over the kingdom to Rama.

As an artificial stream gladdens all the trees of the garden so the news of Rama's installation whom the subjects loved, gladdened every citizen.

The wicked Kaikeyi had all the articles collected for the installation of Rama polluted with the sorrowful tears of the Emperor.

As the earth, soaked with torrents poured by the clouds, sends up a serpent lying inside a hole, so the wrathful Kaikeyi, consoled by the king, prayed for the two boons promised by him before.

With one boon she prayed for the banishment of

Rama into the forest for fourteen years and with another the kingdom which ultimately brought about her widowhood, for her own son Bharata.

In the beginning Rama weepingly accepted the kingdom offered by his father but he accepted with greatest pleasure the command "Go to the forest."

While Rama put on bark the citizens marked the same unchanged countenance which they saw when he put on silken raiment and they were surprised.

Being anxious to repair to the forest of Dandaka along with Sita and Lakshmana to make good his father's promise Rama as if entered into the mind of every pious man.

Remembering the former incident of the imprecation of the Rishi, king Dasharatha, stricken grief consequent upon his separation from his son, regarded the casting off of his own body as the only penalty for his own sin.

The princes going to the forest and the king breathing his last the kingdom of Koshala became an object of temptation to the enemies who were on the look out for a loof-hole.

Thereupon controlling their tears for hiding the calamity the courtiers, whose master was dead, sent the principal minister and brought Bharata from the house of his maternal grand-father.

Returning to his own house and hearing of the miserable end of his father, Kaikeyi's son Bharata, filled with mighty grief, was not only annoyed with his own mother but also desisted from occupying the throne.

Beholding the trees of the hermitage of Rama and Lakshmana pointed out by the ascetics and shedding tears he accompanied, by the soldiers, followed them.

Communicating the demise of his father to his eldest brother Rama who was living in the forest around the mount Chitrakuta, Bharata requested him strongly to accept the kingdom which he had not enjoyed himself.

When he could not dissuade Rama from carrying out the command of his father then in heaven Bharata prayed for his pair of sandal to make it the presiding god of the kingdom. Giving him the sandal and embracing him affectionately Rama sent away Bharata. Without returning to Ayodhya he went to Nandigrama and began to govern the kingdom, as ordered by his eldest brother, like unto a property entrusted by another.

In this way Bharata, devoted to his eldest brother and shorn of avarice for the kingdom, began to expatiate the sin committed by his mother.

Rama too, in the company of his younger brother of controlled self, and Sita, began to spend his days feeding on wild forests] and roots; in youth he followed the foot-steps of old Ikshwakus.

One day making the shade of a tree still by his

own power Rama fell asleep by placing his head on Sita's lap.

At that time Indra's son, a crow, as if marking the defect of the wound inflicted by the nails of her lover, cut off the breasts of Vaidehi with its talons.

Awakened by Sita's cries Rama discharged an arrow at that crow. The crow, stricken with fear, gave one of its eyes and saved its life.

Thinking that Bharata might again come in the neighbouring village Rama left the mount Chitrakuta abounding in anxious deer. As the sun, in the rains, proceeds towards the south crossing all the points of the compass, so Rama too, resting in the hermitage of the hospitable ascetics, proceeded towards the south.

Sita following Rama, it appeared as if the presiding goddess of the kingdom, disregarding the request of Kaikeyi, and won over by his accomplishments, was following him. Sita so perfumed the forest with the scented unguents given her by Atri's wife Anasua that bees, leaving the flowers and humming sat on her person.

As Rahu obstructs the course of the moon so the Rakshasa Viradha, smoke-coloured like the evening cloud, stood obstructing the way of Rama.

As Avagraha pilfers the rain in the months ot Shravana and Bhadra so he stole away Janaka's daughter who was between Rama and Lakshmana.

Having slain Viradha and thought that a bad

smell would pollute the atmosphere if they would leave her there Rama and Lakshmana interred the dead body under the earth.

As the mount Vindhya stood in the same way by the command of Agastha so Rama by his instructions lived in the Panchavati forest.

As a she-serpent, assailed by the rays of the sun, approaches a sandal tree, so Ravana's youngest sister Shurpanakha, assailed by Cupid, approached Rama in the Panchavati forest.

Giving an account of her lineage that Rakshasi requested Rama to marry her in the very presence of Sita, for the growing lust of women does not wait for a proper moment.

Rama, having shoulders plump like the hump of a bull, said to the lustful Shurpanakha :—" O girl, I have my wife with me. Seek my younger brother for your husband."

Lakshmana said :—" Because you first solicited my eldest brother to marry you and therefore I cannot accept your hand." Then she, like a river going to both the banks, appeared again before Rama. Seeing all these incidents Sita smiled. Beholding Sita laugh at her that Rakshasi grew momentarily pale with anger as the still ocean rises with the moon.

" Thou shalt even reap the fruit of this insult. Remember as a she-deer insults a tigress so thou hast laughed at me."

Saying this Shurpanakha assumed a terrific Rakhasi form befitting her own name. Thereat Maithili hid herself out of fear on the lap of her consort.

Lakshmana at first heard her voice sweet like the notes of a coel; but now hearing her terrific voice like that of a she-jackal she took her for an illusive woman.

Thereupon entering into his hut quickly and taking up his drawn sword he cut off her nose and made her greatly disfigured.

With her fingers containing uncouth knots, resembling goads and having crooked nails she, from the sky, roared at Rama and Lakshmana. And immediately going to Janasthana she communicated to Khara, Dushana and other Rakshasas the new discomfiture she had met with at the hands of Rama.

It was really inauspicuous for those Rakshasas to have taken Shurpanakha before them when they marched to fight with Rama.

Beholding the Rakshasas, inflamed with ire, approach with uplifted weapons, Rama, placing his hope of success on his bow and committing Sita to the care of Lakshmana, engaged in battle. Rama was alone on one side and on the other there were thousands of Rakshasas. But in the battle-field the night-rangers saw numbers of Rama equalling them. Rama, the well-behaved scion of the Raghu race, did not forgive Dushana despatched there by the wicked night-rangers. Rama killed Khara and Trishira with the strokes of his arrows. The shafts, discharged by him in regular order, appeared to have been shot simultaneously off the bow. Living in its pure state as before the infallible arrow of Rama, capable of cutting through the body, drank off the life of the three Rakshasas. Drinking their blood the birds justified the existence of their body. There was none amongst those Rakshasas who could rise up except headless trunks. Fighting with Rama who alone shot arrows that great army of the Rakshasas slept for ever under the shadow of the vultures. Then becoming helpless and overwhelmed with dangers Shurpanakha communicated to the king of Lanka, how the Rakshasas had been killed by Rama's arrows.

Hearing of the insult of his own sister and the destruction of the Rakshasas Kuvera's younger brother, Ravana, regarded his heads trampled by Rama. Blinded with anger and deceiving Rama and Lakshmana through Maricha's illusions the ten-headed king of Rakshasas carried away Sita stealthily. Trying his level best Jatayu, the king of birds, could obstruct his course only for a moment. Then searching for Sita Rama and Lakshmana saw the king of vultures with his wings cut off. Communicating to Rama and Lakshmana the news that Ravana had stolen away Sita he died before Narayana himself as if by the force of his piety acquired by his great act of fighting. After the decease of Jatayu the sorrow of Rama and Lakshmana for the death of their sire was kindled anew. Then they performed the obsequial rites of Jatayu.

Rama then killed a Rakshasa by name Kavandha, who being freed from the curse advised him to make friends wfth Sugriva, the king of Vanaras. He then contracted friendship with Sugriva who was like him was also plunged into misfortune. Having killed the highly powerful king Vali by a trick Rama installed Sugriva on his throne which he so long wished for.

Despatched by their king Sugriva the monkeys began to search, like the desire of Rama stricken with sorrow for his wife, for Maithili on all sides.

As a pure man, freed from sins, easily crosses the ocean of the world so Hanuman, the foremost of monkeys, hearing of Sita's whereabouts from Sampati, crossed the ocean and reached Lanka. Searching for her there he gave her Rama's ring, who was surrounded by Rakshasis like a herb girt by a poisonous creeper. When that ring touched Sita's palm she welcomed it with tears of joy. Having consoled Janaka's daughter Sita at the behest of Rama, the foremost of monkeys killed Aksha; and afterwards suffering the oppression of the enemies for some time he consumed the city of Lanka. Having accomplished his work Pavana's son handed over to Rama the jem of insignia given by Vaidehi like unto her very heart. Placing the jem on his breast sent by Janaka's daughter Rama experienced the joy of embrace from his beloved wife for sometime though he could not press her breasts. Hearing of the good news of Janaki and being anxious to be united with her he considered the ocean encircling the city of Lanka as trifling as a ditch. He then advanced with the monkey army for killing his enemy. The soldiers proceeded not only on earth but even in the sky and by other impassable routes. Rama encamped his army on the bank of the ocean. In the meantime oppressed by his brother, Ravana's younger brother, the pious Bibhishana, appeared before Rama. As if out of affection the presiding goddess of the Rakshasas gave him this good sense and sent to him Rama.

Rama promised Bibhishana to give him the kingdom of Rakshasas occupied by Ravana; for policy, when applied in proper time, surely yields fruit.

Rama made the monkeys construct a huge bridge on the watery expanse of the ocean. Thereat it appeared that the serpent Sesha had arisen from the nether region to supply Narayana with his couch. By that wonderful bridge Rama arrived at the city of Lanka and surrounded it by twany coloured monkeys. It appeared that another golden wall had been built around Lanka. Then went on a terrible encounter in the city of Lanka between the Vanara and Rakshasa armies. And victories of Rama and Ravana were announced on all sides. In a fight with trees sticks mounted with iron were shattered into pieces. The clubs were powdered by stone. And the strokes of nails became more dreadful than those of weapons. What more even the elephants were torn by the strokes of rocks. Thereupon one day seeing the cut off head of Rama, the daughter of Janaka dropped down unconscious on earth. Saying that it was the outcome of illusion the Rakshasi Trijata revived her. Learning for certain that her dearest husband was alive Janaki cast off her grief. But she felt great shame that she was alive before when she believed Rama to have been dead.

Ravana's son Meghanada bound Rama and Lakshmana with serpentine nooses. Garuda however cut them off-so the pain was only temporary like that in a dream. Ravana then struck Lakshmana's breast with the mace of Sakti. Thereat although Rama was not himself hurt still his heart was broken asunder by grief. Taking the great medicine brought by Hanuman Lakshmana regained his consciousness and his pain was removed. And again having slain the Rakshasas in battle he taught their women to bewail. As the autumn puts a stop to the muttering of clouds and the display of beauty by tne rain-bow so Lakshmana left no remnant of the leonine roars of Meghanada and of his bow effulgent like that of Indra.

Being wounded with Sugriva's weapon Kumbhakarna, resembling a mountain, and attaining the condition of his sister Shurpanakha, obstructed Rama. Saying as if "you are fond of sleep, Ravana has aroused you untimely," Rama's arrow put him into eternal sleep. As the dust of the field was suppressed by the stream of Rakshasa's blood so the night-rangers of Lanka falling in the midst of the Vanaras met with death. Then promising "the earth will either be divested of Rama or of Ravana" the ten-headed Rakshasa came out of his palace to the battle-field.

Seeing Rama on foot and Ravana on his car, Purandara, stationed in the sky, sent a chariot drawn by ash-coloured horses to Rama, the flags thereon were being unfurled by the wind saturated with the water of Mandakini. Indra's charioteer Matali drove the horses. Holding his hand Rama ascended that *Jaitra* car. Matali put on Rama's person the armour by Indra. The arrows shot by the Asuras became bafled at that coat of mail. As if finding an opportunity to display their respective prowess the fight between Rama and Ravana meeting after a long time was crowned with success. All other Rakshasas had been killed and the king of Lanka was alone, still, on account of his many heads, hands and feet he appeared to have been encircled by innumerable Rakshasas.

Having worshipped Brahma for a long time and afterwards offered his own head as a sacrifice to him the king of Lanka propitiated him and obtained the boon that he would not be killed by the gods. By virtue of this boon he defeated Indra and other guardian deities; and on account of the profusion of his strength he performed the most difficult feat of uprooting the most elevated mount Kailasha. For these reasons the Raghu heroe Rama regarded him as an illustrious enemy. In great anger Dashanana shot an arrow at the right arm of Rama which was shaking indicating his union with Janaki. Riving the heart of Ravana the arrow, discharged by Rama, entered into the earth as if to communicate this glad tidings to the Nagas. They returned words by words and weapons by weapons. And their attempt, like that of two combatants endeavouring to gain victory, increased. As an intervening altar comes equally under the possession of two infuriated elephants while fighting, so success and defeat alternately falling upon them both, the beauty of victory remained equally on the both. The flowers, that were showered by the gods and Asuras on their being pleased with the discharge of weapons or with the act of counteracting them, were obstructed by the incessant arrows discharged by them both. Ravana discharged at Rama the Shataghni covered with golden pikes resembling the club of Yama, which he had acquired by victory. Before it came near their car accompanied with the hope of victory of the Rakshasas, Rama and Lakshmana easily cut it off like unto a plantain tree with crescent-shaped arrows. For striking his enemy, Rama, the incomparable bow-man, set to his bow the infallible Brahma weapon, the medicine for uprooting the mace of grief from his wife's heart. Burning in the sky in a hundred flames that effulgent weapon was seen like the Sesha serpent endued with dreadful fangs. With the strokes of that weapon inspired with mantras Rama cut off the heads of the king of Lanka in a trice. He did not feel the least pain whilst his heads were being cut off. Seeing even Ravana's heads falling in pieces on earth the gods could not shake off their feelings of distrust lest they might be joined together again.

Then showers of sweet-scented flowers, poured by the gods, dropped on the head of Rama, the victor of Ravana and announced his installation. Leaving the temples of the elephants and having their wings laden with temporal juice the bees followed him. Having thus performed the work of gods, Rama, the scion of the Raghu race, loosened the string of his bow. Taking leave of him Indra's charioteer Matali too drove up his car, drawn by a thousand horses and whose flags were covered with arrows bearing the name of Ravana.

Taking Janaki purified by fire and conferring the kingdom on his dear friend Bibhishana, Rama, along with Sugriva, Lakshmana and Bibhishana, started for his ancestral capital Ayodhya on the aerial car gained by him by the strength of his own arms.

CANTO XIII.

On beholding the ocean while proceeding in the flowery car by the etherial way Rama, the scion of the Raghu race, a portion incarnate of Narayana, endued with all attributes, said in stweet words to his most beloved wife Janaki:—"O Maithili, look at the beauty of the delightful autumnal sky adorned with the milk-way and beautiful stars. This ocean, full of foams, has been divided, like the mount Malaya, by the bridge constructed [by me. When the great Rishi, stealing the sacrificial horse of the king Sagara, entered into the nether region, our ancestors, searching for the same, dug the earth and increased the dimension of the ocean. The rays of the sun bear watery conception from it and jems are reared in it. This ocean carries the forest-fire and from it sprang the delightful ambrosia. It is difficult to ascertain the form and limit of this great ocean extending over ten quarters and containing various forms like the various incarnations of Narayana. At the time of universal dissolution the Prime Purusha Narayana enters upon Yoga sleep; and destroying all the worlds he is lauded by Brahma seated on a lotus sprung from his navel. As kings, in fear of their enemies, are freed from the same on seeking refuge with a pious king so hundreds of mountains with their wings cut off by the king of celestials have found shelter in this great ocean, the protector of those who seek refuge with it. When assuming the Prime Boar-form the Lord Narayana upraised the earth from the nether region, its rising pure water acted for some time as the beautiful veil of the earth. This lord of rivers, the only enjoyer of streams and an expert in the distribution of the nectar of mouth, by his natural impudence is drinking the nectar of the mouths of the rivers and making them do the same. Widening their mouths at the mouths of the rivers the Timi fishes are throwing up water with the holes on their heads. Look O dear, the water elephants have all on a sudden swam over the surface of the water. The foaming waves, divided into two parts, are covering their temples for the time being and acting as chowries. The serpents are running towards the bank for drinking the air there. They are appearing like huge waves. The jems on their heads being lighted up by the rays of the sun they are being known as serpents. The pairs of conchs, going in an opposite direction by the Vidrum creepers growing thereon, are with great difficulty coming out of the waves.

The clouds whirling all on a sudden while drinking water it appears as if the ocean is being churned again by the mount Mandara. The blue banks of the ocean being adorned with Tamala and date trees seen indistinctly from a distance they are looking till lines on the salt waves of the ocean. O you having expansive eyes, the wind of the bank is decorating your face with the dust of the Ketaki flowers. Perhaps finding me unable to bear the delay of decorating your person, whose thirst is fixed on your bimba-like lips, the wind is quickly adorning you. O dear, by this etherial car we have in no time reached the bank of the ocean. This sandy bank is interpersed with pearls and the trees are laden with fruits. O you having thighs like the the trunk of an elephant, O you having eyes like those of a deer, look back and see the more we are distanced from the ocean, the more it is appearing that the earth with the forests is moving along with us. O dear, as desired by me this car is proceeding sometimes by the celestial way, sometimes by the cloudy way and again by that of the birds. See the etherial wind, cooled by coming in contact with the water of Mandakini scented by the temporal juice of Airavata, is removing the drops of perspiration caused on your face by the mid-day sun. O dear, as you out of curiosity stretched out your hand from the window the cloud, bearing a bracelet of lightning, put on it a second ornament. O dear, look at this Janasthana once infested with the Rakshasas. Regarding it as shorn of obstacles the pious-souled ascetics, clad in Koupin, have built new huts in their respective hermitages once abandoned by them and are living happily. O dear, there is the part of the forest where searching you I picked up a piece of Nuputra. Separated from your lotus feet it was silent out of grief.

O you timid girl, the trees and creepers, naturally void of the power of speech, pointed out of mercy by their bending branches and leaves the road by which the wicked night-ranger had carried you away. Renouncing their desire for the sacrificial grass, taking up their heads and turning their eyes to the south the she-deer pointed out that road to me who was not acquainted with the etherial way. Look at the summit of the mount Malyavan touching the sky. Here I shed tears in your separation as the new clouds pour down torrents of rain. Here the scent of lakes filled with the water of rain, half blown Kadamva flowers and the sweet notes of peacocks became unbearable to me stricken with your separation. Remembering your former trembling embraces I could with difficulty bear the muttering of clouds. United with the vapour of the earth caused by new torrents of water Kandali flowers, grown on its summit, pained me greatly imitating the bright lustre of your eyes reddened with smoke at the time of wedding. My vision, going down from a distance, is as if out of exhaustion drinking the water of Pampa lake, covered on all sides with Vetasa plants, and filled with fickle Sarasas. O dear, when I was away from you, the pair of Chakravakas, united in this lake, used to give each other filaments of lotuses. Looking at them with eager eyes I used to experience great pain. Seeing the blossoms of the thin Asoka trees on its bank bent down like breasts and thinking

I had got you I was about to embrace it. But Lakshmana prevented me and my breast was filled with tears. Hearing the sound of golden bells hanging inside this car the Sarasas, living on the bank of the Godaveri, are flying in the sky as if to welcome you. O dear, seeing this forest of Panchavati after a long time my mind has been filled with joy. Alas, here, tender as you are, you nourished the new grown Sahakaras by watering them. Look, the antelopes, reared by you, are looking up at the car. O dear, I remember, in the Vetasa groves on the bank of this Godaveri, with my exhaustion, caused by hunting, removed by the watery air, I used to sleep by placing my head on your lap. Look at the hermitage of the great saint Agastya, who is capable of purifying impure water and who by the mere contraction of his eye-brows, prevented the king Nahusha from attaining to the dignity of Indra. Smelling the scent of Havi proceeding in the sky as well as the smoke of the three fires of the illustrious Agastya my soul, freed from Raja Gunas, has become light. The pleasure tank, by name *Panchapsar*, belonging to the great saint Shatakarni, surrounded on all sides with forest, is looking like the slightly perceptible ray of the moon coverd with clouds. Beholding him live on mere Kusa grass and range with the deer, the king of celestials, terrified at his asceticism, resorted to the vile noose of the youth of five Apsaras. Seated at ease inside a palace built on the extremity of the water the great saint Shatakarni is singing in accompaniment with the music of Mridanga. It has resounded the top of the flowery car. Look, O dear, another ascetic, as if holding the sun on his fore-head, in carrying on penances in the midst of four fires. His name is Sutighna. But he is not fierce but of a quiet temperament. Terrified at his asceticism the king of gods despatched an Apsara to break his Yoga. But her smiling glances, beautiful teeth and other lustful gestures could not disturb his mind. Look, another foremost of ascetics is stretching out his right-hand, which cuts Kuca grass, itches the deer and is expressive of favour, to me inorder to welcome me. He is observing the vow of silence and therefore returning my salutation by a slight nod; he is again fixing his pure looks on the solar disc. There is the charming and sacred hermitage of the ascetic Sharabhanga who keeps up sacred fire. Propitiating the fire for a long time with *Samit* he consigned his own body sanctified by mantras to it. Now removing the toil of the travellers by their shade, the trees, of his hermitage, yielding profuse fruits, are serving him like his sons. See, the mount Chitrakuta is looking like a proud bull. The caves are being resounded by the water falls of the springs. Its summits, covered with clouds, are looking like the elephants besmeared with mud. The river Mandakini of pure water, flowing mildly in the valley of the mountain, and looking small from distance, is appearing like a necklace of pearls placed round the neck of the earth. O dear, look at the beautiful Tamala trees grown near the mountain. With their sweet scented leaves I used to make decorations for your ears white like barley stalks. This is the powerful penance forest of the sage Atri. Freed from the fear of oppression the animals have grown humble. And without blossom the trees are laden with fruits. It is said that for the ablution of the ascetics, Anasua, the wife of Atri, brought down the Ganges here, whose golden lotuses are plucked by thy seven Rishis with their own hands and who 'is like the garland of Mahadeva's head. Standing immoveable for the absence of the wind, the trees, grown around the altar of the ascetics engaged in meditation in Vira posture, are as if also engaged in devout contemplation. This the green fig-tree to whom you prayed formerly; see, the fruits of this foremost of trees are shining like the jems of serpents. Look how beautiful the Ganges, being united with Yamuna, is looking. Somewhere the Indraneela flowers look like a garland of pearls. Some where white lotuses are shining. Somewhere blue swans, fond of Manasa lake, are swimming. Somewhere the water is looking like leaves painted with Aguru and sandal; somewhere it looks like moon-light in darkness; somewhere it looks like a white autumnal cloud. And somewhere it looks like the body of Mahesha besmeared with ashes and adorned with black serpents. By bathing at this confluence of the Ganges and Yamuna, men, even without the knowledge of the true nature of god, attain to emancipation. Look at the city of Guha the king of Nishadas. There when we, after casting off our crowns, put on bark and matted locks Sumantra cried saying "O Kaikeyi, your object has been accomplished." Here is my mother-like river Sarayu. The dust of her golden lotuses adorns the breast of Yaksha women. As Prakriti or nature is the source of the principle of Mahat (greatness) so the Brahma saints consider her to be the source of Brahma. Sarayu, on the banks of which sacrificial stakes have been erected, flows near Ayodha. She holds profuse water purified by the kings of the Ikshwaku family when they bathe thereafter the termination of the horse-sacrifice. My mind is welcoming her like the nurse of the kings of North Koshala who grew up by drinking her water and lived happily on her banks. Alas, separated by the worshipful Emperor, she, as if by the arms of her waves raised by the cool breezes, is embracing me like a son away from home. Look again at this side, dense dust has been raised, smoke-coloured like evening. Perhaps hearing from Hanumana of our arrival, Bharata, with his soldiers, is coming out to receive us. As Lakshmana returned you to me when I came back after slaying Khara and other Rakshasas, so forsooth shall Bharata return to me, who have fully carried out his promise, the prosperous kingdom. See, placing the soldiers behind him and our family priest Vasistha, before Bharata, clad in bark, is coming in the company of elderly ministers with *Arghya* in his hand. Although a young man Bharata practised the hardest of vows by not enjoying the kingdom offered him by our father."

While Rama was saying this, the car, understanding his object through its presiding god, came down from the sky. Filled with surprise Bharata's subjects looked up at it. Holding Sugriva, ever intent on serving him, by the hand Rama got down from the car by the stairs of crystal pointed out by Bibhishàna who went before him. Having saluted with reverence Vashistha, the family priest of the Ikshwakus and accepting Arghya Rama embraced Bharata and Satrughna with tearful eyes and rmelt the crown of the former who, out of respect for his eldest brother, desisted from accepting the throne. And casting favourable looks on the aged ministers whose faces were disfigured by growing beards and enquired with sweet words after their well-being.

Rama introduced very respectfully Sugriva and Bibhishana saying "He is the king of monkeys and bears. He is my great friend in calamity. And here is Pulastya's son Bibhishana who always fought before me." Thereat leaving Lakshmana Bharata first saluted Sugriva and Bibhishana. Afterwards when Bharata approached Lakshmana the latter bowed unto him. Raising him up Bharata embraced him placing his breast on his hardened by the strokes inflicted by Indrajit. Then assuming human forms at the command of Rama the commanders of the monkey army rode elephants. And temporal juice trickling down the bodies of the elephants they felt the pleasure of ascending a hill.

By the command of Rama, the king of Rakshasas got upon a car with his followers, beautifully made by his illusory power.

As the moon, beautified on account of the conjunction of Budha and Vrihaspati, ascends a cloud in the night, accompanied with lightning so Rama, with Bharata and Lakshmana, again got upon his beautiful etherial car. As assuming the first Boar-form the Lord Narayana raised up the earth, as the autumn, freed from thick clouds, displays the moon so Bharata saluted the beautiful Sita whom Rama had rescued from the great dangers of Ravana. The worshipful feet of Janaki, which were firm against the salutations of the Ten-necked demon and the head of Bharata, covered with matted locks and deprived of crown for his devotion to his eldest broter, purified each other on being united.

Going half a *Krosha* in the beautiful flowery car followed by his subjects Rama arrived at the charming garden of his capital Ayodhya adorned with a canopy made by Satrughna himself.

CANTO XIV.

Rama and Lakshmana saw their mothers in the garden miserably situated in the absence of their husband like a creeper when the tree, that supports it, is destroyed. With their vision obstructed with tears they could not behold clearly their powerful sons who had come back after killing their enemies but knew them as such by experiencing the pleasure of touching their body. As the water from the springs of the Himalaya falls down and cools the water, heated by the rays of the sun, of the Ganges who purifies the sinful and of Yamuna so their cool tears of joy removed the heat of their tears of sorrow. Touching the green wounds on the persons of Rama and Lakshmana inflicted by the weapons of the Rakshasas Koushalya and Sumitra lost respect for the favourite appellation of the Kshatriya ladies, namely "the mother of heroes." Saying "I am that inauspicious Sita who afflicted my husband," Vaidehi saluted the feet of the both the queens with equal reverence. They however, with truthful and affectionate words, consoled their daughter-in-law, saying "Rise up O child. By the purity of your character only Rama and Lakshmana have been saved from a great disaster." Then with water filling up many golden pitchers collected from many sacred shrines, and with it the tears of joy of his mothers the elderly ministers performed the preliminary part of Rama's installation. The monkeys and Rakshasas too brought water from various rivers, oceans and tanks. The torrents of water, while dropping on the head of the victorious Raghava, appeared like torrents of rain falling on the summit of the Vindhya mountain. It is a mere repitition to say that Rama, who shone exquisitely beautiful when he put on an ascetic garb before, appeared far more beautiful now when he was clad in a royal robe. Delighting the citizens with the sound of bugles, he, in the company of elderly ministers, night-rangers and monkeys, entered Ayodhya, the capital of the Raghu family, abounding in high gateways beautified with fried paddy poured down from the palaces. Lakshmana and Shatrughna fanned Rama who was seated on a car with chowries. And Bharata held the umbrella. It appeared thereat that the incarnate forms of conciliation, gifts, dissension and punishment were united. The smoke of Aguru coming out of the palace and being scattered by the wind it appeared that Rama, who had returned from the forest was, with his own hands, loosening the locks of Ayodhya who was like a woman whose husband had been away. With folded hands which were distinctly seen from the nets of the Palace Windows the women of Ayodhya saluted Sita, the wife of Raghu hero, who had been beautifully decorated by her mothers-in-law. Bearing the permanent marks of resplendent unguents offered by Anasua, and assuming a wonderful beauty as if she had again entered into fire Sita appeared to the females as to have been considered by her husband as pure. Having offered his friends well-furnished houses, Rama, who was the mine of friendship, entered, with tearful eyes, into a house, filled with articles of worship in which only a portrait of his father remained. There with folded hands he said to Bharata's mother Kaikeyi :—

"O mother, it must be admitted that it is by thy virtue only that my father did not violate the vow of truth which yields heaven as its fruit." Saying this he removed her shame. Rama offered so many edibles to Sugriva, Bibhishana and others that though they could gather all at their merest will, they were still filled with surprise. Having duly honored Agastya and other ascetics who had assembled there to welcome him he heard from them the birth-story of his slain enemy Ravana. It mainifested greatly his own personal glory. After the great saints had departed for their respective hermitages Rama sent away Bibhishana, the king of Rakshasas and other monkey chiefs by offering them suitable presents from Janaki. After their departure they spent their days so happily that even half a month was not perceptible to them. Then he ordered the flowery car, the flower of the celestials, which he had acquired by destroying Ravana, to proceed to Kuvera, the king of Kailasha, for carrying him. Thus after the death of his father having spent fourteen years in the forest Rama assumed the reins of the Government and acted impartially towards religion, profit and desire and his three younger brothers. As sucking the breast of the six Kirtikas with his six mouths, Kartikeya, the commander-in-chief of the celestial army, pleased them so Rama, devoted to mothers, served Koushalya and others. Under the regeme of Rama shorn of avarice, the destroyer of obstacles and the remover of sorrow his subjects acquired profuse wealth, performed religious rites and obtained sons. Performing his royal duties in proper time Rama used to spend the rest of his hours happily in the company of Janaka's daughter. It so appeared that the presiding goddess of royal prosperity had been united with him in the person of Janaki. While they enjoyed immensely in the palace embellished with portraits, Rama and Sita enjoyed greater the pleasure the more they remembered their hardships in the forest of Dandaka. Then showing evident signs of conception by her countenance pale like a Sara reed and having beautiful eyes Vaidehi conduced greatly to the happiness of her Consort. Being confirmed in his belief about her conception by her blue nipples Rama, placing her on his lap in a solitary place, enquired after her desire. As ferocious animals musticate Nivara rice offered as food as Vaikhanasa maidens being united show their respective love so Janaka's daughter Sita expressed her desire to behold again the penance groves situate on the banks of Bhagirathi interspersed with Kuca grass. Rama also promised to fulfill her desire.

One day along with his followers he got on the turret of his palace to behold the delightful city of Ayodhya. Beholding the prosperous and crowded high-ways, the river Sarayu filled with boats and gardens inside the houses filled with playful citizens he experienced greatest delight. Inorder to learn the public opinion about his own character the Raghu hero of purified soul, the foremost of orators, victor of enemies and the possessor of serpentine arms, asked his secret spy Bhadra. When he pressed him much Bhadra communicated every thing to him and said:—"O god, the citizens speak highly of all thy actions. They only blame thee for having taken back Sita who had lived in the house of the Rakshasa."

As a piece of heated iron is shattered by the strokes of a massive iron club so Rama's heart was rent asunder by hearing of this charge against his wife. His mind became unsettled like a craddle being himself stupified to decide whether he would disregard the charge brought against him or forsake his own innocent wife. After thinking for a considerable time he decided that no other means would remove this blame except the forsaking of his own wife. Not to speak of the objects of enjoyment, persons, having fame for their wealth, prefer glory even to their own lives. Then Rama, who was shorn of lustre, sent for his younger brothers. When after seeing the pale countenace of their eldest brother they took their seats he communicated to them the news of the censure and said:—

"As a mirror is marked by the watery air so the pure solar dynasty has been soiled with censure through me. Consider it very well. As an elephant-chief regards the pole to which he is tied as a source of great misery so I cannot bear this blame unheared-of before, which has spread amongst my subjects like a drop of oil thrown on the agitated waves. As formerly by my sire's mandate I renounced the kingdom consisting of oceans, so for removing this censure I will forsake Sita even not caring for the hour of my son's birth. I know Janaki to be chaste, but the censure of the people has grown too much powerful for me. There is nothing which men cannot do—they consider the shadow of the earth as a spot for the spotless moon. In vain has not been my attempt to kill the Rakshasas. I have done so for subduing my enemies. A serpent, when trampled under foot, does not bite its aggressor for drinking his blood. If you think that I shall live long after removing this censure then kindly do not prevent me from doing what I have resolved."

When bent upon doing an injury to the daughter of Janaka Rama said this, none amongst the brothers could either prevent him or accept his proposal.

Casting his looks towards Lakshmana his eldest brother, truthful and illustrious in the three worlds, ordered him separately, saying "O gentle one, Sita, who is encient, has expressed her desire of seeing the penance groves. Do you under this pretext take her on a car and leave her in the hermitage of the great saint Valmiki." Lakshmana knew that Parashurama, by the command of his sire, had cut off like an enemy the head of his mother and therefore he accepted such a command of his eldest brother, for implicit submission should be paid to the orders of the elders.

Thereupon Rama's younger brother Lakshmana placed Sita, who was filled with delight on hearing of the favourable news, on a car drawn by fearless steeds and driven by the charioteer Sumantra and set out. While proceeding by charming countries Sita was filled with delight on thinking that her husband was always anxious to secure her pleasure. She did not know that Rama was no longer a Kalpa tree to her but that of sword leaves. The trembling of the right eye, which was for good deprived of the view of a desirable sight, announced on the way the future great calamity which Lakshmana had kept hidden so long. Janaki's countenance grew immediately pale with sorrow for seeing evil omens. She then with a simple mind prayed for the well-being of her most beloved Rama. Raising up her wave-like hands Janhavi prevented Lakshmana who was by the command of his brother about to leave Sita in the forest. When Sumantra stopped the horses Lakshmana helped Sita to get down from the car like a truthful person carrying out his promise and ferryied her across the river in a boat brought by Nishada. Then governing his speech with difficulty which was suppressed with tears Lakshmana expressed the order of the king as a cloud pours down hailstorms. As a flowery creeper drops on earth by the force of the wind, so Janaki, struck by this new wind, dropped down on her mother earth. Her ornaments, at that time, were scattered on all sides. Thinking "why your pious husband born in the Ikshwaku race shall forsake you for nothing" her mother Earth did not allow her to enter into her womb. While Sita was in a fainting state she did not experience the least sorrow. But on regaining her consciousness her mind was consumed with the fire of grief. The consoling words of Lakshmana were more painful to her than her unconscious state. The chaste Sita did not blame her husband the least for forsaking her without any cause but only spoke ill of her own self saying that she was ever unfortunate and sinful.

Having consoled the chaste Sita Rama's younger brother Lakshmana pointed out to her the road to Valmiki's hermitage and said "O goddess, I am dependent upon another. Pray forgive me for this cruel deed which I have committed under the order of my master." Raising him up with her hand from the ground Sita said:—"O gentle one, do thou live long. I am pleased with thee. Thou art not at all to blame. As Upendra is under Indra so thou art under thy elder brother. Communicate my salutations one by one to my mothers-in-law and tell them that they may always think of the well-being of their grandson who is in my womb. And communicate my words to the king saying "Although I proved my innocence before thee by entering into fire still thou hast forsaken me in fear of groundless censure. Is this the becoming action of the Raghu family? Thou art good by nature; I am sure thou hast not acted irresponsibly by me. This is the unbearable thunderbolt of my dreadful pristine sin. Methinks because thou didst forsake before the goddess of fortune and enter into forest with me, therefore she has been unable to bear my habitation in thy house. When the husbands of the female ascetics were formerly oppressed by the Rakshasas I gave them shelter by thy favour, how shall I seek refuge with another while thou art alive? If thy son had not been in my womb whom it is my bounden duty to protect, then I would not have kept this life rendered useless by thy separation. O Lakshmana, fixing my eyes on the sun after delivery I will carry on penances saying that I may even in my next birth obtain as my husband endued all virtues, an incarnation of Narayana and may not suffer separation from him. Manu has said that the duty of a king consists in protecting the four castes, the Brahmanas &c. and the four Ashramas of Bramacharya, &c. And although he has exiled me, he should see me considering me as an ordinary female ascetic."

When after promising that he would communicate all those words to Rama, Lakshmana disappeared from her view Rama's wife Janaki again cried bitterly like a terrified she-deer. At that time the she-peacocks desisted from dancing, the trees cast off their flowers, and the she-deer threw away the sacrificial grass they had taken up. In short sympathising with Sita's grief the entire forest wept. At that time the prime-poet Valmiki was ranging in the forest to collect sacred fuels and sacrificial grass. And following the cries he came where Sita was. He was so very compassionate by nature that he was affected by sorrow when he saw a Krouncha pierced by a hunter. This incident produced his verses. Rubbing the tears off her eyes and desisting from lamentations Maithila saluted that foremost of Munis. He too marking signs of conception blessed her saying "May you have a good son," and said "By my fore-sight I have known, that your husband Rama, his mind affected with fear of people's censure, has forsaken you. Be not grieved for it, O Vaidehi; know that you have come to your father's house, situate in another country. Rama has killed Ravana, the thorn of the world. He is truthful and shorn of pride; still I have felt anger for him for having forsaken you.

unjustly. Your illustrious father-in-law was a great friend of mine. Your father, by delivering divine instructions, shatters the worldly miseries of the pious. You are the foremost of chaste women. Why should you not then deserve my favour? By living in the company of the ascetics even the ferocious animals of this penance forest have grown quiet. You can live fearlessly in this forest; you will give birth to your son without any pain and their Jatakarma and other rites will be duly performed. By adoring your own deity on the back of the sin-destroying river Tamasa, thick set with the cottages of the Rishis your mind will be delighted. The daughters of the ascetics, fearless in speech, with collect season flowers, fruits, ingredients of worship, *Nivara* rice and please your mind who have been assailed with this new grief. By nourshing the growth of the new trees of the hermitage with pouring water according to your might you will experience parental affection before giving birth to a son."

Having said so the kind hearted ascetic Valmiki arrived in the evening at his hermitage full of quiet animals with Janaki, the object of his welcome. As Amavasya consigns the last ray of the moon whose other rays are devoured by the Pitris, to the herbs, so that foremost of ascetics entrusted Sita, who was stricken with grief, to the care of the ascetic ladies who were filled with delight at her arrival. Having duly welcomed Janaka's daughter the female ascetics, lighting up a lamp with Ingudi oil, set apart for her habitation a cottage spread with the bed of deer skin.

Having honoured duly the guests and living on wild fruits and roots for keeping up the line of her husband, Janaki, purified by bathing and clad in pure bark, spent her days in that hermitage.

On the other side discussing in his mind "Has not the king been stricken with repentance by this time?" Lakshmana, the destroyer of Indrajit, communicated to his eldest brother Rama all the incidents ending with Sita's lamentation. Hearing it Rama, like the moon of the month of Pousha pouring down dews, all on a sudden shed tears; for fear of calumny he sent away Maithili from his house, but not from his heart. Then restraining his sorrow, protecting the castes and Ashramas, and enjoying everything equally with his younger brothers Rama governed that prosperous kingdom. After he had forsaken the chaste Sita for fear of calumny the goddess of prosperity, freed from impediments and a co-wife, began to live happily on his breast. Having forsaken Janaka's daughter, Rama, the victor of Ravana, did not marry any other woman. Having heard that he had performed the horse-sacrifice with an golden image of Sita by him, she, with great difficulty, bore that sorrow.

CANTO XV.

Having forsaken Sita, Rama, the lord of the earth, began to enjoy her only whose tongue was the ocean. A Rakshasa, Lavana by name, once obstructed the sacrifice of the ascetics living on the bank of the Yamuna. Thereat they sought refuge with Rama. Finding Dasharatha's son engaged in the work of protection they did not destroy Lavana by their ascetic power, for in the absence of a protector the ascetics, whose weapon is their curse, exhaust their asceticism acquired with great difficulty. Rama, the scion of the Kakustha race, promised to the Rishis to remove their hindrances; because for the protection of virtue the Lord Narayana incarnated himself as Rama on earth. The ascetics suggested to him the means of destroying Lavana. Lavana, the holder of mace, could with difficulty be conquered. He used to invite a person for fight whenever he was divested of his mace. Rama ordered Satrughna to administer to the well-being of the ascetics so that he might justify the root meaning of his name by killing the enemies. As any special injunction is capable of putting a stop to the action of general laws so any one of the Raghu family could destroy the enemies. Having accepted on his head the blessings of his eldest brother the fearless Satrughna proceeded on his car beholding the beatiful forest covered with flowers. As to signify 'Study' the prefix *adhi* follow the root *ing* so the soldiers, at the comand of Rama, follwed him for accomplishing a great work. Preceding the car the ascetics pointed out the road. Proceeding according to their directions the effulgent Satrughna appeared like the sun in the etherial way pointed out by the Balakhilya ascetics. On his way he spent one night in the penance forest of Valmiki abounding with deer with 'heads upraised on hearing the rattle of the car-wheels. Having collected various most excellent articles by his ascetic power, that foremost of Munis, Valmiki, treated to hospitality the prince whose horses were worn out with enhaustion. As the earth gives birth to wealth and soldiers so in that night his brother's wife, who was in family way, gave birth to two sons. Being greatly delighed on hearing of the birth of sons to his eldest brother Satrughna, having saluted that foremost of ascetics with folded hands, set out on his car. Thereupon Satrughna arrived at Lavana's city Madhupaghna. At that time Kumbhinashi's son brought various animals from the forest as a tribute to the king. That Rakshasa was smoky-coloured and from his person emitted smell of fat. His hairs were twany-coloured like fire and he was encircled by Rakshasas who lived on flesh. It appeared as if the fire of funeral pyre was ranging on all sides. Seeing Lavana divested of his mace Rama's younger brother immediately attacked him, for a person who strikes his antagonist on finding a loop-hole, is always crowned with success.

Roaring at Satrughna saying "Perhaps seeing my scanty food the Providence in fear has sent you to me" that Rakshasa uprooted a huge tall tree, at him which was cut into pieces on the way by the sharpened arrows of Soumitri, and could not touch his person, the dust of the flowers only touching it. When that tree was cut into pieces the highly powerful Rakshasa Lavana hurled at Satrughua a huge piece of rock like unto a fist of Death placed elsewhere. Struck by the Indra weapon discharged by Satrughna that massive rock was shattered into atoms minuter than even sand. Then raising up his right hand the Rakshasa ran towards Satrughna like unto a portion of a hill shaken by a tornado. Then with his heart cut off by the Vishnu weapon discharged by Satrughna the Rakshasa dropped down on earth and shook her. But this removed the trembing of the Rishis living in the hermitages. The birds sat on the body of the slain enemy; and celestial flowers were poured dowu on the head of his antagonist. At that time having slain Lavana the great heroe Satrughna regarded himself the worthy younger brother of Lakshmana who had killed Indrajit. The more the ascetics, who were freed from dangers in the performance of sacrifices praised him, the greater was the bashful humiliation of his head which was upraised by his prowess. Satrughna, whose ornament was his manliness, who was shorn of desire for wordly enjoyments and whose form was gentle, made a city, by name Mathura, on the banks of Kalindi. Beholding the prosperity of the citizens under the protection of a good king people thought that the city had been peopled by the extra denizens of heaven. Ascending his palace there Satrughna experienced great delight on beholding the river Yamuna filled with Chakravakas like unto the golden tresses of the earth.

On the other side Valmiki, well-versed in mantras, the friend of both Dasharatha and Janaka, out of his love for them, performed the purificatory rites, of the both sons of Vaidehi. The impurities of the womb of one were cleansed with Kuca, and those of another with the down of the tail of a low. For this reason the Prime Poet named them Kusha and Lava. After they had passed the stage of infancy he instructed them both in the Vedas and then made them sing the Ramayana composed by his own self, the first seeds of poetry. Singing the swbet history of Rama before their mother Kusha and Lava lessened a little her sorrow consequent upon her separation from her husband. Rama's other three brothers, Bharata, Lakshmana and Satrughna, effulgent like three fires, begat two sons respectively on their wives. Having conferred the kingdoms of Mathura and Vidisa on his two sons Satrughati and Suvahu, who were well versed with the knowledge of scriptures Satrughna, who was anxious to behold his eldest brother, started for Ayodhaya.

Considering it unwise to obstruct again the asceticism of the greatest of the Rishis Valmiki, Satrughana passed over his hermitage filled with deer who were rendered motionless by the songs of the two sons of Maithili. The self-controlled Satrughana entered Ayodhya the roads of which were beautifully repaired. The citizens cast respectful looks at him for having slain Lavana. There he saw Rama, the only husband of the earth on account of his having relinquished Janaki, encircled by his courtiers. As delighted at the destruction of Kalanemi Indra received Rama so did his eldest brother receive Satrughana, who bowed unto him, for his having slain Lavana. On Rama's enquiry after his well-being he communicated every thing unto him, but he did not mention the birth of his sons for the Prime Poet asked him not to do so for he would himself return the two sons unto Rama.

One day a village Brahmin placing an infant son before the Palace gate from his lap began to sweep piteously saying—

"O Earth, slipped off the hands of king Dasharatha you were miserably plightedly. But now passing into the hands of Rama you have been visited with greater calamity."

Hearing of the cause of the Brahmana's sorrow Dasharatha's son, the protector of his subjects, was put greatly into shame for premature death had never touched the kingdom of the Ikshwakus. Consoling the sorrowful Brahmana, saying "Tarry a moment" he thought of his flowery car for vanquishing Death. Taking up his weapons Rama, the scion of the Raghu race, got upon that car and started. At that time an invisible voice from the sky was all on a sudden heard before him.

"O great king, some iniquity has prevailed amongst your subjects. Find it out and put it down and you will be successful."

Hearing those confident words and wishing to put down the transgressions of the caste he travelled on all sides on the car the flags whereof were shaken by its velocity. Then, Rama, the scion of the Ikshwaku race, saw that a person of bright eyes was practising penances with his face cast down towards a fire the smoke whereof touched the branches of the tree. When he enquired about his name and lineage that drinker of smoke said "I am a Sudra; my name is Shamvuka, I am practising penances for acquiring heaven." In order to cut off the head of that Sudra who was working the evil of his subjects on account of his not possessing the right of practising penances, Rama who was the subduer of the wicked, took up his weapou. He cut off his head from the neck, the beards of which were scorched by the scintillations of fire and which was like a lotus, the filaments whereof were destroyed by the frost. Being thus punished by the king the Sudra attained to a most excellent state which he had not acquired even by the hardest penances which were not his previlege to practise.

As after the termination of rains the autumn is united with the moon of cool rays, so the lord of the Raghu family, on his way back to Ayodhya, was united with the highly effulgent saint Agasthya. That ascetic son of Kumbha presented to Rama the valuable celestial ornaments which he had formerly obtained from the ocean as his ransom whom he had drunk up. Putting those ornaments on his arms which were shorn of the touch of Janaki's neck Rama returned to Ayodhya.

On the other hand before Rama's arrival the lifeless son of the twice-born one had revived. Regaining his son the Brahmana withdrew his charge by lauding Rama who saved his son from Death.

Thereupon for celebrating a horse-sacrifice Rama let loose a horse for grazing at large. As by pouring down rain clouds nourish crops so Sugriva, Bibhishana and other dependant kings showered on him various articles necessary for the celebration of the same. Not only from the earth but even from luminous spheres the Rishis came from various quarters to the sacrifice of Rama, the foremost of kings and the scion of the Raghu race. The pure-souled Rishis living at her out-skirts the city of Ayodhya, having four gates, appeared like the body of Brahma which creates the worlds. Even the renuncitation of Maithili was an object of glory to him, for at the time of celebrating the sacrifice he did not take a second wife. With a golden image of Sita he had the duties of a wife performed. Then with requisite articles greater in number than what was required by the sacred prescription began the sacrifice of Rama. What more even the Rakshasas who generally obstructed sacrifices, were appointed guards there. Thereupon at Valmiki's command Maithili's sons Kusha and Lava sang about hither and thither the history of Rama known to him only. First of all it was the history of Rama; next it was composed by the Prime Poet Valmiki and thirdly the voice of Kusha and Lava was like that of the Kinnaras. Therefore there was nothing more pleasant to the audience than this. People, appreciating beauty and music, communicated to Rama the excellence of their voice and beauty. Along with his brothers Rama, with a delighted heart, began to behold them and listen to their music. Hearing their song with fixed mind and shedding tears the entire assemblage shone like a forest divested of the wind, in the morning pouring dews. All the people present in that meeting perceived strong resemblance, except in dress, between Rama and those two boys and began to look at them with winkless eyes. The people were not so much pleased with their proficiency in music as they were when they found them reluctant to accept any reward from the king. When the Emperor Rama himself enquired "Who has taught you music? What poet has composed this song?" they mentioned the name of Valmiki. Then Rama with his younger brothers went to Valmiki and made over to him the entire kingdom except his own person. The highly merciful Rishi, saying "Kusha and Lava are your sons given birth to by Maithili" requested him to take back Sita. Thereat Rama said.

"O father, your daughter-in-law proved her innocence before me by the ordeal of fire. But my subjects, on account of the oppressions of the wicked Ravana, do not believe in her purity. If Maithili can create the confidence of the subjects in the purity of her character then I shall, at your command, take her back with the sons."

The king having promised so that foremost of ascetics, as he purifies his own self by self-restraint, brought Janaki from his hermitage through his disciples. Having finished the horse sacrifice Rama, the ornament of the Kakutstha family, collected all the citizens and sent for Valmiki. As the Rishis, with Udatha and other vowels as well as with purified Riks, adore the sun of fierce rays so the great saint, with Sita and her sons, appeared before Rama. Beholding Sita of quiescent form, clad in a silk raiment, with her eyes fixed on her feet they all regarded her as pure. Withdrawing their eyes from Sita the subjects hung down their heads like paddy plants laden with crops. Then taking his seat the foremost of ascetics said to Sita :—

"O my child, remove the misgivings of the people about your character before your husband."

Then rinsing her mouth with the sacred water offered by Valmiki's disciple Maithili pronounced her truthful vow saying "Lady earth, if I have not violated my allegiance to my husband by my speech, mind or words then give me room in your womb." On the chaste Sita saying so, immediately a circle of effulgence like unto lightning came out of the cavity of the Earth. Inside this circle of effulgence the goddess earth, having the ocean for her tongue, was distinctly seen seated on a throne upheld by the hoods of the serpents. Placing Sita, who had her eyes fixed on her husband, on her lap she returned to the nether region although repeatedly prevented by Rama to do so. The family priest Vasistha, who was cognizant of the power of the deity, pacified Rama's anger against Earth, who had taken up an arrow for compelling her to return Sita.

Having sent away his friends and the Rishis with proper honors after the termination of the sacrifice Rama transferred his love for Sita to his two sons.

At the command of Bharata's maternal uncle Yudhajit, Rama, the protector of subjects, conferred the kingdom of Sindhu with immense wealth on Bharata. Having vanquished the Gandharvas there in battle Bharata made them wield Vinas instead of weapons. Having installed his two sons by name Taksha and Pushkala he again returned to Rama.

By Rama's command Lakshmana conferred the kingdom of Karapatha on his two sons Angada and Chandraketu. Having thus distributed the kingdoms amongst their sons the kings performed the obsequial rites of their mothers who had gone to the region of their father.

Afterwards one day Death, assuming the garb of an ascetic, arrived before Rama, and said " Promise you will renounce him who will come here when we will talk in secret." Rama having agreed Yama, assuming his own form, said " By Brahma's command do thou ascend the heaven." In the meantime, Lakshmana, who was at the gate, in fear of the imprecation of Durvasa who had come there to see Rama, broke their secrecy, although he knew the former oath. Having gone to the bank of Sarayu the Yogin Lakshmana, who had violated the promise, gave up his body. His fourth part Lakshmana having gone to heaven Rama lived on earth without any tenacity like righteousness of three legs. Having placed Kusha who was like a goad to the elephant-like enemies in Kushavati and Lava who could please the pious with sweet words in Sharavati, Rama with his other brothers started for the North with fire before them. The city of Ayodhya, out of her devotion to her Lord, followed him. The monkeys and Rakshasas who knew his heart followed his foot steps which were soaked with drops of tears of the subjects big as Kadamva flowers.

Seated on the car, Rama, fond of his votaries, made the sacred Sarayu his staircase for ascending heaven in the interest of his followers. Because at that time for the creatures who were bathing in her the river Sarayu became worthy of even being crossed by the kine, so that part afterwards became the celebrated shrine of *Go-Pratara*. When Sugriva and others, who emanated from the portions of the deities, assumed their own forms Rama created another heaven for the citizens who had obtained immortality. Having thus performed the work of the gods namely the decapitation of the Ten-necked demon, and placed Bibhishana and Hanuman as two pillars of his glory on the Southern and Northern Hills, the Lord Narayana again assumed his own form, the refuge of all the worlds.

CANTO XVI.

Rama having obtained emancipation Lava and six other Raghu heroes conferred on Kusha, who was the eldest and the most accomplished, all the most excellent properties for brotherliness was a hereditary quality in their family. Although they grew powerful by constructing bridges, encouraging husbandry, protecting kine and procuring elephants still they did not go beyond their respective boundaries as the ocean does not transgress its continent. The families of

Kusha, Lava and others the generous sons of Rama and other incarnations of the four-armed Narayana were divided into eight branches like unto those of the eight elephants of the quarters sprung from the Sama Veda.

Once on a time when the wick of the lamp was motionless, and all the inmates of the bed-room were fast asleep Kusha awoke all on a sudden and saw the unforeseen figure of a woman who was dressed like one whose husband was away. Having uttered the word *Jaya* before Kusha, who was powerful like Indra, a victor of enemies and whose wealth was enjoyed by the pious, the charming woman stood with folded hands. Then raising up the upper part of his body the great bowman Kusha, the grandson of Dasharatha, was filled with surprise on seeing the beautiful form of a woman entering into the room locked up like unto a reflection in the mirror and said :—

"O fair one, how have you entered this room which has been locked up. It seems you are not endued with the power of Yoga and your appearance is pale like a lotus assailed with frost. Who are you and whose wife? Why have you come to me in the dead of night? The mental faculties of the self-controlled descendants of the Raghu family are always averse to others' wives. Considering this, reply fearlessly to my questions." Thereat that well-dressed and ault-less lady replied.

"O king, know me as the presiding goddess of that lordless city of Ayodhya the virtuous citizens of which your father had taken away with him at the time of his departure for his own region. Formerly I excelled even the prosperous city of Alaka filled with festivities under the regeme of the king of celestials. But even inspite of the existence of such an illustrious descendant of the solar dynasty, as yourself, I have come by such a pitiable situation. As the period of junction is situated when the sun sets and the clouds are dispersed by a strong wind, so is my condition for hundreds of palaces have become unworthy of habitation, their walls dismantled and houses broken in the absence of occupiers. Formerly in the depth of night unchaste women, with Nupuras ringing on their feet, used to wend the high ways; now jackals are moving about with hideous yells in search of flesh. Formerly the water of the tanks moved by the hands of women while sporting there used to imitate the sound of Mridanga and now that clear water is being agitated by the horns of wild buffaloes. Their houses being broken the sportive peacocks are lying on the trees. They no longer dance now for want of the music of Mridanga. And being consumed by the forest-fire the gardens have come by the condition of the peacocks. The stairs on which formerly the women used to place their feet dyed with red lac are now being printed with the foot-prints of the tigers marked with the blood of the deer killed immediately.

The painted figures of the elephants in the forest of lotuses are now bearing the marks of the claws of the angry lions; the sloughs of the serpents are covering the breasts of the figures of the women painted on the pillars the colour of which has faded away in time. The white colour of the houses has grown pale in time and grass has grown over them. The rays of the moon like unto pearls are not reflected on them in the night. The creepers of my gardens which the sportive women used to bend with great care for plucking flowers are being scattered by the wild monkeys and other animals. No longer the flame of the lamps goes out through my windows in the night, nor are they adorned with the beautiful faces of the women during the day. In time the sacred smoke of Aguru and sandal has disappeared and the houses have been covered with the cob-webs of creepers. Alas! on seeing the condition of the river Saraju now my mind becomes greatly afflicted. Her banks are shorn of food offerings. Her streams no longer carry the scented ingredients of bathing and the Vetasa groves on her bank are not resorted to by men. Therefore O king, as your father having cast off the human body undertaken by him for his own works, has assumed again the form of Vishnu so leaving this city of Kushavati go to your ancestral city of Ayodhya."

Saying 'so be it' the Raghu hero Kusha delightedly accepted her proposal and that beautiful damsel too, with a smiling countenance, disappeared therefrom. The next morning the king communicated that wonderful incident to the Brahmanas assembled in his court. Hearing of it and learning that the capital of his family had accepted Kusha as his lord the Brahmanas welcomed him with their blessings. Then having left his own city Kushavati in charge of the Brahmanas conversant with the Vedas the Emperor Kusha, on an auspicious day, with the ladies of his seraglio and encircled by his soldiers, set out for Ayodhya like unto the wind preceding the clouds. While the soldiers marched the flags imitated the beauty of the gardens, the elephants that of pleasure hills and the cars that of huge palaces. It appeared as if the city was going. Having the white umbrellas for their reflections the soldiers, proceeding towards Ayodhya at the command of Kusha, appeared like the ocean rising up to the bank at the advent of the moon. As if unable to bear the obstruction of the soldiers when Kusha set out the goddess Earth ascended the etherial region in the shape of dust. A portion of the army were busy with leaving the city of Kushavati, another detachment were busy with encamping before and the third proceded on their way. It appeared therefore that all the divisions were united there. With the temporal juice of the infuriated elephants and the strokes of the hoofs of the horses belonging to the Emperor Kusha the dust was converted into mud and the latter was again converted into dust. The soldiers, being scattered while searching the roads on the levelled surface of the mount Vindhya, set up a terrible uproar resounding the caves thereof like the river Reva. Going over the red chalk and other minerals of the mountains the wheels of the cars were dyed therewith and their rattle was mixed with the sound of bugles. In this wise marking presents offered by the Pulindas the king Kusha crossed the mount Vindhya. While at the sacred shrine of the Vindhya he was crossing the river Ganges flowing towards the west with a bridge of elephants the swans, flying in the sky, served for the time being for his chowries, their wings moving without any care. Then the king Kusha saluted the sacred water of the Ganges which was the source of heaven to his ancestors who were reduced to ashes by the anger of Kapila and was shaken by the movements of boats. Thus traversing the roads for a few days he at last arrived at the bank of the river Sarayu and observed the sacrificial stakes by hundreds, erected on the altars, by the Raghu kings who were constantly engaged in sacrifices. Then the extremity wind of his ancestral capital, cooled by its coming in contact with the waves of Sarayu, shaking the branches of the trees went forward to welcome Kusha ircled by soldiers worn out with fatigue of travel.

Thereupon the powerful king, the victor of enemies and the friend of the citizens, encamped, at the boundary of the city of Ayodhya, his soldiers with the hoisting of flying banners. As the cloud with the downpour of rain, vivifies the earth stricken with the rays of the sun, so the artists, engaged by their master, with various ingredients laid out anew the city which was so miserably plighted. Then with the help of persons conversant in the knowledge of adoring Vastu, the presiding deity of the house, the Raghu hero Kusha offered adoration at the spacious temples with sacrifices of beasts. As a lustful person gains the heart of his sweet heart with advances of love so the king Kusha, entering the palace, honored his ministers with offering them houses according to their ranks. With shops filled with various commodities for sale, with horses in the stable and elephants tied to the stakes the city appeared perfectly beautiful. Residing in Ayodhya the capital of the Raghus, rendered again as beautiful as before, Maithili's son Kusha did not aspire after the city of the king of gods or after that of Kuwera. Thereupon set in summer as if for making the beloved wives of Kusha to put on robes set with pearls, to bear necklaces on their breasts and for instructing them to make decorations. When the sun approached nearer from the quarter presided over by Agasthya the North discharged the snowy water of the Himalaya like the delightful cool water. At that time the heat of the day was increased and the night was shortened. So they both appeared like two penitent wives separated from their husband by the quarrels of love. Day by day water of the tanks went down the stairs covered with mosses and the stalks of lotuses rose above water. By and by water, up to the waist of women, was left in the tanks. Unfolding themselves in the evening the Mallika flowers spread fragrance on all sides of the forest. Going to every flower the black-bees were as if counting their number by their hummings. The filaments of Sirisha flowers being stuck on the cheeks of the women filled with perspiration and cut with nails, they did not drop down on earth, although displaced from the ears. Lying on the stone-floors of their houses washed with water and besmeared with sandal the rich people began to ward off the heat of the sun. In the end of the spring, the lustful movements of the hairs of women loosened after bathing, scented with incense, and covered with Mallika flowers, roused the weak Cupid. The twany-coloured blossoms of the Arjuna flowers appeared like the broken bow of the god of love who was reduced to ashes by the fiery anger of Hara. Presenting Sahakara flowers of sweet scent, the fragrant old Siddha and new Patali flowers as well as other charming objects the summer, as if, made himself freed from the charge of spreading painful heat from the pleasure-seeking persons. In this painful season two things were greatly liked by people the moon enveloped with rays capable of removing the distresses of heat and the feet of the prosperous king Kusha capable of removing the misery of people. The king Kusha felt a desire of sporting with his wives in the waters of Sarayu abounding in ganders made restive by her waves and having her bank filled with blossoming creepers. That king, powerful like Vishnu, had a tent pitched on her bank and crocodiles and other ferocious acquatic animals removed by fishermen. He then, as becoming his might and wealth, began to sport in the water. With the sound of armlets, touching one another, of his wives as well as that of the Nupuras when they got down from the bank by the stairs the swans of the river Sarayu were greatly agitated. While seated on a boat the Emperor was witnessing the sport of the women with throwing water at one another he spoke to the two women by his sides who were fanning him with chowries.

"Look with the unguents of hundreds of ladies of my seraglio the stream, of the river Sarayu, is appearing like an evening, assuming various hues by means of clouds. The waters, shaken by the boat, are removing the collyrium of their eyes and imparting in its stead, inebriete glances. Although they are unable to bear the weight of their persons on account of their heavy waists and breasts still out of attachment they are with difficultly swimming with their arms adorned with Keywers. These ear-decorations of Sirisha flowers, made by these women sporting in the water, dropping off their ears, are deceiving the fishes fond of mosses. The pear-like drops of water falling on the breasts of these women engaged in throwing up water it is appearing as if chains of pearls are dropping. The objects imitating their form and beauty have come near them. The eddies are like their deep navels, the waves are like the gestures of their eye-brows and the pairs of Chakravakas are like their breasts. The sound of water like Mridangas struck by these women and welcomed by the peacocks with their notes is filling our ears. The cloth being wetted and tied on their waists the pores of the ornaments, filled up with water and disappearing like stars with the rise of the moon, have become silent. They are throwing water at their friends and who are, in return, throwing the same on their faces. Drops of water, rendered bright with Kumkuma powder, are coming down from their straight hairs. Although their tresses have been loosened and their pearl ornaments have been slackened still their beauty has not suffered deterioration."

As taking up lotuses on his shoulder a wild elephant sports with she-elephants so getting down from the boat Kusha began to sport with them. United with that effulgent king the women appeared greatly beautiful. Pearl is of itself pleasing to the eye. It indeed looks wonderfully beautiful when it is united with the shining Indra-neela stone. The women of large eyes sprinkling the king with water mixed with Kumkuma he looked like a mountain-chief besmeared with red chalk. When he bathed with the beautiful ladies of his seraglio in the river Sarayu he looked like the king of gods sporting in the Mandakini in the company of Apsaras. Rama gave Kusha along with the kingdom the celestial ornament which he had obtained from Agastya. While he sported in the water that Jaitra ornament dropped there against his knowledge. When after performing that desirable ablution he arrived at the tent with those women he found, before rubbing, his arm divested of that celestial ornament. That ornament was the master of victory and used by his father. And therefore he could not bear its loss and not out of avarice. To that wise, rich and considerate king flowery and jewelled ornaments were of equal value. The king Kusha immediately ordered fishermen, expert in diving into the water of the river, to find it out. They tried their best; but being unsuccessful and filled with sorrow they said :—

"O lord, we have tried our best but have not been able to find out your jewelled ornament thrown into water. Forsooth the Naga Kumuda, living in the river, has taken it out of avarice."

Thereupon with his eyes reddened in anger, the great bowman Kusha, stringing his bow, arrived at the bank of the lake and took up the Garuda weapon for killing the serpent. As soon as the arrow was shot the lake was agitated. And as if striking the bank with its hand, the wave, like an elephant thrown into a pit, began to roar terribly. As the Kalpa tree rose with Lakshmi from the ocean when it was churned so the king of Nagas, with a beautiful maiden, came out of the lake the acquatic animals whereof were greatly assailed. Beholding the king of serpents who had arrived there for returning the ornament the king withdrew his arrow, for the anger of the pious does not last long against the humiliated persons seeking their shelter. Then bowing down his head the Naga Kumuda saluted Kusha, the goad of elephant-like enemies and the son of Rama, the king of the three worlds, and said :—

"I know you as the another form in the shape of a son of the Lord Narayana, who had assumed a human form for relieving the earth of her burden. How can I then obstruct your pleasure? This maiden, fickle on account of her youth, was playing with balls. While she looked up to mark them she saw your ornament dropping in the lake like a star from the sky and took it up. Let this jem of an ornament, O king, be united with thy strong arm, extending to the knees, marked with bow-strings and like unto a shelter for protecting the world. O Scion of the Raghu race, now my prayer before you is that you may be pleased to permit this my youngest sister Kumudvati to expatiate her sin by serving your feet for ever."

When Kumuda returned the ornament after saying

this Kusha, pleased, replied :—" O king of serpents, you are an honorable friend of mine, so I cannot disregard your prayer."

Afterwards in the company of his friends the Naga-chief Kumuda duly united Kumudvati, the ornament of both the races, with Kusha. When the king, for securing a helpmate in religious practices, accepted her hand before the flaming fire all the quarters were filled with the sound of bugles and a wonderful shower of sweet-scented flowers fell there. In this way the Naga-chief Kumuda obtained Kusha begotten on Maithili by the foremost of kings, Rama, the preceptor of the three worlds, as his friend. And Kusha too secured Kumuda, the fifth son of Takshaka, as his friend. The first obtained freedom from the fear of Garuda, the destroyer of his father and the latter happily governed the earth divested of the fear of serpents.

CANTO XVII.

As from the third part of the night intellect obtains delight so Kumudvati obtained as her son the Kakutstha prince *Atithi*. As the sun of incomparable effulgence lights up both the north and the south so Atithi of incomparable beauty purified both the families of his father and mother Then his sire, the foremost of all those conversant in the worldly object, first instructed his son in all the branches of learning and afterwards had him married with the daughters of the kings. Having obtained that, powerful and self-controlled son the heroic, self-controlled king Kusha regarded himself fortunate and helpful. Then as becoming his family, he, for helping the king of celestials, killed an invincible Daitya and was himself also slain by him. As a lily follows the moon affording delight to her, so Kumudvati, sister of the Naga king Kumuda, followed him. One of them occupied with the king of heaven the half of his throne and the other shared Parijata with Sachi. Then remembering the last mandate of the king before he set out for the battle the elderly ministers thought of installing his son Atithi on the throne. For his installation the ministers had a new hall erected by the artists supported by four pillars and containing an elevated altar. The subjects brought golden pitchers filled with sacred water before the king Atithi who was seated on an auspicious altar in that Hall. With the calm and deep sound of the bugles at the gate it was ascertained that his auspiciousness would be permanent in his generation. With grass, barley seeds, bark of fig-tree and new leaves the elderly kinsmen performed the rite of Neerajana. First of all reciting the mantrams of the Atharva Veda his priests and other Brahmanas began the ceremony of installation. The water, pouring with a sound on his head appeared like the stream of the Ganges falling on the head of the destroyer of Tripura. As when the clouds appear the Chatakas welcome them so the panegyrists sang his glories at the time of installation. After the termination of the installation ceremony he gave profuse wealth to the priests so that their sacrifices might be celebrated with sufficient presents. The blessings which they delightedly showered on the Emperor were the outcome of his pristine virtue. He set the prisoners at liberty, forgave the culprits who were to have been hanged, set free the beasts of burden and stopped the milching of the kine. By his command the Suka and other birds that were in the cage were set free and fled away at their pleasure.

Thereupon for the purpose of dressing, the king sat, in another room, on a most excellent throne covered with a sheet of ivory. Washing their hands with water the attendants decorated, with scents and garlands, the dried hairs of Athiti. On the pearl chains with which his hairs were tied they put brilliant rubies. Having rubbed his body with sandal scented with musk they put on marks of *Gorochana*. Adorned with all the ornaments and clad in a silk raiment marked with the emblems of swans the king, bearing garlands, looked exquisitely beautiful like the bride-groom of the goddess of regal prosperity. While Atithi saw his decorations in a gold mounted mirror his reflection there looked beautiful like that of the Kalpa tree reflected on the Meru at the time of the rising of the sun. Then exclaiming his victory his attendants, carrying chowries, umbrellas and other parapharnalia of royalty, moved on around him. He then entered the Assembly Hall like unto that of the celestials and sat on the beautiful ancestral throne beautified with a canopy which was marked with the lines of the crown jems of tributary kings. When he sat on the throne that spacious hall, resembling the house of Srivatsa, looked like the breast of Keshava bearing the mystic mark of Srivatsa and adorned with the Kaustava jem. Atithi was installed as heir apparent in his boyhood and therefore early gained the empire. He thereat looked like the full-moon with the immediate termination of lunar curves. His attendants considered the sweet-speeched Emperor, of smiling countenance, as a reservoir of trust. Riding on an elephant powerful like Airavata, Atithi, powerful like Indra himself, converted the city, adorned with Kalpa-tree-like flags, into heaven itself. The umbrella, of pure lustre, which was held over his head, removed the sorrow of the world consequent upon the absence of the late king. The flame of fire issues after smoke; with the rise of the sun its rays appear. But transgressing this natural virtue of luminous bodies, Atithi appeared with all the virtues and accomplishments aggregated. As an autumnal night, with the eye of a delightful star, sees the Dhruva so the beautiful damsels of the city, with eyes expanded with joy, began to look at Atithi. Throned as images in the spacious temple of Ayodya all the deities engaged in meditating on the well-being of Atithi who was worthy of that favour. Before the altar, which was wetted with the water of installation, was dried, the ocean of his power went to the end of the bank. When the counsels of the family priests Vasistha, and arrow of the bow-man, Atithi, were united what was there which was difficult of being accomplished. Encircled by pious friends, he every day, casting off idleness, used to look after all affairs so that without doubt he might ascertain proper persons of favour. Whenever pleasing him with the accomplishment of an object the dependants prayed for rewards they got riches beyond their expectations. By the administration of the previous king the subjects had grown prosperous like a river in the month of Sravana; but now they grew immensely rich like that of Bhadra. Whatever he said never proved otherwise. He never took back whatever he gave away. This rule was violated only in the case of uprooting the enemies and placing them again in their respective positions. Youth, beauty and wealth—any of these three is sufficient to create pride. But all these three were united in him and still he was not puffed up with pride. His subjects grew daily attached to him. Although he was placed newly on the throne still he became invincible like a firmly rooted tree. External enemies are not eternal for they live at a distance and therefore first of all he conquered the internal enemies, the six passions.

The goddess of prosperity, fickle by nature, became constant to that king of pleasing countenance like unto the line of gold on a testing stone. Conduct, shorn of bravery, is the characteristic of cowardice and continual display of bravery is the nature of ferocious animals; considering this Atithi used to do works by both the means. As the sun, after the rains, spreads its rays everywhere so he collected all informations of his kingdom through emissaries. He used to perform duties alloted to the kings both in the day and night as followed by Manu, and other kings. He never neglected them. He used to consult daily his leading ministers. Although discussed continually his secret counsels never saw the wind. Although he used to sleep in proper time still he kept information of his own and foreign countries through secret spies. Thus he was wide awake both day and night. Atithi used himself to besiege enemies' citadels, but his own fortresses were invincible, for a lion, the killer of elephants, does not lie in the cave out of fear. His good works used to pass secretly through deliberations and discussions like the Shali rice. As when the ocean of salt-water rises it does not go by a wrong way but goes to the mouth of the river so though he grew immensely prosperous he never wended evil ways. He was always capable of allaying immediately the displeasure of his subjects but he never gave an opportunity for the same. Although very powerful he used to fight with those whom he could defeat, for a forest-fire, when it is helped by the wind, does not go to the water. He never obstructed religion with desire or profit or the latter two with the former; nor did he obstruct profit with desire, nor desire with profit. In fact, he was equally inclined to all these three. There is no use of making friendship with poor men. And it is dangerous to make friends with rich people. He therefore contracted friendship with middle class people. When comparing his own strength with that of the enemies he found his own sufficient he started for battle. Otherwise he desisted from the attempt. Knowing that every body seeks protection when the treasury is full he used to collect money, for the Chatakas seek the clouds surcharged with water. First throwing obstacles in the way of the enemies, he himself engaged in war. Hiding his own defects he took advantage] of enemies' loopholes and killed them. He never considered, different from his own person, the soldiers trained up in the use of arms by the quiet king Kusha. Like unto the jem on the head of a serpent the enemies could not draw his three-fold power of strength, *mantrams* and good counsels. But as a load-stone draws iron so he used to rob the three-fold power of his enemies. The merchants used to move about in the rivers of their own accord as if in tanks, in the forests as if in gardens and on mountains as if in their own houses. Atithi used to protect asceticism from obstacles and wealth from robbers. And in its stead the ascetics living in the hermitages and the four orders used to confer on him one-sixth of their produces. As he used to protect the earth so she too gave him jems out of mines, corns from fields and elephants from forests. He was clever enough to employ six-fold qualities and armies on their proper objects. Thus gradually employing the four means of regal policy he was crowned with success in all his undertakings. The goddess of victory, who always follows the heroes, used to go to him engaged in righteous warfare like an unchaste woman athough he knew unfair warfare.

As the ordinary elephants, depressed by the smell of temporal juice of other elephants, do not fight with them so his enemies, depressed by his prowess, hardly fought with him. The moon after attaining the highest increase wanes; the ocean rising up to the highest point recedes; but he, although highly prosperous like the both, never knew deterioration. As the clouds are filled with water after going to the ocean, so poor people, beggars and pious men, going to that king, were loaded with riches. He always performed praise-worthy deeds but felt bashfulness when any one praised him. Still his glory, who never liked flattery, spread on all sides. Like the rising sun Atithi used to destroy the sin of his subjects by conducting them into his presence. And he used to destroy their ignorance by instructing them in the reality of things. Thus did he bring the subjects under his control.

The rays of the moon cannot touch the lotus and those of the sun cannot touch the lily, but the virtues of that accomplished king went even to his enemies. The deception practised by the Emperor on his enemies when he set out on an expedition of conquest of celebrating a horse-sacrifice was considered moral. As Indra is the king of gods, so Atithi, wending good ways as sanctioned by the scriptures, became the Lord Paramount of all the kings by his power. By the equilibrium of qualities, he became the fifth guardian deity, the sixth element, and seventh boundary [mountain. As the celestials carry out the commands of Indra so the kings, leaving their umbrellas at a distance, used to carry out his mandate with uncovered heads. With so profuse presents did he worship the priests in the horse-sacrifice that his name became equally celebrated with that of Kuvera. The king of gods used to pour rain, Death used to suppress disease and Varuna made the rivers fordable for the easy passage of the boats. Thus did the guardian deities do his works like those living under his protection.

CANTO XVIII.

Atithi, the victor of enemies, begat on the daughter of Arthapati, the king of Nishadas, a son by named

Nishadha who was strong like the mount Nishadha. As people are filled with joy on seeing ripening paddy in the rains so determining that he would hand over the government to the youthful and powerful Nishada he attained to great delight. Having enjoyed the objcets of the world for a long time and made over the government to his own son, Kumuda's son Atithi repaired to heaven acquired by his pure deeds. The incomparable heroe Nishadha reigned supreme over the earth containing oceans. His eyes were expansive like lotus petals, his mind was deep like the ocean and his arms were long like the bolts of the city.

After his demise his son Nala, effulgent like fire, obtained the kingdom. As an elephent breaks down the forest of reeds so the lotus-eyed Nala grinded his enemies. The king, whose glories were sung by the sky-rangers, the Gandharvas and others, obtained a son by name Nabha who was blue-hued like the sky. Like the downpours of the month of Shravana he became a favourite of the subjects. Having conferred the kingdom of Ayodhya on his worthy son the pious king Nala repaired to the forest in his old age and lived there in the company of the deer. He begat a son by Name Pundarika, unconquerable to the kings, like unto Pudarika amongst the elephants of the quarters. Having left the kingdom in the hands of his forgiving son Kshemadhanwa, ever engaged in the well-being of the subjects, Pundarika, of sure aim, repaired to forest for practising penances.

Kshemadbanwa obtained a god-like son who always went before the commanders in battle. His other name Devanika was also celebrated in heaven. As Keshemadhanwa was greatly happy in obtaining his son Devanika, who was always ready to serve his father so the son too was highly pleased with the affection of his sire.

Having entrusted the charge of his subjects to the care of his son resembling his own self Kshemandhanwa repaired to the region of the celestials. By his sauvity of manners Ahinagu, the self-controlled son of Devanika, became not only a favourite of his own people but even of his enemies; for by sweet words even excited deer are brought under control.

Ahinagu, the highly powerful son of Devanika, conquered the entire world. He never mixed in bad company in his youth and always abstained from the corrupt habits of drinking, gambling &c. After his father Devanika, the clever Ahinagu, who was an expert in studying mankind, became the master of the four quarters by the four-fold means of conciliation &c., like the Prime Purusha Vishnu incarnate in four parts.

After the demise of Ahinagu his son Parijatra obtained the throne. In prosperity he excelled the Kula mountain Parijatra. Parijatra begat a son, liberal-minded and of a spacious breast, whose name was Shila. He conquered his enemies with arrows and felt himself abashed when any one lauded him.

Having installed the wise Shila as the heir-apparent the blameless king Parijatra enjoyed pleasure, for kings, for various pressing works, can never enjoy pleasures like a prisoner. As if growing jealous on seeing the love of women for Shila, who was not satiated with pleasures of life and who was a favourite to] women for his beauty, decrepitude soon overtook him. Shila begat a son by name Unnabha who was well-known, the foremost of all kings and deep-navelled like the lotus-navelled deity. After him Unnabha's son Vajra-nabha, who weilded thunder-bolt in battle, became the king of the Earth who paid him tribute in diamonds. After the departure of Vajranabha to heaven by his piety, the earth, with oceans, began to serve his son Sankhana with presents of jems produed from the mines. After his demise his son, effulgent like the sun and beautiful like Aswin, obtained the ancestral throne. Encamping soldiers and horses on the bank of the ocean he became celebrated on earth by the name of Vyushi-tashwa. He begat a son by name Vishwasaha the friend of the universe who, by worshipping the Lord of the universe, was capable of govering the entire world. As fire, the friend of the wind, becomes unbearable unto the trees, so Vishwasaha, well-versed in polity, having obtained a son by name Hiranya-nabha, a portion incarnate of Narayana, became invincible unto his enemies. Desirous of enjoying eternal happiness in his old age, Vishwasaha, the lord of subjects, who was freed from the debt to his ancestors, installed the long-armed Hiranyanabha on the throne and put on bark. Hiranyanabha, the scion of the solar dynasty, the lord of Ayodhya and the drinker of Soma juice, begat a son by name Koushalya, pleasant to the eyes like unto the second moon.

Koushalya whose fame reached even the Assemblage of Brahma, engaged his son Brahmishtha, who was devoted to Brahma, in the porotection of the subjects and was himself immersed in Para Brahma. The king Brahmistha, the ornament of his family, governing the earth without a hitch. His subjects enjoyed bliss for a long time with eyes full of tears of joy. His son Putra, whose soul was purified by serving the elders, who took after Narayana and was lotus-eyed, made his sire Brahmistha the foremost of those having sons. Thinking that the prestige of his family would be sustained by his son, Brahmistha, who had abstained from worldly pleasures, the future friend of the king of gods, bathed at the sacred shrine of Tripushkara and attained to the dignity of a celestial.

On the full-moon day the queen of the king Putra gave birth to a son, more effulgent than the Pushparaga jem, by the name of Pushya. When he appeared like the Pushya star his subjects grew highly prosperous. Having transferred the earth to his son, the Emperor Putra, afraid of the next birth, received initiation from Jaimini, conversant with the nature of Brahman. And learning the practice of

Yoga from him the great Yogin attained to emancipation. Then Dhruvasandhi, the son of the pious king Pushya, became the lord of the earth. That truthful king never broke treaties with submissive kings. His son Sudarshana, beautiful like the moon of the first day of lunar fortnight, having eyes like those of a deer, became charming even in his infancy. While a-hunting king Dhruvasandhi was killed by a lion. Seeing the wretched condition of the lord-less poor subjects the ministers unanimously installed the infant son of the king on the throne of Ayodhya. The Raghu family, governed by that boy king, looked beautiful like the sky adorned with the new moon, like a forest inhabited by one lion and water bedecked with lotuses. The crowned boy king gradually became powerful like his father. The entire population of Ayodhya considered it so. It is seen, that a piece of cloud of the size of a span, by the help of the preceding wind, enshrouds the entire welkin. When clad in a lustrous royal robe he passed by high-ways on the back of an elephant the elephant-keepers used to hold him and the subjects used to regard him with respect like a father for though a boy of six years he was still their king. Though he could not fully cover his father's throne when he sat on it but it was filled with the golden lustre of his person. Lowering their crowns the kings used to salute his feet dyed with red arsenic, which, hanging a little down from the throne, could not touch the golden foot stool. As it is not improper to call a ruby, of deep violet colour though it has a bluish tint so the appellation of Emperor was not unbecoming of that boy-king. The command, of the mouth of that boy-king, which was decorated with curling locks shaken by the wind of the chowries, suffered no violation up to the bank of the ocean. Bearing the mark of royality on his fore-head adorned with gold that king of a smiling countenance, deprived the beautiful faces of the wives of his enemies, of their paintings. That king, more tender than a Shirisha flower, used to feel pain even in putting on ornaments; but by his prowess he did not experience the least pain in carrying the heavy burden of the earth. Before learning the business of state he had studied Polity by the help of elderly ministers. Not finding an opportunity to sit on the unspacious breast of Sudarshana and waiting for the same for his advanced youth, goddess of prosperity, as if out of shame, embraced him in the shape of the shade of umbrella. The signs of bow-strings were not printed on his arms till then, the sword did not touch his fist still that arm protected the earth. Not only his body was developed in time, but the hereditary qualities of generosity, bravery etc., so liked by people, which lay latent in him, were also developed. Sudarshana, a favourite to his elders, had mastered all the branches of learning in his former birth and now recollecting them he at once regained that learning, the source of the attainment of three objects as well as his paternal nature. While learning the use of arms and studying he used to tie up his hairs. Spreading forward the fore part of his body and bending a little his left thigh he drew his bow and looked exquisitely beautiful. Then he attained his youth, the only place of amusement, which is an object of attachment like honey pleasing to the eyes of lustful women, like the flowers of the tree of Cupid and which is like the natural ornaments for all the limbs. With a view that he might have a good son the ministers brought a princess, more beautiful than a photo shown by a female agent. Becoming the wife of the prince that youthful princess became a co-wife with the goddess of prosperity.

CANTO XIX.

Having installed his son Agnivarna, effulgent like fire, on his own throne, the self-controlled king Sudarshana, the foremost of those conversant in Sastras, repaired to the Naimisha forest in his old age. Forgetting the tank of his house through sacred water, his royal bed through Kuca reed, and Palace through the thatched cottage he practised there desire-less penances. Agnivarna did not experience the least inconvenience in governing his kingdom for having uprooted the enemies by the strength of his own arms his father consigned the earth to him duly for his enjoyment. He did not leave any thorn of an enemy to be rooted out. Having governed the kingdom for a few years the lustful Agnivarna left it entirely in the hands of his ministers and became mad after women. Pleasure-parties held in his Palace filled with the sound of Mridangas and women clouded even the great festivities of his ancestors. He could not spend a moment without any object of sense. Day and night he lived in the inner apartment and never thought of subjects who came to interview him. Even if he, at the request of his ministers, allowed his subjects to see him it was only his feet which they could behold through the holes of the windows. His dependants only saluted his dyed feet like unto lotuses touched by the new rays of the sun. When the lustful Agnivarna used to sport in the water of the tanks, the lotuses thereof were agitated by the rising breasts of the youthful damsels. There was a secret house built in that tank where he used to sport with women. The collyrium of the eyes and the paintings of lips of those women on being washed by water they looked whitish. At that time the natural beauty of their face was perceptible at which the king was more tempted. As an elephant, in the company of his female mate, devours lilies so he, in the company of women, used to drink wine, in a drinking site, sweet-scented with the smell of mango blossoms. The women liked to drink secretly the wine of his mouth; he too, equally anxious, used to drink the wine of mouth offered by them. Vina emitting sweet music and sweet-speeched women used always to occupy his lap. He never allowed it to remain empty. With his body and armlets shaking at the time of playing on the musical instruments, the king Agnivarna, an expert in the science of music, used to charm the dancing girls so much that failing to follow the new method they felt shame before the teacher seated by them. After the termination of dancing he, airing their beautiful faces with breaths, the paintings whereof were washed off with drops of perspiration, used to kiss them. At that time he used to think himself more powerful than the lord of Alaka, the city of immortals. While in the company of that king who, unsolicited, used to enjoy the objects of pleasure, his favourite women showed him half of the same and kept hidden another half. Deceiving the women he used to receive from them rebukes in the shape of the pointing of finger, contraction of eye-brows and the binding with Mekhalas. In the night of sexual intercourse when his favourite women used to come on turns he, hiding himself in the back of one of them, though within the knowledge of the female emissary, used to hear her lamentations, the outcome of the fear of separation. When he felt desire for the dancing girls in the presence of his wives he used to paint their bodies with perspiring fingers and bear himself up with great difficulty. Being jealous of the women who were proud of the king's love aud worked up with passion the queens too, casting off anger, used to invite the king and have their lust satisfied. When Agnivarna used to come in the morning they, finding marks of other women on his body, felt anger and he too propitiated them with folded hands. And again showing laxity of love he used to repent again. When the king mentioned the name of another wife in a dream his other wives expressed their anger by overturning bed sheets, shedding tears and breaking bracelets. Coming to the groves of creepers adorned with flowery beds in the company of the procuress pointing out the way he, trembling in fear of his wives, used to hold sexual intercourse with the maid servants. Whenever he mentioned the name of one of his lady loves his wife said :—"O lustful man, I have got the name of your dearest lady, now I wish to have her good fortune. My mind has grown anxious for it." When the lustful Agnivarna got up from his bed it showed many marks of sexual intercourse. Some part was covered with the powder of Kumkuma, some part was filled with bees, some part was covered with torn waist-chains and somewhere was dyed with red arsenic. He used to dye the feet of his women with his own hands; but when his eyes were fixed on their waist with loosened clothes or on their buttocks he could not concentrate his attention. When newly married damsels used to turn back their mouths when kissing or withdraw their tongues their attempts became like fuels to the fire of his passion. When seeing the marks of sexual intercourse in the mirror he used to laugh behind them his wives bent their bashful heads on the smiling reflections. When after the termination of the night the king attempted to leave the bed his wives, throwing their tender arms round his neck, and putting down his feet with their fingers, used to pray for kisses. Beholding his royal dress, putting the beauty of Indra even into shade, the youthful Agnivarna did not experience that delight which he felt on marking distinctly the signs of sexual intercourse in the mirror. When he attempted to leave their side on the pretext of attending to a friend's business, his favourites said "O cheat! I have come to know your pretext of flying away" and held him by the hairs. Worn out with the fatigue of sexual intercourse the women, embracing him, used to lie down on his breast the sandal paste whereof was removed by the pressure of their rising breasts. Hearing from their secret emissary that another woman was ranging secretly in the night for having sexual pleasure his wives came to him and said "O lustful man, where will you go in this dark night and spend it there." Saying so they used to stop him. Feeling the pleasure of the embraces of women pleasant like the rays of the moon Agnivarna used to keep up nights and sleep during the day; so he imitated the nature of the moon. The lips of the songstresses were cut with his teeth and their thighs with his nails. So feeling pain either in playing on the flute or on the Vina they used to cast frowning looks at him which were objects of temptation to him. Showing secretly before the dancing girls three forms of dancing he used to vie with expert teachers before his friends. Adorning his limbs with Kutaja and Arjuna flowers and painting his body with the filaments of Kadamva flowers in the rains he used to pass his days on artificial hills filled with peacocks. He never attempted to beseech women who showed unwillingness to share the bed with him for quarrels of love but wished that they, terrified at the muttering of clouds, would hide themselves in his breast. In autumnal nights he used to sport in a house adorned with a canopy and remove the toil of intercourse by enjoying the moon lustrous like a pearl. Through the windows of his palace he used to see the river Sarayu imitating the sports of his dear lady having the banks for her waist and the swans for the girdle. With closing eyes and the sound of girdles the youthful maidens used to attract Agnivarna. Casting their looks in the shape of feeble lights in an inner room divested of the wind the nights of the dewy season, just the proper season for the sexual intercourse, used to witness his sexual enjoyment. Beholding the mango leaves and blossons dropped by the southern wind the women, making up differences, used to beseech Agnivarna stricken with their separation. He kept the women on his lap. And advising them to leave off the rope of the craddle he asked his servants to push it. And they, out of fear, used to clasp firmly his neck by their hands. Bedecked with evening decorations—*viz.*, sandal pastes on their breasts, robes thick set with pearls, and jewelled girdles the damsels used to serve him. With the drinking of the wine of Sahakara flowers their sexual desire, subdued with the end of the spring, was again excited. Thus desisting from the performance of other works and indulging in sensual pleasures at the excitement of Cupid Angivarna spent the seasons leaving marks on his limbs. His enemies, although they found him busy with pleasures, did not dare attack him on account of his great power. As the curse of the king Daksha influenced the moon so the dreadful disease of consumption, the outcome of excessive sexual indulgence, attacked him. He grew disobedient to the physicians and did not leave off the company of women and wine although he was aware of their evil effects. It is difficult to withdraw senses from their objects if they are once engaged in enjoying them. His countenance grew pale and he could not walk without any support. When the emperor was attacked with consumption the Raghu family looked like the sky with the last ray of the moon, a tank in summer with only mud left in it, and like a lamp with a feeble light. Keeping the disease of the king secret his courters announced to the subjects that the king was practising *Japa* in the day for procreating a son. Without seeing the face of a son who could keep up the continuity of the line although he had hundreds of wives the king could not bear the attack of the disease which was beyond the skill of the physicians like a lamp unable to bear the gust of a wind. Consulting with priests conversant in last rites his ministers brought his dead body into the garden attached to the Palace and threw it secretly into the burning fire. Then inviting speedily all the leading ladies of the palace they transferred the kingdom to the principal queen who showed evident signs of conception. He embryo was at first afflicted with hot tears begotten by the sorrow of separation from the king; but it was cooled down by the water sprinkled form golden pitchers. As the earth holds seeds sown in the month of Sravana, so she, holding the conception, for the well-being of the subjects who anxiously expected the hour of delivery, sat on the golden throne and governed the kingdom of her husband without any obstruction along with the hereditary aged ministers.

THE END.